DO WHAT I SAY

M. S. Novaes

CONTENTS

JANE

Chapter 1

"But I love you…"

"You don't…. You're beautiful but exhausting. I have to focus on school and my career, and I don't have time for your constant mood swings. Sorry, Jane, it's over."

"No, please, Alan. Don't leave me. I will be better to you, I promise…"

"Bye, Jane. We can be friends…"

"Jerk!" I shouted, slamming the car door shut and stomping toward my building without looking back.

"Asshole! Who does he think he is to treat me like this? I'm not a piece of garbage." I muttered to myself furiously. Once at home, I ate my feelings with a big slice of chocolate cake and cried myself asleep.

#

Late, as always, I got up and went straight to the shower, got dressed in the first outfit I could reach in my closet, and then, out the door, in the elevator, on the street, and finally, at the office.

"I can't believe I've made it!" I said, taking my jacket off, putting my stuff away, and trying to sit on my chair, all at the same time.

"Yeah, you'll be F-I-R-E-D next time you're late. Get a freaking alarm clock! I mean, how difficult can it be to wake up on time?" Ann said as she tied up her shoulder-length, chestnut brown hair in a ponytail and resumed work. "I told you I could call you every morning when I get up…just to make sure…you know?" she added, typing and focusing on the task before her, not even looking at me.

"Oh, never mind, Ann. I really appreciate it, but I have everything under control." I said while still putting my belongings away.

"Whatever! I'm just trying to be nice, not that you deserve it anyway," she said, rolling her eyes.

"Ms. May?" spoke the voice on the intercom.

"Yes, Mr. McKee!" I answered, still trying to manage my things.

"Would you get me a grande caramel macchiato with skim milk and a sprinkle of cinnamon? Ah, don't put any sugar. Ok, honey? Thanks! See you in my office in…what…fifteen minutes?"

"Yes, sir! A grande caramel macchiato with skim milk and a sprinkle of cinnamon is coming right up!"

"Don't forget, no sugar!" he replied.

"No sugar," I confirmed as the intercom conversation ended.

"He's a freak! He drives me crazy sometimes! I can't stand this job anymore. Every day is the same shit. I need to do something else in my life!" I started complaining to myself. "Why wasn't I born rich?"

"Wow! Take it easy, Jane! Do not start your day like that."

"Like that, how? What are you talking about?" I yelled at her.

"Bad mood," she said without changing her voice tone. "You're going to spoil everybody's day with this attitude, and I have to be sitting by your side all day long. Please, give me a break, would you?" She stopped typing to look at me, raising her eyebrow.

"Shut up!" I shouted at her, turning around to reach my purse that I had just placed under my desk. When I lifted my eyes from my desk, I saw this very handsome guy staring at me with his piercing green eyes. Neither Ann nor I saw him coming in. "May I help you?" I asked with an attitude.

He smiled, embarrassed. "Yes, I'm here to see Mr. Poch."

"You were going to get Mr. McKee's coffee, remember, Jane? I'll take care of Mr...?" Ann said, getting up on her feet and pushing me out of her way with a much happier semblance now. It was obvious that she was impressed by his looks.

"Joe," he said, still staring at me. "Joe Garrison."

"Fine!" I said, gritting my teeth and looking at Ann with intimidating eyes. She ignored me, and I left the office reception, stomping my feet through the door. I could hear her giggling from the hall; it was irritating!

I didn't ask Ann about that Joe guy when I got back from the coffee shop. I wasn't in the mood to talk and would rather die than give her a chance to talk on and on about how he supposedly flirted with her. Yeah, right! She's a loser. I feel sorry for her. She's insecure because she knows she's not pretty, and guys always prefer me over her.

She tried to engage me in a conversation several times during the day, but I ignored her. I bet she was proud of herself for having the chance to flirt with the guy. She's so predictable. Anyway, after a while, she finally gave up, leaving me alone. After work, I rushed home, stopping only for cat food and a nice bottle of wine.

#

Ollie was anxiously waiting for me by the door and started purring and draping his whole body around my legs, headfirst and then his entire length, until the tip of his tail. Ollie is a funny cat, I must admit. He can do anything in his power to get whatever he wants, and as soon as he's satisfied — he's done — that's it! No more purring or rubbing legs. He's gone somewhere else to take care of his own business. That's what I like about cats. They have personalities.

They're jerks!

"Ok! Ok!" I said, trying to get into the apartment and closing the door behind me without stepping on him. "Ollie is hungry, isn't he? Look what I got for him! Wow! Tuna flavor, your favorite! Do I deserve a kiss? Huh?" I said, taking the cat food from the grocery bag and showing it to him as he tried to reach it, lifting his body.

I grabbed him in my arms, he kissed me and purred loudly, so excited that he couldn't help but meow nervously. It was funny, and I couldn't resist torturing him for a while, pretending I couldn't open the can. I started laughing. "Poor cat. Jane is so mean to him, isn't she?" I said, teasing him, but I finally gave up when he started meowing loudly and long, "Meoooowww, meeeeooooowwwwww." He had lost his patience with me.

I rushed with his food before the neighbors imagined I was killing the poor cat. Once he was content and out of the way, I poured a glass of wine, took my shoes off, and went to my bedroom. There, I took my clothes off, went to the bathroom and filled the bathtub. A nice bubble bath was exactly what I needed! I looked at myself in the mirror, checking for any flaws. No defects. I'm pretty, hot, and perfect. Who needs Alan? He'll regret dumping me.

Chapter 2

"Do you want to go to the movies tonight?" Ann asked me while typing and staring at the computer screen at the same time without looking at me.

"Movies? I don't know; what do you want to see?" I asked her, also working on my computer, not glancing at her.

"I want to see that new kids' movie. What's its name?"

"A kids' movie?"

"Yep!"

"You've got to be kidding me!"

"No, I'm not! I think kids' movies are cool. C'mon, where is your sense of humor? Let's relax and laugh a bit. I have some poot," she sang the word *pot* to emphasize it. She stopped typing and looked at me with a huge smile on her face.

"Umm…I like the pot part of it. I think it could be fun. Count me in, girlfriend!" I needed to distract myself and forget about Alan anyway.

"Great!" she said, answering the phone. "Good morning, Poch and McKee Attorneys and Associates. This is Ann. How may I help you?"

"Ms. May?" said the voice on the intercom almost at the same time.

"Yes, Mr. McKee?" I answered, already getting up and knowing what he wanted.

"Have Mrs. Goldenberg's documents arrived yet?" The intercom spoke again.

"Yes, sir, I'm on my way." I left for his office with the envelope in my hands.

The day went by smoothly, with no stress. Ann and I had a peaceful and productive workday. We are like sisters. One day, we are the best friends ever, and the next, we hate each other to death; so girlish!

After work, we stopped at my place just to feed Ollie. He was waiting by the door as usual, but instead of kissing him, I pushed him away with my foot. "I guess I can be a jerk, too, huh?" He got dry food today because it was the easiest to get and we were out the door the next minute.

#

I was so high at the movies that Ann elbowed me several times, warning that I was laughing too loud, but actually, I was cracking up at her. She was totally spaced. We decided to stop for a drink at this place close to her house after the movie; she knew the bartender.

"What's up?" she said, pounding her fist on the counter to get his attention while sitting and checking the place out, which was crowded and loud.

"Hey, girl. Where have you been?" he said with a sexy smile on his face, leaning forward and kissing her on the lips. "Who's that?" He pointed at me, but with his eyes fixed on hers, their faces just a couple of inches apart.

"A girlfriend!" she said without introducing me and staring back at him.

"Oh…." he said, still staring at her face. "Does she have a name?"

"Probably, but who wants to know?" she teased.

"That's it!" I said, getting myself in between them and facing him. "Jane May!"

"Hello, Jane May. What can I get you? It's on me," he said with a smirk, showing his nice teeth behind the groomed blond goatee and mustache. His strong, tanned arms with tattoos made me imagine myself being embraced by him; he was hot.

"What about a margarita on the rocks?" I charmed him with my sexy look that always worked.

"Sounds good," he said, leaning sideways to face Ann again. "What about you?"

"I'll have what he's having," she said, pointing to a lonely, miserable man on the opposite side of the bar.

"Ouch! I wouldn't if I were you! He's having very strong stuff!" he warned her.

"Really? Give me a double strong stuff then!" and she pounded on the counter again.

The night was awesome; we got drunk in a heartbeat. And if I remember well, at the end of the night, Ann was giving advice to the lonely, miserable man sitting at the opposite side of the bar and I was kissing the bartender nonstop. I still don't know his name, though!

CHAPTER 3

Late as always, I couldn't believe it when my car didn't start in the morning!

"Argh! I just hate my life! What am I going to do now? Think…think…. Get a cab? Fuck!" I have no time. "Cab, it is," I said to myself, calling a cab company.

\#

"Wow, there she comes again…" was the reception I got from Ann at the office.

"Thanks a lot, bitch!" I replied while making my way to my desk hastily.

"You're welcome, bitch!" she answered without bothering to look at me.

After a while, she got up and left the room, not saying a word. She kept herself busy and never asked if I was ok, ignoring me all day long. I'm sure she's just jealous because of last night. What can I do if the guy liked me better?

At the end of our shift, she said, "See ya!" and left the building. I was astonished by her attitude. *Who needs a friend like that? What a witch!* I left the building with a dark cloud on top of my head and was getting really distressed thinking that I would have to take the bus home since getting a cab in rush hour was almost mission impossible. Ann was gone before I could ask her for a lift.

\#

At the bus stop, I was grossed out by the dirty bench. So, I got a piece of paper in my purse to sit on.

An hour passed by, and I was getting a bit more relaxed, distracted seeing people getting on and off buses that lined up at the bus stop in an organized manner, one after another. It was interesting seeing how people behaved, making a line to wait for the bus driver to open the door, so they could get on the bus without delay.

Finally, I saw my bus approaching. I got up fast to get myself in the bus line, wanting to be the first one on the bus. I wanted to get a nice seat, preferably by the door, so I could get off the bus without having to touch anyone. Oddly, people pushed me out of the line, as if saying, *Wait your turn, bitch!* Feeling threatened by the unfriendly faces, I politely moved myself to the end of the line. I didn't want any confrontation.

When I was finally about to get my turn on the bus, I heard a honk going crazy and someone calling my name aloud: "Jane!"

"What the fuck!" I muttered to myself. Who in the hell could have seen me at the bus stop? Curiously, I looked around and saw that Joe guy, remember him?

"Hey, Jane! C'mon, I'll give you a lift!" he said, waving at me.

"No thanks," I said and turned back, getting ready to step on the bus.

Everybody, including the bus driver, gave me that look as if saying — *Hellooo? Are you getting on or not?* Gosh, I felt intimidated and decided to take Joe's offer.

"Fine." I finally said, walking toward Joe's car. "How's it going?" I asked, getting in his car.

"Fine," he said without hesitation. "Your name is Jane, right? We met Monday at the law office."

"Yeah," I said without enthusiasm.

"What? I was just trying to be nice to you!" he said indignantly.

"Whatever. You can keep driving north on Federal Highway; I'll let you know when you need to turn."

"What? I'm not a taxi driver."

"I thought you said you're taking me home."

"Never said that." He looked at me with this strange psycho expression on his face that made me regret getting in his car without thinking twice.

"Uh-oh," I said, trying to reach my cell phone in my purse. I wanted to have it handy in case he tried to kidnap me.

"What are you doing? Looking for pepper spray?" he said, delighted at my nervousness.

"Just want to call my mom! I call her every day when I get off work." I lied, calling my mom. "Hey, Mom."

"Jane?" she asked, as if not recognizing my voice.

"Yeah! How are you today?" I tried to sound calm and keep her from yelling at me, as she usually does.

"Oh, what do you want?"

"Nothing, I just miss you."

"What is it this time? I have no money to lend you."

"No, no, it's not that…" But she hung up without listening to me, as always. *Who needs a mother like that?* So, I pretended she was still talking to me.

"Ok…ok, Mom. I'm on my way home now. I'll call you when I get home, ok? Love you, too. Bye." I hung up feeling neglected by the person who was supposed to love me the most.

Well, all I wanted was to make sure someone knew where I was in case Joe was kidnapping me. Unfortunately, my mother doesn't care if I'm dead or alive. She never calls or worries about my wellbeing. I'd survived the lack of affection my whole life, and I don't know why I bother keeping in touch. I'm perfectly fine without her!

"Do you have to drive this fast? Where are you taking me, anyway? You didn't ask where I live!" Suddenly, I was bombarding him with all these questions as he was speeding through the streets.

"Yes, I drive fast. I don't know where you live, and I'm not taking you home," he explained.

"What? What do you mean you're not taking me home?" I panicked.

"You talk too much. I was going to invite you to this place. I'm hungry! Aren't you?" he said, keeping his eyes on the road. "Let's have something to eat first?"

"But I want to go home now," I replied.

"Well, I didn't say I would take you home right away. I offered you a lift since you were going in my direction." He focused on the road. "At least, let me buy you a drink, and I'll take you home afterward."

"Thanks, but NO thanks!" I said, irritated. "What made you think I was going in your direction? You don't even know me! Jerk!"

"Wow, I like you already!" he said sarcastically, turning to face me this time.

"Well, I don't!" I crossed my arms with an angry attitude.

He sighed, shaking his head, but kept driving. I felt a heat wave passing through my body, starting at my feet and going all the way up to my face. I blushed with rage. He parked the car on the street in front of this Irish pub, got out of the car without looking at me, and then came around to open my door.

"Would you grant me the pleasure of your company?" he said, making a gesture with his hands and forcing a smile on his pathetic face. "Let's have just one drink to clear the air between us, and I'll take you home. I promise."

I got out of the car, avoiding touching him. He closed the door behind me and rushed to my side as I walked fast toward the street, waving my hand at the first cab I saw, which passed me by without stopping. "ASSHOLE!" I yelled.

Joe started laughing, leaning back against a parked car, holding his right elbow with his left hand and slightly covering his mouth with his right hand in a calming, irritating manner, getting amused by my distress.

"What?" I shouted at him. "I'm going home! Bye!"

"Ok, you know where to find me in case you change your mind. Bye." He left just like that.

"Jerk!" I said to myself, checking the street for another passing cab. A few minutes passed by, but it felt like a whole hour. The street was completely dead, no cars, no cabs, no buses, nobody. Not a soul passed by me, so I decided to call a cab.

"Where is my cell phone?" I tried to find it in my purse — but it wasn't there. In my pocket? No, it wasn't there either. Maybe I dropped it on the street. I looked all over without success and tracked my path back to Joe's car. Still nothing. I peeked inside his car.

"Oh my God! No. No. NOO!" I couldn't believe it! My cell phone was lying there on the car's seat. Fuck!

I sighed and entered the bar. There was an Irish band playing in the pub that night. I looked around, trying to find the jerk who had left me alone in the dark, empty street and far from home. It didn't take me long to spot him sitting at the bar.

"Hey, you finally came in, huh?" he said with a smile of satisfaction on his stupid face.

"Yeah. I came to claim my drink." I said, forcing a smile.

"Please have a seat. What do you want? Do you drink beer?" he asked.

"No, I'd rather drink wine," I said, turning to the bartender, who was already waiting for my order.

"A glass of Merlot, please."

The bartender got a wine glass and an already open bottle of wine from under the counter and poured it for me. Disgusting, but I didn't complain.

"Thanks," I said, turning back to watch the band play.

"Cool, huh?" Joe said, drinking his beer. "Do you like Irish music?" He insisted on trying to engage in a conversation.

Not happening, I thought to myself. *Jerk, jerk, jerk* was all I had in my mind. After he finished his beer, he decided it was time for us to go.

Finally! I thought. I would get my cell phone, call a cab, and never see Joe's stupid face again. That was my plan.

Once we got to his car, he opened the passenger door for me. I bent in, got my cell phone, and showed it to him, taking a step back from the car.

"Oh!" he said, surprised. "So, I guess that's why you joined me at the pub." He went around the car to the driver's side, leaving the passenger door wide open.

"Are you coming?" he said, already inside the car, waiting for me to get in.

"No!" I slammed the car door, turned around, and started walking back to the pub.

"Goddammit!" I heard him cursing.

I kept walking without looking back and called a cab service number.

Chapter 4

"Good morning!" I said, feeling happy when arriving in the office, planning to tell Ann all about my adventure of the night before.

"Someone is in a good mood today!" Ann replied with dubious eyes, not believing I was in a good mood. "What happened? Did you get laid last night?" she asked with a sarcastic look on her face, waiting for my response.

"Nope…" I answered.

"Did you meet someone?" she tried again.

"Nope. Actually…" and a sudden commotion in the office reception interrupted me. Mr. McKee and Mr. Poch were talking and gesturing with excitement at someone who had just walked in right before I did. They came to introduce us to the new associate, Mr. Joe Garrison.

"Ladies, this is Mr. Joe Garrison," Mr. McKee said, patting Joe on the shoulder of his navy-blue suit jacket. "He's the new associate."

My stomach clenched, and bile immediately shot up my throat. I had to swallow down the vomit that threatened to come up and splatter across his nice leather shoes.

"Nice to meet you," Joe said, sticking out his hand toward me.

I paused for a split second. Did I really want to shake this douchebag's hand? I blinked and realized that four sets of eyes stared at me — Mr. McKee, Mr. Pock, Ann, and the asswipe from yesterday.

I put on a fake smile and slipped my hand into his. "Nice to meet you, too, Mr. Garrison." His warm hand lingered a few seconds too long, so I pulled it back, hoping nobody noticed.

Thankfully, Ann jumped in, grabbing his hand and shaking it with enthusiasm. "Nice seeing you again, Mr. Garrison."

"Well, which one of you will grab me a coffee?" Mr. McKee said while the other two men walked back to their offices, talking nonstop.

"I will," I said, in need of fresh air to put myself together. I left, not giving a chance for Ann to make any comment.

After lunch, I was quiet, still astonished by the situation. I couldn't think about what to do or imagine what could possibly happen to me now that the jerk was my boss. Maybe he won't say anything. Why would he? *Anyway, why didn't he say anything about being the new associate at the office last night?* I thought to myself.

"Jane?" Ann called. "Are you alright?

"Yeah…" I said in a self-controlled mode. "What are you doing tonight?"

"I don't know. Nothing, I guess. Why?" She looked at me suspiciously.

"I need some weed!" I said, looking at her with begging eyes.

"Oh! That's what you want, huh? Ok, I never say no to weed; let's party tonight, girlfriend!" She swiveled her chair around.

#

I arrived at her house around nine o'clock. She was all dressed up, ready to go out.

"Where are we going?" I asked.

"Par-tee!" she said, dancing around with her dog, Max, getting inside the house and leaving the door open for me to follow. "Here, grab this." She handed me the already-lit joint she took from an ashtray on the side table.

I grabbed it right away, filling my lungs with smoke. "Umm," exhaling and inhaling again.

"Take it easy, Jane. This is good stuff…" she said, laughing, watching my frantic smoking.

"What?" I said, holding my breath again.

"Really good," she said, taking the joint from my hand and taking a puff herself. "That's it! Enough for you, girlfriend, let's go." She patted Max's head on our way out. "Be nice, kiddo!"

We danced, drank, and had a lot of fun all night long. When we finally went back to Ann's house, where I had left my car parked, she didn't want to let me drive home, so I passed out on her couch.

#

The next morning, I was still feeling wasted and couldn't sleep any longer because her couch was very uncomfortable. So, without making any noise to wake her up, I snuck out and drove home to take a shower, change clothes, and head to work.

After parking in the office garage building as usual, I decided that a double espresso would be good to wake me up before getting to work. I walked to the coffee shop across the street and got into the lengthy line in front of the cashier.

That's fine, it's still early, I thought to myself, gazing at my watch to check how many minutes I had before having to get to work.

"Hey!" someone said behind me, getting my attention.

I turned my head to face the male voice…. I couldn't believe it! It was Joe! All my nightmares from the day before came back to me at once, and suddenly, I was fully awake.

"What do you want from me?" I asked, rolling my eyes.

"I want peace!" he said, making puppy dog eyes. "We can be good friends…we *have* to be good friends since we're going to work together!"

Despite being an obnoxious jerk, he looked handsome in a black suit, which matched his dark hair and accentuated his greenish-piercing eyes, looking at me at close range. His hair was still slightly wet from the morning shower, and his face, recently shaved. He smelled of lotion, not the cheap kind, but the kind that can only be noticed at a close distance.

"Why didn't you say we were going to be working together that night? I don't get it…" I started saying, trying to make my point and sound more friendly now.

"I was going to, but you got so stressed out," he said.

"Just…please don't tell anyone about that night, ok?" I begged, smiling and blinking, surrendering to his charm.

"Ok," he replied. "I wasn't planning to open my mouth, anyway."

"Good! I feel a lot better now." I said, relieved. "You don't seem too awful to me now."

"You've never seemed awful to me…just cute. Friends?" he said, making an irresistibly innocent face and winking at me.

"Friends!" I said content, and then it was my turn to order. "A grande latte, please." I had changed my mind about the double espresso.

We walked to the office together. I told him that I had slept at Ann's house but couldn't sleep at all because of her very uncomfortable couch. He laughed about my story, and I could tell he was starting to like me, too.

#

The day went by smoothly, without complications. Ann was still sleepy and couldn't function well all day long. It was amusing watching her lose concentration and forget what was to be done. I thought about telling her what happened between Joe and me but didn't find the right time…. Maybe another day.

I went straight home after work. I needed to relax and rest since I hadn't slept for more than twenty-four hours. After taking the second shower of the day, I put on my pajamas and went to the kitchen; I was starving.

Ollie and I looked inside the refrigerator, trying to decide what we were in the mood for. "Lobster Bisque?" I asked him, reading the box, but he didn't move and kept staring at me. "No, no, I don't think so, too," I said, putting the box back in the freezer. "Quiche Lorraine?" I read another food packet, he meowed, and I agreed, "Quiche Lorraine, it is! Do you want some salmon tonight?"

He started purring and rubbing my legs as soon as he saw me getting his food from the cabinet. He rushed to his bowl, waiting for me to dump his food, meowing nervously.

"Stay back," I said, pushing him out of the way with my foot and depositing the food in his bowl. I ate while watching TV, and by eleven o'clock, I was in bed sleeping like a rock.

CHAPTER 5

Ann and I had a lot of work to do. We were typing and printing all kinds of documents and answering phone calls nonstop all morning long. By lunchtime, I was exhausted.

I asked Ann if she wanted to grab a bite with me so I could tell her about Joe, but she decided not to take a lunch break so she could finish her work on time.

I didn't care if I had to stay a little longer after hours. I just needed my break. So, I grabbed my purse and left. I went for a walk on Las Olas Blvd. After eating a turkey wrap at the usual place at the corner, I passed by the chocolate store and couldn't resist buying some chocolate for the afternoon snack. The place smelled like heaven.

Back at the office, Ann was desperately trying to manage all bosses and phone calls at once. She didn't say anything, but I could tell she was furious because I had left her alone. I knew she was under a lot of pressure, but it was her fault for not taking a break. Sometimes, she's a nerdhead!

"Here, this is for you," I said, trying to make peace by handing her the small bag of chocolate I had brought her.

"Thanks," she said in disdain, grabbing the bag and putting it away in her drawer.

I got so upset. *Go to hell, bitch!* I thought to myself.

It's not my fault she gets stressed out trying to please the bosses, who, by the way, don't even notice her effort; she's really menial.

We didn't talk until the end of our shift. After she left, I took a deep breath and organized myself. I still had some work to finish. After a while, Mr. McKee, Mr. Poch, and Joe passed by me, leaving for the day.

"Are you staying a little longer today, Ms. May?" asked Mr. McKee.

"Yeah, I still have work to finish. I'm almost done," I said, typing fast, inputting the data into the computer database, very focused on the task.

"This is our best employee," he told the others. "She does what it takes for the sake of the company."

The others agreed with him, and they left, talking loudly as usual and proving my point.

Now that I was by myself, I could concentrate easily and do my work faster. As I said, Ann is such a moron; she stresses herself out trying to impress the bosses but never gets recognized. She should've known by now, after working here for almost six months, that they really don't care as long as the work is done. All she needs to do is pretend she's working very hard when they are around.

"Oh well, whatever!" I said aloud since there was nobody else there.

"Whatever?" Joe said, unexpectedly opening the door.

"Oh! It's you!" I said, surprised.

"Sorry if I scared you. I left an important file on my desk," he said, rushing there to get it.

His unexpected presence made me feel uneasy, especially because we were alone in the office. I kept working fast, pretending he wasn't there…as if it was possible.

When he came back to the reception, he sat down on Ann's chair and started casually going through her stuff. He opened her drawers and checked what was inside.

"Mm, chocolate!" he said, helping himself to the chocolate I had given her earlier that day.

"You can't do that!" I said, after observing him awhile, still astonished, not believing my eyes.

"That what?" he asked with his mouth full and shoving another piece of chocolate into it.

"That!" I said, pointing to his mouth, drawers, and the chair he was sitting on.

"Why?" he said as if it wasn't a big deal.

"Because it's not yours! I don't think Ann would appreciate your behavior. It's not polite. I don't go through people's stuff!"

"Do you know if she goes through yours?" he said and helped himself to a piece of gum now.

"Of course, she doesn't!"

"If you say so…" he said, turning her computer on with a smirk.

"Would you stop that?" I got up to turn her computer off. "Why don't you go home? I still have lots to do!" I said, without thinking about who I was shouting at. The jerk was my boss now….

He leaned back in the chair, letting me shut down Ann's computer, reorganize, and close her drawers, laughing at my irritating mode.

"What?" I shouted, turning around to look at him. His penetrating green eyes looking at me had a sparkle that almost made me jump into his arms. My heartbeat raced, and suddenly, the annoyance feeling was mysteriously gone.

"I like you!" he said, still laughing. "And I'm not leaving you here alone. I'll walk you to your car."

"No thanks! You can go, I'm fine." I replied, going back to my work, trying to disguise my attraction to him.

"No, no, no. I would rather wait for you. What if you decide to go through my stuff?" he said, making an interrogation face.

"You're sick!" I started rushing through my work. He sat up on the chair, rolled it back to the desk, and turned the computer back on. I looked at him in disbelief. He smiled without looking at me.

"I'm done!" I said after fifteen minutes. "Let's go then!" I pushed myself away from the desk, grabbing my stuff underneath it and turning my computer off, all at the same time as I usually do.

"Let's go!" he said, turning Ann's computer off, getting up and grabbing his file.

At the parking garage, I walked fast and didn't look at him once, anxiously trying to get out of there. I had my car key in hand, rushing my last steps to the car, almost running. He giggled, and I blushed but didn't turn to look at him while trying nervously to open the car door. Suddenly, I felt his warm body gently pressing mine against the car.

"What are you in the hurry for?" he asked, whispering in my ear.

I froze and couldn't answer. He stepped back, waiting for my reaction. My heart was pounding fast; I turned to face him, not able to say a word. He approached me slowly, looking straight into my eyes. I couldn't move, I was hypnotized.

He kissed me tenderly.

CHAPTER 6

The next morning at the office.

"What do you know about Joe?" I asked Ann, trying to sound casual and debating in my head if I wanted to tell her about the kiss and everything else or not. At this point, she'll be jealous and try to give me bad advice, such as, *"Are you crazy? He's our boss.... You will get yourself fired...blah, blah, blah...."*

"Not much!" she answered. "All I know is that he's from England but lived in Chicago before moving here because of this job. He's cute, isn't he? I love his British accent!"

A-ha, I knew it! She has a crush on him. Poor Ann, if she only knew that he had already shown his interest in me. I guess it's not a good idea to tell her about Joe and me, at least for now.

"Yeah, he's hot!" I said, agreeing with her.

"Have you eaten my chocolate?" she asked with indignation while still searching her drawer for it.

"Yeah. Sorry, I was starving last night. You know I stayed longer to finish my work."

"Oh, so you're responsible for the mess in my drawers, huh?" she commented.

"Sorry," I said, expressing naivety in my face.

"No biggie," she said, turning to help this delivery guy with an enormous flower arrangement in his hands who had just walked in.

"Hi!"

"Ms. Jane May?" he asked her.

"I'm Jane May!" I exclaimed, getting up and taking the flowers from his hands, feeling puzzled.

"Please sign here!" he said with irrelevance.

I signed the paper, not bothering to look at him. I was frantically trying to find a card, or something, within it. After not finding anything, I stopped the delivery guy, who was already on his way out, questioning, "Who sent it?"

"How should I know?" he said and left, leaving me amazed with his attitude.

"Dickhead!" I said, sitting back at my desk with the flowers in hand. "Who could've sent it?"

"Maybe an ex that is still in love with you? Or the guy you slept with last night…" she said with a grin, coming to help me look for the card.

"No, I don't think so. And I haven't slept with anyone lately, anyway. Alan is out of the picture. We broke up."

"Really? I was going to ask you about him…"

"Flowers!" Joe said when arriving from a late business lunch with Mr. Poch, who also looked content.

"Who sent you these beautiful flowers?" Mr. Poch asked.

"I have no idea, sir! There is no card…" I replied, still trying to figure out where the card could be. Maybe Alan was trying to get back together with me.…

"Maybe there isn't any card because the person who sent it knew you would know who they were from," Joe said, winking at me.

"It makes sense," Ann said. "But I don't think she has a clue…"

They all laughed, but I didn't care. Now I knew who had sent me these beautiful flowers.

#

Friday after work, I was feeling so light and content all day that I didn't realize the day was already over. Ann asked if I wanted to go for a drink, but I turned her down. I just wanted to go home and think of Joe. Alan will regret leaving me. As I strolled to my car, remembering Joe's kiss — such a good kisser, by the way — I heard a voice that sounded like music to my ears.

"Hey."

I turned myself around to face Joe with a huge, pathetic smile of satisfaction on my face that I couldn't disguise.

"Hey," I replied.

"Did you like the flowers?" he said as he approached me.

"I loved them." I sighed.

"Do you want to go for a drink or something?"

"Yeah. I guess," I replied, still with an idiotic smile on my face.

He climbed into my car on the driver's side and closed the door, waiting for me to get in on the other side. It took me a little while to realize what I had to do, but I rushed my way around as soon as I got the insight.

"Ok, let's go then!" I said joyfully. He looked at me, amused. "What?" I didn't understand what he was so amused about.

"Key?" he said, opening his hand in front of me.

"Oh! Here." I handed him the car key, feeling stupid but still smiling ear to ear. He turned the car on, reversed it, and drove us out of there.

He took me to this nightclub in South Beach. It was dark, crowded, and chaotic, with people everywhere and loud music playing. I was somewhat disappointed with his choice because I was expecting something quieter and romantic where we could talk and get to know each other, but apparently, he had something else on his mind. I decided to go with the flow.

We started drinking and dancing all over the place. I was starting to have a fun time when he unexpectedly grabbed my hand and pulled me out of there.

"Too loud, wasn't it?" he said when we were already outside.

"I don't know, I guess. It's still early…. Do we have to go home?" I asked in frustration, glancing at my watch.

"Where do you want to go?" he asked, holding my hand as we started walking. He seemed not to know where to go.

"I don't know…"

Still holding my hand, he pulled me through the crowded street. After several blocks, we got to this much quieter place with lit candles on the tables and suave live music playing. I opened a smile of cheerfulness on my face.

"Are you hungry?" he asked, looking at me while the host directed us to our table.

"A little bit!" I said, a lot more pleased now.

He ordered a bottle of Merlot and steak while I asked for a salad. I was enchanted with the sophisticated place. The server poured the wine and water, which I drank in large gulps. Joe chuckled and sipped his wine, commenting that he'd ordered Merlot because he knew "I'd rather drink wine…" he imitated what I said on our first encounter, making a snobbish face.

"Very funny!" I remarked.

He went on and on, remembering my behavior that day, laughing at my reactions while bringing up everything that had happened between us since we met a few days before. After we ate and finished the bottle of wine, he waved to the server, who came right away.

"Another bottle, please!" he ordered instead of asking for the check. I put a huge, silly smile of satisfaction on my face again.

The couple at the next table got up and started slow dancing, talking, and smiling at each other. Joe looked at me and, with a gesture, asked if I wanted to dance, too. I nodded and got up on my feet. He embraced me and looked deep into my eyes while starting to move with the rhythm of the music.

"I think we can have a really good time together," he mumbled, almost whispering.

"I think so, too…." I said in a hushed tone.

"You're very…funny, sexy, and…moody," he mocked.

"You're embarrassing me…" I mumbled, averting his gaze.

"Look at me," he said. "I was thinking about this game I heard about…"

"A game?" I asked.

"Yeah, game. I think you and I could have a lot of fun together. You turn me on big time. We could play if you want to…"

"What is it called?"

"Do What I Say."

"What?"

"It's the name of the game…"

"Ahhh…"

"Let me explain it to you. It's a couples' game, with only two players and nobody else. It's supposed to be sexy and exciting; there are only three rules in this game," he explained. "First, we can't say no to each other — ever! You have to do everything and anything I ask you to and vice versa."

"It could be fun, but I don't know if I would want to do everything you ask me to…"

"Well, I could say the same about you, but let me finish explaining. It's ok if you don't want to play."

"Ok."

"So, as I was saying, the second rule is, we can't involve other people in the game with us or even use a third person." He went on. "It's a two-person game, remember? We can't tell anyone because that would involve another person."

"I see. Keep going." *Gosh, he smells so good*, I thought to myself, discreetly sniffing his shirt.

"And third, we can't fall for each other — that would spoil the entire game."

"How are we supposed to not get involved with each other? I think that will be the hard part," I said, a little concerned about this rule that seemed unfair to me.

"I have to disagree with you. The hard part is doing what the other asks you to do. Anyway, these are the rules."

"Ahh...ok. What would you ask me to do?" I was still a little confused but dying to be kissed.

"Hmm...I'll think of something. Do you want to play?"

"I do, I do!" I said without thinking, making him chuckle again.

"Seriously now..." he said, "If one of us breaks one single rule, it's over, just like that."

"That's harsh."

"That's what makes the game interesting and exciting."

"I don't know..."

"Just say yes. Please?" he whispered, pulling me even closer to him.

"Yes, yes, yes!" I said, and he giggled again.

It was late when we left the restaurant. We were talking excitedly about the game all the way back to Fort Lauderdale. I had so many questions, and he was delighted to give me more details about the game.

"It's not that you're going to ask me to take my clothes off in the middle of the street or something like that, even because you can't involve other people, making them aware of us or having to give explanations. Let me see.... A good start for you is going home and thinking about your craziest fantasies — the dark and sordid ones. You know, the ones that make you ashamed just to think of them" He was trying to keep a serious tone while my face was turning red. He started laughing at my reaction.

"Wow! I can't share my darkest fantasies with you. I mean…yet. Maybe later when we get to know each other better and I feel comfortable talking to you about them."

"Ooh, I was so curious to know what excites you. Maybe you can start with something lighter to begin with. But you liked the idea, didn't you?" he teased me.

"Jerk!"

We arrived in the parking garage building where his car had been parked almost all night. He kissed me a long and ardent kiss, then told me to go home and think about the game, make plans, and decide my first move. He said he would do the same, and sooner than I had thought, we would be having a lot of fun together. He kissed me goodbye, and I drove home dizzy with my thoughts, excited about what was going to happen next. And since it was Saturday already, I spent the entire weekend planning my first move.

Chapter 7

"How's your weekend?" Ann asked me as soon as I arrived at the office on Monday morning.

"Not so bad. What about yours?" I replied.

"Eh! Nothing much. I went to see my mom and hung out with my sister. We're very close, you know?" She started a conversation about family, which is not my favorite subject.

"Who are you close to, your mom or your sister?" I asked just to be polite.

"My sis…. I don't really get along with my parents," she said with a sad voice.

I didn't want to give her a chance to talk about her family, and I had a very important mission to accomplish anyway, so I excused myself, saying that I needed to go to the restroom. She made an aware face when she saw I was taking my purse with me.

"One of those days, huh?"

I nodded, agreeing with her while walking out of the reception to the restroom but sneaking into the lunchroom instead. I had decided I would be the one making the first game move, so I had to act before Joe did. I felt butterflies in my stomach thinking about what I was about to do, still not sure if I wanted to play that game stuff with him or not. Anyhow, I felt I had nothing to lose. If I changed my mind, I could break one rule, that simple, right?

In the lunchroom, I carefully took out a paper bag with *Joe* neatly written on it from my purse and quickly placed it in the refrigerator, leaving the area as soon as I could. Back at my desk, I had a huge smile of mission accomplished on my face. It was so idiotic that Ann stopped typing to look at me, frowning suspiciously.

Later that afternoon, Joe passed by us, leaving for the day with the paper bag in his hands. My heart jumped up to my throat, and I made a huge effort to swallow it back, trying to control my excitement. In that bag were a plastic container with pineapples, a flier about a luau, and a Hawaiian lei.

#

The luau party at Dania Beach was traditional but known only by locals, so I figured it wouldn't be too crowded, and I made sure that nobody I knew was going. I bought this sexy Hawaiian outfit just for the event and couldn't control myself with such excitement when Thursday night finally arrived.

Once there, I walked around, scanning everybody and everything, eager to see him. Time started passing by, and my apprehension grew. I needed a drink, so I got one called Brainwash, which I thought was a funny name for a drink.

No sign of Joe after the first drink, so I had a second one because I was already feeling stupid. Maybe he thought my luau idea was silly or something. After my third drink and no sign that my plan had been successful, I was determined to relax and enjoy the party. With all that alcohol, I really got brainwashed, and soon, I was dancing and being sociable to anyone who bothered talking or dancing with me.

Suddenly, I spotted Joe sitting by the bonfire, watching me. He smiled and nodded. My reaction was to smile back at what I thought was a hallucination. I kept dancing, making eye contact with him every so often, waiting for the mirage to disappear at any moment. Since it never did, I started walking north on the beach and then to the water, not daring to look back.

I dove under a wave and felt someone grabbing me by my waist when I resurfaced.

"Aren't you afraid to swim at night…in the ocean…alone?" he murmured in my ear, still cuddling me from behind. I leaned my head back against his chest with satisfaction and turned my face to see him; he had a wonderful beam on his most handsome face.

"You really think I'm your catch, huh?" I said, turning my body around.

"Pretty much!" he answered, nodding.

"Actually, you are my catch. I'm a mermaid that seduces men into the ocean and then…I eat them!" I said, jumping over him, holding myself up with my arms around his neck and my legs around his waist.

"I'm scared," he said, thrilled, holding me steady. We took a moment, staring at each other's eyes, and then we kissed.

Chapter 8

The next day, I was in heaven. Ann was looking at me sideways.

"Are you high?" she asked out of nowhere.

"Me? No, why?" I didn't understand the question.

"Well, look at your face. You look pathetic! Did you meet someone? Are you in love?"

"Shh, don't say that. I haven't met anyone else that you don't know about." I wasn't lying.

"Um, ok. Do you want to go out tonight?" she asked.

"Yeah... Why not?"

It was Friday, and Joe hadn't sent me any sign that we were going to do something together anyway.

#

I went home to feed Ollie and change clothes. Ollie was not by the door as I had expected. I looked all over, but he was nowhere to be found.

"Where in the hell that stupid cat can be...." I started calling him. "Here, kitty, kitty.... Oooollie! Ollie..." Nothing. I looked outside in the hallway, and I thought that maybe my good friend and neighbor Mike could have seen him or knew something. I knocked on his door.

"Hey, Jane..." He wasn't surprised to see me. We hang out a lot; he's my building buddy.

"Hey, Mike, have you seen Ollie?" I asked.

"No, not at all. Why? Isn't he in the apartment?"

"Nope. I looked all over for him. He's definitely not in the apartment."

"Strange. How could he possibly have gotten out without you seeing him?"

"I don't know. All I know is when I came home from work, he wasn't by the door as he usually is. I looked all over and called his name, but Ollie is nowhere to be found."

"Have you looked under the bed or behind the couch? Cats love to hide in these places…"

"Ok, Mike, thanks for your help. I'll keep looking. Bye," I cut him off. What was he thinking, I'm stupid? Of course, I looked everywhere!

"Hey, you don't have to be a jerk. I was just trying to help you. And you knocked on my door, remember?"

"Sorry, Mike. I'm really upset right now. And you know me well enough to know that I can be a jerk sometimes."

"Hell yeah, I do," he said, making an unimpressed face. "Let's take another look, may I?" he asked, entering my apartment.

"Sure," I replied and followed.

He went straight to the places he had suggested, but I knew Ollie wasn't there. I rolled my eyes but said nothing because it would only piss him off. He looked everywhere I had already looked, so I didn't help him at all. I just crossed my arms in protest. Suddenly, he had the great idea of getting Ollie's favorite food to see if he was really hiding. It was a genius idea! So, we did. We went around the apartment, calling him with the cat food in hand. We were almost giving up when we heard a weak meow coming from the bathroom.

"Here!" Mike said, pushing me into the bathroom.

"Where in the hell is he?" I asked, going through every little corner.

"Here!" he said, opening the cabinet door and getting his body almost entirely in it.

"Where?" I was freaking out about the idea that he had been there all this time.

"C'mon, little kitty. It's me, your favorite pal. Look what I have for you. Mmm, tuna, your favorite!"

"What in the hell is he doing? Doesn't he want to come out?"

"No, Jane, he's trapped behind the pipe…" he said and pulled Ollie from there. "Poor little Ollie! He's scared," he said, hugging and kissing the cat.

Ollie was shaking, and his eyes were wide open. I took him from Mike's arms and hugged him, too. "Everything is gonna be alright. Poor baby. How did you get stuck in there? Stupid cat!"

We went to the living room, and I led Mike to the door.

"Do you want to go out later?" he asked me.

"Oh, sorry, Mike, I already have a date."

"A boyfriend?"

"Thanks for your help, Mike. Bye." I opened the door for him, ignoring his question, and after a few awkward moments, he left.

I felt bad for him, but what's with guys? They always want something from us, unbelievable! If you smile or ask them a favor, they think you're interested. Even when you say no. All they think about is sex! *Jerks!* Well, Mike and I are friends with benefits. He's cute and adores me dearly. I like it when he's around; it makes me feel protected. So, yes, he gets his way with me sometimes….

I looked at the clock. It was already nine o'clock. I rushed to the bathroom, took a quick shower, changed clothes, and flew to Ann's house.

#

"Welcome, girlfriend!" She was waiting for me with a joint in hand.

We went to Riverside this time because we couldn't agree on where to go, and Riverside has plenty of choices: bar after bar and all kinds of people and music. In the first bar we went to, there was a live band playing this old song that reminded me of my days in high school, one of my favorites, so I started to dance and sing along.

After a while, Ann and I were screaming the song lyrics while dancing. The people in that little place got hooked on us and started doing the same. Suddenly, everybody was shouting the lyrics so loud that the band stopped playing to let us finish the song. We figured they didn't like us very much, so we left for the bar next door, where hip-hop music was playing.

Chapter 9

It was already Thursday, and Joe had made no game move. I was worried; *maybe he didn't like our first date, maybe he found me boring or something, or maybe he found someone else to play with….* I was lost in my thoughts.

"Jane? Are you there?" Ann asked, wheeling her chair around to face me. I didn't know if she was seriously concerned or mocking me.

"What?" I stopped typing and looked at her, confused.

"What in the hell is going on with you? You look so distant. Is something wrong?" she asked.

"No, no. I'm just bored and melancholic. You know, every day, the same boring stuff," I started.

"Ah…don't complain, bitch! You have a pretty good life! Look at you. You are pretty, intelligent, sexy…" she tried to cheer me up.

"I know. I can't complain about my life. Sometimes, I wonder if I'll ever find the right guy. I'm tired of being alone." I couldn't help thinking that Joe wasn't interested in me anymore.

"Let's go out tonight! You will relax and have some fun — maybe you'll meet someone," she said. "You just need to be patient; you're only twenty-one."

"Thanks, Ann, but I'm not in the mood today," I replied, going back to my work.

"Alright then. I tried. Call me if you change your mind," she said, also going back to her work.

"Hello, ladies!" Joe said, entering the reception, looking at Ann and ignoring me.

"Hi, Mr. Garrison, what can I do for you?" Ann asked with a sparkle in her eyes that made me sick; she's so predictable!

"First of all, drop the Mr. Garrison stuff. It makes me look older…and you don't need to be formal with me in the office. Anyway, could you get me a flight to Chicago for tomorrow? Ah, I'll need a hotel room, too."

"Chicago, tomorrow? Sure. I'll try my best, Mr. — oh —Joe," she corrected.

"Thanks, Ann, I'll stay a week. Could you set up my return for next Friday, if it's not much trouble?" he asked her.

"A week? I mean, you'll be gone for an entire week?" She couldn't disguise her disappointment.

"I'll be back!" He teased her, leaving the room without even looking at me.

"Don't you love his British accent?" she sighed.

I didn't answer and kept doing my work. I just hated her and her stupid comments. I hated him, too, for ignoring me. Who does he think he is? Who cares for his British accent…. I wanted to fade away and disappear. I decided it was over, and if Ann wanted him…fine! Good for her. *ASSHOLES!*

#

I went home really pissed with my situation; I couldn't see a way out. *What now? If he doesn't make a move…,what am I supposed to do? Should I take a second step? No, I will not!* I was so very dizzy with my thoughts that I didn't see Mike in the hallway.

"Hello!" he said, getting my attention.

"Oh! Hi Mike!" I replied without stopping and getting ready to open my door.

"What's wrong with you?" he asked. "You seem out in space."

"Just thinking…. That's all. Problems, you know?" I answered.

"Problems?" he asked, making his way into the apartment with me.

"What are you doing?" I asked, annoyed. He was already making himself comfortable on the couch.

"Me? Why?" He wasn't surprised about my nastiness.

"I don't remember inviting you in…" I said, closing the door.

"You never do," he said in a muffled voice. "So, where is Ollie?" He changed the subject.

"I don't know! Where *is* he?" I started looking for him.

"Maybe he's hiding from you again." He cynically smiled at me.

"Very funny! You know what? It's time for you to go!" I said, returning the cynical smile.

"Don't you want to go out?" He tried again.

"NO!" I said with meaning. I really wasn't in a good mood.

"What if I help you find Ollie, and you cook for me in gratitude?"

"Whatever!" I said, giving up. His company could help me take Joe and Ann out of my head. "Chicken and vegetables, it is."

He jumped off the couch, satisfied, and started looking for Ollie. He went straight to the bathroom, thinking that he might be there again, but he was sleeping on my bed under the blanket.

"Found him!" he yelled from the bedroom, coming into the kitchen with Ollie in his arms. "What do you want to listen to?" he asked, putting the cat down and walking into the living room to check the options through my CDs.

Ollie was back to normal and started meowing for his food, rubbing my legs. "Ok, ok, Ollie!" I said, getting his food from the cabinet.

We had some wine, and Mike made me laugh with his stupid jokes. I like him, but unfortunately, our chemistry is not a hundred percent, not even eighty percent, to be precise.

#

The next morning at the office.

"Hi! Is everybody already in?" I asked Ann, rushing to my desk, knowing that I was late again.

"Yep, and Mr. McKee already asked about you…" Ann said, sipping her coffee and going back to typing.

"What did you say to him?" I asked, turning my computer on and putting my stuff away.

"I said you were late!" She didn't bother looking at me.

"Thanks, bitch." I replied. *Why was she doing that to me?*

"What should I say? That you were…where?" She stopped typing to look at me with indignation.

Who was in a bad mood now, huh? I thought to myself.

"I don't know! Something more creative than that!" I couldn't believe she was betraying me.

"What about the…truth?" She made a face.

"Ok, Ann. Whatever! I don't want to argue with you. Just leave me alone." I turned my back to her, starting my workday. I don't know what is going on with her. I bet she misses Joe, too, but betraying me isn't ok. I'm glad I know how to sway the bosses. This should be nothing.

The day went by slowly, and I had to try not to quit. It was getting very difficult to stand Joe's silence. He had been quiet since the luau, and now he was off to Chicago for an entire week! I couldn't take it anymore. What was I going to do the entire week without seeing him?

I drove home, swearing at everyone on my way. When parking at my building, I remembered I hadn't checked my mailbox in a while. The mailroom was empty, but my box full of junk, bills, and an envelope without a sender caught my attention. I managed to open it while opening my apartment door, putting my stuff away, and trying not to step on Ollie.

It was a plane ticket to New York in my name for Saturday morning.

New York, Saturday? I thought to myself. I hadn't bought any ticket…oh! Joe!

"Yes! Yes! Yes!" I started dancing, grabbing Ollie, and kissing him. "I'm going to New York! I'm going to New York!"

#

Saturday morning arrived. My hands were sweating, and my heart raced in anticipation of the weekend ahead of me. It was my first time flying somewhere, too.

How was I supposed to find him in New York? Most likely, he'll be waiting for me at the airport…. I needed a drink. After two glasses of wine, I felt more relaxed and in no time, we were landing at LaGuardia Airport. I wandered around without knowing what to do or where to go. *What if he isn't here?* I was getting nervous, looking all over for a clue, when —

"Hey!" I suddenly heard his sweet and so-expected voice behind me.

"Hey," I said, turning around to face him with a huge stupid beam on my face.

"How's your flight?" he asked, getting my bag.

"Fine…" was all I could say, still with that huge smile on my face and staring at him pathetically without blinking.

"Are you hungry?" he asked, chuckling.

"Not really, but if you're…I mean, I could eat something…" *Oh, shut up, Jane!* I thought to myself.

"Did you eat anything on the plane?" he asked.

"No! I had a drink — actually two," I said without thinking.

"I can tell…" he said and pulled me closer to kiss me.

The hotel was gorgeous, five stars for sure. Our room was big, all white, and decorated in a modern style. The bathroom was impeccable, with a huge round Jacuzzi. The bed…oh, the bed was a modern white four-poster bed with white see-through drapery hanging from the canopy. The all-white bedwear was very cozy, crispy, and sexy. The dozens of fluffy pillows were to die for. I loved it.

#

Later that day, I stayed lying naked there, looking around that wonderful place under the silky sheet, feeling good after having a lovely time in Joe's arms. He came back from the bathroom with his hair wet, putting his shirt on and asking, "Are you getting up?"

"Do I have to? I don't think I can…" I said, trying to lift my body up, pretending I was dizzy and dropping myself back on the bed, teasing him.

"C'mon! It wasn't that bad, was it? I tried my best to please you…" he joked.

"Bad? I'm in heaven!" I pulled him into the bed with me, kissing him all over.

"Wow. We have plenty of time for more of that later," he said, kissing me back, "but now I'm really starving, aren't you?" He held me down, sniggering while I was still trying to kiss him.

"No…. I want more of that now." I said with a begging voice.

"You'll regret that, my dear." He laughed aloud, getting up and finished getting dressed.

"Never, I'll never regret that or anything I would ever do with you, my dear."

We both laughed, and I started dressing as well.

We went to this nice little restaurant on Madison Avenue — cute and romantic. He ordered steak and a bottle of Merlot, of course, and I ordered a salad, as usual. We talked about New York and about what we wanted to do the next day. I wanted to go shopping, but he wanted to go to the Metropolitan Museum. I thought I could do anything as long as I was with him, so I didn't argue and let him do all the planning, also because it was his turn to tell me what to do.

"Are we still playing the game?" I asked him, wondering since we appeared to be getting along as normal people did.

"Sure," he said, calling the server at the same time. "Why are you asking?"

"I don't know; I just get the feeling we're being us, with no…you know, crazy fantasies," I said, a little afraid of what he could think about my question or suspect that I was falling for him big time.

"Don't worry; we'll get there. Just let it be," he said, putting cash on the table.

We went back to the hotel and had a wonderful, unforgettable night together. He's perfect. I love everything about him and would do anything to be with him forever…*for-ever!*

The next day, we went to the Metropolitan Museum as he wanted, and believe me or not, I loved it. He was a gentleman but not a lousy one, just the right type…very handsome, sexy, and rich. Yeah, he can definitely solve all my problems at once. All I had to do was get him to feel the same way about me and forget about the game stuff. That was my goal. He'll fall for me, too, and we'll live happily ever after forever.

Later that day, we kissed goodbye at the airport. I went back to Fort Lauderdale, and he went back to Chicago. It was difficult seeing him going away.

Chapter 10

The week without him went by slowly. I tried to keep myself busy going shopping, going to the beach to get tanned, cleaning my house, doing laundry, and still…time was against me. Friday finally came. I had butterflies in my stomach just thinking about seeing Joe again, and it was my turn to make a move. I needed to plan what I would do this time, so I opened a bottle of wine, put some music on, and relaxed on the couch, planning my next step.

Back from Chicago, Joe was kind of distant, not really showing that he was happy to see me again. But I was on a mission; he would get his interest back in me one way or another. Wednesday, the office was somewhat slow, and I had a plan to set into action after work. But at lunchtime, Joe passed by us, leaving for the day. I had to think fast if I wanted to catch him before it was too late, so I got up almost at the same time, told Ann I was going to buy lunch and rushed my way out of the building in a flash.

I had this sexy black crisscross dress on that could be easily opened by just untying it. It was perfect for what became a last-minute plan. I rushed to the parking garage and waited on the first-floor ramp for his car to come down.

About two minutes later, I saw him making the curve on top of the ramp and coming down in my direction. My heart was beating fast. I hesitated for a second, but I got in front of his car, making him stop. He shook his head in disbelief when he saw me flashing him, opening and closing my dress quickly so no one else could see me but him. He opened the passenger's door and said, "Get in!"

"Are you crazy? What if I weren't alone?" he said, driving away, clearly upset.

"I thought it could be exciting if you were with Mr. Poch or Mr. McKee," I teased him, making a joke.

"You're getting…" he started saying.

"What? Audacious?" I completed his sentence.

"Vulgar! That's the word I was looking for," he said without looking at me.

"C'mon. You said that I should let my craziest fantasies come out for you. Remember? And I knew you were alone…" I complained, feeling a little odd about his comment.

"I know what I said," he replied, and he drove away to a remote street in Dania Beach.

He was nasty. He kept looking out the window while making out with me as if he was afraid that someone would see us. Suddenly, he got off me and started fixing his clothes, leaving me unfinished.

"I can't do this! Someone can see us," he said, visibly annoyed with the situation. "Get out!" he shouted, starting the car.

"What? You're kidding me!" I panicked.

"GET OUT!" he yelled.

"How am I going to get back? You can't do this to me…" I started arguing, almost crying now.

"Here…" he said and tossed a twenty-dollar bill on my lap that he pulled from his pocket.

"Take a taxi or a bus if you want. OUT now."

I got out, and he drove away, leaving me there in the middle of nowhere, alone. I started walking and crying, at the same time feeling dirty and used. I walked all the way to US1, where I could take a cab back to the office.

#

"What happened to you, Jane?" Ann asked, scrunching her forehead together in concern.

"Nothing. I just started walking on the beach and forgot about the time. When I realized what time it was, I rushed back and got all messed up and sweaty." I lied.

"You better go to the restroom and get your face straight, Missy," she advised me.

"Yeah…thanks, Ann." I went to the restroom and cried even more.

I didn't want to talk for the rest of the day. Ann was suspicious that something had happened, but I knew she would wait for the right moment to ask. After work, I went home feeling miserable and stupid. All I could do was cry myself to sleep.

#

The next morning, I overslept again, but I didn't rush as I usually do. I didn't care. Taking my time, I took a shower, put on this beautiful and very classy outfit, had breakfast, and went off to what could be my last day at work. I was already late when I parked my car in the garage, slowly grabbing my stuff and walking to the elevator.

"Hey, gorgeous. You're late." Joe grabbed me from behind and whispered in my ear.

"Let me go!" I said, getting out of his embrace.

"I know you're upset, but you asked for that," Joe said.

"I asked for that? You're kidding me, right?" I reacted.

"No, you acted like a trollop, and I treated you like one. It wasn't my intention, but you wouldn't listen, like now, you never listen…" he replied and started walking to the elevator.

"Wait! Don't leave me here like this! Being a whore wasn't my plan. I only wanted to spice things up a little. I'm sorry if I messed up. Maybe you're right; it was my fault. I shouldn't have behaved like that. I guess it was vulgar.... Sorry."

"That's fine. I didn't behave well either. I shouldn't have left you there alone. I was upset about other stuff going on in my life and ended up lashing out at you. I'm really sorry."

"Do you want to talk about it?" I asked, but he shook his head. "Well, I'm sorry, too," I said, and we kissed in the elevator.

CHAPTER 11

Still not convinced that I wanted to go on with that stupid game thing, I wasn't too excited anymore after the way he treated me. I had this strange feeling about him, but something kept me attracted to him. It's hard to explain, but I still wanted to be with him. I was a little afraid of what could happen next, but at the same time, very excited just to think about it.

A week passed by with no movement on his part. I actually relaxed a little, forgetting about that awful incident. Ann and I went for a walk on Las Olas Blvd after work and decided to stop for a drink at this very cool place we used to go to all the time. They have live music every Friday, and everybody who works on Las Olas Blvd goes there after work for happy hour, so we went for the sake of the good times.

"Isn't it awesome? I miss this place!" Ann said, sitting at the bar.

"Yeah. Cool," I said, doing the same.

"What can I get you girls?" the bartender asked in a friendly manner.

"A margarita for me, please," I said, finding him kind of cute.

"Same for me," Ann said, also interested in him.

"Mm…" she said, elbowing me when he left to go to the other side.

"Yeah. I know! He's really cute." I replied, elbowing her back.

"Let's bet! A hundred dollars that he's going to ask me out tonight!" she said, glancing at him with an enticing face when he looked at her from the other end of the bar.

"He's going to ask me out, bitch!" I said, calling him back with a gesture.

"Hey!" he said, already in front of us.

"Did I tell you I want my margarita on the rocks?" I said in a provocative voice.

"Ok," he said, "on the rocks for you," then he looked at Ann, waiting for her to say something about her drink, too.

"What?" she pretended she wasn't paying attention.

"Would you like your margarita on the rocks?" he asked.

"Oh! What are my options? I mean…what do you suggest?" She blinked at him.

"On the rocks is good…" he said, chuckling.

"On the rocks, then!" she said, dancing to the music's rhythm.

"He didn't like you…" I commented, making her stop dancing when he left again.

"How do you know? Did he say something to you?" she mocked me.

"No! I can tell he liked me…" I started dancing as well.

We laughed and looked around to check the place out. We saw some familiar faces and nodded to them in recognition.

"Here you are!" the bartender said, setting the drinks in front of us.

"Thanks," I said.

"Yeah, thanks. What's your name?" Ann asked, putting that provocative smile on her face again.

"Fred! Yours?" he asked back.

"Ann," she said as if she were a confident woman, "and this is my friend, Jane," she added before he could ask me.

"Nice meeting you two." He winked and walked away to help someone who called him on the other side.

We started talking about what we were going to do to get his attention and win the bet. We were happily finishing our drinks when Fred came back with two more margaritas.

"Yay! More margaritas!" we said at the same time, still feeling joyful and talking nonstop.

Then Ann got up and started dancing. It didn't take long before some guy joined her. They started talking, and I felt a little rejected, so I went back to my margarita.

"So, Jane, are you from here? I mean…I haven't seen you around." Fred started talking to me.

I could tell he was waiting for me to be alone to start a conversation; of course, he liked me better. They always do. Poor Ann.

"Yeah, actually, I am. I used to come here all the time, but…you know? You get tired of going to the same place over and over." I looked at him, content, feeling full of myself, and much better now since I had definitely won the bet.

"I know what you mean. Would you like to go out one of these days?" he got straight to the point, inflating my ego.

"Sure," I said, taking a sip of my drink, showing a little embarrassment just to impress him.

When I lifted my gaze to look at him, I saw Joe staring at me. He was sitting across from us. I gasped, not with contentment but fear. I feared he would think I did that on purpose to upset him as if it were part of the game. He would think I was being vulgar again by flirting with the bartender. I got up at once and left as fast as I could, not looking back. I hope he realized that I wasn't planning anything, it was just a coincidence.

#

"You owe me a hundred dollars, my friend," Ann said at the office first thing Monday morning.

"Why? You didn't. Did you?" I asked her with a disgusted face.

"I sure did, girlfriend!" she said, smiling victoriously. "Where did you go, anyway?"

"I felt sick, so I left. You were so involved with that guy, and I didn't want to bother you. Sorry." I made up an explanation.

"No problem. Actually, it worked well because Fred asked what had happened that you left so suddenly," she started. "We didn't know if you had left for good or just gone to the restroom or something, so he kept me company. And since you never came back, he offered to walk me to my car…. And there you are, a hundred dollars, please!"

"All right, I guess you deserve it." I laughed at her gesture, asking for the money.

"Ms. May?" The intercom spoke.

"Yes, Mr. McKee?" I answered right away.

"Could you make reservations for ten at my favorite restaurant for tonight?" he asked.

"Sure, Mr. McKee."

"Thanks. Could you bring me Mr. Smith's file?"

"Right away." I rushed to do what he asked.

CHAPTER 12

We had one of those harsh days at work, and I was exhausted. I wanted nothing else but to get in my bathtub. Unfortunately, I had to stop at the supermarket to get cat litter and cat food, plus a couple of other things for the house. I was wandering around through the supermarket aisles when I ran into Joe, apparently doing the same thing.

"You…" I said, surprised.

"Do you shop here often?" he asked in a flirtatious tone.

"Pretty much." I didn't know what else to say.

"I'm buying some wine. I have a very special night tonight." He winked, showing me a couple of nice wine bottles he had in his cart.

"Oh!" I felt a little jealous.

"So, what are you up to?" he went on.

"Not much. I'm going home." I said without enthusiasm, feeling rejected.

"O-k!" He looked at me with some kind of indignation.

"Bye," I said, starting to walk away and feeling a little upset about his eagerness for the night he was about to have.

Who was he going out with? We just accidentally ran into each other. He couldn't have been planning this…or could he? I was confused. I got in my car and drove out of the parking lot, still thinking about the encounter.

A quarter mile from my home, this stupid car cuts my way, making me brake, almost crashing behind him.

"Look where you're going, you fool!" I yelled. When the guy got out of the car and started walking in my direction, I realized it was Joe. I opened my window as he approached.

"What's wrong with you?" he shouted at me.

"What? You cut me off, I almost crashed…" I was shouting back when he interrupted me.

"I'm talking about us! Don't you get it? I was giving you a clue. I want you to come with me!" he finally said.

"Oh…really?" I was still confused and trying to make sense of the facts.

"Yeah. Really," he said, striking the car door and stepping back in an irritated mood.

"I'm sorry, I didn't get it. I think I had put off that game stuff for a while," I said, trying to come up with an excuse for my stupidity.

"You had put off?" He leaned in to look at me closely, very serious. "So, you don't want to play anymore!" He was fuming with those irresistible green eyes.

"I don't know…" I was still not sure what to say, but I couldn't look away from his gaze.

"You must decide right now. I want you to come with me. If you don't, that will be a *no,* and the game will be over! What's going to be?" He crossed his arms, leaning against the car door, still staring at me, waiting for my response.

I wanted to say no, but I couldn't resist. I wanted him so bad. I loved his handsome face, his smell, his kiss…. I was ready to forget everything he did to me and melt in his arms again.

"I'm coming with you."

"That's my girl!" he said, tapping on the car door and standing up with satisfaction now. "Why don't you park over there? I'll wait for you at the corner, ok?" and he pointed to a parking space on the street.

"Ok," I said and went to park my car where he told me to and rushed back to his car.

He parked the car at the marina, and we started walking on the dock. At the pier, we passed by those big luxurious boats that made me wonder what he was up to. The very last one was a wonderful, oversized yacht that had its engine already on as if it were waiting for us. He got on the boat first, put his grocery bags down, and reached for me, helping me to get on board. I was amazed just for being there. I had never been on a yacht like that before. The only boat I'd ever been on was a tour boat in Miami that took tourists to see celebrities' houses by the water.

"So, are you surprised?" he broke the silence.

"Cool, I have never been on a boat this big before," I said, trying to disguise my nervousness now that the boat had started sliding away.

"We're going to the open sea. It's a full moon night, and I thought we could swim under the moonlight," he explained his plan.

"I hope you don't make me swim all the way back this time," I said without thinking.

"What was that?" He laughed at me. "If you behave well, as a good girl should, you've nothing to worry about." He completed, still laughing at my comment.

"Am I behaving well so far?" I asked, worried.

"So far, so good…" he said and hugged me, kissing the top of my head as we sailed away.

The boat halted its engine. Only the sound of tiny waves broke the silence, crashing on the boat and making it jiggle a little. He took me inside the cabin, where there was a table set for two and ready for us; the candles were lit, the wine poured, and the food on our plates.

"How did you do that?" I asked, amazed. "Who is driving the boat? Where is everybody?" I asked, puzzled.

"There is nobody but us…" he said, pulling a chair for me to sit.

"What is this?" I asked after taking a look at my plate.

"Escargots à la Bourguignonne."

"Can you ask the chef to make me a burger? Or a salad will be fine, really. I'm not eating snails."

"Why don't you try it?" he said, getting one with this little weird fork and bringing it toward my mouth.

"Nope!"

"C'mon, I bet you'll love it…" He tried again the way someone tries to make a kid open their mouth to take medicine.

I turned my face away as a stubborn child would do. He burst into laughter while having fun with my demeanor.

"Ok, you have to *do what I say* — eat it!" He was threatening me, bringing the fucking game up and having a blast.

I opened my mouth with my eyes closed, and he fed me the disgusting snail. It was kind of chewy but not that bad.

"It tastes like garlic. Why do people like to eat this if they have to add a lot of garlic to make it edible?" I said, willingly feeding myself another snail.

"People eat them because they're exotic and expensive," he lectured.

"Yeah, right! Would you eat a snake or an alligator just because it's exotic?"

"It depends on the chef. Of course, I wouldn't if you were

cooking." he mocked, still having the time of his life.

"Very funny!" I said and resumed eating my food.

He leaned back in his chair and looked directly into my eyes in an easy and happy manner while taking a sip of his wine.

"You're fun to be with. I like you…"

"I'm fun? That's all?"

"No, you are beautiful, too…"

"What else?" I leaned back in my chair and took a sip of my wine, mimicking his actions and staring back at his gaze.

"What else do you want me to say? That you're the most beautiful, sexy, and moody girl I have ever been with?" He had a sensual smile on his gorgeous face now.

"Do you have a girlfriend?" I filled myself with the courage to ask.

"No, do you have a boyfriend?"

"Nope. Are you playing the game with someone else?"

"No. You?"

"No."

"Ok then, let's go to the deck to check the moon…" He got up, grabbed my hand, and off we went.

The warm full moon night was beautiful, and the ocean was calm and flat, reflecting the moonlight. There were a couple of lounge chairs with robes just waiting for us under more candlelight.

"Let's go for a swim?" he asked me, taking his clothes off and diving into the ocean. "C'mon!" he yelled from the water.

I slowly started to take my clothes off, and then I jumped into the water, squealing loudly. He came closer and kissed me tenderly.

"You *are* the most beautiful girl I have ever been with," he said, holding my face in his hand and staring into my eyes.

I felt my heart skip a beat. I melted in his arms and was ready to do whatever he asked me to. All I wanted was to be there with him.

Chapter 13

A week had passed, and I couldn't decide on what to do next. Chills ran over my body every time I had an idea. I had to think it through and reevaluate ten times before just to make sure I would behave as a good girl should. The last thing I wanted was to upset Joe again.

How could I do it without some spice that could appear vulgar to his judgment? Confused, with time running out, I had to think fast, or our relationship would cool down.

"Hey, Jane?" Ann called me while turning to get some papers she had just printed out.

"Yes…" I responded, still typing.

"I'm going to New York this weekend. Do you mind taking care of Max for me? If you could just stop by once a day to let him out and give him some food and water." She asked if I could take care of Max, her sweet dog. "I would really appreciate it."

"You're going to New York, bitch? Alone?" I asked.

"Oh no! With my sister," she said, "It'll be only for the weekend. She found a college that she wants to apply to, and she wants me to go with her to see the place. Look and tour around, check prices and stuff."

"Sure, Ann, no problem. I'll take care of Max for you."

"What are you doing this weekend?" she asked.

"I can't make up my mind…probably nothing," I answered.

Mr. McKee walked into the reception with a big box full of gifts from clients in his hands that we could have if we wanted. We waited until he left the room and hurried to open it and check what was inside. It had all sorts of things: chocolate, candies, cookies, pens, T-shirts, and tickets for the *Cirque du Soleil,* which grabbed my attention.

"I want this if you don't mind," I told Ann, grabbing the tickets.

"What is it?" She took the tickets from my hand. *"Cirque du Soleil,* I want to go, too. Maybe we can go together?" she said, still looking at the tickets. "The tickets are for Sunday night. I'll be back by then."

"I want to go with Mike, don't you get it?" I lied.

"Oh, alright then. Mike who? Your neighbor? I didn't know you had something with him. You've never told me. I bet I would be tired, anyway. Have fun then!"

We kept looking inside the box.

The idea of inviting Joe to the *Cirque du Soleil* thrilled me. What could go wrong? I would dress casually, and afterward, we could go to that restaurant where he took me on our first date in South Beach. I left his ticket on his car windshield and went home as happy as I could possibly be.

#

Sunday night came. I was nervous and tried on my entire closet but couldn't make up my mind on what to wear. I finally decided on a simple top and jeans. Running late as usual, I left in a hurry, parked my car, and rushed inside, taking my assigned seat. The seat on my side was empty, uneasily waiting for *someone* to sit on it.

The show started, and I grew anxious as nobody claimed that seat. I tried my best to pay attention to the show, but it was impossible. He didn't show up.

I was so frustrated that I couldn't take it anymore. With half an hour to the end, I got up and left. I drove all the way to Fort Lauderdale, thinking about what could have happened to him. *Maybe he didn't get the ticket in the first place. Or maybe he decided to break a rule and stop playing the game with me....*

I arrived home feeling miserable. Mike was getting back at the same time.

"Hey," he said.

"Hi."

"Are you ok? You look sad."

"I'm fine," I responded.

"Would you like me to come over? Or if you want, you can come to my place..." he went on.

"Nah.... I'd rather go sleep. Thanks." I searched for my key in my purse.

"C'mon, I can tell you need a friend tonight." He approached me and I threw my arms around his neck and started crying.

"Sorry, I'm just feeling weird tonight...lonely." I sobbed. "I'm so lonely..."

"You don't have to be. You know I have feelings for you, don't you?" he said, and I wept even more. "I really want you..." He kissed me tenderly.

I couldn't react, so I let myself go. He took me to his place, and we had a lovely night sleeping together. I felt rejected by Joe and needed to feel loved. Mike loves me and I feel protected in his company. It is good to know that he's always there for me.

#

"How was New York?" I asked Ann on Monday morning.

"Awesome," she said. "I had such a nice time. How was the *Cirque du Soleil?*"

"Cool," I said without giving more details.

"Was Max sad about my absence?" she asked.

"I guess so…. He's such a nice dog." We had a lot of work to do, so we couldn't keep chatting.

#

At the end of the day, Ann didn't want to go anywhere because she had laundry to do and wanted to spend time with Max. I didn't want to go home, but it seemed that I had no better option, so I walked to my car slowly, trying to decide where to go. I was considering going to watch a movie or just wasting some time at the mall. When opening my car door, Joe embraced me softly.

"Sorry, I couldn't go," he whispered in my ear. "Something came up in the last minute…."

"What happened?" I said, turning around to face him.

"My friend's car broke down, and I had to go get him. It took forever for the towing truck to arrive…."

"Oh, ok. You could've called me or texted, at least…"

"Yeah, sorry. Do you want to go out for a drink or something?" he asked, tucking my hair behind my ear.

I nodded shyly, looking into his beautiful eyes and feeling the warmth of his embrace. He smiled tenderly, kissed me, and then opened the car door, getting in the driver's seat. I hushed to the other side, happy as a butterfly, knowing that the game was still on.

We didn't go far that night. We went to this cute restaurant, and after we ate, he took me for a walk on the beach. Holding my hand, he told me that the game was still on because he hadn't actually said *no* by not showing up; it was an unexpected event that he had no control over. He also said that he would make it up to me somehow for having stood me up. Then, he drove us back to the parking garage, kissed me goodbye, and left. I drove home feeling better; I couldn't wait to see what he was up to next.

Chapter 14

It was already Friday. Joe had made no move, and I was getting tired of this whole game thing.

At the office, he pretended that we were complete strangers to each other. Actually, he was a lot nicer to Ann than to me.

I was freaking out all the time, waiting and waiting for nothing. Why did I agree to play this game in the first place? How stupid I was!

If I hadn't been persuaded to play the game with him that night, he could be my boyfriend by now. I was getting really upset with the situation. So, I decided to tell him that I didn't want to play anymore. All I wanted was to be his girlfriend.

Ann and I went to happy hour at that little place on Las Olas again. I really needed to clear my mind. We wanted to see Fred and have some fun. We planned to mess with him. This time, we were getting a table so we could take turns going to the bar for drinks, hit on him, and then come back to the table. We bet another one hundred dollars on which of us he would prefer and ask out this time.

The music was cool. We got this table close to the band so we could have a better view of the place and the bar without being too visible to Fred. Ann decided she wanted to go first since she was the winner last time. I agreed just to get it started, and I also knew she liked the guy. All she needed was an excuse to see him again.

As she left on the mission, Amber and Steve arrived, asking if they could sit with us since the place was so crowded and they had nowhere else to sit. "Of course," I agreed.

They are old friends of ours. We met when we first started working at the office and used to come here every Friday for happy hour. They also work on Las Olas and apparently haven't broken the happy hour habit like Ann and I have. Catching up and remembering old times, we ordered drinks and appetizers. Ann took a long time to come back, but when she finally did, she had a huge smile on her face.

"I want to see if you can beat me, girlfriend. He's already mine," she said quietly in my ear so no one else could hear her. "Hey! Amber, Steve! How nice seeing you guys?" She kissed them both on the cheek, then sat down at the table, joining the conversation.

I excused myself when getting up to go to the restroom. I stopped by the bar on my way back.

"Hey, Fred!" I called him.

"Hey, Jane, nice to see you again. Can I get you anything?" I could tell he was happy to see me.

"I think I want a beer tonight," I said.

"What kind?" he asked.

"Any kind…"

"Yeah, I have that," he said and turned to get the beer. "So, are you with Ann?"

"Yep. We're sitting over there…" I pointed in our table direction, "We're with a couple of friends. What about you? Are you working a lot?"

"Not that much. I enjoy working here. Where do you work?" he asked.

"Ann and I work at this law office up the road."

"Excuse me for a minute," he said, trying to get something for someone. "Don't disappear again!" He smiled, turning to talk to this guy who was asking him for a drink.

"I'll come back later. Bye."

I headed back to the table. When I got there, I was surprised to see how many people had joined us. Amber and Steve were already there when I left. Now I could count Mary, Susan, Josh, and Justin. I kissed everybody on the cheek and pulled a chair next to Ann.

I don't know Mary, Susan, and Josh very well, but Justin is a nice nerd guy who has a crush on Ann. She met him when Mr. Poch sent her with paperwork to the real estate office he works at down the road. They became friends, but they never had anything, as far as I know.

"Hey, bitch, I think you're going to win again. Fred didn't care much for me today." I told her, taking a sip of my beer.

"Well, too bad for him because I'm really into Justin right now," she said with a grin. I didn't get why she was interested in Justin when Fred was a way bigger catch.

"You.... And here I am, wasting my time trying to make it more exciting for you. Brat!" I complained. She shrugged, turning herself to Justin again.

"So, do you want to dance?" Steve asked me.

"Why not?"

I got to my feet, and he put his hands around my waist. We started dancing to this light jazz rhythm. We chatted about what we had been up to lately and where we worked, but nothing exciting.

After a while, we went back to the table. Justin was still there, but Ann was not. I looked around to see if she had gone to the bar again, but I couldn't see her anywhere. As I swept my gaze around the place to find her, I spotted someone else instead: Joe.

Apparently, Joe had not seen me yet, so I observed him for a while to see if he was with someone. He was alone, looking around and drinking a beer. I didn't know if his presence was because of the game or just a coincidence. The doubt was driving me crazy. It didn't take long for him to see me. He nodded and fixed his eyes on me.

"Have you seen who's here?" Ann asked me when she got back to the table. "Joe."

"Yeah, I saw him too," I said, trying to sound casual.

"Let's invite him to sit with us," she suggested.

"NO! Leave him there. I mean, it could be embarrassing for us if we get drunk or something…" I really didn't know what could be worse than having Joe at the table with us. I didn't know if I could control myself after a couple of drinks.

"Would be embarrassing either way if he sits here with us or stays there watching us. Duh! I'll go talk to him," she decided and left to invite him over.

"No…" I tried to hold her back, but it was too late. I got so anxious about the commotion that I got up and rushed to the bar. I needed another drink and time to think. I thought that being separated from Ann and everybody else would make things easier for Joe if he was planning something for us to be together. So, I decided to stay at the bar, talking to Fred and wait for Joe's next move.

Ann would think that I was still trying to win the bet, and in the end, everything would be fine. From the bar, I could see Ann talking to Joe. They were smiling, and I could tell she was flirting with him. I got jealous and called my friend Fred, who came right away.

"Another beer?" he asked.

"I need something stronger," I said.

"Here, drink this," he said, giggling at my nervousness.

"What's that?" I asked but didn't wait for him to answer. I drank it anyway. "Ugh! Strong!" I made a face.

"So, why do you want to get drunk?" he asked.

"Who said I want to get drunk? Can I have another one?" He was still laughing at my facial expression as he poured another — whatever it was — into my little shot glass.

"What's the deal with you and that guy Ann is talking to? Are you jealous of him or her? Or both? Ann seems to like him." He smirked, making an interrogation face.

"Haha, he's just a coworker. What's the matter with you? Are you a spy or something? Pretending to be a bartender but getting into everybody's business…to blackmail them later…for money or something else?" I teased him.

"Yeah, for something else," he said, nodding seriously.

"What?"

"Maybe for a kiss," he said.

"A kiss?"

"Yeah, a kiss will do," he said, getting closer to my face. He kissed me on the lips, taking me by surprise.

I saw Joe's eyes stabbing me from a distance, and I couldn't move. It was too late. He probably will think I'm provoking him on purpose and will call me a trollop again.

"Just a coworker, huh? He seems to be enraged. Did I put you in a difficult situation?" Fred asked, concerned about Joe's reaction to the kiss. Terror consumed my body as I knew Joe wasn't going to take the kiss nicely. I panicked, not really knowing what to do next.

"No. It's complicated. I wasn't expecting to be kissed, that's all…" With all the alcohol buzzing in my mind, I grabbed Fred's face and kissed him again without thinking twice. I knew that Joe was going to break up with me and say that the game was over, and I really didn't want to go home and cry myself asleep for being rejected again.

Ann came to tell me she was leaving with Justin. Fred promised her he would take care of me and drive me home in case I got too drunk to drive. She agreed with the arrangement and left.

I didn't want to move while Joe was sitting there, so I decided to stay put all night long if required. *He can't be upset with me. After all, we are just playing a game, and as far as I remember, there is no rule forbidding the players to have an affair with others since they aren't technically together.* I was getting lost in my head. Fred noticed my worry and asked if I wanted him to scare Joe away.

"No, you're crazy? He is my boss!"

"Your what?" he questioned loudly as if he didn't believe me. "You better find another job soon, girl, he's pissed."

"I have to go." I suddenly got up and hurried out when I realized that Joe was distracted talking with someone else and not paying attention to me. That was my chance to escape.

I was wrong.

He reached me when I was getting to my car and grabbed my arm with force before I could get in. "Are you scared of me?"

"You are hurting me. Let me go," I said, trying to yank my arm away from his grip, but he held me tight.

"Why? Just tell me why?" It was clear that he was trying to keep his cool, but his eyes were showing disappointment and anger instead. He was speechless for a moment as he waited for me to apologize or say something, but I couldn't think straight.

"I don't know. I wasn't trying to upset you. Believe me, he kissed me unexpectedly…" I was trying to excuse myself for my bad behavior.

"Rubbish!" he said, interrupting me. "I'm starting to think that you like to be a trollop, and you enjoy being treated like one because…"

"No, Joe. Please, he surprised me."

"Do you think I'm stupid? He didn't surprise you. I've seen you flirting with the guy before, but that was before you told me you didn't have a boyfriend. You lied to me."

"No, let me explain…" I was getting frustrated, not knowing what to say or do.

"There is no explanation. You kissed him twice, right in my face! If you wanted to upset me, congratulations, you succeeded. Have a great life. It's over." He pushed me away and started walking away.

"No! Joe! Don't leave me here like this…" He ignored me and kept going. I ran after him and tried to stop him from leaving, holding his arm. "Please, let's talk!"

"Leave me alone, Jane!" he said, pulling his arm from my grip.

"You know what? Yes, I was flirting with him because, as you said, we were just playing a freaking game, right? You never said we were together, and I was tired of waiting for you to make a move. Who knows if you lied to me, too? Maybe you're kissing other people, too!"

"You are sick!"

"No, you are! To my knowledge, there is no rule preventing us from having fun with other people. What did you expect me to do? Do you think I would just sit there and wait for you to get horny and want to fuck me again?" I was yelling at him in the middle of the parking garage, which infuriated him even more.

"You're being vulgar again. I guess you're a slut after all," he yelled back at me.

"I am! And if you leave me here, I'll go back and sleep with him. And you can bet that he'll be very happy to be with me. You're a jerk!" I turned around, making my way back to the bar.

"You're not going back there!" He grabbed my arm again, pulling me toward my car. "You know what? You don't deserve my respect. You're a freaking trollop!"

"Yeah, apparently, I'm your whore…"

"Get in the car, NOW!" he demanded, pushing me inside; then he pushed the seat back, holding my arms up to stop me from slapping him.

"Let me go!" I demanded.

"Nope," he said, looking in my eyes. "Do you still want to fuck the bartender? Do you?"

"No…"

"Liar! Let's play whore?" And he ripped my panties with his free hand, still looking in my eyes. "That's what you want, huh? Being fucked by someone, anyone…"

I was angry, staring back at him without saying a word, when he started to penetrate me with anger and passion. I couldn't resist him and gave in, starting to pant and moan with pleasure.

Suddenly, he stopped, got off me, fixed his clothes, and climbed out of the car, still fuming.

"I bet you're satisfied now…" he muttered, then left without saying another word, leaving me there unfinished and mute. I curled myself up and cried until falling asleep.

CHAPTER 15

I woke up the next morning with Joe opening the car door, getting in, and starting the engine. I had an immediate reaction to get away, but he held me back more gently than he did in our last encounter.

"We need to talk," he said, caressing my hair as I started sobbing again.

"I'm taking you away for the weekend. Are you hungry?" he asked as he drove us off.

I didn't respond. I just lay there, not caring about what could happen next. He took the I-95 and drove south. We passed Miami, Homestead, and Florida City, so I knew we were heading to the Keys.

He veered off on the Marathon exit toward the beach. He finally parked the car at this isolated little house right on the beach. Then, he came around, took me out of the car and we went inside the house. In the bedroom, which was already set for us, there was a fresh dress and a bikini on the bed waiting for me.

"Take a shower, change clothes, and meet me downstairs," he demanded, but with a gentleness in his voice.

I did what he said, not questioning or complaining. When I finished and went downstairs, I couldn't find him anywhere, so I went for a walk on the beach by myself. It was already afternoon, and I thought about what I could do to get out of the situation. I was frightened and starting to think that he could hurt me for real. I sat down on the sand to stare at the light green crystal-clear ocean I loved so much, thinking about what was happening to me. All I wanted was to be his girlfriend and stop playing the stupid game.

"Here you are." I didn't see him coming. "What are you thinking about?" he asked, sitting down by my side. I looked at him but didn't speak.

"Why do you keep behaving like that? Don't you see that I'm trying to be nice to you? Haven't I treated you well, taken you to nice places?" He looked at me, waiting for a response. I nodded shyly, and he went on. "How could you be so vulgar? Why don't you treat me the same way I treat you?"

"I didn't mean to upset you last night. I had a little too much to drink and got carried away. He kissed me by surprise, believe me."

"No, you kissed him and looked at me smiling…"

"Sorry, I was drunk. I love you!"

"No, you don't. I'm very attracted to you and love being with you." I felt happy for a second, thinking that he was going to say that we needed to be together openly. "But this whole game thing has gotten out of control, and I don't think we can have a healthy relationship now. I'm afraid I will end up hurting you."

"No, Joe. We can work it out. I promise I'll be good to you!" I said, almost begging, noticing a change in the tone of the dialogue.

"This game nonsense must stop. You're a nice girl and will find someone to love and love you back, but this person is not me. Sorry. It's going to be really hard for me to see you every day and not touch or kiss you, but it is over, and I think bringing you here was a mistake as well. Let's go back to Fort Lauderdale."

"I think I deserve a chance to prove you're wrong. We don't have to play the game, but I want to be with you." I said with tearful eyes. He reached out for my hand, getting up, and we started to walk back to the house in silence.

Back in the house, he went upstairs to the bedroom and started to grab his stuff, ready to go home. I followed him and sat on the bed, not knowing what to say. My heart sank. The only thing I was sure about was that I wanted him with all my heart and body. He was the best thing that had ever happened to me. I just couldn't let him go like that.

"I don't know what to say. Please, let's stay…" I begged him, with tears running down my face.

He smiled at me with compassion and sat by my side, hugging me affectionately. "Listen, we were drunk and upset last night and said things we shouldn't have said to each other ever. And I'm really sorry for having mistreated you like that. I never thought I could behave the way I did, but there is something about you that really pushes my buttons."

"Please give us another chance. Let's stay here for the weekend. I know we'll feel better tomorrow to talk things through."

"Ok, we can stay the weekend, but I don't think I'll change my mind. You need to understand that."

"Ok…" I said, nodding. Anyway, I was determined to win his heart back. I couldn't live without him, and I was pretty sure he loved me, too. He was jealous of Fred, that's all. It'll pass.

#

The next morning, I woke up to Joe coming into the room with a tray in his hands. He sat the tray down on the bed and opened the curtains to let the sun in. It was a bright morning.

"Good morning! Look what I have for you. Let's see…orange juice, toast, cream cheese, eggs and bacon, and coffee. Have I forgotten anything?" He seemed happy.

"Good morning," I said, sitting up on the bed, feeling better. I was starving and started eating my toast, not bothering to spread cream cheese on it. "Umm…, it's so good. Thanks."

"No problem. Do you want to go snorkeling today?" he suggested.

"Sure!" I replied and kept eating eagerly. He chuckled.

"I'll be waiting for you downstairs," he said softly and left the room.

It was a beautiful day. It isn't by chance that Florida is called the Sunshine State. Joe was by the water and had all the equipment necessary for snorkeling that he started making me wear.

"Ouch!" I said when he accidentally pulled my hair, trying to put my mask on.

"Sorry, sorry…" He bent his face sideways to kiss me, and his mask banged on mine.

"Ouch!" We both said at the same time, then we started laughing. Once I had everything on, I dragged myself into deeper waters.

"Stop that. You're going to scare the fish away and lift the sand up," he said, holding me back.

"What fish? Don't you know you need a coral reef to snorkel? There is nothing to be seen in here…" I said, as if I knew everything about snorkeling, peeking under the water.

"Really, smartie pants? Who told you that?" he said, giggling. "For your knowledge, this is the best beach in the world for snorkeling, and you won't forget this day for the rest of your life. Have a gander right there!" He pointed to under the water.

"Where, where?" I followed his finger, trying to see what he was seeing. "I don't see anything…"

"Here, here…" He showed me a bunch of tiny gray and very ugly fish swimming together. "See? I told you!" he said, trying to sound serious.

"What?" I looked at him, puzzled.

He pointed down again. "Look, look!"

"No, I'm not falling for that again…" I said, laughing.

"C'mon," he said, diving. "It sparkles…" He smirked after resurfacing. I dove to look at the sparkling thing he had seen but saw a black box at the bottom instead; I picked it up and surfaced. Confused, I opened the box to see this wonderful pearl necklace inside. I looked at him, astonished, and a huge smile lit my face.

"Look, over there." He pointed to another location. I dove in the direction he pointed just to find another little box.

"I can't believe you!" I said in disbelief, opening it and finding a pair of earrings now.

"I told you…the best snorkeling place in the world; the clams here do complete work." He was laughing with satisfaction while I kept diving frenetically, looking for more.

We went back to the house. He put on this opera CD, which was too loud, and he sang along, making big gestures and funny faces while cooking. He was happy. I had fun, too, and enjoyed helping him cook. We ate and relaxed a little before driving back to Fort Lauderdale.

On our way back home, he started talking nonsense.

"Jane, we need to talk seriously…"

"What is it?"

"We can't go on with this ridiculous game. I'm sorry. You're beautiful and a nice girl. We're just not a good match for each other. You'll find someone else to love."

"I don't want anyone else. I want you. We can stop playing the game and be boyfriend and girlfriend instead."

"This can't work, Jane. You think you love me, but you're very young and will have many boyfriends before finding the right guy."

"No, Joe. I love you. And you love me, too. I'm sorry I upset you Friday night. I understand you felt angry and jealous when you saw me kissing another guy. I was wrong and deserved to be treated like a whore. I'm sorry, it won't happen again."

"No, you didn't deserve the way I treated you. No one does. I never thought I could do something like that to you or anyone else. It scares me just to think of it. I was furious and really wanted to hurt you."

"I promise it won't happen again." I was crying now.

"Ok, don't cry. Listen to me, let's stop with this game shit and be friends for now. I like you, and we work together. Having said that, we need to be responsible adults and behave ourselves. We'll not be together again, at least for some time. We need a break."

"I don't think I can…"

"Yes, you can. Friends? Look at me. I know you're sad, but it'll pass. You'll see."

"It'll never pass. I love you." I said when we arrived at the parking garage where his car had been parked since Saturday morning.

He looked at me with pity and left without another word. I stayed there in the parking garage, watching him walk away, still not believing that he had really broken up with me. I was determined not to accept that. He said that because he was jealous of seeing me with Fred, of course. He wanted to punish me for having misbehaved. Moving on, I'll be more careful, and I know he'll forgive me. After all, he loves me, too.

Chapter 16

Monday morning, I got to the office early. Ann was already there.

"Where have you been?" she asked agitatedly, walking in my direction.

"Why? I'm on time..." I said, looking at my watch.

"I've been trying to find you all weekend long. Don't you ever answer your cell?" She looked frightened. "Fred died," she said at once.

"What?" I swear my heart stopped for a second. I was shocked.

"Friday night, after he left work. It was a car accident."

"I can't believe it…" I said, sitting down at my desk.

"I freaked out when I was told about the accident because I knew you were supposed to be with him. I tried to call you and even went to your house. Where were you?" she asked, sitting down and turning her computer on, a lot calmer now after seeing that I was ok.

"I was in Marathon…"

"Marathon, what's in Marathon?"

"My friend Laura has a house there and invited me over for the weekend." I lied. "How did it happen?"

"Nobody knows. Apparently, he lost control of his car, and it rolled over several times. He was killed instantly."

"My God… Thank God I wasn't with him. I left right after you.

I remembered that Laura had invited me, so I rushed home to grab a couple of things and rode with her to the beach house. Poor Fred…" I made up that story, still not believing that Fred was gone.

Ann rolled her chair with her feet close to mine and hugged me. "I'm sorry, too. He was such a cute young guy. Let's not talk about that anymore. There is nothing we can do anyway," she said, wheeling back to her desk and starting to work.

I couldn't stop thinking of Fred all day. What terrorized me the most was the thought that I could have been in that accident with him. I could be dead now. I know I wasn't in a pleasant situation that night either, but I'm still alive.

After work, I went home feeling miserable, remembering Fred's face right before I left that night, his kiss, his handsome smile. He was such a nice guy. *Why do people have to die?* I went home crying. I've never experienced anything like that in my life. I know people die all the time, but not someone who I've just seen hours before.

#

Ollie was by the door, and I felt so happy seeing him because I didn't want to be alone. I fed him and went to watch some TV to see if I could distract myself a little when someone knocked on the door.

"Who is it?" I got up to check. "Hi, Mike," I said and left the door open for him, heading back to the couch.

"What's up?" he said. "Where have you been? You disappeared and left Ollie all alone," he said, almost complaining.

"Please, Mike. Not you, too. I don't want to talk — really."

"Ok, are you hungry? Do you want some company?"

"I really need a friend who doesn't ask questions…."

"Anything to be with you." He seemed happy. "I'm making chicken parmigiana for you."

And he went to the kitchen to see if I had all the ingredients needed for the dish he wanted to make. He started opening and closing all the cabinet doors, which got on my nerves, so I went there to help him out, and I ended up cooking for him, of course. After we ate, he went to his apartment to get this wonderful wine and a CD he thought I would like.

"What kind of music is this?"

"It's called *Forró*. It is a Brazilian type of music. Let me teach you how to dance *Forró*." He was excited about it.

"When did you learn to dance Brazilian?"

"I practice Jiu-Jitsu with this Brazilian guy, and we became friends. He invited me over to this party, and I loved it," he said. "C'mon, let me teach you." Mike pulled me closer against his body very, very tightly, moving his ribs, rubbing frenetically his lower body against mine.

"Wow! This is obscene!" I complained.

"I KNOW!" he said with enthusiasm. "Don't you love it?"

"Not really."

"I went to this place up in Pompano, a Brazilian place. It's like heaven…no, actually hell." He was funny. "With all these little devils dressed in these sexy outfits rubbing against me. I want to go to a Brazilian hell when I die!" he said, making a sexy movement and making me laugh aloud.

"I have Brazilian friends, too," I said. "Sandra and Fernanda, we went to high school together. Actually, I bought this pair of Brazilian jeans once. A very low-rise and tight pants that I wore once or twice. Let's see if I can find it." I went to my bedroom on a mission, found them, put them on, and looked in the mirror. It still looked amazing! I had forgotten about this outfit. I was feeling sexy and went back to the living room to show Mike.

"Ta-daaah!" I made a theatrical entrance.

"Wow! Come here, you little devil…" He ran after me.

"AAAHHH!" I screamed, running around the furniture as he tried to catch me. "AAAH!" I squealed.

He caught me by my waist and pulled me down on the couch with him. We were laughing…and then…silence.

"That night we spent together…was the best night ever…" he said, caressing my face.

"Mike, please." I sat up.

"I love you," he said, getting closer and looking into my eyes, ready to kiss me. "I just want you to know that."

"I love you too — but as a friend," I said.

"There is always a *but*." He pulled himself away from me, disappointed.

"I'm sorry. I really enjoy your company… Isn't it enough for you?"

"Honestly? No."

Silence.

"What do we do now?" he asked.

"We go to sleep! Tomorrow is a new day!" I said, getting up and starting to clean up to avoid the conversation.

"Ok, bye," he said, walking toward the door. "I'm here whenever you need me…" He managed to kiss me good night.

I kissed him back and went to bed, feeling a lot lighter. Mike is a very dear friend. It's good to know he loves me that much. It sounds selfish, but I like knowing I have someone there for me. It feels good to have him around.

Chapter 17

Two weeks passed, and I wondered if all of that was a nightmare. Looking at Joe in the office seemed so surreal as if he were someone else. Behaving totally different, very polite, nice but distant, as a working relationship should be.

He was so good at disguising his personal life that I started to think I had created the Joe I knew — as if this other man were a figment of my imagination. Maybe I was getting insane fantasizing about this entire weird story, like a movie or something. He was more distant than ever, with no actions, just silence.

I expected him everywhere, at the parking garage, grocery store, even on the street; everywhere I went, I was alert and eager to see him — but nothing. His absence was driving me crazy. I felt odd, longing for all that tension and anxiousness. My life now was somewhat empty without him, with no emotions or extreme feelings. I felt butterflies in my stomach thinking about being with him again. I loved him and had to act before it was too late.

Ann had called in sick for a couple of days; I texted her to see if she wanted my company, but she dismissed me, saying she was fine.

Joe had left for a couple of days, too, and I felt abandoned, alone. Mike was my only friend. He had become more regular in my life these last weeks. We laughed a lot and talked more openly now. Even so, I couldn't develop any romantic feelings for him. All I wanted was to be with Joe again. I was craving the extreme emotions that only Joe could give me, any kind — good or bad. I just wanted to feel alive again. So, I decided I was going after him. I would keep playing the game with him, no matter what.

#

"What happened?" I asked Ann when seeing that she had a broken arm arriving in the office on Friday afternoon with Joe.

"I tripped on a sprinkler in my backyard while chasing Max. Stupid dog," she said, showing her cast.

"Poor Ann… I missed you, bitch! Why are you here with Joe?" I said, hugging her and finding it odd that they arrived at the same time.

"It's just a cast." She showed me her injured arm. "I was bored and wondered if you wanted to go somewhere after work. Is Joe here, too?" she said, glancing at Joe's office. "Let's smoke some pot and have some fun, girlfriend?"

"Alright!" I said, "Where do you wanna go?"

"Anywhere that makes me forget the last couple of days!" she said.

"I know! What about that Brazilian place up in Pompano that Mike keeps bothering me about? I think it could be fun," I replied.

"That sounds good. I will take the drugs," she said and gave me a thumbs up.

#

Later that day, Ann came over to my place ready to go to the Brazilian place. Mike was funny, thinking he was the king of the hill. I was thrilled to see him so happy.

We smoked pot while Mike charmed Ann. He was high and acting weird trying to teach her how to dance *Forró* before leaving for the place. I couldn't stop laughing watching them trying to get the dance straight.

"You want to teach me what?" she asked while he kept rubbing himself on her body. Ann just cracked up and rubbed against him, too. It was alluring.

Once there, Ann looked at me and said, "What in the hell is this place about? These people…they are almost naked. Look at those bodies. I'm out of here." She turned around as if she was about to leave.

"Welcome to Hell!" Mike said excitedly, pushing her in and starting to dance with her as they entered.

I laughed, feeling just fine in my Brazilian outfit. The place was really overwhelming. It really looked like we were in Hell. Everybody was so gorgeous, and they had no sense of modesty whatsoever. It was really intimidating. I felt a little out of place, too, but I thought that after a couple of drinks, I would blend in just fine and have fun. I had nothing to worry about.

We were having a blast. The music was contagious. Nobody could stand still, and the whole place was dancing, rubbing, sweating, and having fun. *Definitely hell*, I thought to myself.

Some guy started dancing with me. Then, I was taken by the crowd, letting myself go without even giving a thought to what I was doing. I just kept passing from hand to hand, really dizzy but feeling amazed, *if only Joe could see me now…*

I was frightened at the thought that he could be watching me and would strike at any moment, abruptly taking me out of there and making harsh love to me. Chills ran down my spine just thinking about that. I desperately wanted him to see me and get angry at me.

I was deliberately behaving badly. I felt sexy dancing with all those guys and was loving showing off, provoking Joe. It was terrifying to realize that I would rather have the bad Joe — the jealous, reckless, and furious one.

Ann was having the time of her life, too. She was all over the place, dancing and talking to everybody with her cast and everything.

Mike clutched me, saying. "Hi, gorgeous! Are you having fun?" he asked, smelling alcohol.

"I sure am," I said, pushing him away a bit to avoid his breath.

"How do you like this hell?" He held me tight, talking too close to my face.

"I love it…" I said, turning my face. "How many drinks did you have?"

"Who cares? I'm an angel that came down to Earth to rescue you… You slut…you sinner…I'm going to save your soul…and body." He went on, making me laugh.

"And how exactly are you going to do that?" I asked.

"I showed you hell, and now I must show you heaven so you can choose what's better for you. I'll follow you anywhere — hell or heaven. Are you interested?" He yanked me close, holding me tighter. "By the way, you look irresistible in those jeans."

"I think it's time for us to go," I said, laughing at him and looking for Ann, who was nowhere to be found.

"Yeah. Let's go home, baby," he said, still stoned, amazing me. I couldn't find Ann anywhere, and I got really upset when trying to call her cell and not getting any answer.

"You know what? She came in her car, and she can go home on her own." I left a message saying we were taking off. "Let's go, Mike?"

"*Sim meu amor*, you're going to be mine tonight…" He ran after me as I rushed to the parking lot, getting into my car before he could reach me, laughing at his obsession with me.

We drove home, racing on the streets like maniacs. I got there before him, parked my car as fast as I could, and rushed to the elevator as I saw him running in my direction. I pushed the elevator button anxiously for it to close its doors, which closed right before he could reach it. I was shrieking happily and laughing hysterically.

The elevator opened its doors on our floor, and I could hear Mike rushing up the stairs. I ran as fast as I could, overly excited, still screaming gaily. He saw me trying to open my door and yelled, "Come here, you little devil! Let me save your soul…"

"AAAAHHHH!" I shouted, opening my door in a hurry, having a flare with Mike. I rushed in and slammed the door just in time.

"C'mon," he said, punching on the door and trying its knob. "Let me in…"

"Go home, Mike. You'll wake the entire building. Sssshhh, good night!" I said, going to my bedroom with a huge smile of ease on my face.

CHAPTER 18

It was Friday again. Joe apparently was serious when he said it was over because he had been very distant and did not make any move to be with me again. I missed him. I missed his arms around me, his eyes looking at me, his taste, his laughter, his jealousy, and his anger… I could feel him inside me.

My thoughts were driving me crazy. It was very difficult to see him every day and not have him, as he was someone else in the office. I needed to do something to get us back together, and I knew exactly how to do that.

At lunchtime, Ann went to the bank to deposit a couple of checks, and I saw that Joe was alone in his office. It was my chance.

"Hi!" I said, stepping into his office.

"Hi, Jane, do you need anything?" He stopped working to look at me.

"Yeah. I miss you…"

"Stop right there; we're in the office!" he said, getting up in a hurry and walking toward the door, worried that someone could see us.

"I don't care. I need to see you after work."

"No, that will not happen. You must accept that our relationship was a mistake," he said, whispering and closing the door so no one could hear us.

"I can't."

"Listen, let's have lunch on Sunday and talk as friends, but please don't make a scene here in the office. We both need our jobs." He was very serious and afraid that I could have him fired.

"Ok, Sunday," I said and left his office feeling triumphant.

In the afternoon, I was feeling lighter, so I decided that I needed a night out with my bestie.

"Let's go out tonight, girlfriend?" I suddenly asked Ann. She was extremely focused on her work.

"Huh?" She looked at me.

"Let's go out tonight. I want to dance again. Wasn't it great last week at that Brazilian place?" I went on… "I want to do it again."

"Justin has invited me out tonight," she said, going back to her work.

"Oh, shit," I said, disappointed.

"Maybe we can invite more people over," she said, trying to cheer me up. "So, it wouldn't be a date, date. I don't want to rush into a relationship with him anyway."

"Really?" I opened a huge smile.

"Really."

"What about that Spanish place on Ocean Drive?" she asked.

"What about it?"

"It's a fun place with Spanish music. I think they play Brazilian, too. People dance on the tables and everywhere. We can invite more people; it'll be fun."

"Fine with me, " I said and tried to appear more excited than I really was when I realized Joe was entering the reception. He acted as if he wasn't paying attention to our conversation, but by the look he gave me, I knew he had heard the whole planning thing. I felt thrilled and back on the game.

#

I got home early that day and Mike was waiting for me in the hallway.

"What's up?" he said.

"Not much," I responded, opening my door, getting Ollie in my arms, hugging and kissing him.

"Do you want to do something tonight?" he said, getting in and closing the door behind him.

"Not really. I have plans for tonight," I said, going to the kitchen and getting Ollie's food. He meowed, getting eager to be fed.

"You know, I'm trying my best to figure you out. I know you don't have a boyfriend. I know you enjoy being with me, but I can't understand why you keep pushing me away," he started.

"How do you know I don't have a boyfriend?" I asked, finding his conversation interesting.

"Helloo! I'm with you almost every day. More than that, I'm your neighbor. I don't see anybody over, no phone calls, or any sign of another man in your life but *moi*." He was playing detective now.

"Maybe I have a secret life." I smiled.

"In your dreams?" he mocked.

"How do you know I'm not going out with a man tonight?" I tried him.

"So, you're an escort girl — that's your secret," he teased me.

"What?" I laughed at his comment, amused by his wild imagination.

"That's it, I knew it. You go out with different men all the time; that's why nobody comes over to your place…or calls you. They take you to hotels and yachts, and they give you money. Or expensive gifts like the necklace you were wearing the other day. You're a little slut." His imagination took over him.

"Stop that! I'm not an escort girl. I just don't want to be seriously involved with anyone, not yet. I like my freedom and my lifestyle. I'm going out with Ann if you want to know. It's a girls' night out," I explained.

"Prove it. Tell me where you're going so I can show up just to make sure it's a girls' night out, and I promise I'll leave within an hour or so…if you're telling me the truth," he dared me.

"Nice try, Mike. NO. Who told you I care if you think I'm an escort girl or not? Really, you know what? I am! I'm going out tonight with this very rich, old man, but as you know, I can't tell you who he is. It's against the rules."

"Ok. Keep pushing me. You're driving me insane. I can tell you like me and enjoy my company. I just don't know what keeps you from being with me for good. It has to be someone who doesn't care much for you because he gives room for me to be in your life, and he's never around or seems worried about losing you." He said while leaving my apartment, grinning maliciously, not bothering to look back at me.

"Bye, Mike!" I said, slamming the door after him, upset about his comments.

Chapter 19

South Beach was crowded, as usual. It was annoying trying to get there in the first place and then a nuisance to park, but it was worth the trouble, I guess.

Ocean Drive had people everywhere, getting in and out of the many bars, nightclubs, and restaurants. There were people sitting at tables on the sidewalks, not leaving much space for people to walk through, forcing them to walk on the street, backing up the traffic. But the chaos didn't seem to bother anybody. Everyone was there with the same purpose of having fun. I saw Amber smoking a cigarette just in front of the crowded, loud place.

"Hey, Amber. Have you seen Ann?" I asked, kissing her on the cheek.

"Hey, Jane. Yeah, everybody is inside. Can you see them?" she asked and pointed to the table where Ann, Justin, and everybody else were sitting.

"Thanks, see you inside," I said, making my way in.

"What's up, people?" I kissed everyone and sat at the table, taking a sip of Ann's drink.

"What took you so long? I was about to call you," Ann asked.

"Oh, Mike. He was jealous and didn't want me to come."

"What's up with him? He really likes you, huh? He's cute…"

"Well, sometimes he gets on my nerves."

"Yeah, I know what you mean..." she added, nodding.

"What do you want to drink, Jane? I'm going to the bar to get Ann another pina colada..." Justin interrupted our chat.

"Thanks, Justin! A pina colada sounds good!"

He nodded, getting up and leaving for the bar.

"Do you see that guy dancing over there by the bar?" Ann pointed at a cute Spanish guy.

"Yeah. Who is he?"

"That's Justin's friend, Juan Carlos. He's hot."

"Is he with us?"

"Yep. That's your mission, girlfriend. We have to be friends with him — for the future. I'm stuck with Justin. I'm officially his date tonight, and it wouldn't be polite if I hit on his friend. But you can at least get his phone number." She assigned me the mission.

"No problem. What won't I do for you?" We laughed.

When he came back to the table, he sat at Justin's side, and they started to talk enthusiastically. Suddenly, his eye caught mine, and he smiled. I smiled back, and he asked if I wanted to dance.

"Sure, but I don't dance Spanish, though," I warned him.

"No te preocupes, yo te ensino."

"Um, I don't speak Spanish either." I felt stupid.

"Yo te ensino tambien. I'll teach you," he said, smiling and pulling me tight.

"Wow, take it easy." I was getting dizzy as he pushed and pulled me around frenetically in all directions. "You're a really good dancer!"

"You, too. With a little training, you'll be the best..." he said, looking in my eyes and trying to seduce me. Juan Carlos was cute and a very sexy guy. But all I could think about was if Joe had come after me and was watching me dancing, provoking him.

"He is awesome. We can definitely be friends…or…" I said to Ann, sitting back at the table, breathless with the workout.

"OR? No, no, girl. You don't *or* him; I saw him first." Ann said, trying to threaten me, holding back a smile.

"Let's make it fair. We play clean, right? It'll be up to him," I suggested.

"Fair enough. Did you get his number?" she asked.

"Not yet, but I will."

I was getting in the place's mood. People were very sensual, dancing all over, on the tables, on counters, everywhere. Suddenly, Juan Carlos grasped me, and we both were on the table giving a show. The crowd went crazy. It was really cool seeing all these people cheering for us.

I scanned the place for Joe while dancing with Juan Carlos. I could feel his fuming eyes on me, but I couldn't find him since the place was dark and crowded. My gut was telling me he was there and saw the whole performance. I felt chills running down my spine and knew I was going to see him soon.

All that dancing made me gasp for some fresh air, so I went outside looking for Ann since she wasn't by the table when I came back from giving the show of my life. I looked all over, but it was difficult to find someone among so many people. I was trying to find a place to breathe when I felt someone snatch my arm and pull me out of there… It was Joe.

My heart raced, but I was thrilled to see him at last.

"Surprised?" he asked, smiling cynically.

"What are you doing here?"

"What in the hell were YOU doing? I just can't understand you. Today, this very afternoon, you said you missed me, and now you're rubbing yourself all over that stranger? You're disgusting," and he pushed me away, making a repulsed face. I could tell he was drunk.

"What? I was just dancing. There's nothing wrong with that, and I do miss you." I held his arm, stopping him from walking away from me.

"You know what, I know what you're up to... Let's get out of here." He grabbed my arm again, pulling me and asking where my car was. I couldn't think clearly, but I knew he wanted me. Once in my car, he drove us away.

"Please, Joe, don't hurt me..."

"I won't hurt you, babe. Did I ever hurt you? I'm just giving you what you want," he said, driving like a maniac. "Do you want to hurt someone?" An evil grin spread on his face when he saw Juan Carlos passing us by on his motorcycle.

"What do you mean by hurt someone?" I panicked, seeing that his eyes were fixed on Juan Carlos, who was just ahead of us.

He didn't answer and sped even more, almost hitting the motorcycle's rear, pulling away at the last minute, missing Juan Carlos by about an inch, and then he cut him off, making the poor guy fall.

"JOE, STOP! Are you insane? Stop the car right now!" I couldn't believe what I had just witnessed. I started to shake and sweat cold. "Stop the car! We have to go back there and help him. I'll call 9-1-1." I was trying to get my cell out of my pocket but was not able to control my shaking hands.

"You aren't calling anybody," he said, squinting and huffing, clearly angry with me. "Accidents happen all the time..."

"You're a monster... I want to go home."

He started laughing at me.

"No, you don't want to go home. And at least you didn't kiss this one." He looked at me with a sarcastic smile.

"What? What are you saying...? Oh my God. Oh my God. Fred!" I stopped breathing now. "Please tell me you've nothing to do with Fred's death…please."

"Fred, who? What the fuck are you talking about?"

"You killed him…"

"You are drunk. Shut up and be a good girl so we can play whore, would you?"

He took me to a shabby motel on Biscayne Blvd, the kind hookers go with their clients. He parked and, looking at me, still furious, said, "I'm going to get a room for us. If you try to escape, I will hunt you down, and it won't be pleasant for you. Do you understand?"

I nodded, quietly looking at him. I saw him checking us in from the car, thinking how much I loved him. The butterflies in my stomach anticipated what was about to happen next. I couldn't wait to be in his arms again, couldn't wait for him to grab me and make harsh love to me.

He came back and opened the car door, taking me by the arm harshly. Once in the room, he looked at me, saying, "Let's start playing whore, shall we?" and he pushed me on the bed. I tried to get away.

"Joe, wait. Let's talk…"

"No talking, you little slut. Were you going to fuck that guy? Huh? Tell me, how many guys have you fucked since we broke up?"

"I haven't been with anyone, Joe. Believe me…"

"I don't believe you. And I know you have a boyfriend — and he isn't the guy on the bike."

"No, I don't have anyone! Who told you that?"

"It doesn't matter. What matters is that you're a trollop. All you want is to fuck someone — anyone," he said, flipping me on the bed and taking my pants off.

"No, Joe. Please wait. We need to talk. I love you." I tried to look at him, but he held me down furiously and started to fuck me from behind. I gave in, eager to feel him inside me again.

"Joe, I don't know what you're thinking. I wasn't doing anything wrong, and I have no one. You're the only one I want," I said after he finished with me and got up, pulling his pants up.

"Liar! I saw you many times flirting with other guys. You're a slut and don't deserve my compassion," he said, calling a cab.

"I don't understand. You told me it was over and then you get upset seeing me having fun trying to move on with my life? You told me to do just that…"

"See, you admit you were going to fuck the guy. You went outside to meet him and go somewhere you could be his whore!" he yelled at me, still angry. "Yes, move on with your life and leave me alone! Don't keep trying me, woman!"

"No! I went outside looking for Ann. She suddenly disappeared, and I was worried about her. Juan Carlos is a nobody. He asked me to dance with him, that was all. Please believe me."

He didn't listen to me and left.

Chapter 20

I couldn't stop thinking that Joe had something to do with Fred's death. I spent the entire weekend thinking about everything that had happened the night Fred died. *Joe was furious; that's a fact. He left me there in the car for a very long time. Maybe he went back to the bar and waited for Fred to get off, probably until the place closed, and then he followed him, causing the accident just like he did with Juan Carlos…*

No, that's impossible. I'm getting mad. He wouldn't be capable of doing something like killing someone. Or would he? Maybe it got out of control. He didn't really mean to kill Fred, and it happened when he was just trying to cause an accident out of jealousy. But if he loved me that much, we would be dating openly. I couldn't think straight anymore. My theories were driving me insane. I knocked on Mike's door, still trying to make sense of the thoughts in my head. I needed to clear my mind.

"Hey," he said after opening the door when he saw me. "What's up?" He walked back inside his apartment, leaving the door open for me to follow.

"Hi, Mike. Are you still mad at me?" I asked him, making an angelic face and looking at him innocently.

"Furious," he said with a grin, going back to his computer.

"I'm sorry. I didn't mean to hurt your feelings. You're right; I'm a stupid little brat who really needs a friend right now," I started saying, almost crying.

"C'mon, don't cry. What's wrong? I can't stand seeing you

crying," he said, getting up and putting his arms around me. "Tell me, what happened?"

"I don't know. I'm confused. I don't know if anything happened to begin with. I can't explain. Just let me stay here with you for a little while. Please," I begged.

"Sure, you can stay as long as you wish. Are you going to tell me what is going on with you? Has it anything to do with your imaginary boyfriend?" He was no fool.

"I really don't know what's going on with me, Mike. And I don't know what to say because there is nothing to tell you. I'm confused, maybe a little emotional, too. I think I'm going insane," I started talking, not making any sense to him.

"You know what?" he said. "I'm going to get you a cup of tea. You'll feel better, and then you can tell me whatever you want, ok?" He looked into my eyes now, slipping my hair behind my ear gently.

"Ok..." I said grateful for having him in my life.

He went to the kitchen to fix me a cup of tea. I lay down on his couch, and a few minutes later, I was deeply asleep.

"What time is it?" I asked him as he watched TV, waiting for me to wake up.

"It's past midnight," he said, coming closer to me.

"Oh my God, I have to go. I have work tomorrow morning," I said, getting up in a flare.

"Why don't you stay here tonight? I will fix you a wonderful breakfast tomorrow morning." He was almost convincing.

"No thanks. I don't want to bother you. And all my stuff is there, anyway." I said, heading toward the door.

"I will fix you breakfast anyway," he said. "Come over when you're ready, ok?"

"Ok," I said and kissed him on the cheek.

#

The next morning, I woke up late as usual, but instead of getting up right away, I took a while lying there on my bed. I was reluctant to go to work. I didn't want to see Joe and needed more time to think. *I could call in sick*, I thought to myself. No, I had to end this nightmare as soon as possible. I decided to confront Joe about Fred.

"Good morning, Mike," I said when he opened the door with a huge smile on his face.

"Hello there! Please, come in. I hope you're hungry." He led me to the table that was impeccably set and full of goodies.

"Umm, looks delicious!" I said, sitting down and helping myself with orange juice and fresh fruits. "What time did you get up? How long did you take to prepare all this?" I was amazed.

"Early. I had to get up very early," he said, being a martyr.

"You didn't have to." I bit a piece of my toast and took the last sip from my latte. "I got to go!" I said, getting up and gathering my belongings. "Thanks, Mike, I'll see you later, ok?"

"Knock on my door when you're back. We can have dinner together," he shouted while I ran through the hallway.

"Ok…" I replied and dashed out.

Chapter 21

Ann wasn't at her desk when I arrived in the office that Monday morning, but I knew she was there because her computer was on and her purse was under the table as usual. I sat down at my desk and started putting my stuff away, turning my computer on as always when she came to check who had arrived.

"Hey, it's you," she said, going back to the lunchroom; she was making coffee, which started to smell good.

I rushed there to talk to her and grab a cup for myself. I almost screamed when I got face to face with Joe, who was also there talking joyfully and helping her make coffee. They were engaged in a conversation about relationships.

"You?" I couldn't disguise my surprise at having seen him that early with Ann.

"Good morning, Jane, how was your weekend?" he asked with a smile as if he didn't know where I was that very weekend. I almost threw up from how my stomach swirled.

"I'm not feeling well…" I said and ran to the restroom.

Ann followed me. She was clearly worried. "Are you ok? What happened?"

"I'm better. I should've called in sick," I said, leaning over to wash my face with cold water.

"You can go if you want. I'll take care of everything." She's such a nice friend, but I couldn't leave her there with a murderer.

"No, I'm fine. I feel better now, thanks." I said, drying my face with a paper towel.

"If you say so…" She left, blissfully going back to the lunchroom to talk to that demon again. She's so naïve. I have to protect her, and I'll not leave her here with him. He's mine. What is he trying to do? Why is he flirting with Ann? Does he want to make me jealous? If that's what he wanted, well, he succeeded. However, I'm not going to let him use Ann to get to me.

"So, what did you do this weekend?" Ann asked when coming back to her desk and smiling while looking at Joe, who was walking gaily to his office with a cup of coffee in his hands, which made me furious.

"Not much. What about you?" I tried to control myself.

"Not much either," she replied and started to work.

I felt she was a little different — too happy and mysterious. I didn't like it. The morning went by slowly and quietly. She didn't want to talk much, and every time I started a conversation, she would give me short answers, not leaving room for me to continue. I asked if she wanted to go have lunch with me, but she said she already had plans. I was very uneasy and didn't know why Joe was giving her so much attention.

"Let's go?" Joe said to her, and they both left for lunch, happily talking without looking back.

I couldn't believe it! I was astonished. *What in the hell was he up to?* My head was spinning so fast that I felt dizzy and sick again. My heart sank. How would I be able to convince her that he's a psychopath? Even if I told her the entire story, she wouldn't believe me. We're best friends — we work together every day, and she suspected nothing. I've never told her anything. He has never even flirted with me in the office this whole time we worked together. I didn't know what to do.

They took a long time to come back, and when they did, Ann had a sparkle in her eyes. She seemed to be falling for him — sighing and smiling throughout the afternoon. I was so irritated that I almost went to the devil's office and killed him with my bare hands.

#

When five o'clock came, I got my things and ran out of there, literally. I got inside my car in the parking garage and cried with fury and jealousy. I was so angry that I couldn't see Joe coming.

"Why are you crying, Jane?" he said, getting inside my car and showing concern.

"You're an evil, awful jerk. I hate you!" I started slapping him all over.

"Wow, calm down, Jane," he said, holding my arms, preventing me from hitting him.

"Why are you doing this to me? Why are you doing this to Ann?" I asked, crying.

"What? What are you talking about? Ann is my friend. I invited her for lunch, that's all. Are you jealous? Please don't cry. We need to talk. You're a big girl and must understand that I'm free to go out with whomever I want. You and I were just playing a game, which is over, by the way."

"I don't know what to think. What about Juan Carlos? You made him fall... You were jealous because I was dancing with him." I was confused.

"What are you talking about? Who is Juan Carlos?"

"That guy on the motorcycle...on Friday...you made him fall..."

"It was an accident, Jane. I swear to God. He wasn't hurt. I saw him getting up in the rearview mirror, and he rode away, maybe with a bruise or so, that's all. You're the one driving me crazy!"

"What about Fred? You killed Fred..."

"Who? I think you are hallucinating, Jane. Let me take you somewhere so you can calm down. I can't let you drive like this," he said, getting out of the car and going around to the driver's seat.

"Scoot over," he said, and I dragged myself to the passenger seat. He drove us away. He parked by this deserted park with no one around, and I knew he wanted to have me; otherwise, he would have gone somewhere else with lots of people.

"Babe, I don't know what's going on in your head, but I guarantee that I have nothing to do with the things you're accusing me of. I never, ever hurt any of your boyfriends. You need help…"

"I know you did. And why are you charming my best friend, now? Why are you trying to hurt everyone who gets close to me? You don't have to do that. You don't have to hurt anyone just to punish me."

"No, you're wrong. I'm not trying to punish you."

"Yes, you are! You like it when I misbehave, so you have an excuse to fuck me with fury. That's what you like. If I'm a whore, you're a pimp."

"You're wrong!" He was getting upset, just the way I liked it. "You're wrong, and it's over. Please don't say anything to Ann. I like her for real, and if you tell her about us, she'll be very sad…and I'll be very angry."

"You see, you want me to make you angry…"

"Don't be ridiculous. I want you out of my life! We started so well…we could've been together by now, but you kept spoiling everything."

"We still can be together."

"No way. We'll end up killing each other. Please leave me alone!"

"I know what you want — me," I said, lifting my skirt and unzipping his pants, mounting him, then caressing and kissing him ardently. "I can give you what you want…" I whispered in his ear, unbuttoning his shirt and kissing his naked chest. I took my shirt off, and his hands traveled over my body with passion. He squeezed my breasts, looking into my eyes. I couldn't help moaning with pleasure. He kissed me with anger, pulling me down on his lap. I felt him inside me.

"Do you like this? Huh?" I asked, looking into his eyes. He was panting and didn't say a word, but I could see his eyes full of desire. He kept pushing and pulling me up and down until we both groaned in ecstasy. "You know we belong together, and I won't let you go," I said, still panting and letting myself fall over him.

"Go home, Jane, and leave me alone. It doesn't matter if we fucked again. I still don't want you. It's over!" he said, pushing me aside.

"Don't leave me here like this, please. Let me stay with you tonight. I won't say anything to Ann, I promise."

"You need to promise me you'll leave us alone."

"I promise."

"I don't know what to do with you. You're driving me insane."

"Please, I want to stay with you for the last time."

"Ok, but you promise it'll be the last time."

"I promise…" I vowed but lied. *Yeah, right!*

We went to this small boutique hotel in Lauderdale-By-The-Sea; the room was beautiful and very chic, way better than the last place he took me. We ordered food and went to bed after taking a shower. I kissed him good night, and we slept together, feeling cozy with each other.

The next morning, I wanted to take another shower so I could be ready and crisp for him, but he was already dressed when I came out of the bathroom.

"Do we have to go now?" I asked, disappointed.

"Yeah, we need to go work. I have a very busy day ahead of me." He drove us to the parking garage where his car was parked, and without saying a word, he left.

Chapter 22

"Hello, Jane!" Mike appeared from nowhere when I was about to open my door.

"Hey. Hi, Mike." I was surprised to see him so early.

"Where have you been? I've been waiting for you since…seven last night? We were supposed to have dinner together, remember?" And he peeked at his watch.

"Sorry, I didn't know you were waiting for me. I went out with Ann, happy hour, and ended up sleeping over at her house," I said, as it wasn't a big deal.

"LIAR!" he yelled.

"What?" I was perplexed.

"Your hair is wet. Why would you take a shower in her house if you were coming home to change? It doesn't make any sense." And he touched my hair with an appalled gesture.

"Oh, Mike. I'm sorry. Don't be mad at me." I got caught lying and didn't know what to say.

"You don't have to say anything…" He turned around, leaving.

"Mike, please. Come in and let's talk," I said, opening my door and trying to get him in.

"NO! You can't use people like that! I've had enough, and I'm done with you. Do you understand?"

I nodded and started to cry. "Please, Mike. Don't…" I cried as he left me there, astonished. He was my rock, and I couldn't even think about losing his affection.

I couldn't help slipping down to the floor and crying in the hallway. There was a lot going on in my life; I really didn't need Mike to be upset with me, too. I was out of control and didn't care when my front-door neighbor opened her door to check what was going on.

"What are you looking at?" I shouted at her, crawling inside my apartment and closing the door behind me.

Ollie came to check on me and started to rub and kiss me as he could sense my miserable condition. I finally got up, still crying, to take care of him. Poor cat, he couldn't imagine what was going on in my life. "I envy your stupid little life. What do you have to worry about?" I said, getting his food from the cabinet.

I changed and left for work. I was feeling awful.

#

Ann was suspicious that something was wrong. She kept trying to get me talking, smiling at me skeptically, but I couldn't. My face was so terrible that Mr. McKee called me into his office.

"Is something wrong, Ms. May? You look so distressed. Is there anything we can do to help you? Why don't you take the day off?"

"No, sir. I don't need anything. I'm sorry. I shouldn't let my personal problems interfere with my work. I promise it won't happen again."

"No problem. We like you very much, and this is not a warning, but you need to focus on your work and be well if you want to interact with our clients. Are you sure you are fine to stay and work?"

"Yes, I'm fine, Mr. McKee. Coming to work was more than a relief to me right now. I'll do better."

"Oh well, if you say so. Please let me know if there is anything I can do for you, ok?" He's such a nice guy.

"What happened?" Ann was worried. "Did he fire you?"

"No, Ann. He's really cool. He told me to take the day off if I wanted." I explained.

"Really? What did you say?" she wanted to know.

"That I'm fine. Actually, I need a friend." I said, looking at her sadly.

"Sure, anytime. Do you want to go out?" she asked.

"No, can we go to your house? Can I sleep over?" I asked.

"PJ party! I love it," she said.

#

We went to my apartment to feed Ollie and get my things; I didn't want to see Mike, but we ran into him in the hallway anyway...

"Hi, Mike." Ann rushed to hug him.

"Hey, Ann..." He hugged her, too, looking at me with indignation. "Are you guys going out again?"

"What do you mean again? Of course, we go out again and again and again..." She laughed.

"I mean, you just went out yesterday, which was Monday. You guys must have a lot of energy — and make a lot of money..."

"We didn't go out yesterday. Uh-oh...sorry, Jane." She went inside, leaving me out there in the hallway with Mike.

"I knew it." And he turned his back on me.

"Mike, wait! I really want to talk to you. Let me explain." I ran after him into his apartment.

"There is nothing to explain. You never said you loved me, anyway," he said, sitting down on his couch.

"No, I want to — for real. But tonight, I'm going to Ann's house. How about tomorrow? I'll cook for you," I insisted.

"Ok, but you have to promise you'll tell me everything that's going on. Promise?" He looked up to face me.

"I promise," I said, going back to my place.

Chapter 23

"Are you going to tell me what's going on or not?" Ann asked me after we ate and smoked pot sitting on her sofa, already in our pajamas.

"I've got nothing to tell you, Ann, really. I had an argument with Mike yesterday, that's all." I was still thinking that telling her about Joe would be useless. She would not believe me. I had to show her who Joe really was.

"So…where did you go?" She wasn't stupid.

"Nowhere. I just didn't open the door for him. I wasn't in the mood for him, and then I said that you and I had gone for a happy hour, just a little lie." I explained.

"Oh…and why are you so miserable today? It seems that you've been crying a lot. You know what? If you don't want to talk, that's fine, really. I understand. Just know you can count on me, ok?"

"I'm not miserable. As I said, I had a fight with Mike, that's all. I'll be fine tomorrow." I was eager to change the conversation to know about Joe and her. "What about you? You and Joe seem to be getting along after all…"

"Yeah, you know I have a crush on him…"

"When did he start paying attention to you?"

"Why are you asking that? Why do you think he wouldn't be interested in me? You're just jealous."

"I'm sorry, Ann. I just wanted to know if there is anything going on between you two."

"I'm not sure either, but I'll let you know if something more serious happens, ok? Let's smoke pot and forget about Mike and Joe…"

"Ok."

I knew they were getting closer, but why? Why was he doing that? He couldn't be truly interested in her after being with me. That didn't make any sense. He was driving me crazy. I needed to think things over before taking any action. I needed to find out what he was up to.

I was a lot better when we arrived at the office the next morning. I found it strange that Joe was already there. "Hi, girls…" he said with a cup of coffee in his hand, too happy for the time.

"Did you make coffee?" Ann asked him without ceremony. I could swear she blinked her eyes. They looked oddly comfortable with each other.

"I tried…" he said with a smirk.

"Let me try it. I'll tell you if it's bad. Do you want some, Jane?" she asked and went to the lunchroom to get us some coffee.

Joe and I locked eyes but said nothing. Ann came back and handed me a cup. "Good, very good actually…" she complimented his coffee.

"Not bad…huh? See you later?" he said, winking at her and then looking at me.

"Sure…" she said, smiling back at him.

"What's going on?" I almost couldn't wait for him to leave the reception to ask her.

"Nothing. Why?" she said, turning her computer on and organizing herself.

"Nothing? I can tell there's something between you and Joe. Why didn't you say anything last night?" I was astonished.

"C'mon, Jane. You know I have a crush on him. He's so amazing. Nothing really serious has happened…yet. But God is father, and He will provide," she said, lifting her hands up to Heaven, joking.

I couldn't laugh at her stupid joke.

"Oh, well. You're jealous," she said, starting to work.

I was so aggravated that I couldn't say anything. I started working, trying to avoid my destructive thoughts, but I couldn't help it. *If he were taking her out for lunch again, he would have to take me along. I wouldn't make this easy for him. Jerk! And why didn't Ann say anything yesterday? I'm going to show them I'm not that stupid. Enough is enough.*

"Do you want to go have lunch with me?" Ann asked.

"Huh? Aren't you going with Joe?" I tried to sound calm.

"No, we're going out Friday night…" she said, not making a big deal out of it and knowing that I was jealous.

"Really? Thanks, Ann, but I have things to do in my lunch time…bank stuff." I had to control myself.

I left, not knowing exactly where to go or what to do, but I was going to do anything in my power to avoid their date from happening. *Think, think…* I had an idea! After work, I went home, already feeling the taste of my revenge. I had a plan to end their affair at once. In his dreams I was going to let their affair happen! No way! Joe and I belong together, and Ann will not have him.

\#

Mike was waiting for me. "Hey, Mike," I said, opening my door and grabbing Ollie, who was by the door, waiting for me as always.

"Hey." He came after me, helping with my groceries. "Do you want to go out for dinner?"

"Nope, I said I was going to cook for you, and I will. Unless you don't like my cooking…" I replied.

"No, I love your cooking, for real. I'm going to grab a bottle of wine, and I'll be back in a sec, ok?" he said, leaving to his apartment.

"Make it two!" I yelled.

I started cooking; we were going to have caprice salad to start, then salmon with asparagus and roasted potatoes, and key lime pie for dessert to finish it up. The kitchen was a mess. Even though I'm not a really good cook, I really enjoy cooking, and I'm glad Mike enjoys cooking too and never complains. He was with me all the time while I was cooking, keeping me company, and making me laugh, trying to help in one way or another, I enjoy being with him, it's relaxing...

After dinner, we went to sit on the couch, feeling very full. He stretched his legs and looked at me, smiling. "That was good…"

"Anytime," I said.

"So, we were going to have a certain conversation, right?" he started.

"Yeah. Look, Mike, I don't know what to tell you, but I'll try just because I like you very, very much…" I looked at him while sitting up on the sofa. "I'm not going to tell you if I have someone else; it's really none of your business. I mean, what's important for us isn't the fact that I have or don't have someone, but if I want to be with you or not, right?"

"I don't know if I want to hear what you're about to say…" his face saddened, and he just kept staring at me.

"Well, as I have said many, many times, I really like you, but I don't have deep feelings for you. You knew that all along and kept insisting. I tried; I wanted to fall in love with you, but it didn't happen. It's not my fault; it's nobody's fault. You need to give me time, maybe in the future…who knows? But for now, we need to keep things the way they are with no pressure or commitment, ok?"

"Ouch…" he replied and sat up, looking away from me for a minute. "Ok, you're right. I know I insisted on forcing you to commit to a more serious relationship. Sorry," he said, still looking away. "I love you, and I won't give up…" he looked at me now. "I promise I'll respect your deep *feeling-less* for me but will wait for you."

"I hope you do, really. I want to fall in love with you, Mike…believe me."

"I know you have someone else who isn't doing you any good. He's going to hurt you, Jane," he said, changing the focus of our conversation.

"I don't want to talk about my love life now, Mike. Let's just be friends, buddies…?" I finished the conversation.

"So, do you want to watch this movie I've got?" He changed the subject, agreeing to finish the awkward conversation about us.

"Sure, go get it and bring more wine, too." I smiled and felt a lot more relaxed. At least one chapter of my drama was over. Now…it was Joe's turn.

CHAPTER 24

It was the Friday of their date.

"Hi, Ann," I said, sitting at my desk and going through my usual routine.

"Hey, are you ok?" She looked at me, concerned.

"Sure. I'm fine. Has everybody arrived yet?"

"Not everybody. Joe hasn't." She made sure to mention Joe. I had a feeling that she wanted to tell me something about them.

"Is it today that you're going on a date?" I tried to sound casual.

"Yeah, please don't be jealous. I want you to be happy for me, Jane."

"Oh, Ann. I love you very much. You know that don't you? Yeah, I'm jealous because you'll leave me aside to be with him. Who will party with me?"

"I like him, Jane, and I will always be your friend, but life must go on. We need to move on." And she started her work.

"Ms. May?" the inconvenient intercom spoke.

"Yes, Mr. McKee."

"Could you please bring Mr. Greenberg's file? Thank you."

"Right the way, sir." And I rushed to do what he asked.

Joe didn't show up all day. He had a meeting somewhere else that took him all day, but he called Ann. She tried to hide it from me, but

I knew it was him. She was delighted all of a sudden, and her eyes sparkled.

I overheard her saying, "Nine o'clock is fine. See you then."

BITCH!!! JERK!!!

I didn't know who I hated the most. I was getting desperate. *I have to control myself; I have to control myself; I have to control myself.* I kept repeating over and over in my mind…but I just wanted to cry. *Why was he doing this to me? Why was he showing interest in her? He definitely wanted to get to me using my best friend.* I didn't know what to think, but I knew what he wanted me to do: push his buttons.

#

I left the office a little earlier with the excuse that I wasn't feeling well since I had a plan to set into motion. I went shopping for a trashy and very vulgar outfit. I wanted to look like a whore for Joe. *If that's what he wants, that's what he'll get!*

It was kind of fun picking the right clothes in the thrift shop. I ended up getting a miniskirt — black, imitation leather — but it felt rubbery to the touch. A red scarlet, very tight top that allowed a lot of cleavage to show, and a red varnish high heel shoe. Then I stopped to get the most important piece of my costume — a long, curly, and very bleach-blond wig. It was awesome the way I looked, even I couldn't recognize myself. Next stop: car rental shop. I left my car parked on the street and drove home in an economical, quite common silver car. I couldn't risk Ann recognizing my car on her street, which is very narrow and short. She would notice my car by looking out the living room window.

The toughest part of getting dressed was putting the wig on. I almost chopped off my beautiful long, well-treated golden-brown hair because it was impossible to fit it inside that damn cap; it seemed so easy when the wig woman showed me how to do it. I finally got it. I had a lot of makeup on, heavy blue eye shadow and very red lipstick. I saw myself in the mirror — I looked amazing! The plan was to get Joe before he could get to Ann, making him stand her up. She's going to be disappointed and lose hope in their relationship. At the same time, I know he'll be pissed seeing me dressed like the whore he wants me to be, and he'll come straight into my arms. It's a trap. He needs to understand that he doesn't have to use her to get to me. I'm going to show him that I'm the one for him, and Ann...she's just not that kind of girl.

I put the shoes and wig in this big bag and had a raincoat covering my body from neck to ankle to hide my minimal attire from any curious *neighbor*. My hair was rolled inside this tight cap, so a hat would cover it perfectly. I ran to the car as it was already eight o'clock.

I arrived at Ann's address at around 8:30 PM. I parked two houses up to wait for Joe. Her street is a one-way, very calm and narrow. There's only one way in. I had to be fast to get him before he could get to her house; I put the wig and shoes on, got out of the car and waited behind a street tree.

My heart raced when I saw his car turning onto her street. I ran to the middle of the road, making him stop, not recognizing me.

"Hey, baby... Do you want company tonight?" I said, going around and leaning on his window that was rolling down.

"Get off, bitch!" he said, not looking at me.

"C'mon, I bet you'll have a lot more fun with me than with Ann..." I said and smiled, batting my eyelashes.

"Jane? Is that you?" he said in disbelief.

"Here..." I tossed a piece of paper with this bar address at him. "I'll wait for you 'til ten o'clock. If you don't show...I'll tell Ann who you really are."

And I turned my back to him, got into the rental car and drove away. He stayed there, in his car in the middle of the street, for a while. I could see through the rearview mirror as he slammed the steering wheel with rage.

I was afraid to get in the bar dressed like that, but I needed a drink and get acclimated to the place before he arrived. I sat at the bar and asked for a beer. The place wasn't full, with a few middle-aged men and a couple of women playing pool and drinking beers. Nobody seemed bothered about my presence. The bartender asked if I was waiting for someone. I muttered a "yeah…" and he left me alone.

Maybe after ten minutes of feeling down and unattractive, this big, tattooed guy approached me and asked if he could buy me a drink. "Sure…" I replied. I wanted to be having fun when Joe arrived…if that was even possible.

It was 9:30 PM already, and Joe hadn't shown up yet. I had three beers and was feeling funny. My friend, Nicholas — I'm sure that was his name — was already asking me to marry him. It was comical. I was laughing, almost relaxed, with my fiancé, who was showing me all his tattoos. They had meaning, every single one. Do you believe it? He seemed to be a nice guy.

Joe arrived ten minutes to ten o'clock. He sat at the bar across from me, asked for a beer, and fixed his devil's eyes on me. I could tell he was fuming.

I was feeling uneasy with Joe staring at me in that stupid place. I felt idiotic flirting with that ugly guy and wearing that whore costume. Since I couldn't entertain my tattooed friend anymore, he was losing interest in me, I excused myself and went to the restroom. I had to think of a Plan B.

What if I took Joe out of there and had an open conversation? I could open my heart to him… I know he loves me, too. He is dating Ann just to upset me and make me misbehave. That's how he likes me, and I love it, but he needs to leave Ann alone. We could be openly together and keep playing the game for excitement. I know he likes to see me flirting with other guys just to get upset and make harsh love to me. That's his fantasy, and he found someone who is up to do what he says — me.

When I came back, my friend was gone, and Joe wasn't there either. Everybody had given up on me. I scanned around just to find the tattooed guy talking to someone else, and Joe had left. I ran out to check his car. It was still there. My heart was pounding so fast that I thought I was going to faint.

As I walked around the building, something was telling me he was watching me. Suddenly, he grabbed me and threw me against the wall in the alley behind the bar, holding my neck with one hand and choking me. "What the fuck are you trying to do? Do you want to get killed dressed like that in a place like this?" He pressed his body against mine. "I'm really tempted to do so…right now," and he squeezed my throat even more, making me gasp.

"Please, Joe…" I couldn't talk as he pressed my throat against the wall.

"What's that on your face? Look at you. You finally took on your real whore persona, huh?" he said, wiping my mouth with his thumb, smearing my lipstick all over my face, still holding my neck. "You're a horny little bitch. And I know exactly what you want," he said, getting his free hand into my panties. "That's what you want?" He looked into my eyes, still fingering me.

"Yes, Joe. I love you," I said, opening his pants and grabbing his dick, panting with pleasure.

"No, you don't love me. You love my dick. You freak nymphomaniac." He managed to get inside me with passion and anger — just the way he liked — just the way I liked it.

"Ah, Joe…I'm the right woman for you. Can't you see it? Let's get out of here — just you and me. I'll do anything. I'll be your whore if you want me to," I said, kissing him. "You just have to leave Ann alone," I murmured, "I'll do anything for you…"

"No!" he suddenly shouted, getting off me and leaving me unfinished and begging for more.

"Come back," I said, pulling him back inside me.

"No! I don't want you! Can't you understand that? Leave me and Ann alone. I'm warning you!" he yelled, walking away, fixing his clothes and kicking everything in his way while leaving me there, crying.

"I will never leave you alone! Do you hear me? I'm not going to let you go. You're mine, and you know it! JOE!" I screamed, but he left anyway.

I went home feeling depressed. Lost in my thoughts. *It's over. He's losing interest in me. How come? What did I do wrong? He was so much in love with me — and all of a sudden — he started openly dating my best friend. Why didn't he choose her in the first place? He's insane, a maniac, a sick son of a bitch.* I looked toward Mike's door when I was about to open mine, and there he was, looking at me with indignation. He didn't say a word, closing his door in a silent protest.

Ollie was sleeping on my bed and started stretching, thinking it was already morning when I turned the light on. I went to the bathroom and almost had a heart attack seeing myself in the mirror. My face was a mess — all blurred with lipstick and melted mascara, the wig was sideways, and my shirt ripped, showing my bra. "Oh my God, Mike saw me like this…"

CHAPTER 25

"Hi, Jane. Are you ok?" Ann asked when she saw me dragging myself into the office on Monday morning.

"I'm fine…" I replied, sitting down and feeling gloomy. "How's your date?" I wanted to know.

"Well, we didn't go out on Friday. Joe couldn't make it," she paused, and I felt better for a second. "But he came over Saturday. Oh, Jane, he's awesome. I'm in love." She couldn't hide her happiness.

"No, Ann. Listen to me. Joe is not the guy for you. He's evil, he's bad…" I started saying without thinking.

"What? What's wrong with you, Jane? We definitely need to talk!" she said. "Tomorrow night at my place. Ok?"

"No. I need to tell you now…" I didn't want to wait. I couldn't take it anymore.

"Jane, stop it! I know you're in trouble, but we can't talk right now. Tomorrow," she said firmly, holding my hands.

"Ok," I replied. What else could I say?

I was determined to tell her the whole story. I needed to. If she didn't want to talk to me ever again, or if she didn't believe me, it didn't matter. I couldn't just walk away and leave her with him. She had to understand that I hadn't said anything before because it was supposed to be a game. *Oh my God! She would never believe me.* Anyway, telling her the truth will definitely spoil their affair. If Joe can't be mine, he won't be hers either.

#

I drove to her house, remembering the last time I was there. My eyes blurred with tears. I took a deep breath and walked to her door and knocked.

"Hey, Jane," she said and left the door open for me to walk in. I shut the door behind me and followed her to the living room.

"Mike?" I was surprised to see him sitting on the couch.

"Hi, Jane," he said, and they both looked at me with concern on their faces. I was bewildered, not knowing what Mike was doing there.

"What's going on here?" I was getting upset, feeling trapped.

"Please, Jane. Listen to us. Calm down, sit down, please." Ann said, pulling me down to sit by her side on the sofa. Mike sat on my other side and stroked my hair with tenderness.

"We need to talk," she said. "Mike and I are very worried about you. You've been acting really strange lately," she said, looking at Mike, who nodded, agreeing with her. "Mike told me how awful you looked when you arrived Friday night. You weren't with me. Where have you been? Who are you seeing? What have you been doing?" She peppered me with questions that I didn't want to answer.

"Mike thinks you're seeing someone that has been abusing you. If you are, that's ok. There's nothing to be ashamed of. I will not ask why you didn't tell me about him. We just have to take you out of this situation before you get hurt." She looked into my eyes and then at Mike.

"You can trust us, Jane. We're not going to judge you, no matter what you've done..." It was Mike's turn to talk now, I was getting dizzy. "If you want, I can take you to New York, to my brother's condo. We can stay there as long as you want..."

"Yeah, Jane, go with him. I'll take care of Ollie for you and then come see you on the weekend. What do you think?" she added.

"No, I can't. You guys are wrong. I don't want to go to New York," I said.

"So, tell us!" Mike was getting anxious for an explanation.

"Ann…" I looked at her, desperate to talk about Joe, but felt helpless. "Remember when we planned to go to California? Come with me; let's quit our jobs, sell our stuff, and go. I would go to California with you," I almost begged her.

"Jane, I can't quit my job and go to California just like that. Go to New York first, and then we'll see. Maybe we can go to California afterward, too." She tried to calm me down.

"No, Ann. You must come with me. You can't stay here with Joe. I can't leave you here with him…" I stammered.

"Jane, stop that! What part of *I like him* you didn't get? It's not my fault that you got yourself in trouble, but please don't spoil my happiness. It's not going to work. I know him better than you do, and he's a wonderful man. Actually, he told me everything…"

"He did?" I was incredulous.

"Yeah. Joe said he saw you at this nightclub…wearing that awful outfit and the wig stuff. Don't try to deny it. Mike saw you wearing just that on Friday night, and he told me you were with this disgusting tattooed guy. Jane, we know…" she said. "I know you wanted to tell me you saw Joe in one of those places. And it's been difficult because you would have to explain what in the world you were doing there — that's why you were going around without the courage to say it."

"No, Ann…listen to me…" I was desperately trying to tell her the truth, but she kept going.

"I know…Joe was really embarrassed at having to tell me he was there when he saw you, but he likes you and knows you're my best friend. Oh, Jane! He cares about you."

She thinks he's a wonderful man? Oh my God, he's trying to make Ann turn against me. Now, she would never believe me and would be upset if I told her the truth.

Oh, Jane! He is a wonderful man — he cares about you. Yeah, right! JERK! I thought to myself, not able to control the tears that started coming down like a river.

"No, Ann. You're wrong. He's awful, evil…" I couldn't stand that conversation any longer, so I ran out of there in a flash, not giving them a chance to follow me.

I just wanted to be in the dark forever, never leave my bedroom again, ever. I drove home without bothering to control my sobbing. My phone started to ring nonstop, and Mike knocked on my door late that night, but I didn't answer either.

CHAPTER 26

The next day, I woke up feeling heavy. I felt a hole in my chest, and my head was spinning around when getting up from the bed.

"Oh my God! I look terrible." I tried to fix my messy hair and my face a little in front of the mirror with my hands. It was difficult to see my face with my eyes so red and swollen.

The phone started ringing early in the morning, but I didn't care. Mike also came to my door before going to work.

"Jane, are you there? Please open the door…" he tried.

I stayed there all day feeling miserable. I didn't change my pajamas or eat breakfast…or lunch. I sat there on the kitchen floor, not being able to move or even think. I was feeling empty and lost.

What was Joe trying to do? Why does he want us both? Am I not enough for him? He can't handle me. The only explanation is that he needs her to make me upset, so I would trigger him and make him angry so he could have me the way he likes it, with anger and passion. There is no other explanation.

It was six o'clock in the evening when they started knocking on my door again: Mike and Ann. "Jane, please open the door," Ann urged.

"If you don't open the door, we're going to call your mom…and the police…" They were losing their patience.

"Go away. I don't want to see anyone…" I shouted from the kitchen.

They insisted for a while, and then it got quiet. I got up to look through the peephole; they were gone. *Good!* I thought to myself, and then I realized I had to stop feeling defeated. There was only one thing to be done. I knew it was going to be hard on Ann, but I had no choice. I had to show Joe that I wouldn't give up and if he thinks he'll make Ann believe him, he's totally wrong. I'll play by the same rules. It's my turn to get Ann on my side and against him.

I got up on my feet, took a long, warm, healing shower, put on the first clothes I could find, and headed to Mike's apartment.

"Jane…hi." He was surprised to see me.

"Can I come in?" I asked, already getting into his apartment.

"Sure…" he replied, and he followed me in.

"Where is Ann?" I asked.

"She had to go walk her dog. She'll be back in an hour or so," he said.

"Maybe it's better this way. I need to talk to you, Mike," I said.

He sat down and looked at me, waiting for a confession. I sat at his side, took a deep breath, and started…

"Please, Mike, listen to me without interrupting. Don't ask questions or make any comments, ok?" I asked him, and he nodded. "I'm not the one that needs help right now. Ann is in danger. That Joe guy she's in love with and just started dating is the reason for my nightmares and this whole mess. Ann knows nothing about it because everything was supposed to be a game. A stupid game he proposed to me a while ago just to have me under his control…"

"What? I knew something was shady. Let me call Ann. Don't you want to wait for her to come back so you can tell us both?"

"No, not yet. She won't believe me. I need to make her see with her own eyes."

"Ok, so let me text her saying that you have opened the door for me and that she doesn't need to come back right away," he said, typing on his phone quickly.

"Ok," and I resumed telling him the story.

"I don't know what he has planned for her, but I don't trust him. I know he isn't in love with her because he's dating me as well. He just wants to use her like he's using me…"

"What? You were dating him all this time? What about us?" He was getting upset. "Why didn't you tell Ann, your best friend, that you were having a relationship with him?"

"Be-cause it was all part of a game that he proposed to me when he started working in the office. We weren't supposed to let anyone know…"

"Very convenient. And you were very stupid to fall for his BS…"

"Whatever, Mike. It just happened. I was excited about the game's thrill and went for it. Anyway, apparently, he couldn't handle seeing other men hitting on me and started to become aggressive, to the point he hurt two of those guys… One ended up dead."

"My God! He's fucking dangerous. Why didn't you tell me? I would have protected you!"

"I know you would, but everything happened so fast. I'm sorry, Mike."

"We have to think fast, Jane. We don't have a lot of time. We can't tell Ann this story now. She wouldn't believe it, right? She's already too involved with him." He was thinking aloud.

"Yeah, I know she won't believe me. See my problem?" Finally, I was getting some support.

"Let me call her and say that you've agreed to go to New York with me, that I gave you a couple of sleeping pills, and you're asleep, so she doesn't have to worry about you for now. I'll call for some food delivery, open a bottle of wine, and you'll tell me exactly what happened, ok?"

"K."

So he did, and I told him about the game and about Fred and Juan Carlos.

"We have to have a plan to get him. I don't want you taking any risks," he said, hugging me. "What was in your mind that made you fall for this psycho? I just want to understand…" he said, looking at me with indignation.

"I don't know, Mike. Things got worse little by little, and he was always so convincing. He has the skills to convince you that you're the psycho one, not him. He's a predator…" I didn't know how to explain.

"He's dangerous — and violent. We have to be careful because we don't want anyone to get hurt. How are we going to ambush him? You know him well. Tell me what's the easiest way to bring him to us." He started laying out a plan.

"Whatever we decide to do, it has to be done fast. You told Ann that we're going to New York tomorrow, right? I don't know how I could approach him outside of the office. I have to stop by there early in the morning."

"No, it has to be another way. Maybe it would be even better if he thought you were gone. He would be caught off guard, which could be an advantage for us." He was thinking aloud again.

"Maybe you're right. I could get him by surprise so he wouldn't have time to plan anything…" I completed it. "So, here is what we're going to do…."

And we started to lay a plan to trap Joe and save Ann.

CHAPTER 27

A week later, I couldn't believe I had on that awful whore outfit again. This time, I had to improvise a top because the original one was totally ruined. I had this nice sleeveless V-necked black T-shirt that wasn't that appealing, but it would suit the circumstances well.

I was once again waiting for Joe on Ann's street. His car was parked right in front of her house, as we predicted it would be. The plan was to get him leaving her house since we knew he didn't want to be part of the conversation Mike had set up with Ann. He would be mad when he saw me wearing that whore outfit again and then he would take me out of there in a rage. Mike would get Ann and follow us. I needed Ann to see with her own eyes since she would never believe me if I told her that Joe was a sociopath.

I was scared but relieved that Mike was nearby. I knew Joe would be extremely mad at me this time, especially when he realized that Ann was following us. I'm sure that Ann will break up with him when she sees for herself the type of jerk he is. She would have to digest the situation for a while but will get over it eventually, and Joe will be mine.

"Mike, are you there? What if he gets suspicious?" I called Mike in the middle of the street, just wishing to disappear. We knew Joe was going to leave her house any minute now.

"Relax, Jane, I'm right here. He isn't going to hurt you, I promise. I brought my baseball bat just in case he gets violent." He calmed me down.

"Ok…" I was still talking when Joe left Ann's house. I panicked but knew exactly what to do. "Joe," I called him.

"Jane? Bloody hell! What are you up to? Get in the fucking car… NOW!" he yelled at me, getting in his car. "What are you trying to do? What's this about? Have you lost your mind?"

"I just want to be with you, Joe…"

"It's over, Jane. Don't you get it? I'm not into you anymore. I'm tired of this game shit. Let's forget everything and pretend it never happened."

"I can't pretend it never happened. You've just turned my life upside down, and now you're trying to get my best friend's life also screwed up. Sorry, but I can't let you."

"Jane, you don't understand. If you don't let go…I'll have to make you." He drove us away, taking I-95 South. I knew he was taking me to Marathon.

"How? Are you going to kill me?"

"Don't try me, woman! And why are you wearing this slut outfit again? Do you want to play whore?"

"I want you. I can be your whore if you like."

"I can't take this anymore. Jane, please leave me alone. For the last time, I'm asking you to LEAVE ME ALONE!"

"NO!" I yelled back at him. "Don't hurt me, please."

"Why do you keep saying that? I never hurt you; it's all your imagination. You keep pushing me over my limits. You like to see me angry and out of control. We've had enough of this craziness. I really don't want to hurt you."

"You can't leave me. I don't know how to live without you. Where are you taking me?"

"Let's go to Marathon. You and I are going to talk and find a satisfactory solution that suits us both… Ok?"

"You mean we're going to fuck…" I knew exactly what he wanted.

"That too! Isn't that what you want?"

"You can't play with people's minds. It's wrong. I'm a human being, and I have feelings."

"You know what? It was my mistake, really. I should've known that you were too young for this type of thing. You're just a little spoiled brat; that's what you are."

"No, Joe. I'm the type of girl you like. I'm the right woman for you. You also can't live without me."

"NO, you're wrong. You disgust me. Look at you. You really like to be treated like the whore you are. I'm just the one that fell for your angel's face and ended up bringing the slut out of you. Didn't I?"

"Don't you understand? I'm doing what you wanted me to. You started treating me this way. I could've been just a girlfriend to you, just like Ann…"

"Ann is not like you. She's a good girl."

"Why are you saying that? What do you know about her? She's a normal girl, just like me…"

"No, she's nothing like you. She's genuine. She has no hidden side like you do."

"WHAT? You really are a son of a bitch, a psycho, and an asshole. I can't believe you're saying that to me. I'm doing what you wanted me to; I'm doing it for you. And you love it, you know that."

"For me? Give me a break, Jane. We were doing so well until you started playing dirty. I'm a guy; I can't control myself. You knew I was crazy for you, and you kept pushing my buttons to see me furious. Say it…I want to hear you say that I made you hornier than you've ever been in your life, freaking bitch. You're playing with my mind — you're the psycho. You knew my weakness and pushed me to the point that I really wanted to kill you."

"I can't believe my ears. You're trying to make me feel guilty about everything that happened to me since I met you."

"You are guilty, Jane. Admit it. You can't have a normal relationship. It would make you bored. You like to incite and feel the adrenaline running in your veins…taking risks. You love to fuck in filthy alleys… You make me want to hurt you. And you like to be abused by me. I couldn't see this side of you before it was too late. Is your boyfriend following us?" He looked in the rearview mirror, squinting. "Is he not enough for you? Doesn't he fuck you like I do? Of course, he doesn't."

"You're insane! How could you think I wanted to be abused? I'm just playing your fucking game. You asked me to play with you. You said it was supposed to be sensual and thrilling, remember? You wanted to fulfill my fantasies — and I just wanted to fulfill yours. I had to provoke you because it was the only way to make you come to me. That's the way you liked it. And Mike is not my boyfriend. I love you."

"Jane, I'm sorry, but I don't love you. I just wanted to have a good time. You're so beautiful and sexy, and it seemed to me you were up to enjoy some adventure. And I don't believe you. I bet you fucked the guy. Why is he following us?"

"They're following us so they can witness with their own eyes the jerk you are. Why did you go that far? Why did you try to hurt Juan Carlos and kill Fred if you weren't jealous and desperate in love with me?"

"They who?" He was puzzled, looking through the rearview mirror, not knowing who was in the car with Mike. "Are you insane? I never tried to hurt Juan Carlos and don't even know who Fred is. You need help…" He pulled over to look at me. "Jane, believe me, it's all in your head. I've done nothing to hurt anyone, not even you.

I thought we were enjoying a good time together, but every time I tried to be nice to you, you turned the table to trigger me. That's what you wanted, not me."

"I did it for you, Joe. I would do anything for you, and I can't stand seeing you with Ann."

"So then, we have a problem. I really like her."

"NO! You will not be with her, I promise," and I started crying again.

Mike's car caught up and pulled over behind us.

Chapter 28

Before they reached us, I held Joe's hand and said, "Please, Joe…I need you. We can start over somewhere else — just you and me."

"I wish we could, but no matter where we are, we can't change what already happened. It's too late for us. One of us has to go," he said, pushing me away.

"NO! I won't let you go. You can't leave me. Please, please don't say it's over. I'd rather die!"

"Jane! Listen to me; we must move on. There's no other way. And you're not going to die. You'll find someone else."

"NO…" I opened the car door and ran away onto the highway. I needed to make Ann see Joe attacking me.

"Jane! Come back here…" He caught me and held me tight. "Jane, please don't make a scene."

"You said you loved me!" I yelled so Ann could hear me as she approached us.

"It will not work. We can't see each other ever again. If you don't quit the office, I'll have to. I don't want to hurt you or anybody else. You need help, Jane." And I started to cry hysterically.

"Let her go!" Mike yelled, approaching us with the baseball bat in his hands, and Ann was right behind him.

"What's going on? Jane, let's talk. We can clear all this misunderstanding, I'm sure," Ann said, getting closer.

"Ann, Joe is a jerk. He hurt me and killed Fred, tried to kill Juan Carlos, and now he wants to hurt you! Believe me." I needed to tell her before he could convince her I was the nutty one. If he doesn't want me, he will not have Ann as well.

"No, Jane. I don't believe you. Come here," she said, stretching out her hand to me. Joe let me go, not believing Ann was there, seeing that scene. "Why are you wearing this costume?" She had an inquiring look on her face.

I ran to her crying, "That's how he likes to see me…we're playing this game that I'm his whore. He's a psycho!"

"Game?" She was getting upset and looked at Joe in disbelief.

"Well, what the fuck, man! Why did you do this for? Why did you mistreat her like that? She's just a girl…" Mike was confused and tried to keep Joe away from Ann and me.

"I meant no harm," Joe said, not believing his eyes and anxious to take Ann away from me.

"I guess it's too late, huh? Do you think you can just play a game of your choosing, set the rules, and end the game when you're tired? I don't think so, not with my girl. I love her and will not let this happen again. You are an asshole."

"I may be. Let's talk, all four of us. We can clear up all this freaking story, shall we?" Joe said, taking control of the situation.

"Yeah," Ann said. "I want to clean this mess up."

"Ok, but you need to stay close to me," I told her, holding her hand tight. She nodded.

"I have a house in Marathon. It's about one hour from here. We can talk there. Follow me," Joe said, going to his car.

"Come with me, girls. I don't trust the guy," Mike called us to get in his car.

"I'll go with Joe. We need to talk,"

Ann said, all serious, and getting in his car.

I got in Mike's car, concerned about what Joe was going to tell Ann. "Can you speed up, Mike? I want to get there as soon as possible…"

"We're right behind them. Don't worry, he will not hurt Ann…"

"What did you tell her?"

"I told her you and Joe were having an affair, and he asked you to keep it a secret. I thought it was weird, but she knew you and Joe had something in the past but didn't know that it was still going on."

"Was she upset with me?"

"I guess she's upset with him, of course."

"I hope she believes me now that she could see with her own eyes."

"Yeah, he can't hide anything else from her, not anymore. But I bet he's telling her you're the one to be blamed… The son of a bitch!"

"He'll try, but she's my best friend, and I know she loves me more than anything…"

"She would be an idiot if she chose to believe in him."

"I hope you're right," I whispered, mainly to myself, as we arrived at the house.

ANN

CHAPTER 29

"C'mon, Max, inside now. I know you want to stay outside, but I have to go work. C'mon!" I was trying to make my darling dog come inside the house. It was time for me to leave. He came in slowly as in protest. "Good boy!" I tried to cheer him up without success. I locked the door and looked at the living room window. There he was, looking at me with sad eyes, but he was quiet as he understood that I had to go. It broke my heart.

I was the first one to arrive in the office, as usual. Jane, my friend and coworker, is always late. I tried to talk with her several times, but she's just irresponsible, that's a fact. I walked into the office, turned all the lights on, put my stuff away, turned my computer on, and went to the lunchroom to make coffee. I can't function before having my coffee.

"Good morning, Ms. Martinez!" Mr. McKee said, walking into the office.

"Good morning, Mr. McKee! I replied with a smile.

Five minutes later.

"Good morning, Ms. Martinez!" Mr. Poch said, arriving next.

"Good morning, Mr. Poch!" I said, still smiling.

Twenty minutes later, Jane comes in in a hurry, as always.

"I can't believe I've made it!" she said, taking her jacket off and putting her stuff away.

"Yeah, you will be F-I-R-E-D next time you're late. Get a freaking alarm clock! I mean, how difficult can it be to wake up on time?" She looked at me, getting annoyed. "I told you I could call you every morning when I get up…" I tried again to convince her that arriving on time is important.

"Oh, never mind, Ann. I really appreciate it, but I've got everything under control," she said as if this were the first time that she's late.

"Whatever! I'm just trying to be nice, not that you deserve it, anyway!" I said, going back to my work.

"Ms. May?" spoke the voice on the intercom.

"Yes, Mr. McKee?" she answered, still putting her stuff away.

"Would you get me a grande caramel macchiato with skim milk and a sprinkle of cinnamon? Ah, don't put any sugar. Ok, honey? Thanks! See you in my office in…what…fifteen minutes?"

"Yes, sir! A grande caramel macchiato with skim milk and a sprinkle of cinnamon is coming right up!"

"Don't forget, no sugar!" he replied.

"No sugar, sir," she confirmed.

"He's a freak! He drives me crazy sometimes! Every day is the same. I'm so sick of it. I need to do something else in my life! Why wasn't I born rich?" I love Jane to death, but sometimes she really gets on my nerves.

"Wow! Take it easy, Jane! Do not start your day like that."

"Like that, how? What are you talking about?" she yelled at me.

"Bad mood! You're going to spoil everybody's day with this attitude, and I've got to be sitting by your side all day long. Please, give me a break, would you?" I was getting irritated.

"Shut up!" she shouted again.

"May I help you?" she said to someone who had just entered the office without making a noise. I think he was embarrassed about the situation and all the yelling.

"Yes, I'm here to see, Mr. Poch," he said timidly.

"You were going to get Mr. McKee's coffee, remember, Jane? I'll take care of Mr...?" I had to interfere before she could burst at the poor guy.

"Joe," he said, "Joe Garrison."

"Fine!" she said and left the office stomping her feet.

"I'm sorry about Jane. She's just having a bad day." I tried to make things better, looking at him a little shy; he was quite handsome.

"No problem," he said with a smile on his face. "Everybody has a bad day once in a while, I understand."

"Mr. Poch? Mr. Joe Garrison is here to see you," I spoke on the intercom, still smiling at Joe.

"Please make him comfortable in the conference room. I'll be right there," the intercom replied.

"Ok. You can follow me." I directed Mr. So-Cute to the conference room.

The meeting was short. After fifteen minutes, they came out of the room, talking loudly and smiling. Joe waved goodbye to me when leaving since I was on the phone. I waved back with a smile, wishing I could talk to him a little longer. *Oh well, I guess I'll see him again. He may be a client or work for a new client.* I thought to myself.

Jane came back twenty minutes after Joe left. Why did she take that long? The coffee shop is just across the street. Anyway, I tried to talk with her normally, but she kept the bad mood attitude, so I decided to leave her alone. Tomorrow, she'll be better.

CHAPTER 30

The next morning, she was back to herself and arrived on time. So, I pretended nothing had happened the day before and acted normally.

"Do you want to go to the movies tonight?" I asked her.

"Movies? I don't know. What do you want to see?" she replied.

"I want to see that new kids' movie. What's its name?"

"A kids movie?"

"Yeah…I think kids movies are funny. C'mon, where is your sense of humor? I have some pooot," I said with a huge smile on my face. I know she can't resist weed.

"Umm, I like the pot part of it. I think it could be fun. Count me in, girlfriend!" And just like that, she was happy and in a good mood for a change.

"Great!" I said and answered the phone, "Good morning, Poch and McKee Attorneys and Associates; this is Ann. How may I help you?"

#

The day was busy but fun. We left at 5:00 PM in a hurry because she needed to feed her cat, Ollie, before going to the mall. At the movies, she was really high and laughing loudly, so I had to elbow her several times to make her calm down without success. She was elbowing me back; maybe I was being loud, too, but who cares?

I didn't want to go straight home after the movie, so I thought that a pit stop at the bar for a drink would be great. We went to this bar close to my house. The bartender, Peter, is my friend. Once we arrived, I called his attention by pounding my fist on the counter. He put a huge beam on his face when he saw me.

"Hey, girl. Where have you been?" he said, kissing me on the lips as usual. "Who's that?" He pointed at Jane without looking at her.

"A girlfriend!" I said without introducing her, staring back at his face.

"Oh…" he said, still gazing at me. "Does she have a name?"

"Probably, but who wants to know?" I teased.

"That's it!" she said, getting in between us. "Jane May!"

"Hello, Jane May. What can I get you? It's on me," he said, looking at her face.

"What about a margarita on the rocks?"

"Sounds good," he said, leaning sideways to face me again. "What about you?"

"I'll have what he's having," I said, pointing at this sad man on the other side.

"Ouch! I wouldn't if I were you! He's having very strong stuff," he warned me.

"Really? Give me a double strong stuff then!" I pounded the counter again.

I got my drink and went to sit at the sad man's side. "What's up?" I said. He looked at me and nodded without saying a word. I could tell that he was in pain. "You look so sad. You know, sometimes speaking to a complete stranger can help…" I tried again.

"You don't really want to know," he said after a while.

"If I'm asking, it's because I want to know. Sometimes, all you need is a pair of good ears," I replied.

"You seem to be a nice girl. How old are you?" he asked.

"I'm twenty-four."

"I think you're too young to understand my problems. Have you been cheated on before?" he started to talk.

"Yeah. I have, believe me…"

"My story is like many, nothing special. It just hurt so much," he starts saying. I looked at him, nodding, saying nothing. "You know, I'm only forty-two. I have been married for ten years. We have two kids together, and I don't understand what I did to deserve this. I love my family and still love my wife, even though she cheated on me with the husband of her best friend. Can you believe?" He looked at me.

"I believe you. I was betrayed by my best friend once."

"But you're only twenty-four."

"Yeah. I know how it feels. How did you find out?"

"I followed her," he said, asking for another drink. "I got suspicious when she started to care about how she looked, going to the gym, and buying new sexy clothes. I thought that she was doing it for me in the beginning, but at the same time, she was losing interest in me. We were not having sex anymore, and she wasn't being herself at home. And she started to hang out with her 'friends,' if you know what I mean."

"I know what you mean. In my case, I started to suspect that something was going on between my best friend and my fiancé when they also started to hang out a bit too much as 'friends.' And thinking that I was called neurotic for questioning their sudden closeness makes me feel really mad." I had this unpleasant flashback crossing my head.

"Really? Your fiancé and best friend?"

"Yep, they're a happy married couple now."

"Wow! I'm sorry to hear that."

"You see, you're not the only one. And believe me, time will soothe the pain, but the scar will always be there."

"I guess you're right. Life must go on…"

"Give her some time. I know it'll be difficult but, in my opinion, you need to think about your kids. It must be terrible and scary for them to see you down like this. You must be strong."

"Yep, I have to be strong and move on with my life. Thanks for the conversation; it brought me some comfort."

"No problem. I wish I had someone to help me back then…"

"You're a nice girl, and I wish you all the happiness in the world from the bottom of my heart…"

"Thank you!" I smiled at him compassionately.

He nodded and asked for the check, then looked at me, making a gesture asking for a hug. I got up and hugged him goodbye, feeling that I had done something good for someone that day.

I looked around for Jane. She was already inside the bar, helping herself with drinks and making out with Peter. Why am I not surprised? Sigh.

Chapter 31

It was difficult to wake up the next morning. I couldn't take the time to let Max out as I usually do, so I had to ask my best friends and neighbors, David and Matt, to help me out. My sweet boy, Max, is a pit bull rescue, and the breed has been banned from Miami-Dade County, where I lived before. There were a couple of dog attacks, and unfortunately, all involved pit bulls, so they passed legislation, making it illegal to have pit bulls in the county. My mom wanted me to get rid of Max, but I couldn't. Instead, I moved to Broward County, where pit bulls are legal. But some people prefer to keep a distance from us. David and Matt are not one of these awful people; they love Max and me.

"David! Matt!" I yelled from my backyard.

Matt opened the back door, "Hi, Ann. What's up?" he asked.

"I'm sorry to bother, really, but I don't have time to wait for Max to come in. Can you? Please?" I begged.

"Sure, sweetheart, no problem at all. We love Max, you know that." And he opened the gate to let Max into their backyard.

Their pug dog, Luna, came right away to meet Max. Even though they are different in size, Max and Luna love each other and play very well together.

"Thank you very much, Matt. When he's done, will you let him in? The backdoor is open," I said, sending them kisses.

"No worries, girl, go!" he said when David came out to see what was going on.

"Hi, David!" I said, waving at him.

"Hey Ann. Hi, Max!" he said, greeting Max, who was happy with the commotion. "We're having a movie night. You're welcome to join us," David added.

"Will do!" I sent them both lots of kisses.

#

At the office, Jane was late as usual and in a bad mood…as usual. Sometimes, I just want to get another job, so I don't have to see her every day. Don't get me wrong, I love her, but she's difficult to deal with.

I wonder how she manages to have real relationships because her mood swings are very constant and exhausting. I feel sorry for her. She comes from a broken home; her mother had her very young, and she never knew her father. She was raised without guidance and moved from house to house as her mother kept moving in with friends or new boyfriends. Now that she's officially an adult — she is twenty-one — her mother asked her to move out. She never calls or cares to know if Jane is doing well. I guess I'm the only one who really cares for her.

When she comes in cursing and complaining, I just ignore it. That's the best thing to do, so she minds her own business and leaves me alone. So, I did exactly that: kept myself busy and didn't even look at her all day long.

At the end of the day, I got my stuff and said, "See ya!" and left. I could feel her eyes fixed on me with indignation, but I was out of the door. Tomorrow will be a new day, and hopefully, she'll be fine again.

#

Max wasn't home when I arrived, so I went to my neighbors. David opened the door, saying, "Hi, Ann, you're early." Max and

Luna came to greet me. They were so happy. Max loves Matt and David and adores Luna.

"Let's go home, boy?" I asked Max. He understood the command and came out the door as if saying, *Ok.*

"Are you coming for the movie later?" David asked. "We're going to watch *Titanic* for the thousandth time," he laughed.

"Yes, of course, I love *Titanic.* I'll be over around, what, eight?" I asked.

"Yeah. Eight is fine. Bye, Max. And see you later, Ann." He closed the door. Max and I went home.

The movie night was fine. I had seen *Titanic* many times, but it was always fun to watch sad movies with David and Matt. They get so emotional and cry. So sweet. I love them.

As customary, I was sitting in between them, holding the popcorn bowl, and they were holding hands behind me on top of the couch's back. I could feel them squeezing each other's hands hard when the emotional moments came up. I cried, too, not because of the movie but because of them. Love is beautiful, and you can consider yourself incredibly lucky if you find your other half. Unfortunately, it hasn't happened to me yet, at least the way I deserve.

I'm Cuban-American, and my family finds marriage very important. More than that, a good daughter must be married or engaged by the age of twenty. At twenty-four, I'm considered a lost cause, and everyone looks at me as the old unmarried aunt. I was engaged once, but he left me to marry my best friend. I was betrayed by the people I loved the most. It has been exceedingly difficult for me to trust anyone after Sam.

I hate it when the memories of them invade my mind. I get depressed, and all I can do is cry. But not tonight. I went home feeling blue, took a warm shower to relax, smoked pot to forget, and meditated to get sleepy. This ritual always works. I'll be feeling better tomorrow.

CHAPTER 32

The next day in the office, I was surprised when Joe showed up early in the morning with a huge smile on his most gorgeous face.

"Hi, how are you?" he said, looking at me.

"I'm fine; you?" I smiled back. "Are you here to see Mr. Poch again?" I added.

"Yes, can you let him know I'm here?"

"Sure!" I said, getting the intercom and pushing Mr. Poch's extension key. "Mr. Poch? Mr. Garrison is here."

"Yes, yes, tell him to come to my office. Thanks, Ms. Martinez," the voice on the intercom said.

"You heard the man. Go in, Mr. Garrison. You know where his office is, right?"

"Yes, I do, Ms. Martinez…" he said and left for Mr. Poch's office, walking gaily. He seemed happy, so I figured he wasn't a client.

Jane came in late as usual, but not that late. She seemed to be in a very good mood, which made me very suspicious.

"Someone is in a good mood today, huh?" I told her. "What happened? Did you get laid last night?" I asked, being sarcastic.

"Nope," she answered.

"Did you meet someone new?" I tried again.

Suddenly, Mr. McKee and Mr. Poch came into the reception

with Joe.

"Ladies, this is Mr. Joe Garrison! He's the new associate." Mr. McKee said.

"Nice meeting you!" Joe said, sticking out his hand toward Jane.

"Nice meeting you too, Mr. Garrison," she said.

"Nice seeing you again, Mr. Garrison," I said, smiling and welcoming him to the office. I was excited to know he was going to be working with us. Who knows if it wasn't destiny working its way through?

"Well, which one of you will grab me a coffee?" Mr. McKee said while the other two men walked back to their offices, talking nonstop.

"I will," Jane said without hesitation. She grabbed her purse and left.

Jane was very strange when she came back. I wonder if something had happened at the coffee shop since she was fine when she came in this morning, and now, she looked distressed.

"Jane? Are you alright?" I asked.

"Yeah," she said. "What are you doing tonight?"

"I don't know. Nothing, I guess. Why?" I was intrigued.

"I need some weed!" she said, blinking her eyes.

"Oh! That's what you want, huh? Ok, I never say no to weed. Let's party tonight, girlfriend!" I tried to cheer her up.

#

Jane arrived around nine o'clock. I was ready, waiting for her.

"Where are we going?" she asked.

"Par-tee..." I said, getting inside and leaving the door open for her. "Here, grab this." I handed her the already-lit joint after taking a puff.

She took it and started to smoke frenetically. "Take it easy, Jane. This is good stuff…"

"What?" she said, holding her breath. "It's good," she said, nodding.

"Really good." I took the joint from her hand and took my last puff. "That's it! Enough for you, girlfriend, let's go." I said, holding my breath and patting Max's head on our way out. "Be nice, kiddo!"

We went to this hip-hop nightclub, not really my type of music, but very trendy now. Anyway, it was fun; we danced all night long.

We headed home around 2:00 AM. "You are not driving, my friend," I told her while parking in front of my house, where her car had been parked all night. "You can stay over or call a cab."

"I'll stay," she said, collapsing on the couch without changing or brushing her teeth.

#

When I woke up the next morning, she was gone. I had breakfast with Max outside, then changed and went to the office feeling tired.

The day was dragging on. I could not wait to go home and have a good night's sleep. At 5:00 PM sharp, I was gone.

Chapter 33

Monday was a really busy day at the office. We had a lot to do, and the phone didn't stop ringing. I was exhausted, trying to handle everything at once. Jane didn't bother. She kept working as normal and took her lunch break earlier at 11:00 AM, leaving me alone to deal with all the bosses, phone calls, and the public.

We had a few clients coming in, and besides the regular work, I had to make sure they were comfortable while waiting to be seen. I smiled, pretending everything was under control, but kept looking at the clock. Jane didn't come back until almost 12:30 PM. I wanted to kill her. After her long lunch, she came back with a bag of chocolates for me, as if asking for forgiveness. I didn't want to argue with her; there was no point, so I said thank you and put the bag in my drawer. At 5:00 PM sharp, I was out of there, gone.

#

When I arrived home, David was watering the plants in the front yard. He saw that I was a little stressed. "Hey, girl, do you want to come over for dinner? Matt is cooking spaghetti carbonara. It's delicious."

"Mm, I love his cooking. Do you have wine?" I asked.

"We do, but you can bring another bottle if you want. You know, we love drinking!" he replied.

"Me too! I should drink less, but today, I really need a good meal, wonderful friends, and a glass of wine — maybe two or maybe three!" I said, and we laughed.

We always leave our back doors open so we can come in and out of our houses without knocking. As I walked into their kitchen, I was amazed by the smell of the food. Actually, the whole house smelled like heaven. The table was impeccably set, and the room was lit by candlelight. They are amazing!

"Almost ready!" Matt said, manning the stove like a real chef. He was funny, wearing this cap on his head to prevent hair from falling on the food. He also had this fun apron on that said: *Best Cock Ever* instead of *Best Cook Ever*. The second *o* had a faded red sauce stain on it that made the *o* turn into a *c*. I love them both. They make me laugh and feel welcome, always.

"Ok, you two, out of my kitchen!" Matt yelled at us. David and I were discussing which wine was better, Californian or French. Of course, David knows a lot more than I do, but it's always fun to debate with him. He goes on and on explaining about the climate, region, grapes and so forth. All I know is that there is a cheaper one.

"Oh my God! It's wonderful, Matt! Really delicious. Why aren't you a real chef already? I mean, you should have your own restaurant." I praised him after starting to eat.

"I wish. Unfortunately, I have to work to pay the rent and have no money to open a restaurant," he said, taking a sip of his wine.

"Anyhow, we love to cook for ourselves, and good friends like you," David added.

"Aww, guys, I love you so much. You can never leave me. You're not allowed to move. If you do, I'll follow you. I don't care where," I said.

"We'll take you with us anywhere we go, I promise," Matt said, sipping his wine and making me smile.

"And Max," I added.

"Of course, Max, as well," Matt completed.

The night was delightful, as usual. I went home feeling better and decided to watch some TV before going to bed. *Why do I have a TV? There is never anything that I would like to watch.* I kept changing channels until I could find something interesting — it was either the *American Pickers* or *Boardwalk Empire* — I chose Boardwalk.

Max came to sleep at my side, and I stayed there, staring at the TV, not really paying much attention. I feel so lonely sometimes. I wish I had someone to love and be loved, like David and Matt. They're so much in love, and they can care less about what other people say or think about their relationship, which, by the way, they make sure to keep open. Everyone knows they're a couple. I think they're very courageous to assume their relationship in public with so many haters out there.

However, I think that the people they let in their lives are special, people they trust and genuinely love. I feel lucky to have them as my friends, and I would do anything for them; I know they would do anything for me, too.

I looked at the clock. It was already 12:30 AM. I needed to go sleep. So, another hot shower to clear my mind and meditation was the solution. I put my mantra CD on and got in the lotus position with my legs crossed and relaxed arms. I closed my eyes and cleared my mind, breathing in and out deeply, focusing on my muscles, which were relaxing with the ritual. After a few minutes, I was ready to go to bed.

Chapter 34

"Have you eaten my chocolate?" I asked Jane with indignation when I realized my drawer was a mess, and the chocolate she'd given me the day before was gone.

"Yeah. Sorry, I was starving last night. You know I stayed longer to finish my work."

"Oh…so you're responsible for this mess, huh?" I asked, looking at the disarray.

"Sorry," she said, embarrassed as a delivery guy came in with a huge flower bouquet.

"Ms. Jane May?" he asked me.

"I'm Jane May!" she said, taking the flowers from his hand without excusing herself and searching for a sender's card.

"I can't believe there is no card!" I said, helping her look for a card or a note.

"I know!" she exclaimed. "Who could have sent it?"

"Maybe an ex that is still in love with you? Or the guy you slept with last night," I teased her.

"No, I don't think so. And I haven't slept with anyone lately, anyway. Alan is out of the picture. We broke up," she explained.

"Really? I was going to ask you about him…" I wasn't surprised to know they had broken up. Her relationships never last long. I wonder why…

"Flowers!" Joe said when arriving from a late business lunch with Mr. Poch, who also had a smile on his face.

"Who sent you these beautiful flowers?" Mr. Poch asked.

"I don't know! There is no card with it," she said, still trying to figure out where the card could be.

"Maybe there isn't any card because the person who sent it knew you would know who they were from," Joe said.

"It makes sense. The problem is that my friend here has no clue," I teased her again.

I don't know if she ever found out who had sent her the flowers, but she was really happy and in a very good mood for a change, which made me happy for her.

#

On the weekend, I went to see my mom and sister. I used to go more often, but since I can't take Max, I feel guilty leaving him alone for too long. I already leave him all day long during the weekdays when I go to work, so during the weekends all I want is to spend some quality time with him.

Pets don't have a choice. They have to cope with whatever they're given. I find it really sad that some pets must beg for love and care, which they rarely get the way they deserve. They're little angels that love us unconditionally, no matter what. There should be a pet care agency to control and check the animal's wellbeing. I know you can make a complaint if you see an abused animal, but how long must they suffer until help arrives? If I could, I would rescue every single animal in need.

My poor Max was going to be put down if I hadn't adopted him. No one wants a pit bull. People fear them, which is nonsense. My Max is the most loving dog I ever had. Sometimes, I think he bears with me in gratitude. He knows I saved his life.

My mom was annoying, as always. I feel sorry for my sister, who's still at home with her. My parents divorced two years ago and now we're all my mom cares about, and since I moved out, my sister has been her only daily concern.

"*¿Por donde andas? ¿Por qué no viniste a visitarnos antes?*" she started questioning me.

"*Lo siento mamá, tengo estado ocupada,*" I replied.

"*Ocupada con que? Con el perro?*" she went on.

"Working, *Mamá,*" I said, leaving the kitchen and following my sister to her bedroom.

"How are you, Stephanie?" I asked.

"I'm ok. This is my last year of high school, and I should start looking into colleges. But I'm not sure where to go or what to do. Can you help me, sis?"

"Sure, what do you have in mind?"

"Not really sure. I would like to move to New York. I've been looking at NYU. I need to apply online, but I would like to see it first, you know, check the place out and feel its vibe," she went on. "Can you find some time to go with me? I really don't want to go with Mom."

"Sure, I would love to go to New York, and we can go watch a Broadway musical, too! What do you think?" I added.

"That would be great! When can we go?" She was getting excited.

"Let me check with my boss, or maybe we can go for a weekend. We're just checking the place out and looking around. One weekend should be enough, and if we need to go back another time, we go. What do you think?" I asked.

"I think it's wonderful! Yay! I'm going to New York!" She started to jump around.

"*¿Quien va a Nueva York?*" my mom asked, walking into the room.

"*Nosotras Mamá ,*" I replied. "Stephanie wants to check out this college and asked me to go with her," I added.

"*¿College? En Nova York. ¿Por qué?* Why can't she go to Miami-Dade like you did?" She started answering in Spanish and then switching to English…as usual.

"Because Miami-Dade doesn't have the program I want!" Stephanie answered.

"And what do you want?" she asked.

"I was thinking about environmental studies, you know? About global warming and climate change. I think it'll be a good profession in the future, I would get a good job," she tried to convince Mom.

"Yeah, Mom. It's a good profession," I assured her.

"Let's see…" she said and left the room, going back to the kitchen.

"Do you want to go out? We can go have *un helado* on Calle Ocho…" I suggested.

"Sure, let's go!" She was happy.

We went to *Azucar*, this little ice cream place on Calle Ocho that we used to go to with Mom and Dad. It brings me good memories from my childhood. I love Little Havana, where I grew up. Nothing ever changes here, and you feel like being in another country. The stores' names and signs are all in Spanish. Everybody speaks Spanish everywhere. Some residents have been living in the US for decades but never bothered to learn English. There's no need in Little Havana. We're all Cubans or Hispanics, anyway.

The place is always crowded, but we made our way through and got our ice cream. *Yum*! When we were about to leave the small, busy place, someone stopped me by tapping on my shoulder.

"Ann? Is that you?" I turned around to see my ex-best friend, Cristina.

"Cristina? Hi…" I anxiously looked around to see if Sam was with her. He was not, to my relief.

"Hi, Ann! What a coincidence. I'm so happy to see you so well," she said and kissed me on both cheeks as Cubans do.

"Yeah. Good to see you, too, so…pregnant!" I couldn't disguise my surprise.

"Yeah. Isn't it wonderful? Sam and I are very happy!"

"Congratulations! I'm sorry, we were about to leave, but it was nice seeing you again."

"Yeah, nice seeing you, too. Let's get together one of these days?" She tried to sound casual.

"Sure, bye now…" I wanted to disappear.

"Bye," she said, smiling and making sure to show me her growing belly.

I almost got killed crossing Calle Ocho without looking, as I was in such a hurry to get away from there. Stephanie ran after me.

"Hey, Ann. I'm so sorry you had to see her. I wasn't going to tell you that she was pregnant…"

"That's ok, it's not your fault. That's why I don't like to come here."

"If it makes you feel a little better, I heard that their marriage isn't going well; that's the reason for her pregnancy, to try to save their marriage…"

"I can care less, really! I hope they find happiness somehow far away from me, *pendejos!*"

"Yeah. Do you want to talk about it?"

"No, they're snakes. They betrayed me, both of them. I was so naïve and in love with the bastard that I didn't see it coming, but the red flags were there. I was an idiot!"

"You were not. You couldn't imagine that your best friend was having an affair with your fiancé."

"I don't want to talk about this anymore. Let's plan our trip to New York."

"Yay, New York!"

#

Back at home, I felt guilty leaving Max alone all-day Saturday, so I decided to treat him by taking him to the beach on Sunday. We had to go early in the morning so he could run freely before people started to arrive. I usually take him to Dania Beach where dogs are allowed, but today I went to Hollywood Beach because it's usually empty at this time in the morning, only a few early bird joggers. Max loves it. I swear he was smiling all the way there, so happy he was.

"Let's go, Max. Run!" I said, opening the car door for him. He went off, running up and down the beach. I felt so happy for him.

The day was gorgeous. I started to walk by the water. Max would go back and forth as if saying, *Can you run with me? Can you run?* So funny.

"Hey, Ann?" I heard someone calling me. "Yes…oh, hi, Mr. Garrison!" I said, realizing that it was Joe from the office.

"Joe, call me Joe, please. Do you come here often?" he asked, walking fast to reach me.

"Not really. I came today because it's usually empty. I brought my dog to run free a bit," I explained, waiting for him to get closer.

"That's your dog?" he asked, pointing at Max.

"Yes, this is Max." I introduced him.

"What a beautiful dog," he added.

"Thanks…and do you always come here at this time?" It was my turn to ask questions.

"Not really. I was supposed to meet someone to run with, but he didn't show," he explained.

"What a coincidence! I usually take Max to Dania Beach, but today, I felt like changing locations. Dania Beach gets busy early, and Max can't run free for too long." I explained.

"Yep, a good coincidence, I hope!" he said, smiling, "Can I walk with you and Max?"

"Sure," I replied, and we started to walk down the beach.

He was surprisingly pleasant, very funny, and more handsome than ever. I could see his muscular and tanned arms and legs since he was wearing only a T-shirt and shorts.

"So, Ms. Martinez. Are you from here originally? Where the Martinez come from? I know it's a Hispanic name, but I have no idea of which country," he asked.

"Ann, call me Ann, please…" I mocked him, and he chuckled. "I'm Cuban-American," I explained. "I'm the second generation born in America. My grandparents, from both sides, came to America, fleeing the Castro Regime in 1960."

"Oh, wow. You know, I learned in school all about the Cold War and the Cuban military coup, but it always seemed to be so far away from my reality. I never imagined meeting someone who had experienced this part of history firsthand." He was really interested in me and my heritage.

"I was born and raised in Miami. A lot of Cubans live there. I'm just another one. What about you? You're from England, right? What brought you to America?" I was also interested.

"Yeah, I'm from London, born and raised…" he said and giggled. "I came to America to study. I went to Princeton in New Jersey. My father is also a lawyer, but I didn't want to make a career working for him, so I took the opportunity to come to the US to study. When I graduated, I got an internship at this law office in Chicago, which is a beautiful city, but I had always heard how wonderful Florida was, so I applied for the job I have now, and here I am!"

"Very interesting! So, you don't know the area very well," I added.

"Nope, I would really appreciate if you could show me Miami. Maybe a tour around your favorite places? But no pressure. Only if you can, of course…" he replied.

"It'll be my pleasure!" I said, smiling.

We had an enjoyable time together. Max was so happy, and I was feeling a lot lighter now. I really enjoyed Joe's company, and I think we could be very good friends — or maybe something else. My only concern is that we work together, and that's unfortunate. I don't think it's a good idea to mix professional and personal lives. Especially because he's my boss, and who knows if he even liked me the same way.

Chapter 35

The week went by without stress. Jane seemed happy, which I thought was strange, but I'm not complaining. I love her when she's in a good mood and happy. She can be fun to be with. On Friday, I asked if she wanted to go out during the weekend, but she turned me down. She said she was planning to clean her apartment, which desperately needed a deep cleaning. Well, I decided to do the same.

Saturday, I did laundry, cleaned the bathroom and the kitchen, put all the rugs outside, and even cleaned the windows. Matt and David were in the cleaning mood, too. They had loud music playing in the background, Matt was cleaning inside, and David was taking care of the garden.

"Hey, guys, do you want to come over tomorrow for lunch? I'll cook this time!" I invited them.

"Sure! We'll come over. Let us know if you need any help!" David said.

"Maybe you can help me put the table outside so we can eat in the backyard and let the dogs play around," I suggested.

"Sure! I'll bring dessert," Matt added.

#

I made *arroz con pollo*. They came over around noon and helped me set the table outside. The dogs were thrilled with the commotion.

"We need to get a grill," Matt said. "I would love to have barbecues outdoor, especially with the nice weather."

"That's a great idea, Matt. I'll check the prices and let's get one for your birthday. We can have a barbecue party!" David was getting excited about the idea.

"Count me in!" I was also interested in the grill. "Let's eat?" I said, sitting at the table and mixing the salad.

"Mm, it's delicious, Ann. You could work in my restaurant!" Matt smiled.

"Yeah, I could," I said, smiling back.

"How's your week? We haven't seen you since last week." David asked.

"Yeah, we didn't see you last weekend and all week," Matt completed.

"I went to see my mom and sister in Miami last Saturday. It took all day, so on Sunday, I decided to take Max to the beach. Poor kid stayed all alone Saturday," I explained.

"If we knew, we could've taken Max to Pompano Beach with us. We went to visit a friend of ours; he loves dogs, too, and wouldn't have minded," David said.

"Oh, thanks, guys, but that's fine. You know that not everyone is comfortable near a pit bull." I said sadly.

"So, how was the beach?" Matt asked.

"It was great. I ran into my boss. I mean the new associate," I'm sure I had a sparkle in my eye remembering that wonderful morning.

"What, who?" Matt was curious. "Tell us all about the new associate!"

"Yeah, girl, how old is he? Is he handsome?" David wanted to know.

"I guess he is twenty-seven or so, very handsome and charming." I smiled.

"Wow! And you didn't say anything? We want to know everything," Matt replied.

"Nothing really happened. We ran into each other on the beach and talked a little about our backgrounds and stuff… He said he's from London and came to America to study. He went to Princeton."

"Princeton! Wow…"

"Yeah, he's a lawyer, so I guess he's well-off," I said.

"Is he married?" David wanted to know.

"I don't think so, and I didn't ask. He asked if I could show him around since he's not really familiar with South Florida. Miami specifically. I, of course, said yes, but he didn't say anything else during the week."

"Don't worry, he will."

"Yeah, Ann, I'm sure he will, and you need to keep us posted! I want to know everything!" David added.

"Of course, I'll tell you guys, but I'm not sure. You know, we work together, and we all know that, statistically, most times, office affairs end badly."

"Nonsense," David said. "I know many cases in which the boss ended up marrying their assistant."

"True," said Matt.

"Well, no one is thinking about marriage. I don't even know if he really liked me, but I don't want to say or tell anyone — especially Jane — until I'm sure that he also liked me. Right now, it's nothing."

"I'm sure it will be. You deserve a nice guy for a change. We want to see you happy!"

"And married!" Matt added, and I smiled at the comment.

After we ate, they helped me clean and stayed a little longer for a glass of wine. We decided to watch an episode of *True Blood* before calling the night off. I was exhausted.

Max was tired, too, and went to his bed without waiting for me. I walked Matt and David out and went to take a nice, long shower. Tomorrow will be a wonderful day, and this week, Joe will ask me out. I just knew it.

Chapter 36

The following week was smooth, with no big mood changes for Jane. Actually, she was in an exceptionally good mood for a while, which I found strange, but I was not complaining. Joe didn't ask me out or even talk to me besides work stuff. He keeps his distance at the office, which is understandable since we work together, and it would be odd if he asked me out, even as friends. I guess he was just trying to be polite and would never ask again. *Oh well, he's too good to be true anyway…*

When Friday finally arrived, Jane and I decided to go out. She went home to change and feed her cat before coming over to my house to smoke some pot while we decided where to go.

We went to Riverfront, a stretch of road that has several bars, one after another, and lots of people going around from bar to bar. Everybody hangs out on the street since you're not allowed to enter a bar with a drink in your hands.

We entered the first bar on the street. It was ok, but we didn't stay too long. The plan was to make our way down to the very last one.

The next bar was playing hip-hop. We sat at the bar counter and asked for two beers. There weren't a lot of people inside. We danced a little and decided to move on to the next.

After finishing our beers outside, it was time for the next bar. Two guys who were flirting with us outside followed us in. At the counter, we asked for beers. They sat close enough to start a conversation.

"We saw you singing down the street. You were good."

"No, we were not. You must be mocking us, right?" I replied with a smile and took a gulp of my beer.

"Of course, they're mocking us. It's just a weird way to start a conversation." Jane clearly didn't like them.

"I'm sorry about that, but yes, we are trying to get to know you. My name is Paul, and this is Rick," he said, pointing at his friend, who wasn't even paying attention to us.

"I'm Ann, and this is my friend Jane." I introduced ourselves, pointing to Jane, who was already talking to someone else.

"Well, I guess she didn't like us."

"Yeah, you can say the same about your friend…"

"See you around then," he said and turned away to talk with his friend, leaving me alone there.

I guess they were interested in Jane, the cute and sexy one, not me, the unattractive and boring one. Sometimes, I get concerned about being friends with Jane. She's beautiful, sexy, and irresponsible. She reminds me of Cristina, who stole my fiancé. Maybe I was really naïve back then, but not anymore. I learned my lesson and if I get another boyfriend, Jane will not be around us, no way.

We finally got to the end of the street, and at the last bar, we were drunk and tired. It was already 3:00 AM, but we didn't care since the next day was Saturday, and we had nothing better to do. At least I had nothing planned. We stayed a little longer to sober up.

"Hey, girls!" Our friends from earlier came to talk with us and probably do the same: sober up before driving home.

"Hi!" Jane replied. "It was a fun night, don't you think?" she added.

"Yeah, as usual. Where are you guys from?" Paul asked.

"From here," I said, "You?"

"I live in Pompano Beach. He lives here in Fort Lauderdale."

"Rick, nice to meet you!" said his friend.

"I'm Ann, and this is my friend, Jane!" I introduced us again since he wasn't paying attention when we were first introduced.

Jane wasn't really in the mood to talk with them. They were ok, but she was ready to go home, so she cut the conversation short. "Nice meeting you two. Let's go home, Ann?"

"Yeah, let's go. Sorry…" I said, shrugging, and we left.

#

The next week started normally. Nothing really happened until Thursday when Joe came in with a huge smile on his handsome face.

"Hello, ladies!" he said, entering the reception.

"Hi, Mr. Garrison, what can I do for you?" I replied, happy to see him content, thinking that he was finally going to say something about going to Miami.

"First of all, drop the Mr. Garrison stuff. It makes me look older…and you don't need to be formal with me in the office. Anyway, could you get me a plane ticket to Chicago for tomorrow? Ah, I'll need a hotel room, too," he went on saying.

"Chicago, tomorrow? Sure. I'll try my best Mr. — oh — Joe," I corrected.

"Thanks, Ann, I'll stay the week. If not too much trouble, could you set up my return for next Friday?" he asked.

"A week? I mean, you'll be gone for a whole week?" I couldn't disguise my disappointment.

"I'll be back!" he teased me, leaving the room.

"Don't you love his British accent?" I sighed.

"Well, I think he's a jerk!" Jane said. "A really handsome jerk!"

"Why is it? Why do you think he's a jerk?" I was curious.

"No reason. It's just that sometimes he talks to us as if he's a close friend, and sometimes, he passes by us, not even saying good morning. He's weird but a very handsome weirdo."

"No, he's not. He's just preoccupied with work sometimes, you know? He's new and wants to impress the bosses."

"Nonsense, he can be a jerk when he wants to."

"Oh well, let me book his trip to Chicago."

CHAPTER 37

The week without seeing Joe was boring. I tried to keep myself busy and pretend I didn't care. Jane was kind of bored as well. I think we both feel the place kind of empty without him. I know it seems stupid, but I look forward to seeing him every day. His smile, his presence…I waited and waited for him to invite me out, but nothing. Maybe he didn't like me as I liked him. Oh well, let's keep moving on. One day, I'll find the right guy. I know I will.

When Joe came back, Jane and I smiled again. Jane was so happy that she couldn't hide it. I guess we both have a crush on him. I can't judge her, but she's too obvious. Anyone could see.

By Wednesday, I was getting annoyed with her, so I decided to be quiet and leave her alone. She left for lunch and, as usual, took a long time to come back, almost two hours. She was a mess when she entered the office after lunch. Her hair was messy, and she was all sweaty. Her mascara was smudged, too.

"What happened to you, Jane?" I was worried.

"Nothing, I just started to walk on the beach and forgot about the time. I rushed back and got all messed up and sweaty," she said.

"You better go to the restroom and get your face straight, Missy."

"Yeah. Thanks, Ann."

She was really distraught and kept quiet for the rest of the day.

#

On Thursday, I was getting irritated with Jane again, so I decided to go for a coffee in the afternoon. We didn't have much to do, and Jane's silence was killing me. I was planning to go get a coffee and stroll down Las Olas window shopping.

"Hey, Ann!" Joe was getting a coffee as well, to my pleasant surprise.

"Hi, Joe!" I could not disguise my contentment.

"There's not much to do in the office, right? I need a coffee to keep me awake!" he joked.

"Me too, I'm done with my work…so I thought I could have a coffee break!" I tried to keep the conversation going.

"I've been thinking about you," he said, getting his coffee from the barista's hand.

"Really?" I smiled, almost saying that I couldn't stop thinking of him.

"I remember you promised to take me around Miami. I'm waiting…" he said, gesturing his hand.

"Any time!" I said, "I was waiting for you to ask."

"What about Saturday?" he suggested.

"Saturday is fine." I was so happy and couldn't wait for our date.

#

It was finally Saturday. I was so nervous waiting for him in the parking garage that my hands were sweaty, and my stomach turned. We agreed that I would leave my car there and go with him. Ten minutes later, there he comes, looking handsome as always.

"Hi!" he said while I was getting in his car. "Sorry, I'm late."

"No problem, I just got here as well." I lied.

"So, where are we going?" he asked, driving us away.

"I thought about taking you to Coconut Grove. Have you been there?"

"No, I've been to South Beach and the Keys. I just passed by Miami."

"Oh, ok. I think you'll love it! Miami's really cool."

"I bet it is."

We drove around Coconut Grove before parking to walk in the historic main street. He was amazed by the vegetation. Usually, people think that Miami only has palm trees and beachy kinds of buildings. We ate lunch and walked around while I told him a little about the history of the place. He was interested and listened to me with attention.

In the car driving back, we passed by Vizcaya.

"Have you heard of Vizcaya?" I asked him.

"No, what's that?" he asked.

"Here, make a right turn here," I said, pointing at the parking lot entrance.

"Ok," he said, turning onto the driveway.

"I know you'll love this place," I said, getting out of the car. "It's one of my favorite places in Miami!"

He was delighted and loved everything about it. After we were done with the guided tour inside the house, we went for a walk in the amazing garden. I was getting anxious, expecting a gesture showing that he liked me too…maybe a kiss?

"This place is incredible!" he said. "Thank you for bringing me here. And for the lovely time…"

"Any time!" I said shyly, feeling butterflies in my stomach in anticipation of what should come next.

"You're really nice, Ann. I really want to spend more time with you." I was getting even more nervous hearing that. "I think we could have a great time together." I couldn't contain my excitement now…

"There's this game that everyone is playing. It's a couples' game called *Do What I Say*." He started to explain to me this weird game.

"What? A couples' game?" I was confused, not getting where he was trying to get with that conversation.

"As I was saying, it's a couples' game. Only two players, nobody else. It's supposed to be very sexy and exciting." I couldn't disguise my disappointment. But he kept going.

"There're only three rules in this game. First, we can't say no to each other — ever. You have to do everything and anything I ask you to, and vice versa."

"What?" I said, frowning.

"Second, we can't involve other people in the game with us or even use a third person." He went on. "It's a two-person game. Remember, we can't tell anyone because that would involve another person," he explained. "And third, we can't fall for each other, as that would spoil the whole game." He was so excited telling me the rules of this stupid game that he didn't even notice my annoyance.

"You've got to be kidding me, right?" I lashed out at him. Here's another jerk trying to sleep with me, having no strings attached. I thought that he came up with this ridiculous game stuff so he could have sex with me and keep it a secret in the office.

"I'm not kidding you. I just thought it could be fun…" He was clearly surprised by my reaction.

"I don't think so…" I answered.

"Why not? We can have an exciting time together," he insisted.

"Yeah, right, so you can sleep with me without committing. I'm not that type of girl," I added.

"No commitment for you, too. You can stop the game at any

time. All you have to do is break a rule," he said, showing some regret for bringing the game stuff up.

"Yeah, no commitment, but I've to be available any time you want. It doesn't make sense. Does anyone fall for that? I can't believe it. And anyway, I like to be free to do what I want, whenever I want! I don't like to obey anyone..."

I was really upset about the whole game shit. I bet he thought I was an easy prey, the type of girl who would do anything to be with someone like him until he finds someone better and ditches me.

"You're taking it too seriously. People playing the game just want to spice things up and have some fun," he added.

"Ok," I said. "I'm saying no! See, I'm breaking a rule even before we start playing. Game over!" I forced a smile, trying to disguise my disappointment, but obviously couldn't.

"I'm sorry, I shouldn't have..." he apologized noticing my change of mood.

"No problem," I said. "Let's go?"

I felt awkward and almost didn't talk on our way back. I was really disappointed and upset. I thought we could be at least good friends, but unfortunately, he's just another jerk. Jane was right; he's a very handsome jerk!

Chapter 38

Finally, it was Friday again. Jane and I decided to go for happy hour. We used to go more often, but then, we kind of got tired of the same old people all the time. The usual place to hang out after work is on Las Olas Blvd, just a couple of blocks down the street from the office. A lot of people who work in our building go there regularly so we knew almost everybody.

It was a surprise to find a new and cute bartender. So, we sat at the bar to hit on him. We bet one hundred dollars on who he would choose, me or her. It was game on!

"Here you are!" he said, setting the drinks in front of us.

"Thanks… What's your name?" I asked.

"Fred, yours?" he asked back, smiling.

"Ann, and this is my friend, Jane."

"Nice meeting you two." He smiled and walked away to help someone who had called him on the other side, across from us.

We started to talk about what we were going to do to get his attention and win the bet. It was fun. We laughed aloud, drinking our margaritas. Suddenly, Fred came back with two more margaritas.

"Yay…more margaritas!" we said at the same time, still laughing and talking nonstop. Then, I saw this cute guy staring at me, so I got up and started to dance. It didn't take long for him to join me.

"You're Ann, right?" he started a conversation.

"Yep, do I know you?" I didn't recognize him.

"It was a while ago. I work at the real estate agency down the street. I'm Michael. Justin introduced us maybe a month ago?" he explained.

"Yes, I remember now!" I lied. Taking a closer look at him, he wasn't my type at all. Therefore, easily forgotten.

"Do you want to have a drink with me?" he asked.

"No, thank you. I'm with a friend, maybe another time," I excused myself.

"No problem. I hope to see you again," he added, leaving and hitting on another girl who was dancing by herself. *Oh well, men…*

I went back to the bar, and Jane wasn't there.

"Hey, Fred, have you seen Jane? She was here just a minute ago…" I was looking for her everywhere.

"Nope, she left a little while ago and didn't come back…" he replied. "Do you want another drink?"

"Sure, why not!" I said, and he started making another margarita while talking with me.

"I haven't seen you around. Do you work close by?"

"Yeah, I work up the street. I used to come here all the time but decided to take a break to try different places, meet different people, get different vibes," I answered. "You weren't here like a month or so ago."

"No, I wasn't. I moved to Fort Lauderdale two weeks ago. I've always wanted to move to South Florida. I'm from Minnesota," he said.

"Wow, big change!" I was surprised. "How do you like it?"

"I love it!" He looked cute saying that. "Especially, the people. I love the diversity," he said. "And you? Are you from here?"

"Yes, pretty much, born and raised in Miami," I told him. "But I live here now and work at this law office."

"Cool, I hope to see you and Jane more often," he added.

"Yeah, we'll definitely come here more often," I said, smiling. "I think I should be going…"

"No, don't go just yet. It's getting late. Let me walk you to your car. I'll be leaving in an hour or so." He was asking me to stay, which I found sweet.

"Don't you have to close the bar?" I asked.

"No, today is John's turn. I can leave at nine," he said.

"Ok then, I'll wait," I said, taking a sip of my margarita, feeling happy that he was flirting with me.

He walked me to my car. We talked about how much Americans move around the country. I was skeptical since I didn't, but maybe it was a cultural thing. Even though I was born in America, I was raised as a Cuban, and Cubans don't move. I mean, only when they can escape the island. We laughed.

"It was really nice meeting you, Ann!" he said, getting close to me.

"Same here!" I smiled back, opening my car door.

Before I could get in, he held and kissed me. I smiled and said, "It was a lovely night, Fred! Bye, I hope to see you around." And I got in the car, closing the door.

"Bye, Ann, drive safe!" he said, tapping the door and smiling back at me.

#

Monday morning at the office, I was feeling happy.

"You owe me a hundred dollars, my friend," I said, opening my left hand and tapping with my right indicator finger, asking for the money.

"Why? You didn't...did you?" Jane was skeptical, looking at me sideways, not believing Fred had actually flirted with me.

"I sure did, girlfriend!" I said, smiling with satisfaction. "Where did you go, anyway?"

"I felt sick, so I left. You were so involved dancing with that guy that I didn't want to bother you. Sorry," she explained.

"No problem. Oh well, it worked just perfectly because Fred came to talk to me, asking about what happened that you left so suddenly. We didn't know if you'd left for good or just gone to the restroom, so we waited for you to come back, and since you never did, he offered to walk me to my car. And there you are, a hundred dollars, please!"

"All right! I guess you deserve it," she said, getting the money from her wallet.

CHAPTER 39

My sister called, asking if I could go to New York with her the next weekend. "Of course, I'll go!" I said, but I needed to plan properly, buy the tickets, book the hotel, etc. Matt and David were going to Orlando and couldn't take care of Max for me…so, I had to ask Jane.

"Hey, Jane?"

"Yes," she said, still typing.

"I'm going to New York this weekend. Do you mind taking care of Max for me? If you could just stop by once a day to let him out and give him some food and water, I would really appreciate it."

"You're going to New York, bitch, alone?" she asked.

"Oh, no…with my sister. It'll be only for the weekend. She wants me to go with her to see a college she wants to enroll in. Take a tour around, check prices and stuff."

"Sure, Ann. No problem, I'll take care of Max for you."

"What are you doing this weekend?" I asked.

"I can't make up my mind…probably nothing," she answered.

Mr. McKee walked into the reception with a big box in his hands. Jane and I rushed to help him carry it. He put it down, saying that we could have the box full of gifts from clients. We waited until he left the room and hurried to open it and check what was inside. It had all sorts of things: chocolate, candies, cookies, pens, T-shirts, and some show tickets.

"I want to have this, if you don't mind…" she said.

"What is it?" I said, taking the tickets from her hand. "*Cirque du Soleil*, I want to go, too! Can we go together?" I asked, still looking at the tickets. "The tickets are for Sunday night; I'll be back by then."

"I want to go with Mike, don't you get it?" she said.

"Oh, alright then. Mike, who? Your neighbor? I didn't know you guys were together. You've never told me. I think I'll be tired, anyway. Have fun!" I was a little disappointed, but she could have fun with her new boyfriend.

#

On Saturday, I went to get my sister in Miami. We would take the bus to the airport since my mom doesn't drive.

"*Ustedes dos, chicas, tengan mucho cuidado, no hablen con extraños…*" My mom was funny, giving us advice.

"*¿Que pasa con extraños mamá?*" I was laughing at her concern.

"*Mira, hay muchos secuestros allí, eso es lo que escuchamos en las noticias ¿comprendes?*" She went on.

"*Si mamacita, lo prometo.*" We got our bags and off we went.

"I'm so happy," Stephanie said.

"I think it'll be great for us to hang out like in the old times." I smiled at her. I just love my little sister.

New York was chilly, around forty-five degrees, which is really cold for us Floridians. I hate cold weather! We went to the hotel, checked in and out we went. I didn't want to waste any time.

Our first stop was Central Park, of course. We walked around and went to the zoo, which is in Central Park. *Do you believe it?* New York is just wonderful. We went down Park Avenue and stopped to eat at this little Italian restaurant. We also went to the Central Station, strolled through 5th Avenue, and checked out The Plaza

Hotel. I was mesmerized, taking a million pictures. Then, around 5:00 PM, we headed back to the hotel. I was exhausted, but we had to be ready for the Broadway show I had booked online, *The Phantom of the Opera* — I was so excited. We loved it, and before going to bed we stopped to eat pizza, New York style, obviously.

The next day was kind of difficult to wake up. We had to be at the NYU campus at 9:00 AM sharp. So, we packed and checked out at 8:30 AM; we wouldn't have time to do anything else. After the tour, we had to go to the airport; our flight back was at 3:30 PM.

Stephanie loved New York and decided that she was going to apply. She would check with Dad later to figure out the cost after she got accepted. I know she'll be accepted since she's an A+ student, but it doesn't hurt to be cautious. She's right. Why stress Mom out before being certain? Smart kid.

#

"How's New York?" Jane asked me on Monday morning.

"Awesome! I had such a nice time there and how did the *Cirque du Soleil* go?"

"Cool."

"Was Max sad about my absence?"

"I guess so. He's a nice dog," she replied, but we were busy and had to cut the conversation short.

At the end of the day, all I wanted to do was go home and spend some time with Max. I needed to do the laundry, too.

#

The following week was smooth, with no big events. Joe was distant and didn't talk to me except for work stuff. He's very professional in the office and didn't show any remorse about what happened that awful day. I think I'm cursed. It's hard for me to believe that someone like Joe would be interested in me. Maybe I was stupid getting offended when all he wanted was to spend time with me. What's wrong with that? I'm really an idiot! I could be in his arms by now. Sigh… Oh well, I'll be smarter next time, and if I have the chance to run into him out of the office again, I'll let him know I'm interested. I have nothing to lose.

CHAPTER 40

On Friday, Jane and I decided to go for a happy hour on Las Olas again. We wanted to flirt with Fred and have some fun. We decided to get a table so we could take turns going to the bar for drinks separately. We bet another hundred dollars on who he'll ask out this time.

After we got a table, Amber and Steve arrived, asking if they could sit with us since the place was so crowded that they had nowhere else to sit.

"Of course..." Jane said.

I went to the bar counter to order a drink and see Fred, who opened a huge smile when he saw me.

"Hey, Ann! Nice to see you again," he said, preparing drinks.

"I'm glad to see you, too. How are you?" I asked.

"Busy!"

"Which is a good thing, right?" I added, curling the tip of my hair with my finger and looking at him with sensuous eyes.

"Can't complain. What can I get you?" he asked, noticing my intention.

"I guess I want a Long Island Iced Tea… No, maybe a daiquiri." I said, showing insecurity. Men usually fall for that.

"Is Jane here, too?" he asked without hesitation.

He was curious and looked around, eager to see her. I confess I didn't like that he asked about Jane. It was obvious that he was more interested in her — the pretty one. He kissed me last time just because I was the one on hand, and he tried to get lucky. Sigh…

"Yeah, she is. We got a table by the band. See her there?" I pointed in the table's direction, knowing that my effort to charm him didn't work.

"Yes, tell her to come and say hi."

"I will," I said, getting my drink and heading back to the table.

"I want to see if you can beat me, girlfriend. He's already mine," I lied to her just to get her excited about winning. She smiled, getting up. It was her turn now. I started talking to Amber and Steve when Mary, Susan, Josh, and Justin arrived, joining us at the table.

Justin is a nice guy who has flirted with me before. We met when my boss was defending his boss in court. I had to take the paperwork back and forth. It was cool having the chance to stroll up and down Las Olas during work hours. Justin was always happy to see me, and we went out for drinks a couple of times, but it didn't go anywhere.

I decided to give Justin a chance since I was feeling down and rejected, first by Joe and now by Fred. I needed to feel good about myself somehow.

"I haven't seen you in a while," he said, sitting closer to me.

"Yeah, I've been busy." I said, "I just came back from New York!"

"New York? I love New York!" He started a conversation. "I've been there several times. A little bit too cold for me, but it's a wonderful place to visit, not to live in!"

"I agree with you, too cold for me, too. I'm a beach gal!" We laughed.

"Hey, bitch. I think you're going to win again. He didn't care much for me today," Jane said, coming back from the bar.

"Well, too bad for him because I'm really into Justin right now."

I felt a little better that they didn't hook up right away.

"Justin? Really?" she asked with disdain. I ignored her and kept talking and drinking with our friends at the table, not really paying much attention to Jane or Fred. But I kept checking the bar just to see if he was looking at her or at me. He was not. While looking around, I saw Joe sitting at the bar, and we locked eyes.

"Have you seen who is here? Joe," I told Jane.

"Yeah, I saw him too," she said.

"Let's invite him to sit with us," I suggested, hoping that she would go ask him to come over and join us.

"No! Leave him there. I mean, it could be embarrassing for us if we got drunk or something..." she went on.

"It would be embarrassing either way if he sits here with us or stays there watching us. Duh! I'll go talk to him." It was my chance to talk to him.

"Hey!" I smiled.

"Hey, Ann..." He wasn't surprised. He'd seen us and was just finishing his beer before leaving.

"Do you want to come and sit with us? I can introduce you to our friends. I mean, I know you're new in town." I was trying to sound casual.

"Yeah. Thank you, Ann! I better be going."

"Look, I'm sorry about the way I behaved in Miami. You caught me by surprise, that's all."

"No problem," he said, smiling. "I shouldn't have asked you. It was my bad, really. Who's that guy you were talking with, your boyfriend?"

"Who, Justin? No. He's just a friend, but he has asked me out..."

"I'm jealous," he said, smiling and trying to make me feel better about him. I smiled back, feeling good for his effort. Apparently, he's a nice guy after all.

I was feeling good now, Joe wanted to make amends, and Justin was all over me. I felt confident and happy and decided to give Justin a chance just to make Joe and Fred see that I'm not begging for their attention.

"Hey, Justin, do you want to dance?"

"Sure!" he said. We danced and talked for a long time. I was feeling pretty and thought I could let Justin think I was interested in him, too. Deep inside, I wanted Joe to be really jealous. After a while, I looked around and saw Jane at the bar, talking to Fred. Joe was there, too, finishing his beer.

"I guess it's time to go home!" I told Justin.

"I'll walk you to your car," he said.

I got up and went to let Jane know I was leaving. Fred smiled and said that I didn't have to worry about Jane because he would take care of her. I acknowledged it and left.

When we got to my car, Justin asked if I wanted to go out the next day, Saturday, for dinner or something. "Yep." I gave him my cell number and then he politely asked if he could kiss me. *What the hell?* Anyway, I smiled and murmured, "Sure."

He kissed me goodnight and waited for me to get in my car and drive away before leaving. On my way home, I was thinking that he was not really a good match for me. *Why do I have to be so picky? Anyway, apparently, Joe was trying to make things right between us, and I feel that we're off to a good second start. I'll make sure everything goes smoothly from now on.*

Chapter 41

On Saturday morning, I was feeling happy and energetic. I decided to inflate Max's pool and let him play in the water while giving him a bath. My garden needed some TLC, so I put on shorts and a bikini top since I could use a little tan as well.

"Hi, Ann!" Matt was outside getting some mint for his iced tea. "Do you want a glass of iced tea?" he asked. "It's passion fruit with lemon and mint."

"How can I say no to that?" I smiled. "Yes, please!" I followed him into his kitchen.

"How's everything? How's the new associate?" He had a malicious smile on his face.

"Well, the new associate, his name is Joe, ended up being just another jerk. Well, sort of."

"No way! Tell me everything. What happened?" he said, preparing my drink.

"Thanks," I said, taking a sip. "We went to Miami, right? Did I tell you that?"

"Nope!"

"Ok, we went to Miami. I took him to Coconut Grove…"

"Wonderful choice…" He stopped cleaning the kitchen counter and sat down close to me at the table, showing interest.

"We walked around, had lunch, and had a nice time together.

When we were driving back, we passed by Vizcaya, so I suggested a pit stop."

"Vizcaya! I love Vizcaya. Keep going; so far, so good. He seems to be a gentleman." His eyes bubbled with curiosity.

"Up till now... Then, he started to talk about a game — a couples' game that was supposed to be kept a secret; the players could tell no one, had to do any and everything the other asked, which means they could never say no, and were supposed to not to fall for each other..."

"What? You've got to be kidding me..." Matt's complexion changed to indignation.

"Believe me, I couldn't disguise my bad reaction. I was so fucking upset. If he only knew that I already liked him, there was no need for a game to make me want to sleep with him..."

"Well, definitely! I just don't understand why he thought you would fall for that. Actually, who would? Maybe people looking for a little suspense. I could play the game for the spice and hot sex..." He lifted his eyebrows twice while having fun about my situation.

"Well, don't forget that we work together. I really think he came up with this freaking game idea to be able to sleep with me and keep it a secret."

"I guess you're right; you shouldn't get involved with him, not like that..."

"So, there's more..."

"More? Tell me, tell me!" he said, dragging his chair even closer to me, curious to know what else I had to say.

Suddenly, Max and Luna burst into the kitchen, making a mess. They were soaking wet, and their paws very dirty.

"Oh my God! Out of my kitchen, you two..." Matt was having a fit.

"Come, Max. Let's go home right now!" I commanded, getting him out.

Matt got Luna in his arms and followed me to my backyard. We closed the gate so the dogs could stay in my yard playing.

"So, you were saying…" He said, putting Luna down on my side of the yard.

"Yes…so yesterday, Jane and I went to this bar after work for happy hour. Everyone goes there, so we knew most people. We wanted to flirt with this cute new bartender and have some fun. Then, I ran into an old crush, Justin, who has a crush on me. Long story short, we kind of hooked up."

"Justin?" He was confused.

"Yes, Justin. After a while, I saw Joe at the bar. So, I went to invite him over to sit with us and say that I didn't have hard feelings about the stupid game proposal. Do you know what he said?"

"No!" he said, getting Luna in his arms again and looking at me with intriguing eyes.

"He said that he was jealous seeing me with Justin. Can you believe that?"

"No way! You go, girl! I think he really liked you, and you should give him another chance," he said, nodding. "I mean, he's hot, right?"

"I don't know. I'll think about it. I really like him, and he's very handsome and charming and hot…" We both laughed.

"You keep me posted!" he demanded, leaving to help David, who had just arrived with groceries. "Talk to you later. Kisses."

"Bye. Kisses," I said, taking Max to the pool for a bath.

Justin called me around 3:00 PM.

"Hey, Ann, how's everything? Well, I'm calling because I said I would, but I understand if you don't want to go out tonight after what happened."

"What happened?"

"Don't you know? Fred, the bartender, he was your friend, right? He died last night in a car accident…"

"What?" I was astonished. "What about Jane?"

"I think he was alone…"

"Oh my God! I have to find Jane! Thanks for letting me know, Justin. I got to go."

I started calling Jane's cell, but she never answered. So, I went to her house; she wasn't there either. I was desperately worried that she could be dead, too.

Since I couldn't find her anywhere, I stopped by the police and asked about the accident. All they could tell me was that Fred was alone. I asked three times, explaining that my friend was supposed to be with him, but they confirmed Fred was the only one in the car. I wondered where in the hell Jane was…

Chapter 42

On Monday morning, I got to the office earlier than usual, anxious for Jane to arrive. I was pacing back and forth until she walked in…

"Where have you been?" I asked when she came through the door.

"Why? I'm on time…" she said, checking her watch.

"I've been trying to find you all weekend long; don't you ever answer your cell? Fred died," I said at once.

"What?" she shrieked, clearly in shock.

"Friday night, after he left work. It was a car accident."

"I can't believe it…" she said, sitting down.

"I freaked out when I was told about the accident because I knew you were supposed to be with him. I tried to call you and even went to your house. Where were you?" I said, sitting down at my desk and starting to organize my files nervously, but relieved that she was alive. I was angry that she didn't even know what was going on.

"I went to Marathon," she said.

"Marathon? What's in Marathon?"

"My friend Laura has a house there and invited me over for the weekend. How did it happen?" she questioned.

"Nobody knows. Apparently, he lost control of his car, and it rolled over several times. He was killed instantly."

"My God… Thank God I wasn't with him. I left right after you. I remembered that Laura had invited me, so I rushed home to grab a couple of things and rode with her to the beach house. Poor Fred…"

I wheeled my chair to hers and hugged her. "I'm sorry, too. He was such a cute young guy. Let's not talk about that anymore. There's nothing we can do, anyway."

She nodded, still in shock.

I rolled back to my desk and went back to work. All I wanted was to forget the weekend, and I was happy that she was fine.

#

On Tuesday afternoon, I left a little earlier because I needed to stop by the supermarket. Joe was leaving at the same time.

"Going home earlier today?" he asked while we awaited the elevator.

"Yeah, I need to get some groceries."

"What a coincidence, I'm going grocery shopping, too. Where do you shop? Publix?" he asked.

"Yes, Publix."

"Do you mind if I go with you?" he said casually.

"Sure, do you want to go in my car or yours?" I tried to sound normal but felt my heart racing in my chest.

"My car," he said.

"Ok, Publix is on my way home. Do you mind following me to my house? I can leave my car there and go with you; I need to let Max out a bit." I started talking fast to control my nervousness.

"Ok, I'll follow you."

Excited about our grocery shop date, I was debating with myself if I should ask him to come in or if I should ask Matt to keep an eye on Max for me and leave right away. I guess Joe thought about it, too, since he parked his car and followed me inside.

"I'm sorry, the house is a little messy. Do you want a beer?" I said, opening the back door for Max and avoiding making eye contact with him. I didn't want him to notice my uneasiness.

"Hey, Max!" He petted Max, who came to say hi, recognizing him. "Yeah, a beer would be great!" he added. "I like your house; it's cozy…"

"Thanks," I said, handing him a beer and going out to the backyard. I needed fresh air.

"Hey, Ann!" David was outside working in their herb garden.

"Hi, David. This is Joe…" I introduced him. I was happy that he was there to help ease the awkward situation I was in.

Matt showed up right away when he heard I had company. "Hi, Ann," he said, drying his hands on his apron. He came closer and whispered, "Is he the new associate?"

I nodded discreetly and introduced him, too. "Hey, Joe. This is Matt."

"Nice meeting you guys," Joe said, smiling at them and looking at David's garden. "I was thinking about planting a raised herb garden on my balcony but had no idea how to begin," he paused and put his hands on his trim waist. "I even got a couple of books, but they are difficult to follow…"

"No, it's very easy. Of course, you need to take care of it." David started to talk, and he never stops talking when he's given a chance to discuss a subject he knows about. Matt felt my despair and came to the rescue.

"Hey, Ann…and Joe, do you guys want to have dinner with us? I'm making chicken marsala with roasted potatoes," he said. "Actually, that's what I came out here for. David, where is my thyme?"

"Oh, yes, let me get it for you," David said, going to get some thyme in the herb garden.

Joe looked at me, trying to see if I was ok if he stayed for dinner. I smiled at him and said, "Do you want to stay for dinner? Matt is a wonderful cook; we can go grocery shop after." I couldn't be happier with the outcome. I love my friends; they really go out of their way to make things easier for me.

"Ok, if you think it's fine. I would be delighted," he said, going inside with Matt; David and I followed.

"Give me that," Matt said, taking the beer from Joe's hand. "We are having wine." He poured the beer into the sink.

Joe laughed, putting himself at ease. "Do you need help? I can wash the potatoes or do anything else that you prefer," he added.

"I prefer you go help Ann set the table and get out of my kitchen. No offense, it's just too small and drives me crazy when I have to cook while trying to get around people in my way."

"No offense taken. Let's go set the table," Joe said to me.

The dinner was marvelous. We had such a great time. Joe and David got along well. Matt was satisfied, and I was in heaven. I had totally forgotten about the stupid game stuff. I guess we could be together—if he wanted; at least I was ready to try.

After dinner and lots of talking and laughter, Joe asked us if we wanted to go to his house in Marathon.

"Marathon?" I said, "Do you have a house in Marathon? I guess Marathon is getting popular now; I need to check it out," I said, practically accepting the offer, not believing in what was happening.

"Yeah. It's not really mine. I rented it for the entire year. I have this friend in Chicago who told me how wonderful the Florida Keys were, so I had to check it out. Of course, I fell in love with the place and couldn't resist getting a little house for the weekends."

"For the weekends," Matt enforced.

"Well, the plan is to live there. I really don't have to go to the office every day. I can easily work from home and only go to the office for meetings and court days," he explained. "Of course, I can't do it now since I'm new in the office, but I'm sure I will convince the bosses," he said, smiling at me. "Don't you think, Ann?"

"I know nothing!" I said, chuckling. "I would love to go with you…guys?" I looked at my friends, almost begging them to say yes.

"How many days are we talking about?" David asked.

"As many days as you guys want to stay. I have an important meeting on Friday afternoon, but you can stay. I'll go back afterward," he added.

"Yeah! We want to go. We'll need to get a few days off, but I don't see any issues, right, David?"

David shook his head.

"What do you need from us? Should we go buy some groceries?" Matt added.

"We're going grocery shopping now," I said, jumping up to my feet as happy as I have ever been in my life.

"Now?" David asked. "Ok, let's go then."

The four of us went to the grocery store. Matt and David bought a lot of food and planned meals for a whole week. Joe was happy, and I was enchanted.

We were planning to go to Marathon the next day, Wednesday, but I had to work.

"You can always call in sick," Joe said. "How many sick days have you taken so far?"

"None, I'm never sick."

"Ok, I won't tell anyone…" Joe said with a smirk on his face.

"I guess I could call in sick. The office is kind of quiet now, and Jane always takes time off, leaving me alone."

"Great! I'll come over around nine o'clock so everyone can be ready on time?" Joe added.

Matt and David were so excited for me and for the trip. They started to discuss what to take and the excuse they would give their bosses.

"For God's sake, Matt, we're staying for just a couple of days…" David said.

"Four whole days!" Matt replied.

And they said goodbye, getting inside their house with the grocery bags, still discussing what they were going to take.

"They're awesome," I told Joe, trying to keep the happy atmosphere between us.

"Yeah, I loved them. It must be nice to have neighbors like them."

"They are life savers. I can't tell you how many times they've helped me. I love them as brothers," I said, scooping up a couple of grocery bags and started walking inside my house. Joe grabbed a few others and followed me.

I started to put the groceries away when Joe got closer and embraced me, turning me around to face him. I felt my stomach fluttering.

"I had such a wonderful time today! It feels like I have known you guys forever, really. I felt welcome and relaxed. Thank you!" he said, looking into my eyes. "Let's have a new start in Marathon. I really hope we can put that game stuff behind us…"

"Joe, you need to stop bringing that shit up, really. It turns me off every time I remember it. You know, I really liked you since the first day I saw you," I confessed without thinking.

He smiled, getting closer to me.

"We can be good friends for sure…" I tried to amend it.

"But I want you," he said, approaching, and kissed me fondly.

My heart raced; I couldn't believe it was really happening. "I guess I want you, too," I said timidly, staring at his beautiful, deep-green eyes at close range, "but I'm not sure if we should get involved…" I said, trying to sound mature but feeling thrilled inside.

"Let's have a good time together, and then we'll see," he said, hugging me tight. "See you tomorrow at nine?"

He smiled, kissed me again and left.

I had to pinch myself to check if I wasn't dreaming. I was in heaven!

Chapter 43

The next morning, I was up at 7:00 AM since I couldn't sleep at all and needed to get ready for the mini vacation. I made coffee, let Max out, called Matt and David to make sure they were up (they were) and started to pack. I called Mr. Poch before Jane arrived, but she texted me as soon as she knew I was ill. She was so nice that made me feel guilty for lying to her. Then, I rushed to the shower and shaved my legs, armpit, and everything else. I tried my bikini on to make sure everything looked good and felt awful looking at myself in the mirror. I needed to lose at least five pounds, and my Cuban butt was a little too big… I turned around trying not to think about it and be positive. There was nothing I could do about it, and there's nothing wrong with being a little heavy. By nine, I was ready.

I left the house at exactly nine o'clock. My hands were sweating, and I was really anxious. Matt and David were locking their door as well.

"Hey, guys… are you ready to go?" I asked, waving at them.

"Yeah! Are you?" Matt said, coming close to me and holding my hands. "You can do this! Everything is going to be perfect. Believe in yourself, girl!"

"I don't know if this is a good idea…what if…"

"Stop that! Nothing is going to go wrong. He likes you."

"Do you think so?" I said, biting my lower lip and frowning, still doubting.

"C'mon girl, everything is going to be won-der-ful!"

"Yayyyy!" Matt and I started jumping, holding hands. "Yaaaaaay!"

"Alright, enough, you two!" David had to put a break on our enthusiasm.

Joe arrived at nine-ten. David, Matt, Max, Luna, and I were waiting for him at the front of our houses, making plans for the day. We got in the cars and drove off. Max and I went with Joe, while Matt, David, and Luna followed us.

The four-hour drive was fun. Joe and I talked about growing up in Miami and in London, two totally different worlds. It was cool listening to him. We didn't stop talking, and when we least expected, we were there.

The small house was right on the beach and isolated. A back sliding door opened to the white sand and crystal-clear blue ocean, an amazing location! Once inside, I was a little concerned to see Joe taking my things to his bedroom and directing the guys to the guest room. I thought he was being precipitated, but he explained that he was going to sleep on the couch. *Good!* I thought to myself, the decision of whether we sleep together was up to me.

The rest of the day was spent putting things away and talking, a lot of talking and drinking. By 3:00 AM, we were exhausted and went to bed.

#

"Morning," I said to Joe, walking into the living room/kitchen. Both were in just one room.

"Morning!" he said with energy, ready to start the day. "Are you hungry? I'm making breakfast."

"Starving," I replied, sitting at the table. "Can I have coffee? I can't function before having my coffee." I was feeling a little odd, but at the same time, happy as a butterfly.

He brought me a mug of fresh brewed coffee and said, "Here, you can help me when you're done."

I took a sip and got up to help him. "What you want me to do?"

"You can set the table. Everything you need is in the upper cabinet above the counter, the first one to your right."

"Ok."

I was almost finished when Matt and David showed up.

"Morning!" we said almost at the same time.

We sat at the table for breakfast, which was delicious. We got Matt's approval for Joe's satisfaction. After we ate, I went to change, and when I came back, they were already outside with the dogs. David went to the ocean but came back running since the water was too cold. "No shit!" We laughed at him and went for a walk. I started to feel more at ease and comfortable in my skin.

Matt made lunch, which was amazing, as always. After the long and pleasant lunch full of conversations, jokes, and laughter, they decided to take a nap. I went outside and made myself comfortable on the lounge chair by the firepit. Joe followed me.

"I shouldn't have eaten that much. I feel like a pig, a fat lazy pig," he said, tapping his stomach and sitting close to me.

"Me, too. I'm so full, but don't worry; the second round should start around five o'clock."

"Bloody hell! You've got to be kidding me. I already ate for the whole month!" he said, chuckling.

"Can we light up the fire pit? It's kind of chilly." I was shivering but content for being there with him.

"Sure." He lit the firepit and went inside to get a blanket for me. He dragged his chair closer to mine and got under the blanket as well, embracing me in his arms and making me feel warm.

"So, did you like the house?"

"Yes, it's really nice." I tried to control my voice to sound normal, but I was freaking out, not believing I was there…with him.

"Would you live here—with me?" he asked with a mischievous smile, waiting for my reaction.

"I'll give it a thought. The house is nice, and you're adorable…" I smiled shyly. *Of course I would*, I thought to myself.

He smiled back with satisfaction and kissed me tenderly. We stayed there talking, laughing, and making out until around five o'clock. As I predicted, Matt and David came down and were already looking for what to do next.

"Firepit! Let's make s'mores! I'm sure I saw marshmallows somewhere…" Matt went to the kitchen to grab the ingredients.

I looked at Joe, saying, "Did I tell you? I know my friends, just relax. We can go for another walk afterward to burn all the extra calories…"

"I'll need to run a marathon," Joe said, getting up to help Matt find the stuff he was looking for.

David sat down and poked the fire. "I'm so happy for you. Joe seems to be a nice guy."

"Yeah, I just hope I'm not dreaming. It's kind of too good to be true…"

"Nonsense, stop being negative. Everything will be fine!" he reprimanded me, and I nodded agreeing, trying to get my confidence back.

After dinner, Joe and I went for another walk under the stars. The dogs came along, but Matt and David decided to clean up the kitchen and go to bed early.

We started to walk under the moonlight; so romantic. He made me feel calm and comfortable; it seemed that we had known each other for a long time. I was totally relaxed and falling for him big time.

"I'm having a great time!" He broke the silence and grabbed my hand content.

"Me too…" My heart started to pound fast again. "This place is really paradisaic."

"Yeah, especially when you're in such good company…" he looked at me and winked.

I smiled nervously, and I knew he could tell I was blushing. He chuckled but said nothing. He put his arm around me, and we kept walking in silence, enjoying the moment and nature. Max and Luna were so happy, running and splashing water back and forth as kids do.

I wanted him and decided that I wanted to take it to the next level. When we got back to the house, I went to take a shower, changed into my pajamas, brushed my teeth, and then went down to the living room, where Joe was trying to make himself comfortable on the sofa.

"Do you want a glass of water?" I asked.

"No thanks, I'm fine," he said, tossing around on the couch and fluffing his pillow that fell off on the floor, making me laugh.

"Well, I'll buy a more comfortable couch tomorrow," he said, getting the pillow back and covering himself with the blanket. He was funny.

"Why buy another couch? I thought you wanted me to move in with you…" It was my turn to put a mischievous smile on my face. "Do you want to come up with me?" I batted my eyelashes at him.

He rushed to my side and pulled me in his arms, looking into my eyes, not saying a word. He took me to the bed and made love to me as I had never experienced before. We couldn't look away from each other's eyes. I can't describe the feeling, but I can assure you that it was a unique experience for us both. He's amazing, and I won't let anyone spoil my happiness this time. I want him to be the one.

#

On Friday morning, the weather had changed. It was raining. Matt, David, and Joe were already in the kitchen when I woke up.

"What's up? What are we going to do today?" I asked, getting my coffee.

"Eat!" Matt said, smiling. "What else?"

"Drink?" David complimented. "What else?"

"We could play cards. Do you guys play poker?" Joe suggested.

"Yeah! Let's play poker for real money when you come back from your meeting!" David said, nodding.

I decided to let the dogs out since it had stopped raining. I opened the door, and the dogs ran outside. I didn't want them to go far, so I tried to hold Max by grabbing his collar. Big mistake, he was so happy that he didn't stop. I fell and hurt my arm.

"Joe!" I screamed, "Joe! I think I broke my arm!"

"Ann! Oh! Let me see..." Joe said, checking my arm with concern.

"What happened?" Matt and David said at the same time, rushing to check on me.

"Let's take her to a hospital!" David said.

Joe grabbed my purse and shoes, and they took me to the nearest emergency room. I was in a lot of pain, but didn't want to cry. I got a cast. However, my bone wasn't really broken; it was just a bad sprain—as if knowing that would make me feel any better.

"Do you want to go home?" Joe asked.

"Yes. Let's go…right, Matt?" David said, looking at Matt, who nodded, confirming.

We changed, packed, and left. Matt and David took Max in their car since it would be difficult for me to handle him with the cast. I went with Joe to the office because he was already late for the meeting.

#

"What happened?" Jane asked when she saw my arm in a cast.

"I tripped on the sprinkler in my backyard while chasing Max. Stupid dog." I lied.

"Poor Ann. I missed you, bitch! What are you doing here with Joe?" she said with an inquiring face.

"Oh well, it's just a sprain. I was bored and wondered if you wanted to go somewhere after work. Is Joe here, too?" I tried to disguise the fact that we had arrived together. "Let's smoke some pot and have some fun, girlfriend?" I tried to change the conversation before she asked more questions, and I was feeling guilty for lying to her.

"Alright! Where do you want to go?"

"Anywhere that makes me forget the last couple of days!" I said as if I had had a terrible time.

I couldn't tell her I was with Joe in Marathon. I'm such a bad liar but determined not to make the same mistake again. She can't know about Joe and me until I'm certain that he loves me for real and makes our relationship official. I need to be sure he's not another Sam in my life.

"I know! What about that Brazilian place up in Pompano that Mike keeps bothering me about? I think it could be fun," she said, thinking that I was probably in need of going out after being sick for a couple of days and hurting my arm.

"Fine, I'll take the drugs," I said, feeling happy.

Jane left at 5:00 PM sharp since she had to get Mike ready to go with us. I waited for Joe to come back and take me home.

"Sorry, I got out as soon as I could!" Joe said, looking at his watch. It was 5:15 PM.

"No problem, let's go?" I said, grabbing my purse and turning my computer off.

I told him I was going out with Jane. I wanted to cheer her up a little and somehow compensate her for managing the office by herself, but he had other plans.

"No, I'm taking you to my place for the weekend. I want to take care of you, my poor baby," he said, kissing and hugging me when we left the office.

"Sorry, Joe. I told Jane I was going out with her tonight."

"What?" He had an upset expression on his face now.

"She asked what I was doing there with you! I had to come up with an excuse. I said that I was bored and asked her if she wanted to go to the movies or something…pretending I didn't know you were there, too."

"Oh, and then you got excited about going out with your little brat friend…pretending I wasn't there."

"What are you talking about? Jane isn't a brat; she's my friend. And she invited me to go out with her and her boyfriend…"

"Her boyfriend?"

"Yes, why? I told her I wanted to go with them for the sake of our little secret…"

"I don't want you to go. Stay with me." He kissed me again, trying to convince me to stay with him.

"Sorry, I have to go with her. We can talk tomorrow, ok?"

We made it to my home in silence; he was clearly upset. I tried to kiss him goodbye, but he pulled his face away.

"Ok, you're mad at me. I'll call you tomorrow then."

He left without waiting for me to get inside the house. David and Matt came out with Max.

"Where is Joe going? I was going to invite you guys for dinner," Matt said, frustrated.

"He's being a jerk. He'll be better tomorrow, I hope," I explained, getting inside my house in a hurry. "I have to go. See you guys tomorrow."

#

I arrived at Jane's house around eight. We smoked pot, and my arm was just fine. The painkiller was working.

Once there, I couldn't believe how crowded the place was.

"What in the hell is this place about? These people are almost naked. Look at those bodies…I'm out of here." I was startled.

"Welcome to hell!" Mike said, smiling, pushing me in and starting to dance.

We had a lot of fun. It was impossible to stop dancing. At some point, I lost Jane and Mike, so I decided to go home. I was tired anyway and in need of sleep. My arm started bothering me as well.

I went straight to bed and slept like a rock.

Chapter 44

On Saturday morning, I woke up feeling better and had a lot to do, so I started with laundry. I called Joe to see if he wanted to come over, but my call went straight to his voicemail box. I left a message saying that I was going to stay home if he wanted to come over later. He never called me back. *How immature!* I can't believe he was giving me the cold shoulder just because I went out with Jane, and I did it to keep our romance a secret, just as he wanted. He really pissed me off, and I decided that I wouldn't call him again; let's see how long he would hold the grudge.

A week passed by, and Joe was silent. He never called me back or came to my house after work. He behaved politely in the office but not a word or even a smile. I decided that I didn't want to get involved with someone who was such a baby and could not respect or trust my decisions. I really thought that he could be the one, but apparently, he just doesn't care about me that much. I actually had the feeling that he was jealous of Jane, not me...I guess Joe was just a one-night-stand kind of affair and not worthy of my heart. Deep inside, I had this feeling that he was too good to be true. I guess it's better this way before I get too involved and not able to cope with another heartbreak.

Conveniently, Justin called and asked me out. I said yes, and I was ready to go for him. At least he's sincere and truly likes me. He's a good man with a good heart, and that's what is important. I decided to give Justin and me a chance and couldn't wait for Friday night to come.

#

"Let's go out tonight, girlfriend?" Jane took me by surprise at the office on Friday afternoon.

"Huh...?" I said, looking at her, still lost in my thoughts.

"Let's go out tonight. I want to dance again. Wasn't it awesome last week at the Brazilian place?"

"Justin has invited me out tonight." I looked at her with sorrow.

"Oh, shit." She sighed.

"Maybe we can invite more people over..." I tried to cheer her up.

"Really?" she said, putting a huge smile on her face.

"Really. I guess it would be good to have more people around. I don't want to rush into a relationship with Justin anyway."

"Ok then!"

"What about that Spanish place on Ocean Drive?" I suggested.

"What about it?"

"It's a fun Spanish place. I think they play Brazilian, too. People dance on the tables and everywhere. It can be fun."

"Fine with me..."

Joe entered the reception right in time to hear the last part of our conversation. I pretended that he wasn't there, but I'm sure he heard our plans for the night. I felt victorious.

#

Ocean Drive was packed as usual; however, we made our way into the place. Justin had reserved a table for us. Not too long after, Amber, Ann, Erik, and Steve arrived. Jane, as usual, was late; she arrived around 10:00 PM.

"What took you so long? I was about to call you," I asked her.

"Oh, Mike. He was jealous and didn't want me to come."

"What's up with him? He really likes you, huh? He's cute…"

"Well, sometimes he gets on my nerves."

"Yeah, I know what you mean…" I added, nodding.

"What do you want to drink, Jane? I'm going to the bar to get Ann another pina colada…" Justin interrupted our chat.

"Thanks, Justin! A pina colada sounds good!"

He nodded, got up, and left for the bar.

"Do you see that guy dancing over there by the bar?" I said, pointing at Juan Carlos and getting back to Jane.

"Yeah. Who's he?"

"That's Justin's friend, Juan Carlos. He's hot."

"Is he with us?"

"Yep. That's your mission, girlfriend. We need to be friends with him—for the future. I can't do it because I'm stuck with Justin. I'm officially his date tonight, and it wouldn't be polite if I hit on his friend. But you can at least get his phone number," I asked her, smiling.

"No problem. What won't I do for you?" We both laughed.

We were having a lot of fun, and Juan Carlos was into her. They danced and were talking nonstop. I felt good for her. I went to the restroom and ran into Joe when coming out. He grabbed my arm and held me against the wall.

"Are you having fun? I thought we had something special…" He was upset and really drunk.

"Joe! What are you doing here?"

"What do you think? I followed you. I needed to see with my own eyes that you're a little slut just like your bestie throwing herself at that guy over there…" he said and pointed at Jane.

"What? You're drunk!"

"Can you tell?" He lifted his eyebrow, making a face.

"Go home, Joe. I don't want to talk with you like this…"

"Apparently, you don't care how I feel. Wait, Jane is more important to you, right?"

"I called you. You never called me back or came over. You're so childish," I said, very upset, pushing him away.

"Why did you have to go out with Jane last Friday? I wanted to stay with you and take care of you. You disgust me." He was definitely drunk and out of control.

"Ok, Joe. You're not in any condition to have a conversation. Go home, we can talk tomorrow. Justin and I have no romantic spark. We're just friends," I said, pushing him out of my way and going back to the table. Jane and Juan Carlos were gone.

I waited for Jane to come back, but she didn't. Juan Carlos had left as well; I figured they were together somewhere. So, it was time for me to go home; I had had enough for the night.

"I had such a great time," Justin said when parking in front of my house, probably waiting for me to invite him in.

"Me too. Thank you." I said, kissing him on the cheek and opening the car door. I couldn't take the affair further and was still feeling troubled about Joe's behavior a little earlier.

"Wait! Don't I deserve a real kiss?" he said, holding my arm.

"Look, Justin, you're a wonderful guy…really, but I'm just not ready for a serious relationship."

"I can make you like me if given a chance…"

"I bet you can. But I have recently gotten out of a very painful relationship, and I'm not ready for a new one. Let's be friends for now?"

"What can I do?" he said, disappointed.

I kissed him on the cheek again and said, "Good night, Justin!"

"Good night, see you around…" he said and left.

Chapter 45

On Saturday morning, I was feeling miserable. I kept worrying about Joe. He was way too drunk, and I shouldn't have let him drive like that. I texted to check on him because I didn't want to call. I had no idea where we stood, and I wasn't in the mood to keep arguing with him. However, he called me right after getting my text.

"We need to talk!"

"Yes, I guess we do!"

Not even ten minutes had passed by, and Joe was at my door.

"Hi!" he said, coming in.

"Hi!" I said, waiting for him to start talking.

"I'm sorry about yesterday. I was drunk and upset…"

"Upset about what?"

"About what? About you going out with Jane when all I wanted was to take care of you after we had such a wonderful time together. And you were hurt, remember? You shouldn't have gone out anyway. Then you go out on a date with that Justin guy—that's why!"

"I didn't want to tell Jane our secret, and she asked what I was doing in the office with you that Friday."

"Who said it's a secret? Did I ask you to keep it a secret?"

"No, but we don't want the whole office knowing just yet, right? Especially Jane."

"Why Jane? I don't get it. Did she say anything about me?"

"Like what?" I was getting curious to know what he was thinking…

"I don't know. I think she has a crush on me."

"Yeah, she does."

"You don't have to worry about her. She's not my type of girl. I want someone who I can trust and love. She's a slut!"

"She's not a slut! She's a little irresponsible and birdbrained, but she's my friend, and I love her very much."

"Ok, I take it back. I guess I'm jealous that you prefer her company instead of mine."

"You're wrong. I want to be with you, but I'm not sure about the office situation."

"What are you talking about? I know it can be a little weird, but we're adults capable of keeping our professionalism at the office."

"I don't know. I have a bad feeling about the office, and I can't lose my job."

"Oh…you can't lose your job or your bestie, but it's ok to give up on me?"

"I didn't say that! I need time to think." I was getting dizzy with his accusations; maybe I was overthinking.

"You know what? I'm done. You can keep your job and your friend. And yes, I think she's a spoiled brat."

Matt and David showed up at the back door to check on me when they heard us arguing.

"What's up, guys? Is everything alright?" David asked.

"Yeah, I was leaving anyway," Joe said, looking at me, squinting with anger, and stomping to the front door.

"Wait! We haven't finished yet. I still have things to say to you…" I grabbed his arm, making him stop. I just couldn't let him go without saying everything that was stuck in my throat.

"Guys, you need to calm down." David came in between us, gesturing down with his hands, worried about the situation.

"Yeah. Why don't you come with me, Ann? Let's make coffee and give Joe a little time to settle down. David will stay here with him."

"Yes! Good idea, Matt. Go with him, Ann. Joe and I will come over in a little while."

I looked at Joe and apparently, he thought it was a good idea because he came back to the living room and sat down without complaining. So, I nodded and left.

"What in the hell is going on with you two? You were so much in love just a week ago. I don't get it." Matt couldn't wait for us to get into their house to start asking questions.

"Well, he got mad because I went out with Jane last Friday."

"Last Friday? The day we came back from Marathon The day you broke your arm?"

"Yeah…"

"Well, you were hurt, and he was worried about you. I think it's just normal that he wanted to be with you. Why did you go out with Jane instead? Sorry, I don't get it," he said, shaking his head.

"I didn't do anything different. I thought we were supposed to keep everything a secret. Jane and I usually go out almost every weekend, and I also wanted to cheer her up for handling the office all by herself while I was in Marathon, having fun instead of being at work."

"I understand, but Joe deserved an explanation, at least."

"I tried! I called him, but he didn't answer and never called me back. He was very distant at the office too, and never said anything until today.”

“And he’s very upset!”

“As you can tell, I don’t know what to do. I’m not sure we should go on with this relationship—if you can call a one-night stand a relationship…”

“Well, you’ll need to decide soon if you want to be with him or not…”

“I think you ’re right. I keep seeing red flags everywhere because I’m afraid of being hurt again. He doesn’t know about Cristina and Sam…”

“I think it’s time for you to tell him.”

“Ok, I will. Thanks, Matt. You’re the best. Love you, *ciao,* ”I said, going home, longing to make peace with Joe. I felt guilty for treating him that way, and I should’ve told him about Sam.

Joe and David were talking when I walked into the living room from the backyard. They stopped and looked at me, puzzled. Silence. I looked at Joe, and we locked eyes.

“Well, I guess Matt forgot to bring my coffee. I’ll go. Bye,” he said, and off David went, leaving Joe and I staring at each other quietly.

“I’m sorry, Joe! I really am…” I broke the silence.

“I’m sorry, too,” he said.

“I think I’m terrified of being hurt because someone hurt me badly in the past. I’m scared of giving myself and being betrayed again.”

“Shh, I understand. I have been hurt, too. Let’s not talk about the past now…” He embraced me affectionally, looking deep into my eyes. He kissed me softly, taking me to the bedroom. “I’ll never hurt you, Ann. I really want to be with you and take our relationship to the next level. I want you…"

"No secrets?" I asked.

"No secrets…" we promised to each other falling on the bed, craving for each other.

Chapter 46

The next morning, I was feeling a lot better. I got up and went to the kitchen to make coffee. Joe was lazy, not wanting to get up. "C'mon! Time to get up, Mr. Garrison," I said, pulling the blanket off and revealing his naked body. *"Ouh là là!"* I said, biting my lips.

"Come here, you," he said, pulling me into the bed with him. He was going to kiss me, then stopped and said, "Did you make coffee for us?"

"Whaaat?" I said, tittering and slapping him on the chest.

He smiled and pretended he was going to kiss me again, stopping just before saying, "I would like some scrambled eggs, too."

"Get up!" I said, smacking him with joy. "You can make your own coffee and eggs!" I added, going to the kitchen to fix him a nice breakfast while he went to the bathroom.

"Mm, I smell eggs and bacon. All that for me?" he said with a cynical smile on his most gorgeous, handsome face that made me melt. "You shouldn't have. I don't want to be any trouble."

"You better eat everything I made," I said, sitting at the table with him and starting to eat. I was hungry.

"So, what do you want to do about the office? As I said, I'll do whatever you decide." He started the inevitable conversation by helping himself to coffee.

"Well, I think we should start dating openly as if nothing has happened between us yet. Jane is my best friend, and she'll feel betrayed because I didn't tell her that you and I were seeing each other."

"How do you know she has no secrets? I mean, everybody does. She may be hiding something from you, too."

"No, you don't know Jane. She's scatterbrained, naïve, and impulsive, but she has a great heart and is a loyal friend. I love her very much."

"I hope she loves you as much," Joe said, taking a sip of his coffee.

"Of course, she does. So…we can start showing that we're dating. We can go have lunch together. You can bring me candies, jewelry…" I said with a smirk. He smiled. "She's going to ask if you and I are seeing each other. I'll tell her the truth that you have asked me out and we're dating. It'll be good to go slowly to check Mr. Poch's and Mr. McKee's reactions as well. I mean, if they say to you that they think it's not appropriate for us to get involved, we'll know how they feel about office romance and then decide what to do next."

"We could run away! Just leave town and no one would ever hear from us again. We can go to England. My mum will love you," he suggested.

"I wish…"

"Ok, I guess we have a plan then!" he said, eating his breakfast and giving a piece of bacon to Max.

"I wonder why he loves you that much," I said, astonished.

#

On Monday morning, we arrived at the office early, and Joe came to the lunchroom with me to make coffee. Jane arrived a little later. She was on time for a change and came to the lunchroom, following me and the coffee smell.

"You?" She couldn't disguise her surprise at having seen Joe there with me.

"Good morning, Jane. How was your weekend?" Joe asked with a smile on his face.

"I'm not feeling well," she said, running to the restroom. I was concerned and followed her.

"Are you ok? What happened?"

"I'm better. I should've called in sick," she said, washing her face with cold water.

"You can go if you want. I'll take care of everything."

"No, I'm fine…I feel better now, thanks."

"If you say so." I thought she needed some time to feel better.

"So, what did you do this weekend?" I asked, just to change the conversation.

"Not much. What about you?"

"Not much either."

She was quiet all morning, so I decided to let her be. Joe and I were going out for lunch together. I was curious to see how Jane would react. I really hoped that she would be happy for me.

At 12:30 PM, Joe came to the reception casually saying, "Let's go?" I grabbed my purse and left with him.

After lunch, I was happy. Jane knew it, but she was quiet. I guess she was still feeling sick. I asked her again if she wanted to go home. She rejected. So, I left her alone.

I was going to Miami after work to help my sister convince our father that she must go study in New York, which we knew wasn't going to be easy. Joe was ok with that since he had stuff to do, too. He had a get together in his building with the guys that he usually works out with.

#

On Tuesday morning, Jane was a mess. We were all worried

about her. Even Mr. McKee called me into his office to talk about her.

"Is everything ok with Jane?" He was worried.

"I know she has been a little distressed lately, but I'm sure she'll be fine soon." I was worried that they were planning to fire her.

"Please tell her to come see me…"

"Yes, sir," I said and left his office, worried about Jane.

"Jane, Mr. McKee is calling you in his office…"

"Really?" She got up at once and went to Mr. McKee's office.

Not long after, she came back still looking worrisome.

"What happened? Did he fire you?" I wanted to know.

"No, Ann, he's really cool. He wanted to know if I needed to take the day off…"

"Really? What did you say?"

"That I didn't need anything. Actually, I need a friend," she said, looking at me and making a sad face.

"Sure, anytime. Do you want to go out?"

"No, can we go to your house? Can I sleep over?"

"PJ party! I love it!" I cheered her up.

#

After work, we went to her place so she could feed Ollie and grab some stuff. When arriving, Mike was in the hallway and I was happy to see him—maybe he knew what was going on with Jane, or maybe he was the reason for Jane's distress. I was trying to get a hint.

"Hi, Mike." I rushed to hug him. "Hey, Ann. Are you guys going out again?" he asked.

"What do you mean again? Of course, we go out again and again and again…" I was confused.

"I mean, you just went out yesterday, which was Monday. You guys must have a lot of energy and make a lot of money…" he said, making a disbelieving face and looking at Jane.

"We didn't go out yesterday. Uh-oh…sorry, Jane." I think I shouldn't have said that. I rushed inside her apartment, leaving them in the hallway so they could talk. Jane went after him and took a little while to come back. Meanwhile, I called Joe. I didn't want him to be upset again.

"Hey, Joe, I'm at Jane's. She needs a friend, and she's going to sleep over at my house. You know, girls' night. I think she needs to talk…"

"What? Why? Did she get fired today? I heard a conversation that she wasn't doing very well," he said.

"Yeah, Mr. McKee called her in his office, but apparently, he gave her another chance."

"Really? I think it would be good for her to take a vacation to think things over."

"Yes, that's actually a good idea. I'm going to suggest that. I think she is having issues with her boyfriend…"

"Boyfriend?"

"Yes, Mike. He's her next-door neighbor. She's there now talking to him; he seemed to be very upset with her. Hopefully, they don't fight, poor Jane. I need to go; she's back. Talk to you tomorrow. Bye."

"Ok."

We hung up.

Chapter 47

"Are you going to tell me what's going on or not?" I asked her after we ate and smoked pot, sitting on the sofa, already in our pajamas.

"I've got nothing to tell you, Ann, really. I had an argument with Mike yesterday, that's all."

"So, where did you go?"

"Nowhere. I just didn't open the door. I wasn't in the mood for him, and then I said that you and I had gone for a happy hour, just a little lie."

"Oh…and why are you so miserable today? It seems that you have been crying a lot. If you don't want to talk, that's fine. I understand." I didn't want her to feel pressured to open up to me. I know she will when the time feels right.

"I'm not miserable. As I said, I had a fight with Mike, that's all. I'll be fine tomorrow. What about you? You and Joe seem to be getting along after all…"

"Yeah, you know, I've a crush on him." Why was she bringing Joe up? I didn't know where she was trying to get.

"When did he start paying attention to you?"

"Why are you asking that? Why do you think he wouldn't be interested in me? You're just jealous." I got a little upset with her comment. Why does she think a guy like Joe wouldn't like someone like me? I know she's more attractive; however, Joe is mature and looking for a woman, not a brainless teenager-ish girl like her.

"I'm sorry, Ann. I just wanted to know if there is anything going on between you two."

"I'm not sure either, but I'll let you know if something more serious happens, ok? Let's smoke pot and forget about Mike and Joe…" I didn't like the path that the conversation was taking, and I wasn't ready to talk about Joe yet.

"Ok."

We were high and decided to watch TV. We wanted to watch this new series that everyone was talking about, *The Walking Dead*. After we watched the first episode, we wanted to eat again.

She opened my refrigerator, checking what was inside. "No ice cream?" She was desperate for sweets.

"No, I don't have any ice cream. What about a granola bar?"

"Eww! Don't you have anything better?"

"We can order pizza!"

"Yay! I want pizza. Pepperoni, please! Can we order chocolate fudge as well?"

We had a fun time after all, and it was good to see Jane a little better.

#

The next day, Joe was already at the office when we arrived.

"Hi, girls." He had a smile on his face and a cup of coffee in his hands.

"Did you make coffee?" I was happy to see him and crazy to kiss him good morning.

"Yeah, I made coffee…" He smiled.

"Let me try it. Do you want some, Jane?" I went to the lunchroom to grab a coffee, waiting for Joe to follow me, but he didn't.

"Good, very good actually…" I said, coming back with two mugs, one for me and one for Jane.

"Not bad, huh? See you later?" he said, smiling at me and going to his office.

"Sure." I smiled back at him.

"What's going on?" Jane looked at me astonished, not believing that Joe was flirting with me.

"Nothing, why?" I tried to act normally.

"Nothing? I can tell there's something between you and Joe. Why didn't you say anything last night?" She twisted her lips, scowling and looking at me with distrust.

"C'mon, Jane. I told you I have a crush on him. He's so handsome and cool. Nothing serious has happened yet. But God is father, and He will provide…" I said, lifting my hands up to heaven, joking. She didn't laugh. "Oh well, you're jealous," I said, starting to work.

Later, I invited her for lunch.

"Do you want to have lunch with me?" I asked her. I really wanted to tell her that Joe had asked me out.

"Huh? Aren't you going with Joe?" She was confused.

"No, we're going out Friday night…" I tried to sound casual.

"Really? Thanks, Ann, but I have things to do in my lunch time…bank stuff," she said, getting her purse and leaving.

"Ok. Bye."

Joe came to the reception and saw me alone. "Weren't you going to lunch with Jane?" He was confused.

"Yeah, but she said she had other plans and left. I'm free if you are…"

"Yeah, I'm ready to kiss you good morning," he said, stealing a quick kiss.

"Let's go then?"

"Yep," he said, waiting for me.

We went to this popular restaurant on Las Olas Blvd. It was crowded, but we managed to get a table. After ordering our food and drinks, he asked about Jane. He was curious to know what we talked about last night at my house.

"So, how's Jane? Is she ok?"

"No, I think she's going through a hard time, but she didn't want to talk last night."

"Did you say that she was having problems with her boyfriend? The neighbor?"

"Yeah, apparently, they're fighting a lot, which is weird because she never cared for Mike that much, so I'm not sure why she's so distressed."

"Maybe she's having money issues?"

"No, she's stressed because of someone. I'm not sure if this person is Mike. He was asking where she went the night before, and apparently, she lied, saying that she was with me…"

"I hope she gets better and really doesn't disturb the office atmosphere. Mr. McKee was talking about letting her go, and to be honest, she may be better off somewhere else…"

"Don't say that. She's my friend and I love her. I know she can be a pain sometimes, but I don't want her to leave."

"Well, I won't let her interfere in our relationship. If she keeps having an attitude, I'll have to agree with Mr. McKee. I won't defend her."

"I'll talk with her. I'm sure she'll be fine soon."

"You're an incredible friend. I just don't have your patience, and

I'm not sure she deserves that much loyalty from you. I don't know, but I feel she's not being honest with you, and I think she wouldn't do the same for you."

"You don't know her…" I was a little sad to hear Joe talking that way about Jane. After all, he didn't know her that much to draw conclusions about her character. We went back to the office and kept ourselves busy. Joe left at four. He had a meeting with a client. Jane was quiet and didn't want to talk. Oh, well, I went home to Max.

Chapter 48

It was finally Friday.

"Hi, Ann," Jane said, walking into the office.

"Hey! Are you ok?" I had to ask.

"I'm fine. Has everybody arrived yet?"

"Not everybody. Joe hasn't," I made sure to mention him so we could start talking about Joe and me at once.

"Is it today that you're going on a date?" She wanted to make sure.

"Yeah, please don't be jealous. I want you to be happy for me, Jane…"

"Oh, Ann. I love you very much. You know that, don't you? Yeah, I'm jealous. I don't want to lose your friendship. You'll leave me aside to be with him. Who will party with me?"

"I like him, Jane. I'll always be your friend, but life must go on. We need to move on." I needed to tell her that I was going to be with Joe, no matter what.

"Ms. May?" The intercom spoke.

"Yes, Mr. McKee."

"Could you please bring Mr. Greenberg's file? Thank you."

"Right the way, Sir." And there she went.

Joe was in the courthouse. He had a case to defend, and I knew it was going to take all day. It was an important real estate dispute. But he called me when he had a break.

"Hey, love! How are you? I miss you so much. Can't wait to see you tonight. I'll pick you up at nine."

He called me love for the first time! I couldn't disguise my happiness.

"Nine o'clock is fine. See you then." I knew Jane was paying attention to my conversation, but she didn't say anything.

We had a smooth, slow day at the office, and I left at 5:00 PM sharp. I had a lot to do before *my love* arrived.

#

I was going to sleep at Joe's for the first time; so exciting! I had to think about what to take. I didn't want him to think that I was moving in, but at the same time, I needed to have everything I could possibly need—what a dilemma.

At nine o'clock, Joe knocked on my door, "Hey, gorgeous!" He embraced and kissed me, taking me inside and closing the door behind us with his foot.

"Hey, I'm ready to go," I said, showing him my not-so-small bag.

He chuckled and said, "How long are you planning to stay?"

"Forever!"

"Forever is good…" He kissed me again. "I've got some not-so-good news…"

"What happened?"

"Larry, Mr. Poch, called me, and he wants me to join him at the country club for a reception. He wants me to meet this new client. I'm sorry, I have to go and can't take you with me…"

"Oh no!"

"I'm sorry, babe, I can come over afterward…"

"That's ok, we can do something tomorrow. I'll cook for you, and we can invite Matt and David, too. What do you think?"

"Sounds like a plan…"

#

On Saturday morning, I went grocery shopping with Matt. He was going to help me prepare the food; we decided to make a BBQ using their brand-new grill. The day was beautiful, perfect for an outdoor gathering.

"Do you think we should grill some corn as well?" I asked Matt. I always eat corn with BBQ, but he might have a different idea for a side dish.

"We can't go wrong with corn, but I want to do something different… Have you ever heard about grilled watermelon?"

"Whaaat? Watermelon on the grill? No way."

"It's delicious, and we're having avocados for dessert…"

"You know I love you, but I'll buy my corn and fruits for a fruit salad, you know, regular dessert…"

I filled the cart with chips, corn, salsa, beer, hamburger, hamburger bread, and fruits. That's my idea of BBQs. He laughed and got his stuff. "Ready?"

"Yeah, let's go!"

Joe arrived around 11:30 AM, and he seemed to be a little stressed out.

"What happened? Is anything wrong?" I was concerned.

"Yeah…I don't know how to tell you this, but I feel I need to. It's about Jane…"

"What happened to her?"

"Well, yesterday, when I left the party, I went to this nightclub. Look, I know it can seem odd, but the guys and I usually go there for fun. We don't go there to pick up hookers. We just go for a good time. It's kind of cool, the people are great, the girls are beautiful. But no lap dancing for me, believe me…"

"I'm not getting…"

"As I was saying, it's a strip club. Anyway, Jane was there, and she wasn't normal. She was wearing this very sexy, trashy outfit and a long bleach-blond wig…"

"No way!"

"Yes way, and there's more…"

"What?"

"She was with this old, tattooed guy; very scary. I had to come closer to make sure that it was her, and it was. She panicked when she saw me. I tried to talk with her, but she left in a hurry…"

"It can't be. I don't believe you…"

"Believe me, I wouldn't tell you if I thought it wasn't serious. I told you, I always thought that she was hiding something."

"Maybe that's the reason for her fights with Mike. He must have found out…"

"It could be. I know she's your friend, but as I said, she doesn't hold you to the same standard."

"I need to digest this story. Thank you for letting me know anyway."

"Hey, guys! A little help here…" David called us outside to help. Matt was freaking out with the grill. I'm happy that I bought chips and salsa.

After we ate, drank, talked, and had a lot of fun together, it was time to clean up. Joe and I helped David and Matt, and when it was already getting dark outside, we went inside to relax.

"Do you want to go to my place as we had planned before?" Joe asked me.

"No, it's ok. I have Max to take care of and want to check on Jane tomorrow, if you don't mind…"

"Nope, I can go with you if you want."

"No, I'll talk with her alone. Actually, I want to talk with Mike first."

"Mike, who? The boyfriend?"

"Yes."

"Ok, *muchacha, ven aquí con papi…*" I couldn't believe he was speaking Spanish to impress me. Even knowing that at least basic Spanish is a must in South Florida, I was stunned that he was learning very fast!

"Aww, you're so cute speaking Spanish! C'mon, say more, you're turning me on…*papi…*" I started kissing him all over.

"*Guapa! Chica hermosa…*" he said, smiling and kissing me… "*Te extraño.*"

"More," I murmured, turned on by his British accent trying to speak Spanish.

"That's all I know."

"Please keep going. Don't stop."

"I promise I'll buy a Spanish dictionary tomorrow…" I couldn't help but laugh. He went on, "*Te quero mucho.*" He laid me down on the couch, undressing me. "*Te quero mucho, guapa hermosa,*" he repeated since he didn't know any other word to say. He amuses me.

"*Yo también te quiero,*" I said, unzipping his pants and caressing him.

"*C'mon, niña. Let me show you papi.*" He was on fire!

"*Basta, ven aquí,*" I said, pulling him on top of me.

"What?"

"Shh, stop talking," I said, kissing him.

"All right, all right, say no more..." he said, gobbling me with his eyes, crazy to have me. I was in love and just wanted to be with him. Forever.

Chapter 49

On Sunday, after Joe left to meet his friends for a jog on the beach, I decided to call Mike.

"Hey, Mike! Do you have a minute? I want to talk to you about Jane."

"Sure, Ann. Do you want to come over?"

"No, I don't think it's a good idea."

"Yeah, you're right. She can see us here. Where do you want to meet? I can go over to your house."

"No, she can show up in here, too. Let's meet at Dania Beach. I want to take Max to the dog park. I know she would never go there."

"Ok, I'll meet you there in about twenty minutes?"

"See you there!"

I took Max and Luna with me; they were so happy, running around like crazy. Mike arrived not long after I did.

"Hey, Mike!"

"Hi, Ann!" he said, kissing me on the cheek and sitting by my side on the park bench. "What's up with Jane? I'm really concerned about her…"

"Me, too. That's why I called you. Can you tell me what were you guys fighting about? She seems to be so distraught lately. I'm worried."

"Yeah, I know something is wrong. She must be in some kind of trouble. I tried to talk with her, but she avoids conversations and doesn't give me explanations. I think she's involved with someone who doesn't care about her. I never saw anyone coming over or calling her, but she goes out, sometimes for days…"

"Oh my God! Joe said he saw her at this strip club on Friday night…"

"Friday night, I saw her coming home around midnight. She was deplorable! She was wearing this trashy outfit that seemed to be torn, her makeup smudged, and a bleach-blond wig…. I don't know what else I can do to help her, really."

"Joe said she was wearing the exact same thing. Oh my God, what are we going to do? I need to help her. Do you think someone is blackmailing her? How did she get to this point, and why she didn't say anything?"

"I don't know. I like her very much, and I know she has a good time with me, too. I love when she's herself: goofy, funny, air-headed, irresponsible, but adorable…"

"Yeah, I love her, too. We need to help her somehow."

"What about an intervention? You know? When family and friends trap the person and force them to talk about an issue that's destroying them."

"Great idea! What if I invite her over to my house as I always do, and you'll be there, too? She'll be trapped and forced to talk with us…"

"It may work. I'm willing to try. When?"

"The sooner, the better. I'll talk to her and let you know."

"Fine with me. Give me a call just to confirm when, and I'll be there."

"Ok, bye, Mike!" I said, getting up and calling the dogs. I knew it would take at least an hour for the dogs to obey and agree to go home.

#

In the afternoon, we were sitting outside, having beers, chips, and salsa. Matt was quiet; he was still distressed about the BBQ. Joe tried to lift his spirits up, saying that he had never eaten grilled watermelons. "It was delicious, really!"

"Thanks, Joe. I'm glad you liked it, but I'll never do that again! No more BBQs for me!" We all laughed.

"What are you guys doing tonight?" David asked. "What about a movie night?"

"Thanks, David, but I have something to talk about with Joe," I said, looking at Joe.

"What? I hope you guys are not fighting again," Matt said.

"No, it's about Jane."

"Oh, poor girl! You told me she's going through a tough time. We feel sorry for her; she's like a stray kitten. Let us know if there is anything we can do to help her, ok?" David added.

"Sure, thanks."

Joe and I went inside. He helped to put the stuff away in the kitchen while I washed the dishes.

"What did you want to talk about, Jane?" he asked.

"I spoke with Mike this morning, the boyfriend…"

"And?" He was curious.

"And we decided to have an intervention session with her. I'll invite her over, and Mike will be here, too; not sure if tomorrow or when, so it's better that you don't come or sleep over for a couple of days. I'll let you know."

"Wait a minute, intervention like the TV show?"

"Yes, something like that!"

"I don't know."

"Well, Mike told me he saw her coming home Friday night wearing the exact outfit you described, but worse, she was a mess. Her makeup smudged, and clothes torn…"

"Oh my God…I told you…"

"I need to do something. She's my friend."

"I know," he said. "I need to tell you one thing before this intervention takes place."

"What?"

"Come sit down here on the couch with me."

"You're making me nervous. What is it?" I was getting apprehensive.

"Well, I didn't tell you before because I thought it wasn't important. Actually, if she didn't tell you, it's because she didn't want you to know."

"What?" I was getting confused.

"I met Jane before starting to work in the office. We had a night out affair kind of thing. It was really nothing."

"How come you never told me?" I could not believe my ears.

"I'm telling you now."

"How come she never told me, either?" I didn't know what to think—memories of Cristina and Sam invaded my mind, and my heart sank.

"I don't know, but it's nothing you should care about. We know that her situation now is way more important than my affair with her. I just wanted to let you know before it came up and seemed like I was hiding something terrible from you."

"You hid a very important detail from me."

"You hid our relationship from her, too. That makes us equals."

"Equals how? I never lied to you."

"You hid our affair from Jane, your best friend."

"Because you wanted me to. You wanted to keep it a secret."

"I never asked you to keep our relationship a secret. You didn't want to tell her, not me."

"Maybe you're right. I was afraid that she could betray me like another best friend I had once did." I was trying to digest the facts. "I need to think…"

"Ok, I'll see you tomorrow at the office," he said, kissing my head and leaving.

I was confused. I really didn't know what to think. *Yes, Joe hid their affair from me, but I didn't want to tell Jane about my relationship with him either. I guess he kept the secret for our sake, but Jane? Why didn't she tell me about Joe? I think she knew I was going to freak out because of what happened with Cristina. Maybe she was just trying to protect me, and it was only a one-night-out affair after all, as Joe said.*

I needed to clear my mind and knew it was going to be impossible to fall asleep without relaxing first. I smoked pot, got my iPod, and started to meditate, relaxing my muscles, breathing in and out, slowly and deeply, until I was ready to go to bed. Tomorrow will be a better day, and everything will be explained.

CHAPTER 50

On Monday morning, I was early at the office, as always, but super eager to see Jane. Joe came in right after me. "Hi, babe. Are you still planning to go on with the intervention thing?"

"Yeah, definitely."

"Is there anything I can do? I mean, do you want me to be there, too?"

"No, you shouldn't be there. I'll call you afterward, ok?"

"Ok."

Jane arrived late, as usual, and she looked terrible. She was literally dragging herself in and didn't even apologize for being late this time.

"Hi, Jane. Are you ok?" I tried to make her say something.

"I'm fine. How was your date?" she asked cynically, as if doubting it had happened.

"Well, we didn't go out on Friday…Joe couldn't make it, but he came over on Saturday. Oh, Jane, he's awesome. I'm in love." I wanted her to know that Joe and I were together.

"No! Ann, listen to me. Joe isn't the guy for you. He's evil, he's bad." She started saying this nonsense about Joe.

"What? What's wrong with you, Jane? We definitely need to talk!" I said, cutting her off. "Tomorrow night at my place…ok?" I demanded.

"No. I need to tell you now…"

"Jane, stop it! I know you're in trouble, but we can't talk right now. Tomorrow, ok?" I said, holding her hands and looking at her seriously. We needed to have a very thorough conversation about her and our friendship. She can't keep secrets from me, and the office was not the place for this kind of talk.

"Ok," she agreed and nodded.

#

I called Mike when I got home. "Hey, Mike. Can you talk?"

"Yeah, tell me!"

"So, she's coming over tomorrow night. She can't know that you'll be here, too, ok?"

"Sure! What time do I've to be there? What should I say?"

"At eight o'clock, and don't worry, I'll start. You just go with the flow, ok?"

"Ok! I'll be there."

Then, it was Joe's turn.

"Hey, Joe!" I called him right after hanging up with Mike.

"Hey, love…" he answered, calling me love again. It sounded like music to my ears.

"So, we're having the intervention thing tomorrow night, just to let you know."

"I think I should be there, too."

"No, you shouldn't. I'll call you after, ok?"

"I'm not liking this shit."

"Everything is going to be fine. I love you." I said with meaning.

"Love you, too. I'll wait for your call." He didn't pause or sound awkward saying that he loved me, too. I started feeling really good about us.

#

On Tuesday, Mike and I were waiting for Jane. At 8:00 PM, she knocked on my door.

"Hey, Jane!" I left the door open for her, and she followed me.

"Mike?" She was surprised.

"Hi, Jane," he said with a very concerned face.

"What's going on here?" Her face went white, and her eyes suspicious. She didn't understand what Mike was doing in my house.

"Please, Jane. Listen to us. Calm down. Sit down, please." I said, pulling her down to sit at my side on the sofa. Mike sat on her other side. "We need to talk. Mike and I are very worried about you. You have been acting strangely lately…"

Mike nodded, agreeing with me.

"Mike told me how awful you looked when you arrived home Friday night. You weren't with me. Where have you been? Who are you seeing?"

She was shocked, looking at me with her eyes wide open.

"Mike thinks you're seeing someone who has been abusing you. If you are, there's nothing to be ashamed of. We just have to take you out of this situation before you get hurt…" She still looked puzzled.

"You can trust us, Jane. We're not going to judge you, no matter what you've done," Mike said, taking her hand. She turned her face to look at him now. "If you want, I can take you to New York, to my brother's condo. We can stay there as long as you want."

"Yeah, Jane, go with him, and I'll come see you on the weekend. I'll take care of Ollie for you, and then we'll switch. Mike comes back to work, and I stay with you a little. What do you think?"

"No, I can't. You guys are wrong. I don't want to go to New York." She was getting agitated.

"So, tell us." Mike was getting frustrated.

"Ann, remember when we planned to go to California? Come with me; let's quit our jobs, sell our stuff, and go. I would go to California with you." She started talking nonsense.

"Jane, I can't quit my job and go to California just like that. Go to New York first, and then we'll see. Maybe we can go to California another time."

"No, Ann, you've got to come with me. You can't stay here with Joe. I can't leave you here with him."

I couldn't believe that all she could worry about was Joe and me…? "Jane, stop that. What part of I like him, didn't you get? It's not my fault that you got yourself in trouble, but please don't spoil my happiness. It's not going to work. I know him better than you do, and he's a wonderful man. Actually, he told me everything."

"He did?" She was incredulous.

"Yeah. Joe said he saw you at this nightclub, and you were wearing that awful outfit and the wig stuff. Don't try to deny it. Mike saw you wearing just that on Friday night. And he told me you were with this disgusting tattooed guy. Jane, we know…" She was turning pale, looking at me, speechless. "I know you wanted to tell me you saw Joe in one of those places, and it's been difficult for you because you would have to explain what in the world you were doing there. That's why you were going around without the courage to say it. We know…Joe was really embarrassed for having to tell me he was there when he saw you, but he likes you and knows you're my best friend. Oh, Jane! He's a wonderful man—he cares about you."

"No, Ann, you're wrong. He's awful, evil," she shouted, getting up and running out the door, leaving Mike and I confused, not knowing what to do.

"What the hell?" Mike said, looking at me, bewildered. "It's worse than we thought. I don't know what else we can do."

"We need to keep trying. I'll not give up on her!"

"Me neither!"

Chapter 51

The next morning, Jane didn't show up at work. I was really concerned and started to call her, but she didn't pick up. I called Mike to see if he could go to her apartment and check if she was alive. "Hey, Mike, Jane didn't come to work today. I'm very worried."

"I'll go to her apartment now and will call you back…"

"Hey, love, how was the intervention thing last night?" Joe was concerned and asked when he arrived at the office, "Why didn't you call me?"

"It wasn't good. I'm sorry I didn't call you. She felt trapped and stormed out of the house…"

"Wow. Did she say anything?"

"She said that you're evil."

"I think she needs professional help."

"Yeah, we're coming to this conclusion, too. Mike is going to try to take her on a vacation to New York so she can at least calm down a bit."

"That's a wonderful idea. She needs to get out of here."

"I'm going to tell Mr. McKee that she called in sick, and I'm planning to go there after work."

"I can go with you."

"No, Mike and I have her under control. She's jealous of us, and your presence will only stress her more."

"Ok, call me if you need anything."

#

After work, I went to her apartment. Mike and I knocked on her door, but she didn't answer. We were scared that she was up to doing something drastic.

"Jane, please open the door!" Mike and I almost knocked the door down. "If you don't open the door, we're going to call your mom and the police." Mike was losing his patience.

"Go away. I don't want to see anyone!" she finally answered.

We kept knocking and asking her to open the door, but she didn't want to cooperate.

"I need to go. I need to take care of Max."

"Go. I'll keep trying and will call you if she opens the door."

"Ok, I'll be back in an hour or so…"

I took Max for a walk around the block. When I was coming back, I saw Joe waiting for me at my doorstep.

"Hey, love, I stopped by to check if you were home and saw your car. I knocked… I was going to call you."

"Hey, babe. I'm fine. Mike just called me, saying that she finally opened the door and agreed to go to New York with him. I'm relieved."

"Well, that's wonderful news! She really needs to get out of here. It's going to be good for her and, to be honest, good for us, too."

"Don't say that…"

"I don't want to talk about Jane anymore. What if we order food and have a nice, relaxing, loving night together—just you and me?" he said, embracing me from behind and walking with me inside the house.

"I think it's a wonderful idea. I miss you," I said, turning around to face him.

"I miss you, too," he said, kissing me and taking me to the bedroom.

"Wait! Let's order the food?"

"Food, right…" he said, getting his cell phone. "What are you in the mood for? Greek?"

I nodded, and he placed the order.

"Ok, it's done. Where were we?" he said, grabbing me again.

"We need to wait for the delivery guy," I said, trying to get out of his embrace.

"The guy said approximately one hour…"

"One hour is not a lot of time, and sometimes they come faster."

"Sometimes they come later. Anyway, I can do a lot of things to you in one hour…" He pushed me on the bed, holding my arms above my head and trapping my legs between his. I couldn't move. He was on top of me, keeping me hostage.

"You can do a lot of things *with* me," I said, amused, trying to kiss him. He turned his head away from my mouth, smiling.

"No, I'll do things *to* you. You're going to be the passive receptor of my actions," he explained and started kissing me all over.

"Joe, stop. It tickles…"

"Now, I'm going to unbutton your shirt. I'm using just one hand. See?" He showed me his free hand that went down my body, unbuttoning my shirt, making me anxious.

"No, Joe. Wait. I want to take a shower. I need to brush my teeth."

"I like you dirty!" he whispered and looked into my eyes, caressing my breasts.

"Mmm…kiss me already!" I begged him.

"No."

"Please, let me kiss you, let me touch you. You're torturing me…"

"That's the intention," he said, kissing my neck and unzipping my pants with his free hand. "Do you like this?" he said, looking into my eyes, getting his hands under my panties and caressing me. I was ready for him.

"Do you want me to stop now?" he asked, smiling and still looking into my eyes.

"No…don't stop…" I said, panting.

"On second thought, I think you're right. Let's wait for the delivery guy…" he said, chuckling, letting me go, and sitting up at the bed's edge.

"Whaaat? No fucking way! Come back here!" I grabbed him from behind and pulled him back onto the bed with me. I took his shirt off and pulled his pants down so I could feel his skin against mine, kissing and touching his strong body. He stayed, lying there, looking at me with desire and letting me do whatever I wanted. I did, and it was awesome. Never felt that sexy before in my entire life. *Oh God, I love him!*

Chapter 52

The following week was peaceful without Jane. I have to confess that I needed a break from her as well. Joe was right. It has been better for all of us now that she was away. Don't get me wrong, I love her and truly miss the old Jane, my best friend Jane, not this paranoiac, secretive person who she had become recently. I hope she gets back to herself, and everything is back to normal.

Joe and I were doing amazingly. For the first time in a while, I felt I could trust someone again and get married, have kids, the whole nine yards. Sometimes, I have to pinch myself to make sure I am not dreaming. Some nights, I stare at Joe sleeping on my side, not believing that it was finally really happening. I'm a lucky girl! I love him with all my heart.

Saturday morning, I was lazy in bed when Joe came in, opening the bedroom curtain and handing me a freshly brewed coffee mug. "Morning, love!"

"Morning, love," I said love, too, smiling and grabbing the coffee. "What do you want to do today?"

"I'm going for a run with the guys on the beach if you don't mind."

"Of course not. I'll do some cleaning and laundry and chat a bit with David and Matt. I miss them. I also have to give some attention to my kid, Max. So go and have fun."

"Ok, I'll grab lunch with Jamal. We can go out tonight if you want…do you want to go dance?"

"Yeah, I guess we could do something different."

"Ok, bye!" He kissed me goodbye.

I got up, gathered the dirty clothes to wash, and opened the backyard door for Max to go out and all the windows. I also put the rugs outside to get some sun.

"Hey, girl!" Matt came outside with Luna. "How's everything? I was thinking about calling you, but I was afraid to interrupt something. How's Jane?"

"Hey, Matt. I miss you, too. Jane is a mess, but she finally agreed to go to New York with her boyfriend on vacation so she could calm down a bit."

"New York? Not bad, huh?" He was being sarcastic. "Well, what about you and Joe? Apparently, you guys are keeping yourselves busy. I haven't seen you all week long."

"Yep, we're doing fine. Finally, everything is getting settled. I just hope that Jane comes back to normal and accepts that Joe and I are together."

"What's that? She doesn't want you to be with Joe? Why?"

"She is jealous. She thinks I'm going to dump her and not be her friend anymore, which is nonsense."

"I always found her a little immature, to be honest with you."

"Yeah, I know. She is immature and…" I was talking when my cell phone rang. "Sorry, it's Mike. I need to get this." And I walked away to answer the phone.

"Hey, Mike. Is everything ok? How's Jane?"

"Everything is fine. Jane is fine. We're coming back today. Are you going to be home?"

"Actually, no, why?"

"I thought we could come over to talk with you."

"Can we do this tomorrow? I have plans for tonight, and you guys are going to be tired from the trip, right? Unless it's something urgent."

"No, today. Joe can be part of the conversation as well."

"Ok, I'm not sure he'll want to be part of the conversation, but I'll let him know. Bye."

I was puzzled about Mike wanting Joe to be part of the conversation. How could Joe possibly help them? Maybe Jane told Mike about their affair, and he blames Joe for her breakdown. I will not allow this nonsense to keep going. She needs to stop with the accusations and leave us alone for real. I'm tired of this shit.

I was really upset all afternoon. I cleaned the house, gave Max a bath, took care of the garden, took a shower, and was eager for Joe to come home. He finally arrived.

"How was your day?" he asked, going to the bathroom to take a shower. I followed him.

"I did a lot. It was a busy day. Mike called. He said they're coming back today…"

"Today?"

"Yes, and they want to come over to talk. They want you to be part of the conversation…"

"No fucking way!" He opened the shower box door to look at me in disbelief. He was very annoyed by the situation. "I really thought the vacation would calm her down. We will not let her keep going with this neurotic behavior…"

"Yeah, I hear you. I'm upset, too."

"Let's go out and enjoy our Saturday night," he said, coming out of the shower and drying himself with the towel, dropping it on the floor when finished.

"I agree. Please don't leave the towel on the floor," I said, giving him the look, the Cuban look.

"*¿Qué pasa, niña? estás loca?*" He laughed, taking the towel from the floor and hanging it on the towel bar. He looked at me, saying, "I wasn't going to leave it on the floor…"

"Better!" I said, satisfied.

"*Hey, Chica, yo stoy hablando Español…*don't you find it hot?" he said, making a sexy and inviting face showing his naked body to me. I wanted to laugh but contained myself. I had serious issues to address.

"It doesn't work when I'm mad…*vete hombre,*" I said, making a gesture with my hand for him to go away.

"*Oí ¿Estás loca mujer?* Ok, I'm going, I'm going…" He was laughing, going back to the bathroom, when my phone rang.

"It's Mike! I'll get it in the living room.

"Mike said they're coming over around 8:00 PM, and he wants to talk with us both," I told him when he walked into the room, combing his hair.

"No way, I'm out of here. Let's leave before they arrive," he said, upset, glancing at his watch. It was already 7:30 PM.

"I can't. Why don't you go for a drink? I'll let them talk, and we'll go out afterward."

"I'll give them one hour. If they're still here when I come back, I'll tell them to leave. One hour is more than enough," he said, grabbing the car keys abruptly and leaving, shaking his head in annoyance.

Chapter 53

Not even five minutes passed by when someone started to knock on my door. It was Mike, and he was alone.

"You've got to come with me. Let's go. We can't lose them from sight."

"What? Lose who? Go where? Where is Jane?" I was totally confused.

"Come with me. I'll explain in the car," he said, pulling me out the door.

"You better have a good explanation for dragging me out of my house like this. Where is Jane?" I said, getting in Mike's car.

"She's with Joe, we're going to follow them…" he said, speeding to reach Joe's car.

"Jane is with Joe?"

"Yes, I know it's confusing. I'll explain," he said, looking at me. "Did you know that Joe and Jane are having an affair?"

"You mean *had* an affair—in the past, before he started working in the office…"

"No, they never broke up. He's the reason for Jane's distress, and apparently, he's very dangerous. He tried to kill a guy and killed another." He was driving me crazy with this nonsense.

I laughed. "What? Look, I don't know what Jane told you, but what you're telling me makes no sense at all. We know that she's delusional and in need of professional help. I'm going to call Joe and tell him to come home. We can talk tomorrow."

"Believe me, Ann, you'll be surprised. Don't call Joe just yet. Let them talk. Jane needs that, and we're right behind them. Nothing is going to happen; they just need to talk." Mike was determined that Jane and Joe needed to sort things over.

"I'm not sure…" I was really upset with Jane and Mike. How could they trap us like that? I'll have a serious conversation with Jane. This was not ok.

"Look, they pulled over!" Mike said, pulling over behind them and leaving the car to check on Jane. As a precaution, he grabbed a baseball bat he had in the back seat. I was shocked. I couldn't believe what was happening. I got out of the car and walked toward them. Joe was holding Jane, and she was crying hysterically.

"Let her go!" Mike yielded, approaching them with the baseball bat in his hands.

"What's going on? Jane, let's talk. We can clear up all this misunderstanding, I'm sure." I stretched my arm to her, and she ran to me. "Why are you wearing this costume?" I didn't understand what was going on.

"That's how he likes to see me…we're playing this game that I'm his whore. He's a psycho!" she told me, whispering.

"Game?" Now I get it, he proposed the fucking game to me too, and it was supposed to be a secret. I couldn't believe he was doing that to me! I wanted to disappear. *Please, God, not again!*

"Ann, Joe is a jerk. He hurt me, and he killed Fred, tried to kill Juan Carlos, and now he wants to hurt you! Believe me, he's a liar!" she screamed.

Meanwhile, Mike was keeping Joe distant from us. At this point, he didn't know what to believe.

"Well, what the fuck, man! Why did you do this to her? She's just a girl. They both are just nice, naïve girls looking for some fun. You're a fucking bastard one way or another," Mike said to Joe.

"I meant no harm," Joe said, looking at us.

"I guess it's too late, huh? Do you think you can just play a game of your choosing, set the rules, and end the game when you get tired of it? I don't think so, not with my girl. I love her and will not let this happen again. You're an asshole!"

"I may be," Joe said, trying to calm Mike down. "Let's talk, all four of us. We can clear up all this freaking story, shall we?" Joe proposed. He was looking at me with begging eyes. I knew he wanted to talk and clarify the facts.

"Yeah," I said, "I want to clean this mess up."

"Ok, but you need to stay close to me," Jane said to me, and I nodded, confirming.

"I've got a house in Marathon. It's about one hour from here. We can talk there. Follow me," Joe said, walking to his car.

"Come with me, girls," Mike said. "I don't trust the guy."

"No, I'll go with Joe. We need to talk." I said upset with the situation.

I got in Joe's car without saying a word. I needed him to tell me that all this commotion was a misunderstanding. He got in the car, saying nothing as well, and took off to Marathon.

Suddenly, he said, "Listen, Ann, Jane is hysterical. She's delusional, thinking I killed this guy, Fred, and tried to kill this other one, Juan Carlos, out of jealousy because she kissed one of them or both. I don't really know."

"Was it just a one-night-out affair, Joe?" I needed to know.

"It was more than that. She became obsessed with me and couldn't let go, especially after you and I started dating. I told her it was over, but she stalked me. She was everywhere—in the supermarket, in the garage, even in front of your house…"

"Please tell me I'm sleeping and having a nightmare. This can't be true!"

"She's crazy, you saw her. I did nothing because I was afraid that she could harm herself. I was really losing my patience when you and Mike realized she was not acting normally and tried to get the help she needs."

"Why did you lie to me?"

"I didn't lie…"

"Why didn't you tell me?"

"Because I thought I could handle her and because she's your friend."

"I don't know what to think. What about the game? Don't keep lying to me."

"I know, it was wrong. I shouldn't have proposed that freaking game to either of you, but it happened…sorry."

I couldn't believe my ears and started crying, lowering my head in despair as he kept talking.

"Ann, please listen to me," he said, lifting my head with his hand under my chin, "I do love you, don't forget that."

"I don't believe you. You're a liar. Jane is right: you're a jerk, and I can't trust you anymore. You had every chance to make it right, but you decided to keep your dirty little secret from me. Leave me alone, and don't touch me!" I said, pushing his hand away from me and looking out the window to avoid his gaze.

"Please, let me explain," he said when arriving at the house. "Whatever happens, whatever they say, just remember that I love you," he said, trying to hold me back while I was getting out of the car.

"Let me go. I have nothing to say to you." I got out of the car without looking back, rushing to Jane and Mike, who were just arriving as well.

JOE

Chapter 54

"Joe, I'm sad that you have decided to leave our firm. I want you to know that our door will always be open for you, and if you ever decide to come back, please call me." My boss was disappointed that I was determined to move to Florida. "Here is a bonus in appreciation for your excellent work. It's just something to help you settle in Miami." He handed me an envelope containing money, for sure. I was curious to know how much was in there, but I had to hold myself together until I was back in my cubicle.

"Thank you, Mr. Spenser. I really appreciate it, but it's time for me to move on." I was grateful but really determined to go. I couldn't stay in Chicago.

Once in my cubicle, I opened the envelope and found ten thousand dollars. Wow! I was sad about leaving my friends and an excellent job, but also excited to be starting a new life away from here.

"Hey, Joe!" Bill, my best friend, said, coming into my cubicle. "We're planning a farewell party for you on Friday. What time is your flight to Florida on Saturday?"

"Saturday at 9:00 AM," I said. "Who is coming? Please don't invite Amy."

"I didn't invite her, but she already knows. And I don't know if she's planning to go, sorry. You know that Suzy and Amy are best friends, like you and me." Bill and his fiancée, Suzy, and me and Amy were inseparable best friends.

"Oh, well…" I said, frustrated, "I hope she doesn't show. I don't know if I can hold myself together if I see her. I'm going to the apartment tomorrow afternoon to get the rest of my stuff; I know she won't be there. It's better this way," I added. Bill was sad about my current situation. He nodded and left my cubicle, saying nothing.

Amy, my ex-girlfriend, ex-roommate, and ex-future-wife is the reason that I'm moving to Florida. I just can't stay here once she's gone. Everything and everywhere reminds me of us. All my friends are her friends. We were inseparable until she decided to go to Iraq and leave me behind. She's a young journalist starting her career and was offered an opportunity to cover the recent attacks in Baghdad. She thinks that her career is worth the risk of getting killed. I'm heartbroken, upset, and desperate to make her stay with me. I keep thinking that if I move faraway before she leaves for Iraq, she might realize that she can't live without me and change her mind… I'm probably dreaming. I know her very well; she's stubborn and obsessed about her career. I just can't watch her going to a war zone. I need to be as far as I can from here before she leaves.

Thursday after lunch, I went to the apartment I used to share with Amy to get the rest of my stuff—books, CDs, and other things. Even though she works a lot from home, I knew she was going to be at the office this day. I opened the door, got in, and my heart sank. Everything was exactly how it was a month ago when she told me she was going to accept the offer to go to Iraq. We fought, and I left. Now, it seems impossible to take it back. What is done is done. She accepted the offer to go to Iraq, and I decided to move to Fort Lauderdale, Florida.

I had little left. One box was all I needed. I was taking the last look around when the door opened, and she came in.

"Hi!" she said, looking at me with the box in my hands, ready to leave.

"Hi. Sorry, I thought you weren't coming back until later…" I tried to justify still being there.

"Joe, I came earlier because I wanted to see you," she said, taking her shoes off and putting her stuff down.

"Amy, there is nothing to talk about unless you have changed your mind." I hoped she was going to stay with me.

"No, I haven't," she said. "But we don't have to end it like this. I love you."

"Stop! You're only making things more difficult for me—for us. Please, just say that you accepted to go because you fell in love with someone who is going with you, so I can hate you for a good reason…"

"No, I don't have anyone else. It's only you, and I love you."

"Get out of my way. I'm already gone," I said, making my way to the front door.

"Please understand that I'm not moving to Iraq forever. It's only for six months, and I'll be back to you, or you can come with me. I never wanted to be apart from you," she said, getting herself in between the door and me, blocking my way out.

"I don't know if you're that stupid or that naïve. If you go, if you come back…? I said *if* you come back, you'll be another person. You'll be changed. There will be no us as we know it. Can you understand that?"

"You're wrong. I'll always love you."

"You have no idea what you're getting yourself into. I don't know what to do. I want to lock you up in the house and hold you captive until you understand what I'm saying." I was getting upset.

"Why are you moving so far away? Please stay here. I'll come back to you," she said, crying.

"No! Please understand that you're taking a huge risk of getting killed, being held hostage, being tortured. Who knows? If you come back, you won't be the same person. The experience, the suffering, the reality you're about to witness will change you forever. Please,

please, please don't go. I love you so much. I just want us to be us,"
I said, hugging her, caressing her beautiful face, and wiping her tears
with my thumbs.

"I don't know what to say. I want to prove you are wrong. No
matter where you are, I'll find you when I come back. I promise," she
said, kissing and hugging me tight.

I couldn't resist her touch, her smell, her taste. I took her in my
arms and carried her to the bedroom. We made love one more time—
for the last time—passionately, tenderly, apologetically.

The next morning, I woke up and stayed there, gazing at her
beautiful face sleeping at my side. I wanted to make this moment last
forever. I needed to memorize every freckle and detail. She woke up,
and her eyes met mine. I got my face closer to hers, and we stayed
there, staring at each other without saying a word. It was goodbye.

#

Friday finally came. I was feeling weird about moving to a place
where I knew no one. I was frustrated and excited at the same time.
Amy didn't come to the party, which was a relief to me since it would
be difficult if I had to see her again.

"So, Joe, are you sure you're taking the right step? I know it's too
late to ask that, but I've got to try. We'll miss you, man," Bill said,
hugging me. He was already a little drunk.

"I know... I'll miss you guys, too, but this isn't really a goodbye.
I'll be back for the wedding, and you can come visit me in Florida as
well."

"Hey, everyone! I want to make a toast to Joe's future! I wish him
all the best and that he finds what he's searching for!" Bill said, calling
everyone's attention.

"To Joe! Cheers!"

"Cheers!" All my friends cheered for my new life to come.

Chapter 55

Saturday was a bright, sunny day in Fort Lauderdale. I went straight to the hotel after renting a car at the airport. Once in the hotel room I had booked online, I started my research for flats for rent in the area. I needed to move fast. There was no reason for procrastination, and I didn't want to give myself a chance to have regretful thoughts. After finding a couple of potential places, I hit save on my laptop and went for a stroll to check around. I was also kind of hungry. The hotel was close to my new job at Las Olas Blvd.

After eating something at this charming bistro, I walked down Las Olas Blvd all the way to the beach. The area was beautiful. I crossed a few small bridges over the various canals on my way and was amazed to see that almost every house on the canals had a nice boat anchored by their backyard. It was incredible. I finally arrived at the beach. Oh, the beach. I love the ocean and couldn't resist taking my shoes off and going to the water, which was chilly but refreshing. I found it very weird that no one was on the beach, and people were wearing jumpers and boots on the streets. The temperature was around fifty degrees, very pleasant, but I guess too cold for the locals.

On Sunday, I visited a couple of buildings that had furnished flats for rent, and since I had nothing specific in mind, I decided on the nicest one closest to the beach. I thought the ocean view would be a plus. The plan was to move after my first in-person meeting with my new boss on Monday morning.

\#

When getting to the office Monday morning, I was a little hesitant to walk in because I heard people yelling. I peeked inside and saw these two girls arguing with each other. *What the fuck! Nice start, huh?* I thought to myself and discreetly sneaked in.

One of the girls saw me and asked, "May I help you?" with an attitude. I didn't know what to do, so I smiled at her and said that I was there to see Mr. Poch. Thank God, the other girl, who seemed a lot nicer, came to my rescue and made the rude girl leave. She smiled and apologized for the situation. Then, she announced my arrival through the intercom and made me comfortable in the conference room.

"Hey, Joseph! Nice to finally meet you in person!" Mr. Poch said, walking into the room.

"Nice meeting you, too, Mr. Poch! Please, call me Joe," I said, getting up and shaking his hand.

"Ok, Joe. I know you've got a lot to do still. Have you found a place to live yet?" he asked.

"Yes, I'm planning to move there today. I don't have a lot of things and rented a furnished flat by the beach," I said, telling him my plans.

"Yes, yes, take your time. There is no rush for you to start; you can take a few days to settle. All we need now is to get this paperwork signed and done."

"Thank you. I really appreciate it. I guess I would need just a couple of days," I said, signing the paperwork he had put in front of me.

"Well, I'm happy to have you onboard," he said, shaking my hand and patting my back.

"See you on Wednesday? Thursday? Which is a good day?"

"I guess Thursday morning, thank you," I said, shaking his hand.

"A couple of days will be enough."

He started walking me out, and halfway to the reception, his cell phone rang. He tapped my back, saying, "See you on Thursday, Joe. I have to answer this call."

I nodded and looked at Ann, the assistant, to say bye, but she was also on the phone, so I waved her goodbye and left.

#

I took the rest of the day to settle in my new home. I really enjoyed the flat, the view, and the location. The furniture was nice as well, but I still had to buy things for the kitchen, bathroom, bed, etc. So, I went shopping. It was difficult to choose from so many choices. Amy was the one buying everything we needed for our home. God, I missed her terribly. I had to stop thinking of Amy.

At around 6:00 PM, I went to the building's gym on the second floor. I headed straight to a treadmill close to the window with an ocean view. Only a few people were there exercising. Suddenly, this guy got on the treadmill by my side and started a conversation.

"My name is Jamal," he said, looking at me.

"Joe."

"You're new here, right?"

"Yep, just moved in."

"From where?"

"Chicago."

"Wow, cool. For a job?"

"Yeah."

"You're going to love it. Are you married, engaged, single?"

"Why do you want to know if I'm available?" I asked with a smirk on my face.

"No! No, I'm not hitting on you, man," he said, laughing, "I just wanted to know so we could hang out sometime. I'm single…and straight, and also kind of new in the area."

"Oh, ok! Yes, single and straight as well."

"We could go for a beer or something on the weekend."

"Sure," I said, "I would love that."

#

On Tuesday morning, I still had a lot to do in the flat and spent almost all-day organizing stuff; I kept moving things around until it felt right. It is so hard to organize a home! The kitchen was another nightmare. Of course, I had gone to the supermarket and bought a lot of goodies without thinking, so when I was ready to cook my lunch, I realized I had no salt, no olive oil, and no skillet! So, I had to go back to the supermarket.

Around 6:00 PM, I headed to the gym since I needed to get out of the flat, and I wanted to see if Jamal was there. He was.

"Hey, man," I said, getting on the treadmill next to him.

"Hey, Chicago man!" He smiled at me, still jogging.

"How was your day? Busy?"

"Not really. I work at this wealth management company, and as you know, the economy is not really in good shape. We've managed to keep our head above water, but it has been difficult. I hope it gets better soon. You? What do you do?"

"I'm a lawyer."

"Great! I may need your services," he said, chuckling.

"Anytime!" I replied with enthusiasm. "I have a question. I need to buy a car. Where should I go? Do you recommend any dealer?"

"Yes, actually, I have a wonderful friend who works at a car dealership. I can take you there if you like."

"Yes, please. Can we go tomorrow?"

"Sure. But it must be early in the morning because I've a lunch meeting with a client."

"Sounds good to me."

"Give me your number. I'll call you tomorrow morning when I'm ready to go."

"Sure, thanks."

Wednesday morning, Jamal called me at 8:00 AM so we could go return the rental car first and then go to his friend's dealership. The guy was already awaiting us with excitement.

"Nice meeting you, Joe. So, what do you have in mind?" He was ready to show me all the options.

Jamal was looking around and pointed to this brand-new black Mustang GT convertible. "Wow! I would love to have this baby," he said. "How much?"

"Well, that would depend on the final options…. Let's go for a test drive?"

"Yeah, definitely!" I said, agreeing with Jamal.

We went for the test drive, and I loved it. "I'll take it!" I said when we got back to the dealership. Jamal left for his meeting, and I stayed to complete the paperwork, which took forever. However, I was motorized and thrilled when I left the place around 1:00 PM. I couldn't resist driving my new toy around, so I drove all the way to Miami Beach for lunch. It was fantastic.

#

The afternoon was amazing. I drove up and down A1A by the beach when back from Miami Beach, feeling the nice sunny weather, stopping only to fill-up the car tank on my way north to Lauderdale-By-The-Sea for a beer. When taking US1, I saw that cute, grumpy girl from the office…what was her name? I think it's Jane. Yes, Jane.

I was feeling good, so I decided to give her a lift and invite her to join me for a drink; apparently, she was about to get on a bus.

"Jane! Hey, Jane!" I yelled. She looked around and made an annoyed face when she saw me. "C'mon, I'll give you a lift!" I yelled, waving at her. She resisted a bit but accepted my offer.

"How's it going?" she said when getting in the car.

"Fine. Your name is Jane, right? We met Monday at the law office."

"Yeah," she said with a not-so-polite attitude.

"What? I was just trying to be nice to you!"

"Whatever. You can keep driving north on Federal Hwy. I'll let you know when you need to turn."

"What? I'm not a taxi driver."

"I thought you said you're taking me home."

"Never said that." Returning her not-too-friendly manner.

"Uh-oh," she said, starting to look for something in her purse anxiously, which made me laugh.

"What are you doing? Looking for pepper spray?"

"Just want to call my mom! I call her every day when I get off work."

"Ahh…" I kept driving, waiting for her to finish the call so I could ask if she wanted to go for a drink or something, but she kept talking…and I kept driving.

After finally hanging up, she suddenly started talking nonstop, complaining about my driving. "Do you have to drive this fast? Where are you taking me, anyway? You didn't ask where I live!" She's cute, but I started to find her a little annoying.

"Yes, I drive fast. I don't know where you live, and I'm not taking you home."

"What? What do you mean you're not taking me home?" She looked at me as if I was about to kidnap her or something.

"You talk too much. I was going to invite you to this place. I'm hungry! Aren't you? Let's have something to eat fir—" and she interrupted me, not letting me finish my sentence.

"But I want to go home now."

"Well, I didn't say I would take you home right away. I offered you a lift since you were going in my direction." I tried again to be nice to her. "At least, let me buy you a drink, and I will take you home afterward."

"Thanks, but no thanks!" she said, irritated. "What made you think I was going in your direction? You don't even know me. Jerk!"

"Wow, I like you already!" I said, looking at her with indignation.

"Well, I don't!" and she crossed her arms and made a grumpy face.

I had to laugh at her angriness. I parked the car on the street in front of this Irish pub I'd heard about. She was still cranky, not looking at me, so I got out of the car and went around to open her door, saying, "Would you grant me the pleasure of your company? We won't take long, I promise…and I'll take you home afterward."

She got out of the car and started walking fast toward the street, waving to a passing taxi, which didn't stop. "ASSHOLE!" she yelled.

It was funny. I couldn't help but laugh.

"What?" she yelled at me, "I'm going home! Bye!"

"Ok, you know where to find me in case you change your mind. Bye." I left; she was just too much.

About fifteen minutes later, there she comes as if nothing happened.

"Hey, you finally came in, huh?" I said with an ironic smirk.

"Yeah. I came to claim my drink," the little brat said.

"Please have a seat. What do you want? Do you drink beer?"

"No, I'd rather drink wine. A glass of Merlot, please." She ordered from the bartender.

I tried to have a civilized conversation, but she was in a terrible mood. To be honest, I have no patience with girls like this. They're exhausting, even if pretty. They're just not worth it. I lost my appetite.

After we finished our drinks, I was ready to go home. When we got to the car, I politely opened the door for her and went around to the driver's side. She had left her cell phone in the car, and that was the reason she had joined me in the pub…as if I cared.

"Are you coming?" I asked for the last time.

"No!" she said and slammed the door of my brand-new car.

"Goddamnit!"

Chapter 56

The next day, Thursday, was my first day in the office, and I wanted to be there early.

"Hi, how are you?" I said to Ann, the nice girl at the reception, when arriving in the office.

"I'm fine, you? Are you here to see Mr. Poch again?" she said, smiling.

"Yes, can you let him know I'm here?"

"Sure!" she said, getting the intercom. "Mr. Poch, Mr. Garrison is here."

"Yes, yes, tell him to come to my office, Ms. Martinez," the voice on the intercom said.

"You heard the man. Please go in, Mr. Garrison. You know where his office is, right?"

"Yes, I do, Ms. Martinez." I went in to meet with my boss happily.

"Joe! Welcome, welcome!" Mr. Poch said, shaking my hand, smiling, and talking loudly.

"Thank you!" I said, shaking his hand.

"Let me show you around." We started to walk in the hallway. "This is your office," he said, opening the door of my new office. "Do you like it?"

"Yes, it's really nice."

"And here is John's office," he said, knocking on Mr. McKee's office door and entering. "John, today is Joe's first day. I'm showing him the office. Let's sit down in the afternoon to talk about work?"

"Hi, Joe, welcome aboard!" Mr. McKee said, getting up and shaking my hand, "Yes, we have a lot to talk about. Have you met the girls yet?" he said, walking to the reception.

"Ladies, this is Mr. Joe Garrison! He's the new associate," Mr. McKee said, introducing me to Ann and Jane, the grumpy girl.

"Nice meeting you!" I said, shaking Jane's hand with a sneering smile. She was surprised to see me.

"Nice meeting you too, Mr. Garrison," she said awkwardly.

"Nice seeing you again, Mr. Garrison," Ann said, smiling as always.

"Well, which one of you will grab me a coffee?" Mr. McKee asked the girls. Mr. Poch and I walked back to the office.

"I think you'll find everything you need in your office. We were eager to have a new associate. We've got a lot of work, Joe. Those files on your desk are the cases that we want you to handle. Please take a look, and let's discuss how to proceed at our afternoon meeting. The girls, both of them, are here to help you, so don't hesitate to ask them if you need anything."

"Thank you, Mr. Poch," I said, getting to my desk and checking the files out. There were quite a few, but I was not complaining. All I wanted was to get myself busy and not have time to think about Amy.

"Well, I'll leave you alone for now so you can check everything out to see if you need anything else. Let's talk in the afternoon. Please read the case files, or at least a couple, so we can start strategizing how to proceed in our meeting this afternoon, ok? Come see me if you have questions, and please call me Larry."

"Will do, thank you," I said, sitting down on my new executive chair. Once he left the room, I took some time to appreciate my new office. Neat! I can definitely get used to this new life. I turned on the computer and started to read the cases, making notes. I wanted to impress my bosses from the beginning.

#

It was already 6:00 PM when I left. I was the last one to leave the office. I went straight home, took a nice shower, put some music on (opera, of course), and headed to the kitchen. I must confess that I'm a terrible cook; I needed to get a few recipe books. However, I was tempted to try without following a recipe. How difficult could it be? I looked inside the refrigerator to see what I had to work with. "Let me see…" I grabbed a few things: chicken, bacon, tomatoes, and basil.

Together, the ingredients looked colorful and yummy, so I decided to create something new. All I had to do was add together things I like, right? Wrong! Whatever I had just cooked was inedible and went straight to the garbage after the first bite.

Got dressed again and went out to grab a bite and walk around Las Olas Beach. After eating a delicious meal, I went for a walk on the beach but didn't go far since it was already dark. Back in the building, I ran into Jamal and this other guy getting into the lift.

"Hey, Chicago! This is Brian, my friend. He also lives in the building," Jamal said, introducing me to his friend.

"Hey, man, how are you?" Brian said, shaking my hand.

"Joe. Nice meeting you."

"So, how's the new car? We need to go for a ride, man. We can go to the Keys if you like," Jamal said, smiling. This guy just bought a brand-new Mustang GT convertible!" he told Brian.

"Wow, nice!" Brian agreed.

"We can go to the Keys if you want, Jamal. I was planning to go there. A friend of mine said that it's beautiful." I was getting excited about having a weekend plan.

"Really cool, I'm in." Jamal said, "How's the new job?"

"So far so good, can't complain."

"Ok, see ya," he said, getting out of the lift to his floor.

"Bye, Jamal, see you tomorrow. Nice guy," I said to Brian, trying to make a new friend.

"Yes, he's very nice. So, you just moved in from Chicago?" Brian started a conversation.

"Yep, my first week here, and I'm loving it!"

"Yeah, man, it's paradise. Let's hang out sometime."

"Sure. See you around!" It was my turn to get out of the lift.

I went home and felt depressed walking into an empty place, nice but lifeless. I think I need a pet or a pet plant to keep me company— or maybe a new girlfriend. Yeah, a new girlfriend would be nice, someone to talk with, care for, and worry about. I miss Amy. God, I miss her so much. I needed to find a way to forget her. I tossed around in bed all night thinking about Amy, our house, our friends, her smile—I needed to move on.

You can miss someone who died, but nothing will bring them back. I feel the same way about Amy. No matter what happens next, we'll never be the same. She's dead to me. She betrayed me, and I can never forgive her for that. My only way out is to find a new love and new friends, and I'm determined to do just that. It's just a matter of time.

CHAPTER 57

Finally, it was Friday. I stopped by the coffee place across the street from the office to grab a coffee and a bagel before starting my day. Once in line to order, I realized that Jane, the little brat, was just in front of me. *Lucky me!* I thought to myself. I actually thought about leaving before she had the chance to see me, but I decided that we needed to be friends. After all, we work together.

"Hey!" I said to get her attention.

She turned around and, of course, made an annoyed face when she saw me. "What do you want from me?" she said, rolling her eyes.

"I want peace! We can be friends. We *have* to be friends!" I said, smiling, trying to change the unpleasant atmosphere between us.

"Why didn't you say we're going to be working together that night? I don't get it." she started talking nonstop.

"I was going to, but you got so stressed out—"

She cut me off again to add, "Just please…don't tell anyone about that night, ok?"

"Ok! I wasn't planning to open my mouth, anyway." There was no point in arguing with her.

"Good! I feel a lot better now. You don't seem too awful to me now." She made a cute face, to make peace with me, I guess.

"You never seemed awful to me…just cute. Friends?" I smiled back to be polite.

"Friends!" she said, smiling and ordering her coffee.

We walked to the office together, and she was telling me all about the night before, saying that they (Ann and her) went to this hip-hop nightclub and that they went home very late; she slept over at Ann's house, and today she woke up very early since Ann's couch is very uncomfortable, went home, took a shower, and stopped to grab a coffee.

Gosh, she never stops talking. She is beautiful, though.

#

The day went by quickly. I kept myself busy trying to get every detail about my assigned cases. We had a very constructive meeting in the afternoon, and I was feeling confident and great about myself. It seemed that I would get through this phase and be happy again, at least professionally. After work, I stopped to get some groceries. I had researched some easy recipes online and was determined to cook my meals, at least dinner. I got all the ingredients and a nice bottle of wine to pair with the delicious fettuccine alfredo with chicken and broccoli, which seemed yummy and pretty easy to make.

Before cooking, it was time to go to the gym and exercise a little. Jamal, my Fort Lauderdale best friend, was already there and smiled when he saw me.

"What's up, Joe?"

"Hey, man. How are you?"

"Not bad. Let's go out for drinks tonight?"

"Yeah, I can drive us…"

"Sure, I want to go in your new Mustang, man. We can drive around a bit with the roof down…to show off and impress the girls, right?" We both laughed.

I went home and cooked my meal, which was very good, by the way. I guess cooking is not that hard if you follow instructions. Then, a nice shower and off to Riverside we went. The Riverside area was packed with people everywhere. I guess that's how life by the beach is. The weather was wonderful, beautiful people all over, and the girls were very sexy and pretty. This place differs totally from every city I've lived in before; I can definitely get used to it.

#

Saturday at 8:00 AM, my phone rang. It was Jamal, ready to go to Key West as we'd planned the night before. "Oh, man, can I sleep five more minutes?" I begged him.

"No, if you want to go, we need to hit the road. If we leave now, we'll be there by lunchtime. Let's go, man!"

"Ok, give me fifteen minutes." I jumped out of my bed, took a cold shower to wake up, got dressed, and left.

The trip was delightful, and the highway beautiful. We crossed the seven-mile bridge, an endless bridge over the crystal-clear blue ocean. We passed through several islands until getting to the last one, Key West. Once parked, we walked around until deciding where we wanted to have lunch. We chose this very nice small restaurant that was packed. One thing I've learned in life is that if the restaurant is busy, the food is good. Never enter an empty restaurant, trust me. We got a table, and the waitress came to take our order. She was cute and had a wonderful smile.

"What can I get you guys?" she asked without looking at us.

"Hey, Monica…" Jamal said, reading the name tag on her shirt, "Can I ask you a question?"

"Sure." She looked at him.

"Are you single?"

"No. Sorry," she said with a bigger but shy smile on her face.

"Of course not. A gorgeous girl like you would never be alone. Today isn't my lucky day," Jamal said, staring at her face, embarrassing her. She shyly averted his gaze but was still smiling.

"Sorry, I didn't want to embarrass you. I'll have the fish and chips with a nice cold beer," he finally said.

"Sounds good to me. Make that two, please." I added, and off she went.

"Hey, man, how can you get away with hitting on girls like that? You're very aggressive. Does being aggressive and direct work for you?" I was curious about his flirting strategies since I was available and eager to get involved with someone.

"Yeah, man, you have to let them know you're interested since the beginning. You snooze, you lose. Get it?"

"Hm, I usually go slower; get to know them first. Beauty isn't the only characteristic I look for when flirting with someone."

"What do you want to know? If she's rich?" He laughed at me.

"Well, I like smart girls."

"Gosh. Smart girls are usually trouble, and if they're pretty, even worse. Double trouble!"

"Yeah, I guess they're more difficult to entertain, but they're more exciting, too."

"You say tomato, I say tomato. How long have you been single?"

"Not long, I have just broken up with my girlfriend of two years. Actually, that's why I moved to Florida. I wanted to get away from everything that reminded me of her."

"Oh, man. Sorry to hear that."

"Well, I must move on, right? I'm looking forward to getting myself a nice girlfriend."

"Well, if you have to get to know them first before making a move, I can say that it'll take you some time around here. Is your ex white?"

"Yeah, redhead, with big blue eyes and lots of freckles…"

"You know, I'm a black man and love black women. They're just straight to the point; they never mess around. If they like you, they let you know. If they don't, oh man, they're not wasting their time. Believe me, I don't discriminate against women. If they're pretty, they can be any color and nationality. Anyway, there's something about white girls; they're never sure of what they want."

"How's that?"

"If you ask them if they like this or that, they'll say: 'I don't know.' Do you like me? 'I don't know,'" he said, making faces imitating a white girl talking.

"You may have a point. Many girls may seem insecure, but I think it's just part of their charm. And I had a black girlfriend in England. She was neither assertive nor self-confident, but I guess English girls differ from American."

"Yeah, I agree. It's a cultural thing. American girls are demons, no matter the color!" We laughed. "You should start playing this game. Have you heard of the *Do What I Say* game?"

"No."

"Here's the thing, only two players, you and someone who you have a sexual attraction to. No one else can get involved or know about the affair."

"Hmm…interesting."

"The players choose what they want the other to do. You could go crazy if you wanted. But no falling in love, those are the rules. So, two people only, can't say no, and can't fall for each other. If any of the rules are broken, the game is over."

"Do you play this game?"

"Yeah, it works very well, especially if you aren't sure about getting really involved with that person. The game gives you the chance to get to know her a little better before committing. If the girl is a pain, just break a rule, and that's it. If she's interested, the relationship can go to the next level. It's a win-win situation, and you get laid!"

"I like that. I think I'm going to try."

Chapter 58

Monday was a busy day. We had a lot to do preparing for court day. I got my first case to defend in court, and I was determined to win. We met with the client to explain the strategy and make sure I knew every single detail. The case was a property line dispute, not really a complicated case, but I wanted to impress my bosses.

We left the office around 5:15 PM, still discussing the case. When we got to the lift, I realized I had forgotten the case file with the documents I wanted to take home to study on my desk, so I had to go back to my office to get it. Jane was still there, working and talking to herself. I heard her saying "Whatever" when entering the reception.

"Whatever?" I said with a smirk on my face.

"Oh! It's you!" she said, surprised.

"Sorry if I scared you. I left an important file on my desk," I said, rushing in to get it.

When I came back to the reception, I sensed she was nervous about being alone with me in the office, which was very stimulating to me. She can be annoying, but she's very beautiful and sexy. Could we, maybe, play that game Jamal told me about?

Maybe. I needed to get to know her a little better. So, I decided to tease her to see what she would do. I sat down on Ann's chair and started casually going through her stuff, opening her drawers and checking what was inside. "Mmm, chocolate!" I said when I found some chocolate in her drawer, helping myself with a couple.

"Yummy!"

"You can't do that!" Jane said, astonished to my delight.

"That what?" I asked with my mouth full of chocolate and shoving another piece into it.

"That!" she said, pointing to my mouth, drawers, and Ann's chair that I was sitting on.

"Why?" I asked, enjoying her uneasiness.

"Because it's not yours! I don't think Ann would appreciate your behavior. It's not polite. I don't go through people's stuff!"

"Do you know if she goes through yours?"

"Of course, she doesn't!"

"If you say so…" I said, turning Ann's computer on, enjoying the way things were going.

"Would you stop that?" she said, getting up to turn the computer off. "Why don't you go home? I still have lots to do!" she said, almost slapping me.

I could not stop laughing. She was very annoyed, and I was getting more interested in her. I leaned back, letting her shut the computer down, reorganize, and close the drawers. She was so close to me I could smell her perfume.

"What?" She turned around to look at me with her big blue eyes inches from my face. Her silky, long, golden-brown hair was loose, covering half of her beautiful face, and her mouth, small and sexy.

"I like you! And I'm not leaving you here alone. I'll walk you to your car," was all I managed to say, wanting to kiss her right there.

"No thanks, you can go. I'm fine," she said, going back to her desk.

"No, I'd rather wait for you. I don't trust you. What if you decide to go through my stuff?"

"You're sick!" she said, going back to work. I sat up on the chair, rolled it back to the desk, and turned Ann's computer on again. I could feel her fiery gaze toward me, and I smiled victoriously. It was getting fun.

"I'm done! Let's go then!" she finally said, turning her computer off and grabbing her things.

"Let's go!" I said, turning Ann's computer off.

We were quiet all the way to the parking garage. I could feel that she was nervous and uncomfortable with the situation. Her body language told me she liked me. Suddenly, she met my gaze and looked away instantly, embarrassed. I could see her blushing; she was cute and interesting. Yes, she had a bad temperament, but this made her unique and challenging. I guess I can handle her mood swings. *Would she play that couples' game with me? Should I try?* I wasn't sure if it was a good idea since we work together, but it could be fun for both of us. So, I decided to go slowly, which is my way of approaching girls, anyway. I'll kiss her and see how she responds. If everything goes well, I'll invite her out. Let us take one step at a time.

When the lift door opened at the garage level on which her car was parked, she rushed out and started walking fast, almost running in front of me, not looking back. Once by her car, she was nervously trying to open the car's door; I thought she was adorable. Then, I approached and gently trapped her between the car and my body. Her hair smelled wonderful.

"What are you in the hurry for?" I said, whispering in her ear.

She turned around, and I could see that she was apprehensive, so I stepped back to give her room to leave if she wanted or to stay and welcome my advances. She stayed, and I kissed her.

I went home feeling good. Jane is gorgeous, and she turns me on big time. I definitely wanted to give us a shot. I decided to treat her very well, making it impossible for her to have another mood swing attack when with me. I'll propose the game to her.

#

The next day in the office, she diverted her gaze shyly every time our eyes met. Her uneasiness excited me. I decided to surprise her by sending flowers to be delivered to the office with no sender's card, eager to see her reaction.

"Flowers!" I said when arriving from a late business lunch with my boss and seeing that she had received the flowers.

"Who sent you these beautiful flowers?" Larry asked.

"I have no idea, sir! There is no card," she replied with an ear-to-ear smile on her face.

"Maybe there isn't any card because the person who sent it knew you would know who they were from," I said, winking at her.

She blushed, and I knew she realized I was the sender.

"It makes sense," Ann said. "But I don't think she has a clue." We all laughed.

Chapter 59

When leaving for the day on Friday, I realized that Jane's car was parked close to mine in the parking garage. Excitement took over me. This could be a good opportunity to invite her out. Looking around, I saw her coming toward her car, not noticing my presence.

"Hey," I surprised her when she opened the car door.

"Hey," she replied, turning around to face me.

"Did you like the flowers?"

"I loved them. Thank you."

"Do you want to go for a drink or something?"

"Yeah. I guess," she replied.

I got in her car on the driver's side, and she went around and got in on the passenger side.

"Ok, let's go then!" she said, excited.

"Key?" I said, opening my hand, requiring the car key. She amazes me.

"Oh! Here." She laughed aloud and nervously handed me the key, embarrassed for being goofy. She's cute.

We went to this nightclub in South Beach; it was crowded and chaotic, with people everywhere and loud music playing. It was an awful choice; we were not having fun. Jamal had told me that the place was cool and played all kinds of music, but it was not to my taste, so we left and started walking on Ocean Drive.

"Too loud, wasn't it?" I asked her.

"I don't know, I guess. It's still early. Do we have to go home?" She was kind of frustrated for having to go home so early.

"Where do you want to go?"

"I don't know."

I held her hand and pulled her through the crowded street. I needed to find a nice place to take her. We walked two streets down on Washington Ave, and then, a couple of blocks to Espanola Way. We came across this place which seemed to be a lot more tranquil, romantic, and nice. The small restaurant with candlelit tables and smooth live jazz playing was more my style kind of place.

"Are you hungry?" I asked her while the host welcomed us.

"I don't know; a little, I guess!" she said shyly while the host directed us to our table.

Once we ordered and were finally given a chance to hear each other, I reminded her of our first encounters. She was uncomfortable but had a friendly attitude for a change. The food and wine arrived. We were still talking about how she slammed my brand-new car's door. "Goddamnit, girl!" She giggled, relaxed and happy, amazed at my recollection of events. *God, she's so beautiful when she relaxes and smiles that I forget how annoying she can be.* I just wanted to kiss her again. I guess I was ready to take the next step.

The couple at the next table got up and started slow dancing. I made a gesture with my hand, inviting her to dance. She promptly got up, I embraced her, and we started to dance. She smelled so good, her hair and skin silky and smooth.

"I think we can have a great time together," I finally said, looking into her beautiful blue eyes.

"I think so, too."

"You're very funny, sexy, and…moody."

"You're embarrassing me," she said, turning her face away timidly.

"Look at me; I was thinking about this game I heard about."

"A game?" she looked back at me curiously.

"Yeah, a game. I think you and I could have a lot of fun together; you turn me on big time. We could play if you want to."

"What is it called?"

"Do What I Say."

"What?"

"It's the name of the game."

"Ahhh."

"Let me explain it to you. It's a couples' game with only two players and nobody else. It's supposed to be very sexy and exciting, and there are only three rules in this game. First, we can't ever say no to each other, and you have to do everything and anything I ask you to and vice versa."

"It could be fun, but I don't know if I would want to do everything you ask me to."

"Well, I could say the same about you, but let me finish explaining. It's ok if you don't want to play."

"Ok."

"So, as I was saying, the second rule is, we can't involve other people in the game with us or even use a third person. It's a two-person game, remember? We can't tell anyone because that would involve another person."

"I see. Keep going." She showed curiosity to know more about the game, which made me more excited about playing with her.

"And third, we can't fall for each other, as that would spoil the entire game."

"How are we supposed not to get involved with each other? I think that will be the hard part."

"I have to disagree with you. The hard part is doing what the other asks you to do. Anyway, these are the rules."

"Ahh. What would you ask me to do?"

"Hmm. Let me see. I could think of a few things."

"Like what?" She had this sensual look on her face that made me shudder.

"Hmm! If you play with me, I'll think of something. Do you want to play?" I was ready to kiss her.

"I do, I do!"

"Seriously, now, if one of us breaks one single rule, it's over. Everything will be over. Just like that."

"That's harsh."

"That's what makes the game interesting and exciting."

"I don't know..."

"Just say yes. Please?" I pulled her tight and looked deep in her eyes, almost begging her to say yes.

"Yes, yes, yes!" she finally said gaily.

On our way back to Fort Lauderdale, we were making plans to play the game. She had a lot of questions, and her interest encouraged me. I had to hold myself together to not take her straight to my place and make love to her.

"It's not that I'm going to ask you to take your clothes off in the middle of the street or something like that, as you can't involve other people or make them aware of us or have to give explanations. Let me see...a good start for you is going home and think about your craziest fantasies—the dark and sordid ones. You know, the ones that make you ashamed just to think of." She blushed, making me laugh at her reaction.

"Wow. I think I can't share my darkest fantasies with you. I mean, yet. Maybe later when we get to know each other better and I feel comfortable talking to you about them."

"Ooh. I was so curious to know what excites you…. Maybe you can start with something lighter, to begin with…. But you liked the idea, didn't you?" I teased her.

"Jerk!"

At the parking garage, I kissed her good night and left content. I was making progress. I went home, smiling to myself and feeling happy. Jane is beautiful. I can't wait to play the game with her and have her in my arms. I'll gladly fulfill her fantasies.

Chapter 60

The weekend went well. I was relaxed and happy. Saturday morning, I ran into Brian, Jamal's friend, in the lobby. We chatted for a while, and he invited me for a jog on the beach the next morning.

"Sure, I would love that. Where are we meeting?" I was happy with the invitation.

"We like to run at Hollywood Beach. There's a nice oceanfront boardwalk."

"Count me in. What time?"

"We usually go early before it gets too hot, around 8:00 AM."

"Ok, see you guys there."

I went home, and for the first time in a while, I could relax and not feel miserable about missing Amy. I put some opera music on and decided to cook for myself, so I made stroganoff. It was good, not awesome, but edible. In the afternoon, I went to get some plants to keep me company since the house seemed so empty, cold, and lifeless. It needed something alive for me to take care of. I went to this nursery close by. I knew they had a good indoor plant selection and ended up getting a few more plants than I was planning to. I was feeling blissful anyway.

#

The next morning, I woke up early, feeling energetic and happy, changed into my new running outfit, and drove all the way to Hollywood Beach. Once at the agreed location, at the agreed time, I felt a little uneasy since Brian was not there. The boardwalk was empty, and there were just a few people around. While waiting for him, I was warming my muscles up, getting ready for the jog. Time passed by. It was already 9:00 AM, and Brian was a no-show. So, I decided not to wait for him any longer and started walking on the beach. The day was gorgeous, and I was too happy to be upset about being stood up.

Not long after, I ran into Ann, the nice girl from the office. What a coincidence.

"Hey, Ann?" I called, rushing my steps to reach her.

"Yes. Oh, hi, Mr. Garrison!" she said, stopping to look at me.

"Joe, call me Joe, please. Do you come here often?" I said, a little breathless, reaching her.

"Not really. I came today because it's usually empty. I brought my dog to run free a bit."

"That's your dog?" I pointed to the dog running around.

"Yes, Max."

"What a beautiful dog."

"Thanks, and do you always come here at this time?"

"Not really. I was supposed to meet someone to run with, but he was a no-show."

"So, what a coincidence! I usually take Max to Dania Beach, but today, I felt like changing locations."

"Yep, a good coincidence, I hope!" I said, smiling. "Can I walk with you and Max?"

"Sure!"

We walked down the beach. She was very pleasant, and I wanted to know more about her.

"So, Ms. Martinez, are you from here originally? Where the

Martinez come from? I know it's a Hispanic name, but I've no idea of which country…"

"Ann, call me Ann, please," she mocked me. "I'm Cuban-American. I'm a second-generation born in America. My grandparents, from both sides, came to America fleeing the Castro Regime in 1960."

"Oh, wow. You know, I learned in school all about the Cold War and the Cuban military coup, but it always seemed to be so far away from my reality. I never imagined meeting someone who had experienced this part of history firsthand."

"I was born and raised in Miami; a lot of Cubans live there; I'm just another one. What about you? You're from England, right? What brought you to America?"

"Yeah, I'm from London, born and raised." It was my turn to mock her. "I came to America to study. I went to Princeton in New Jersey. My father is also a lawyer, but I didn't want to make a career working for him, so I took the opportunity to come to the US to study. When I graduated, I got an internship at this law office in Chicago, which is a beautiful city, but I've always heard how wonderful Florida was, so I applied for the job I've now, and here I am!"

"Very interesting! So, you don't know the area very well."

"Nope, I would really appreciate it if you could show me Miami. Maybe a tour around your favorite places? But, no pressure; only if you can, of course."

"It'll be my pleasure!" she said, smiling.

We walked together, talking. It was a pleasant morning. Ann is way more mature than Jane, and it seemed to me that she is a down-to-earth kind of person—totally opposite from Jane. I think we could be good friends, nothing more. Jane is way more exciting and more of my type, not that Ann isn't pretty; she is. However, she doesn't stand out and there's some sort of sadness in her personality that kind of turns me off. Jane, on the other hand, is spicy, temperamental, angry, unpredictable, beautiful, and really, really sexy. I was determined to pursue Jane. Play the game with her to see where it'll take us. I just couldn't wait to start.

#

Monday morning, Jane had this spicy look in her eyes. I knew she was up to something, and excitement took over me just thinking about it. *What did she have in mind?* I couldn't wait to start playing for real. In the afternoon, I went to the lunchroom to get a water bottle and saw this brown bag with *Joe* written on it in the refrigerator. It wasn't mine, but it was definitely for me. I peeked inside, and it had a Hawaiian lei, pineapples, and a flier for this luau event. *Oh, Jane, you're incredible!*

The luau was on Thursday night in Dania Beach. I knew the location and was keen to meet her. Trapped in a meeting with my boss and a client until 7:30 PM, I managed to get there as soon as I could. After going home to eat something quick and change clothes.

At the location, it was easy to spot her dancing with a group of people. She seemed a little intoxicated but happy and beautiful in this Hawaiian outfit, with a hibiscus flower in her hair. I sat by the bonfire and watched her having fun, not aware of my presence. After a while, she saw me and flashed a huge smile but kept dancing while looking at me. Suddenly, she started walking north toward the ocean, not calling or even making eye contact. *So irresistible!* I got up and followed her. She dove into the ocean, compelling me to follow her in.

"Aren't you afraid to swim at night…in the ocean…alone?" I whispered in her ear, grabbing her waist from behind once she surfaced.

"You really think I'm your catch, huh?" she said, turning her face around to look at me.

"Pretty much!" I answered.

"Actually, YOU are my catch. I'm a mermaid that seduces men into the ocean, and then I eat them," she said, jumping up into my arms, her arms around my neck and legs around my waist.

"I'm scared…" I said, laughing, holding her tight and kissing her, wishing to have her right there. But I'm a gentleman, and since she was a little tipsy, waiting for the right time was the right thing to do. She must be sober and able to remember our first time for the rest of her life. I was already falling for her.

CHAPTER 61

Saturday afternoon, Jamal and I went to South Beach for a beer. I knew I wasn't supposed to tell anyone about the game, but I had to talk to someone. I told him about Jane and our first encounter playing the game. He was excited for me and wanted to know more details. The only thing I said was that it was really fun and that we were having a good time together. I thanked him for the game idea. My phone rang. It was Bill from Chicago.

"Hey, man, how's everything?" I said, answering the call.

"Not bad, man. You? How's your new life going?"

"Great, I'm great. What's up?"

"Well, I'm calling to remind you that my wedding is in two weeks, and you're my best man. I hope you haven't forgotten."

"Of course not. Wow, two weeks. I need to get everything arranged."

"You better! Be here at least two days earlier since we'll have the wedding rehearsal on Monday evening, and you have to be there."

"Of course, I'll be there. Love you, man. Bye."

My heart sank after we hung up. Amy is going to be there, too. She is Suzy's maid of honor, and we both will have to enter the church together.

"Are you ok, man?" Jamal brought me back to reality.

"Yeah, I need to go to Chicago for my best friend's wedding, and

Amy, my ex, will be there, too. I was just thinking that it would be hard for me to see her again. I don't know if I'm ready yet."

"Well, at least you have someone else now. Why don't you take Jane with you?"

"No, I can't do that."

#

The week passed by slowly. I was anxious and reluctant to go to Chicago, but I couldn't disappoint my best friend. I would have to endure and face the situation. The whole week, I was distant and feeling down. I couldn't think of a way out and definitely could not take Jane with me; that would be dreadful. I thought about calling Amy to check on her and see if she was anxious about seeing me, too, but I dropped the urge. She hadn't called or texted me since I left, so why should I bother? But at the same time, I was really into Jane and wanted to be with her before going to Chicago. I thought everything would be a lot easier for me if I had Jane on my mind when facing Amy at the wedding.

I had a plan. I would go to Chicago on Friday, see my friends, and have a good time. Saturday, I would fly to New York to meet with Jane, and this would be my first game move. We'll have a wonderful weekend together, and on Sunday, she'll come back to Fort Lauderdale, and I'll head to Chicago to face Amy and endure the wedding circus. I felt relieved.

#

"Hello, ladies!" I said, entering the office on Thursday morning.

"Hi, Mr. Garrison. What can I do for you?" Ann asked with a huge smile on her face, as always.

"First of all, drop the Mr. Garrison stuff. It makes me look older, and you don't need to be formal with me in the office. Anyway, could you get me a ticket to Chicago for tomorrow? Ah, I'll need a hotel room, too."

"Chicago, tomorrow? Sure, I'll try my best, Mr. —oh—Joe."

"Thanks, Ann. I'll stay a week if not much trouble. Could you set up my return for the following Friday?"

"A week? I mean, you'll be gone for an entire week?" she said, changing her facial expression, the smile was suddenly gone. I guess she was a little disappointed knowing I was going to be out for a week. Her reaction made me realize that she may have a crush on me. It felt good.

"I'll be back!" I teased her, leaving the reception area and not looking at Jane. Jane looked distraught, I could tell, but that was the plan. The trip was meant to be a surprise. I had bought an airplane ticket for her to meet me in New York on Saturday. The flight purchase confirmation and instructions were delivered to her house. I couldn't wait to spend the whole weekend with her.

#

Friday came, and to Chicago, I went. Feeling nervous in the hotel room, I called Bill to check where we were going to meet that evening. I couldn't stop thinking about Amy. *What could I say to her to sound normal and not a complete idiot?* I had a couple of drinks at the hotel bar since I needed to relax before calling a taxi to go meet them.

"Hey, everyone!" I said, arriving at the restaurant and greeting everybody.

"Hey, Joe!" Bill got up and came to greet me with a tight hug and a pat on my back. He was already a little sipped. I can't judge him. I would do the same in his situation.

"Hi, Joe!" everyone else said, including Amy. She was also nervous about seeing me, I could tell. I know her very well; she usually plays with her hair when in a situation that makes her nervous. She looked at me shyly, smiling, playing with her beautiful red hair, looking adorable as always.

I sat far away from her. I didn't want to give myself a chance to have a relapse and beg her to take me back. The night was smooth. It was great seeing my friends.

Back in the hotel, I was feeling good and proud of myself for my good behavior. Tomorrow would be a new day, and everything would be wonderful with Jane at my side.

#

I got to New York early, checked in at the hotel, took a nice shower, and went back to the airport to find Jane. She was arriving on the 11:00 AM flight.

"Hey!" I said when I found her walking around, looking for me in the LaGuardia Airport.

"Hey." She smiled, looking at me.

"How was your flight?" I said, hugging her and grabbing her bag.

"Fine."

"Are you hungry?" I asked, and we started walking toward the exit to take a taxi.

"I don't know. But if you are…I mean, I could eat something."

"Did you eat anything on the plane?"

"No! I had a drink—actually two," she said delightfully.

"I can tell," I said, chuckling and then kissing her.

We went to the hotel, dropped her bag in the room, and out we went to grab a bite. I was hungry and wanted her to relax and feel comfortable with me. We walked around Park Avenue and had lunch at this Italian restaurant. The food was delicious, and after two more glasses of wine, Jane was herself again, being goofy and spontaneous. We went back to the hotel and had a wonderful time together. It was amazing. We spent all afternoon making love and having a good time.

"Are you getting up?" I asked her, sitting on the bed and putting my shoes on after taking a shower. It was already getting late.

"Do I have to? I don't think I can…" she trailed off, lifting her body a bit and falling back onto the bed. She was being silly.

"C'mon! It wasn't that bad." I teased her.

"Bad? I'm in heaven!" She pulled me on the bed with her and started kissing me.

"Wow. We have plenty of time for that and more of that later," I said, kissing her back, "but now, I'm starving, aren't you?" I held her down so she couldn't kiss me anymore.

"No, I want more of that now," she said, whispering and trying to kiss me.

"You'll regret that, my dear," I said, laughing aloud, and finishing getting dressed.

"Never. I'll never regret that or anything I would ever do with you, my dear." We both laughed.

We went to this little restaurant on Madison Ave., which was nice and romantic.

"Are we still playing the game?" she suddenly asked.

"Sure," I said. "Why are you asking?"

"I don't know, I just got the feeling that we're being us, with no, you know, crazy fantasies?"

"Don't worry. We'll get there. Just let it be." I was feeling confident that we were going to have a great time together, and she might be the one to make me forget Amy. On Sunday, we had a lovely day. We went to the Metropolitan Museum and had another pleasant afternoon, making love and getting to know each other before heading to the airport.

"Are you going to miss me?" I asked her while waiting to check her in.

"I'm already missing you. Do you have to stay all week long in

Chicago? Can I go with you? Pleeease."

"I wish I could take you with me." I kissed her tenderly and saw her getting through the security gate and disappearing. She went back to Fort Lauderdale, and I went back to Chicago.

Chapter 62

On Monday, at the wedding rehearsal, I was feeling good and more relaxed. Amy was happy as well and looked beautiful as always. Rick, the bride's brother, was timing the whole thing. We had a certain time to walk down the aisle and get put at our assigned locations on the altar.

First, five little girls would run in, tossing rose petals on their way to the altar, then Amy and I would stroll down the aisle in the music's rhythm, and finally, Suzy, the bride, would walk in with her father. The groom and the other parents were to be already at the altar. After the ceremony, the bride and groom would walk off the altar first, followed by his parents, then her parents, and lastly, Amy and I, the best man and the maid of honor. We were supposed to stay aligned outside the church to greet the guests, and only after greeting everyone we could head to the reception.

"I guess we're good," Rick said after we repeated the whole process three times.

"Yes, I'm happy with the rehearsal," Suzy said, giving us a thumbs up. "Let's go have dinner, everybody!"

We went to this bar/restaurant that we used to go to all the time. I had a déjà vu moment, remembering the best time of my life with my friends and Amy on my side. I almost felt like crying but stayed strong. Amy was sitting at Suzy's side, talking enthusiastically, laughing, and having fun.

After a few drinks, I was feeling stupid and awkward. My reality had changed. I was living a different life now with Jane—my beautiful Jane. *Who needs Amy?* I thought to myself, staring at Amy. She looked so beautiful, as always. I loved the freckles on her gorgeous face, her mouth, and her perfect teeth. I could smell her perfume and feel her warm body on my skin. She met my gaze and smiled at me. *She still loves me, and I still love her.*

Without thinking twice, I got up, went to the stage, asked the band singer's permission, and grabbed the microphone. "Here I go. For you, Amy," I said and started singing our favorite song to her.

Amy got emotional, and tears ran down her face. She got up and came to me. I hugged her tightly.

"I love you. I love you so much," I whispered in her ear.

"I love you, too," she said, looking into my eyes now.

I kissed her. I couldn't let her go. I needed her embrace. I needed her love.

Everyone clapped. Suzy and Bill were crying, too. They always wanted to see us getting married as well. The four of us were the best friends ever, and we belonged together. We should be neighbors and raise our kids together as families do. I need to be with them forever; I need Amy. I belong here. I belong with Amy.

Amy and I went to my hotel room. I was craving her love. God, I missed her so much. She was thirsty for me as well. We couldn't stop. We were so much in love; we always had been. I decided not to ask about Iraq. I knew she hadn't changed her mind, and I didn't want to spoil my happiness. I just wanted to be with her and enjoy our time together without fighting.

The next morning, when I woke up, she was sitting on the bed's edge, looking at me.

"Good morning, love," she said.

"Good morning!"

"Listen, I know the pain I've caused you, and I'm very, very sorry. I wish you could understand and be with me for good or for bad. I understand your concerns, and I love you even more for that, but I need to go. I need to fulfill my dream and know that I'm making a difference in the world. Please, let's enjoy each other's company without fighting, ok? I can't fight you. I need you to love me. I need to have you on my mind while I'm there, and I need to have someone to come back to. Please love me without judging me. I'll be back to you, and we'll get married and live happily ever after."

"I'll wait for you for six months. Six months is all you have. If you don't come back, I'll go get you, I promise!"

#

The wedding was beautiful. We had such a good time. Amy and I were together as if we had never been apart. We didn't talk about her trip to Iraq or me leaving for Fort Lauderdale after the conversation we had the morning following the rehearsal night. Everything seemed as it was before when we were happy together. However, the week passed by quickly, and here we were again, having to say goodbye to each other. Friday morning, when I woke up, she was already gone. I tried to see if she was still in the hallway, but she wasn't.

When I was in the airport awaiting my flight, she sent me a text message. *My love, I'm already missing you with all my heart. I couldn't stand having to face you saying goodbye again. Last time was really hard for me. I want to have the image of you sleeping on our bed after a wonderful night together. I love you, I love you, I love you. We'll see each other again soon. I can't wait to be back to you and find comfort in your arms. Love, Amy.*

Chapter 63

The first week back in Fort Lauderdale was very hard for me. Hating everything and everyone, I didn't want to see or talk to Jamal or Jane. I just wanted to be left alone with my grief. Jane was anxious to see me, but I just couldn't do it, not yet. I needed some time alone, and I hoped she would get it. I decided to stop that game nonsense. It wasn't fair to her, and I wasn't in the mood to play it anymore.

On Wednesday, I left the office for the day at lunchtime. I wanted to go for a jog. I needed some physical activity to release the angry energy trapped in me. When coming down the garage ramp, I saw Jane in the middle of the way, waiting for me. She flashed me and opened up a huge smile, probably thinking that she was being sexy. It pissed me off. I found it vulgar and irresponsible. *She is nuts!* I thought to myself. I had no option but to let her in my car, and we drove away. She was happy and eager to touch and kiss me. I just couldn't.

"Are you crazy? What if I weren't alone?" I asked her, driving away.

"I thought it could be exciting if you were with Mr. Poch or Mr. McKee," she said as if it weren't a big deal.

"You're getting…"

"What? Audacious?" She cut me off, finishing my sentence as always.

"Vulgar! That's the word I was looking for." I couldn't even look at her.

"C'mon, you said that I should express my craziest fantasies to you, remember?"

"I know what I said," I replied, driving without knowing where to go, wishing her out of my car and out of my life. Once I parked the car in a remote area in Dania Beach, I was ready to have a frank conversation with her to put an end to the whole game thing, but she was horny and all over me, touching, kissing, and pulling me over her. I let myself go for a moment; she's beautiful, after all.

"Did you miss me?" she whispered, unbuttoning and unzipping my pants, looking into my eyes, caressing my body, and pulling my shirt up. She started kissing my chest, pushing my pants down, and getting me inside her. I was panting, looking into her eyes, not believing what was happening. She was acting so boldly, in broad daylight—that's a felony!

"Stop!" I yelled and pulled myself away from her. She groaned and looked at me, surprised but still panting.

"What's wrong?"

"Are you crazy? If the police catch us, we'll go to jail," I said, fixing my clothes.

"No one will catch us. Come back here," she said, whispering and trying to pull me back over her.

"What the fuck! Don't you understand? I don't want to do this. It's crazy, you're fucking mad! And I don't want to play this stupid game anymore. Get out of my car and out of my life."

"What?" She was shocked, looking at me with those big blue eyes wide open, trying to catch her breath and fixing her clothes.

"Get out!" I said, starting the car.

"What? You are kidding me!"

"GET OUT!"

"How am I going to go back? You can't do this to me!"

"Take a taxi or a bus if you want, OUT now," I yelled at her, tossing some money for the taxi. She got out, and I drove away without looking back. After a while, I felt bad for treating her like that. She didn't deserve it, so I decided to make it up to her somehow. At that time, I had just wanted to run, run nonstop until dropping dead exhausted.

#

The next morning, I felt really guilty for having mistreated Jane. She didn't know about what was going on in my life and didn't deserve the way I behaved. I waited for her in the car park.

"Hey, gorgeous, you're late," I said to her when she finally arrived.

"Let me go!" She was angry and in a bad mood, as predicted.

"I know you're upset, but you asked for that." I was trying to tell her that flashing me in the middle of the garage wasn't ok and having unprotected sex in the car, on the street, in broad daylight was stupid, but, as usual, she replied without letting me finish my sentence.

"I asked for that? You're kidding me, right?"

"No, you acted as a trollop, and I treated you as one. It wasn't my intention, but you wouldn't listen, like now; you never listen." I started walking toward the lift. I thought it wasn't a good time to talk with her, and I was getting annoyed. *Why can't she understand we were both wrong?*

"Wait! Don't leave me here like this. Being a whore wasn't my plan. I only wanted to spice it up a little. I'm sorry if I messed up. Maybe you're right; it was my fault. I shouldn't have behaved like that. I guess it was vulgar. Sorry," she said, calming down.

"That's fine. I didn't behave well either. I shouldn't have left you there alone. I was upset with other stuff that was going on in my life and ended up lashing out at you. I'm really sorry."

"Do you want to talk about it?" she asked. I shook my head in silence. "Well, I'm sorry, too," she said, looking at me with an angel's face that I couldn't resist. We kissed in the lift.

#

There wasn't much to do in the office, and I could've taken the day off. But once I was there, I took the time to organize my files, thinking about taking Jane somewhere nice and telling her that this game stuff was a stupid idea. I wanted to tell her I had someone else in my life and that I was sorry for having proposed the game to her.

In the afternoon, I went for a walk on Las Olas to clear my mind and grab a coffee. Ann was there, lucky me. I needed a good friend to talk with.

"Hey, Ann!"

"Hi, Joe!"

"There is not much to do in the office, right? I need a coffee to keep me awake!" I tried to start a conversation.

"Me, too. I'm done with my work, so I thought I could have a coffee break!"

"I have been thinking about you." I was preparing to ask about Miami.

"Really?" she said, putting a bigger smile on her face.

"I remember you promised to take me around Miami. I'm waiting." I smiled back.

"Any time," she said. "I was waiting for you to ask."

"What about Saturday?" I suggested.

"Saturday is fine."

I went home happy, thinking that Ann was the friend I needed now. She's smart and lovely. We get along well, and that was exactly what I needed: a good friend.

#

On Saturday morning, she was waiting for me at the parking garage as we agreed.

"Hi! Sorry, I'm late," I said when she got in my car.

"No problem, I just got here as well."

"So, where are we going?"

"I thought about taking you to Coconut Grove. Have you been there?"

"No, I've been to South Beach and the Keys. I just passed by Miami."

"Oh, ok. I think you'll love it! Miami is really cool."

"I bet it's."

We went to Coconut Grove, which is south of Miami. Ann explained to me that Coconut Grove was once an independent city that was incorporated by the City of Miami in the early 1900s. It was a surprise for me to see so much vegetation and no palm trees for a change. It actually felt like a mid-Atlantic city with beautiful historic architecture. We had a pleasant lunch. Ann is a very cool girl and knows a lot about Miami. I enjoyed her company, and after lunch, we went for a cortadito, which is a type of Cuban coffee, mostly espresso with a little milk and lots of sugar. It was delicious.

Driving back home, Ann suggested a pit stop at this house museum called Vizcaya. We did. It's a wonderful place. The gardens amazed me; I have seen gardens like that only in Italy. Ann told me that the parties held there are the best if you have money to pay for the ticket, of course. She's so knowledgeable and interesting; we could talk forever without boredom. I really wanted to go out with her again and get to know her better. All sorts of thoughts passed through my mind. I thought that between Jane and Ann, Ann was a better match for me. I know Jane is gorgeous and sexy, but that's about it; it's only sex. Ann, on the other hand, could be a real companion, a friend with benefits. *But how do I get rid of Jane? They're friends, and we all work together. Maybe, if we played the game…not for the game per se, but to keep our relationship a secret.… Should I? Yes, I'll try.*

"This place is incredible! Thank you for bringing me here and for the lovely time."

"Any time!" she said with satisfaction, looking happy and relaxed.

"I think you're really nice, Ann. I really want to spend more time with you. I think we could have a great time together. There's this game that everyone is playing; it's a couples' game." I started talking about the game to her.

"What? A couples' game?"

"As I was saying, it's a couples' game: only two players, nobody else. It's supposed to be very sexy and exciting. There're only three rules in this game. First: we can't say *no* to each other ever. You've to do everything and anything I ask you to and vice versa."

"What?" she said, frowning.

"Second, we can't involve other people in the game with us or even use a third person. It's a two-person game, remember? We can't tell anyone because that would involve another person. And third, we can't fall for each other as that would spoil the entire game."

"You got to be kidding me, right?" she said in disbelief.

"I'm not kidding you. I just thought it could be fun…" I wasn't expecting this reaction from her.

"I don't think so?" She was clearly upset. Her face was aggravating, and she started to walk faster in the car park direction.

"Why not? We can have an exciting time together," I insisted, trying to keep up with her fast pacing.

"Yeah, right, so you can sleep with me without committing. I'm not that type of girl." She stopped walking to look at me. She was serious and snorting with anger.

"No commitment for you, too. You can stop the game at any time. All you have to do is break a rule." I was confused. She didn't get it.

"Yeah, no commitment, but I have to be available any time you want. It doesn't make sense. Does anyone fall for that? I can't believe it, and anyway, I like to be free to do what I want, whenever I want!" She was really upset now.

"You're taking it too seriously. People playing the game just want to spice things up and have some fun." I tried to calm her down. It wasn't a big deal.

"Ok, I'm saying no! See, I'm breaking a rule even before we start playing. Game over!" She had a cynical smile on her face, which turned me off.

"I'm sorry, I shouldn't have," I apologized.

"No problem, let's go?" She was dry, no more smiling. We were quiet all the way to Fort Lauderdale.

Chapter 64

Girls. You can't live with or without them. Why do they have to be so complicated? Gosh, sometimes I just don't know what to do. I needed a break from them. I had a lot to deal with lately and couldn't handle any more drama in my life.

That's it. No Jane, no Ann, and no Amy for a while. *Oh Amy, where are you?* I thought about calling Bill to ask if she was already gone but didn't have the strength. Sometimes, I turn on the telly to watch the news, hoping to see her on camera covering an event or something. I miss her.

I had promised Jane that I would do something nice to make up for our disastrous last encounter. I looked online and saw that I could rent a yacht per hour with all services included, which could be a good idea and a nice treat for her. I called a few and checked them out before booking one for two weeks away because I wanted to enjoy some time alone to relax and not think about women for the time being.

On the weekend, I went back to the Keys. I wanted to take my time exploring the beautiful islands on the way to Key West. I stopped at Marathon, which is on a small island, before entering the seven-mile bridge. A friend from Chicago had told me how wonderful this place was. Beautiful and serene and close to Key West, which is a more dynamic city.

I rented a little house on the beach, literally. The house's backyard is the beach. All you need to do is open the sliding door in the living room and step on the white sand. I don't even need to say that I fell in love with the place so much that I ended up signing a year's contract. The paradise was mine for the whole year. It was good to have a place to come to and relax. I thought about moving there since I really didn't have to be in the office every day. I could go to Fort Lauderdale for meetings and court days only. It became my plan for the near future.

The weekend alone in Marathon was awesome. I went for long walks on the beach, swimming and cooking for myself; it was just what I needed to de-stress. The following week in the office was smooth. Jane and Ann were quiet, and everything was looking good. On Friday, I went for a beer after work at this place on Las Olas Blvd with live music, nice people and good food; everyone goes there, so you see lots of familiar faces, and of course, Jane and Ann were there. Jane was flirting with the bartender.

I confessed I didn't like to see Jane charming the guy. Ann was dancing with someone and seemed happy; I was just observing both from a distance. Suddenly, Jane saw me looking at her, and I could tell that she was surprised and uncomfortable about seeing me. Right there, I realized I was being stupid for thinking that I was being unfair to her because of Amy. Apparently, Jane has other love interests as well, and she's clearly not concerned about my feelings. What a slut! So, game on, I will not break up with her. She's beautiful, and I want her.

#

The following Friday was the day I had planned to take Jane on the yacht. I wasn't really in the mood after seeing her flirting with the bartender but decided to keep with the plan anyway. After work, I followed her. She had no clue I was right behind her and stopped at the grocery store. I followed her in and started shopping as well; eventually, we ran into each other.

"You," she said when she saw me.

"Do you shop here often?" I said, smiling and touching her hair gently.

"Pretty much."

"I'm buying some wine. I have a very special night tonight." I showed her favorite wine in my trolley and winked at her with an inviting smile on my face.

"Oh!"

"So, what are you up to?" I was expecting her to say that she was up to whatever I wanted, but she didn't get it.

"Not much, I'm going home."

"O-k!" I was astonished that she had no clue about my intentions.

"Bye," she said and left.

I had to count to ten before going after her. How could she be so birdbrained? Following her in my car, I overtook her car and made her stop.

She yelled, "Look where you're going, you fool!" She did not recognize my car or even me. Unbelievable!

"What's wrong with you?" I shouted, getting out of my car and walking toward hers.

"What? You cut me off. I almost crashed," she said, lowering her tone now that she saw it was me.

"I'm talking about us! Don't you get it? That was a clue; I want YOU to come with me!" I was getting irritated.

"Oh, really?"

"Yeah, really."

"I'm sorry, I didn't get it. I think I put off that game stuff for a while."

"You put off?" I was astonished. "So, you don't want to play anymore!"

"I don't know…"

"You have to decide right now! I want you to come with me. If you don't, that's a *no*, and it'll be over! What's going to be?" I gave her an ultimatum.

"I'm coming with you," she said after a moment.

"That's my girl! Why don't you park over there? I'll wait for you at the corner, ok?" I was feeling better now that she decided to come with me.

She was amazed when she realized we were getting on the yacht.

"So, are you surprised?" I asked, helping her to get on board.

"Cool, I have never been on a boat this big before."

"We're going to the open sea. It's a full moon night, and I thought we could swim under the moonlight…"

"I hope you don't make me swim all the way back this time," she said spontaneously, making me laugh.

"What was that?" She stuns me. "If you behave well, as a good girl should, you've nothing to worry about," I said, still laughing at her comment.

"Am I behaving well so far?"

"So far, so good." I teased and hugged her, kissing the top of her head as we sailed away.

When the yacht stopped, I took her to the cabin where our dinner was served.

"How did you do that? Who is driving the boat? Where is everybody?" she asked delightedly.

"There is nobody but us," I said, pulling a chair for her to sit.

"What is this?" she asked, taking a look at her plate.

"Escargots à la Bourguignonne."

"Can you ask the chef to make me a burger? Or a salad will be fine, really. I'm not eating snails."

"Why don't you try it?" I couldn't help but giggle at her reaction. I took one on my fork and tried to make her eat.

"Nope!"

"C'mon, I bet you'll love it." She was funny, behaving like a kid, refusing to take medicine.

"Ok, you've to *Do What I Say*. Eat it!" I threatened her, having fun looking at her face in repulsion. Then, she closed her eyes and opened her mouth. I quickly fed her the escargot, curious to see her response.

"Hm…. It tastes like garlic. Why do people like to eat this if they have to add a lot of garlic to make it edible?" she said and willingly fed herself another one.

"People eat them because they're exotic and expensive."

"Yeah, right! Would you eat a snake or alligator just because it's exotic?

"It depends on the chef. Of course, I wouldn't if you were cooking."

"Very funny!"

She diverts me. I feel so relaxed with her, and for a while when we're together, I forget about all my troubles. I looked at her with ease, leaning back on my chair, feeling content.

"You're fun to be with. I like you," I said, looking at her.

"I'm fun? That's all?"

"No, you're beautiful, too."

"What else?" she asked and leaned back on her chair, too, looking into my eyes with those big, blue, irresistible eyes.

"What else you want me to say? That you're the most beautiful, sexy, and moody girl I've ever been with?

"Do you have a girlfriend?" she asked me out of the blue.

"No, do you have a boyfriend?" I also wanted to know.

"Nope. Are you playing the game with someone else?"

"No. You?"

"No."

"Ok then, let's go to the deck to check out the moon."

I grabbed her hand and took her to the deck, where two lounge chairs were waiting for us.

"Let's go for a dive?" I took my clothes off and dove into the ocean. "C'mon!" I yelled from the water; I couldn't wait to have her in my arms. She took a little while to start taking her clothes off, but when she did, she held her nose with one hand and jumped into the water, squealing. She turns me on big time and makes me happy. I want her to be the one making me forget Amy. I'll give us another chance.

CHAPTER 65

Things were getting better, and I was kind of content again with my new life. *I've got a good job, live in a beautiful place, have good friends, and a purported girlfriend who is gorgeous. What is there to complain about? Nothing, right? But somehow, I still felt empty and lonely. I feel that I don't belong here; it's a weird, melancholic feeling that I can't explain.* I was lost in my thoughts at the pub, having a beer, when someone tapped on my back.

"Hey, man! Where have you been?" Jamal brought me back from my deep thoughts.

"Hey, Jamal. How's it going?" I was happy to see him and to have someone to talk to.

"Not bad, not bad. You disappeared, you don't go to the gym anymore, and I haven't seen you around lately…"

"Yeah, I went to Chicago for the wedding. I told you about it, right?"

"Yep, how was it?"

"Good. I've been busy with work and went back to the Keys."

"Awesome!"

"I actually rented a place in Marathon for the whole year. It's nice and peaceful. We can go this weekend if you like to check it out."

"I would love to, man. Let's go."

#

On Saturday, Jamal and I drove to Marathon. The weather was beautiful, and the ocean was flat and crystal clear. In the afternoon, we went to Key West to have some fun. There was this weekend party that celebrates the sunset with artists performing, beautiful people, and many tourists enjoying the fantastic place. Jamal and I were having a blast when two girls came to talk to us out of nowhere.

"Are you having fun?" one asked Jamal.

"Yeah. I'm Jamal, and this is Joe. What's your name?" Jamal never wasted a minute when he had a chance to flirt.

"Nice meeting you. I'm Nicole, and this is Samantha," she introduced.

"Where are you from, Nicole?" Jamal started talking with one of the girls, leaving me and the other girl, Samantha, feeling awkward.

"Samantha, right?"

She nodded.

"Where are you from?" I asked.

"I'm from Boston. You?"

"I'm from England originally but live in Fort Lauderdale now."

"I could tell you're British; your accent is undeniable." She smiled at me.

"That obvious, huh?"

"Yeah. I've been to London. It's a big, crazy city. Are you from London?"

"London."

"Cool."

"Do you want to grab a beer or something?" I asked her, looking at Jamal and Nicole, who were already getting acquainted with each other.

Samantha smiled and said, "Yeah, sure."

We went to the bar, got our drinks, and walked back to the beach. We sat by the bonfire and talked about our lives. She said she was a nursing student and was on vacation with her friend, Nicole, who was also a nursing student. They were in Key West for the week and were going back to Boston on Monday. This was their last weekend in Florida. She was a smart and cute girl. We had a nice conversation and a couple of beers when Jamal and Nicole were ready to go home.

I looked at Samantha, and she nodded as if to say it was fine with her. We went home and had a very cool night. The girls were fun and had no shame whatsoever. Jamal was in heaven, and I... I was fine. It was a fun, lovely night. On Sunday, we went for a walk on the beach; the girls were happy. We had a nice time together, and after lunch, they left for Miami to catch their flight.

Jamal and I went back to Key West before heading home.

"Hey, man, aren't you afraid to be in that remote house all by yourself?"

"No. Should I be?"

"I don't know. Do you have a gun? I mean, just in case."

"I don't. But I think it's a good idea to get one."

"Yeah, just in case, right?"

"Right!"

When I got home on Sunday night, I remembered that Jane had plans for us. She had left a ticket to the *Cirque du Soleil* on my windshield that I totally forgot about. Now, it was too late. I was feeling guilty again for having stood her up, but who knows what she was doing behind my back? As I remember well, she's not shy when seeking company. I'll make an excuse; hopefully, she'll accept, and everything will go back to normal.

#

Monday after work, I waited for Jane at the garage.

"Sorry, I couldn't go. Something came up at the last minute."

"What happened?" she said, turning around to face me.

"My friend's car broke down, and I had to go get him. It took forever for the towing truck to arrive."

"Oh, ok. You could've called me or texted, at least."

"Yeah, sorry. Do you want to go out for a drink or something?"

We went to Lauderdale Beach, just down the road. We walked on the beach, and she was fine, back to normal and not upset with me, which was a relief. I told her I was planning something nice for us on the weekend. I didn't tell her what, but I was planning to take her to Marathon. After a nice walk, I drove her back to the garage where her car was parked and kissed her good night.

#

On Friday, after work, I saw Ann and Jane going down to Las Olas; they were probably going to Friday's usual happy hour. I decided to go as well after stopping at the ATM to get some cash for the trip to Marathon with Jane. I wanted to surprise her, so I sat at the bar as usual and observed them both from a distance. Ann was flirting with a guy. I think I knew him from the real estate agency. *Yes, that's him, his name is Justin.* I was disappointed with Ann because she turned me down and now is flirting with this nerd. *What's wrong with her?* Suddenly, she saw me and came to talk.

"Hey!" she said, smiling.

"Hey, Ann."

"Do you want to come and sit with us? I can introduce you to our friends. I mean, I know you're new here." She was friendly.

"Yeah. Thank you, Ann! I better be going."

"Look, I'm sorry for the way I behaved in Miami. You got me by surprise, that's all."

"No problem. Who's that guy you were talking with, your boyfriend?"

"Who, Justin? No, no. He's just a friend, but he has asked me out." She said making a sexy but shy face to tease me.

"I'm jealous." I said to lift her spirits up. She was flirting with me and probably regretted not accepting to play the game with me.

She smiled, contented, going back to her table. Ann is a sweetheart. I like her.

On the other hand, Jane was getting on my nerves. She saw me and came to the bar to flirt with the bartender again—in my face! I couldn't believe it! Not only was she all smiling and making cute faces at him, but she also kissed the guy twice, knowing that I was watching her. *What the fuck!* I felt like killing her. She was pushing my buttons and making me go over my limit. I was furious. She left in a hurry when she saw me distracted, thinking that I would let her go without confrontation. I paid for my tab and ran after her in the garage.

"Are you scared of me?" I grabbed her by the arm before she could get in her car.

"You're hurting me. Let me go."

"Why? Just tell me why?" I tried to contain my frustration.

"I don't know. I wasn't trying to upset you. Believe me, please."

"Rubbish! I'm starting to think that you like to be a trollop, and you enjoy being treated like one."

"No, Joe. Please, he surprised me."

"Do you think I'm stupid? He didn't take you by surprise. I've seen you flirting with the guy before, but that was before you told me you didn't have anyone. You lied to me."

"No, let me explain."

"There's no explanation. You kissed him twice, in my face! If you wanted to upset me, congratulations, you succeeded. Have a great life. It's over," I said, pushing her away and walking off.

"No! Joe! Don't leave me here like this!" she shouted and rushed after me. "Please, let's talk!"

"Leave me alone, Jane!"

"You know what? Yes, I was flitting with him because, as far as I'm concerned, we were just playing a freaking game, right? You never said we were together, and I was tired of waiting for you to make a move. Who knows if you didn't lie to me, too?"

"You are sick!" I said, disgusted. I stopped to look into her eyes, not believing my ears.

"No, you are! As far as I know, there is no rule preventing us from having fun with other people. What did you expect me to do? Do you think I would just sit there and wait for you to get horny and want to fuck me again?" She was shouting at me in the middle of the garage, which made me even more furious.

"You're being vulgar again. I guess you're a slut, after all."

"I am! And if you leave me here, I'll go back and sleep with him. And you can bet that he'll be very happy to be with me. You're a jerk!" she yelled, then turned her back to me, leaving to go back to the bar.

"You're not going back there!" I grabbed her arm again. "You know what? You don't deserve my respect; you're a freaking trollop!"

"Yeah, apparently, I'm your whore."

"Get in the car, NOW." I was so furious that I couldn't control myself. I pushed her inside the car and held her down when she started hitting me all over. I wanted to hurt her for real.

"Let me go!" she screamed.

"No." I was enraged. "Do you still want to fuck the bartender?

Do you?"

"No."

"Liar! Let's play whore?" And I ripped her panties with my free hand, still looking into her eyes and holding her down. "That's what you want, huh? Being fucked by someone, anyone…"

I could not think straight; she really got me mad. If she wanted to fuck, I was going to give her what she wanted. I pushed the seat back and got on top of her. She tried to get off, but I held her arms up tight and lifted her skirt up with my other hand. "Do you like this?" I said, looking in her eyes.

"Joe…" She looked back at me, still upset but giving up.

"Let's play whore," I said, holding her leg spread up so I could see myself entering her without mercy. She didn't say a word or fight me off. She was angry but gave in. When I was satisfied, I climbed off her and fixed my clothes to leave, still feeling aggravated.

"I bet you're satisfied now. Go home!" and I left without looking back.

Chapter 66

I was so furious that I couldn't sleep. I had planned a nice weekend for us in Marathon, and she had to spoil the whole thing. *What a fucking bitch, how could she?* I had so much anger going around my body that I needed to relieve it somehow. I went to the gym, and I ran and ran until exhaustion, but despite that, I still couldn't relax.

Around 6:00 AM, I was feeling better and decided to go to Marathon, anyway. It would be great to walk on the beach and be out of Fort Lauderdale. I stopped by the office to grab a couple of case files I needed to study for court day next week. When I parked in the garage, I noticed that Jane's car was still there, parked at the same spot it was the night before. I was getting upset again, thinking that she actually had gone out with the bartender and had a wonderful night fucking him after being with me. I got closer to her car and saw that she was still there, sleeping. It broke my heart.

I got in her car and checked her forehead to see if she was warm. She woke up and flinched away from me. She was scared and mad, of course.

"We need to talk," I said, caressing her hair. She started sobbing, and I felt miserable.

"I'm taking you away for the weekend. Are you hungry?" I asked, starting the car, reversing it, and driving us away. She didn't say a word and just stayed there all the way to Marathon.

When we arrived, I took her inside and told her to take a nice shower and meet me downstairs. She nodded. I had bought a couple of things for her since my original plan was to get her by surprise and bring her here for the weekend. The whole house was ready and prepared for her. I got groceries, a couple of dresses, and a bikini for her. I also bought some jewelry for her—nothing expensive, just a nice treat, really. But now, I wasn't so sure that she deserved all the nice things I'd gotten for her. She can be a bitch, after all.

While waiting for her, I went to check the mailbox in front of the house. It was full of junk and a couple of bills. I needed to ask someone to come get the mail and clean the house once a week. I called the real estate agent who had rented me the house to see if she knew of someone.

"Sure, Joe, I would try to find someone." She's such a nice lady.

Back in the house, I also had to find a safe place to hide the gun I had purchased. I decided to hide it in the fireplace shaft behind the dumper. It seemed to be a good and accessible place.

Jane wasn't in the house, so I went out to the beach, and there she was, sitting on the sand, looking at the ocean. I sat by her side, saying, "Here you are."

She looked at me without smiling.

"Why do you keep behaving like that? Don't you see that I'm trying to be nice to you? Haven't I treated you well and taken you to nice places?"

She nodded shyly in response.

"How could you be so vulgar? Why don't you treat me the same way I treat you?"

"I didn't mean to upset you last night. I had a little too much to drink and got carried away. He kissed me by surprise, believe me."

"No, you kissed him and looked at me smiling."

"Sorry, I was drunk. I love you!"

"No, you don't. I'm very attracted to you, and I love being with you. But this whole game thing has become out of control, and I don't think we can have a healthy relationship now. I'm afraid I'll end up hurting you."

"No, Joe, we can work it out. I promise I'll be good to you!"

"This game nonsense must stop. You're a nice girl and will find someone to love and love you back, but that person is not me. Sorry. It's going to be really hard for me to see you every day and not touch or kiss you, but it's over, and I think bringing you here was a mistake as well. Let's go back to Fort Lauderdale." I reached out for her hand, got up, and we started to walk back to the house.

"I think I deserve a chance to prove you're wrong. We don't have to play the game, but I want to be with you." She was apologetic, trying to convince me to give her another chance, but I had made up my mind.

Back in the house, we went upstairs to grab our stuff and go home. She sat on the bed quietly, looking at me.

"I don't know what to say. Please, let's stay," she finally said, almost crying. I could see that she was genuinely sorry. I felt bad for having behaved badly as well.

"Listen, we were drunk and upset last night and said things we shouldn't have said to each other ever. And I'm really sorry for having mistreated you like that. I never thought I could behave the way I did, but there's something about you that really pushes my buttons."

"Please give us another chance. Let's stay here for the weekend. I know we'll feel better tomorrow to talk things through."

"Ok, we can stay the weekend, but I don't think I'll change my mind. You need to understand that."

"Ok," she said, nodding. She stopped crying and looked at me with those beautiful, big blue eyes.

#

"Good morning!" I was feeling happy, "Look what I've got for you. Let's see… we've orange juice, toast, cream cheese, eggs and bacon, and coffee. Have I forgotten anything?" I said, bringing her breakfast.

"Good morning," she said, sitting up on the bed and taking the breakfast tray. "Thanks! It looks so good," she said, smiling.

"No problem," I said. "Do you want to go snorkeling today?"

"Fine," she said, eating frenetically and making me chuckle.

"I'll be waiting for you downstairs," I said and left the room.

I was preparing the snorkeling equipment when she came to meet me. She looked gorgeous in the bikini I had bought for her. It was just perfect for her perfect body. I helped her with the mask and flipper, and then she dragged herself into deeper water clumsily, making me laugh.

"Stop that! You're going to scare the fish away and lift the sand up." I said, holding her back.

"What fish? Don't you know you need a coral reef to snorkel? There's nothing to be seen in here," she said, taking a pick under the water.

"Really, smartie pants? Who told you that?" I said, laughing. "For your information, this is the best beach in the world for snorkeling, and you won't forget this day for the rest of your life. Have a gander right there!" I said, pointing in one direction.

"Where, where?" and she dove to check it out. "I don't see anything…" She was disappointed when resurfacing.

"Here, see? I told you!" I tried to be serious, showing her a shoal of small gray fish.

"What?" she said, puzzled.

"Look!" and I pointed it down again.

"No, I'm not falling for that again," she said, laughing.

"Take a look," I said before diving. "It sparkles," I said when resurfacing.

She dove and finally found this little jewelry box I had placed there for her to find. Confused, she put a huge smile on her face when she opened it and saw this beautiful pearl necklace inside. She looked at me with disbelief.

"Look, over there," I pointed to another location, and she dove in that direction, finding another little box. "I can't believe you!" she said, opening it and finding a pair of earrings now.

"I told you. The best snorkeling place in the world. The clams here do complete work…"

It was a happy day. We enjoyed each other's company. She's wonderful when she acts normally. *Why does she have to screw everything up all the time?* She could be perfect, but unfortunately, she's a beautiful airhead who can't discern right from wrong. Even though we had a nice weekend together, I was convinced to end our affair. The whole game thing was a mistake, and I was going to make myself clear to her; it was over.

On our way back to Fort Lauderdale, it was a good time to have the frank conversation I was planning to have with her for a while.

"Jane, we need to talk seriously."

She looked at me apprehensively. I guess she knew I was going to break up with her.

"What is it?"

"We can't go on with this nonsense. I'm sorry. You're beautiful and a nice girl, but we're just not a good match for each other. You'll find someone else to love…"

"I don't want anyone else. I want you." Her eyes teared up.

"You think you do, but you're very young and will have many

boyfriends until finding the right guy.”

“No, Joe. I love you. And you love me, too. I’m sorry I upset you Friday night. I understand you felt angry and jealous when you saw me kissing another guy. I was wrong and deserved to be treated like a whore. I’m sorry, it won’t happen again.”

“No, you didn’t deserve the way I treated you. No one does. I never thought I could do something like that to you or anyone else. It scares me just to think about it. I was furious and really wanted to hurt you…”

“I promise it won’t happen again.” She was crying now.

“Ok, don’t cry. Listen to me. Let’s stop with this game shit and be friends for now. I like you, and we work together. Having said that, we need to be responsible adults and behave ourselves as such. We’ll not be together again, at least for some time. We need a break.”

“I don’t think I can…” She was still crying.

“Yes, you can. Friends?” I said, looking at her. She was still crying and didn’t say another word until we got back to the garage where my car was parked. Before getting out of the car, I tried again to convince her that the breakup was the best solution for us.

“Look at me. I know you’re sad, but it’ll pass. You’ll see.”

“It’ll never pass. I love you,” she said, facing me now.

I caressed her head, slipping the hair off her face. She turned her face away from me, saying nothing, when she realized I wouldn’t change my mind. I understood that there wasn’t anything I could say to her that would make her feel better, so I left. I knew she would be fine again in a couple of days.

CHAPTER 67

It was a relief getting everything straightened and clarified with Jane. I knew she was going to be sad for a while, but as I had witnessed, she doesn't stay alone for too long. She's pretty and interesting. She's just not for me and I'm ready to move on with my life.

Coming home Sunday night after the weekend in Marathon with Jane, I was surprised to have an email from Amy.

My love,

I hope everything is well with you and that you miss me the same way I miss you. It has been difficult to be far away from you, and everyone I love and care about, but you guys are always in my mind and heart. Before I say what I need to say, I want you to know that my feelings for you haven't changed a bit. I love you. However, I got a job proposal to be the correspondent in Syria for the Chicago Tribune, and I can't refuse. Please don't hate me, but I accepted the offer and am not coming back to Chicago. Love, Amy.

I couldn't believe my eyes, and my heart sank. *Why?* I didn't understand why this was happening to me. We had it all, and we were happy, Amy and I. She changed my life completely twice: once when we fell in love and had the best years together, and now when she abandoned me. It's impossible not to hate her, but I can't stop loving her either. This had to end. I'll not let her ruin my life, not this time.

I was feeling miserable about everything. I couldn't stop thinking about Amy and was very remorseful for Jane as well. The truth, I guess, is that I didn't want to be alone, not now. I needed someone to trust and have a fresh start with, someone to make me feel stable and loved. Someone to have a normal life with and someone I could rely on, and I knew exactly who this person was: Ann.

#

On Tuesday, leaving the office, I ran into Ann in the office hallway.

"Going home earlier today?" I asked her while we waited for the lift to arrive.

"Yeah, I need to get some groceries."

"What a coincidence! I'm going to the grocery shop, too. Where do you shop? Publix?" I asked her.

"Yes, Publix."

"Do you mind if I go with you?" I took the opportunity to get closer to her; destiny was smiling at me.

"Sure, do you want to go in my car or yours?"

"My car," I said, feeling lucky.

"Ok, Publix is on my way home. Do you want to follow me to my house? I can leave my car there and go with you. I was planning to stop by my house first anyway. I need to let Max out a bit."

"Ok, I'll follow you."

I was determined that she was a good match for me. She's loyal, sincere, trustful, intelligent, and cute and would never betray me. I followed her to her house and was curious to see her environment, so I parked and followed her inside. Max was happy to see her and was jumping all over her. Cute.

"I'm sorry, the house is a little messy. Do you want a beer?" she said, opening the back door for Max.

"Hey, Max! Yeah, a beer would be great!" I said, petting Max. "I like your house; it's cozy."

"Thanks," she said, handing me a beer and going out to the backyard.

"Hey, Ann!" her neighbor greeted her from his backyard.

"Hi, David. This is Joe," she introduced us. "And this is Matt," she introduced me to this other guy who came out of the house to check what was going on.

"Nice meeting you, guys," I said, smiling at them and noticing the wonderful herb garden David was working on.

"I was thinking about planting an herb-raised garden on my balcony but don't know how to begin. I even got a couple of books, but they are difficult to follow," I said, trying to fit in and be sociable with her friends.

"No, it's very easy. Of course, you need to take care of it…"

David and I started talking about gardens, but Matt cut us off.

"Hey, Ann and Joe. Do you guys want to have dinner with us? I'm making chicken marsala with roasted potatoes," he said. "Actually, that's why I came out here. David, where's my thyme?"

"Oh, yes, let me get it for you," David said, going into the herb garden to get some thyme.

I didn't know what to say. The invitation was so unexpected. I looked at Ann to see how she was feeling about me joining them because I didn't want to be inappropriate.

"Do you want to stay for dinner? Matt is a wonderful cook. We can go grocery shopping after."

"Ok, if you think it's fine. I would be delighted." I was happy that she wanted me to stay. Everything seemed to be going well for me.

"Give me that. We're having wine," Matt said, grabbing the beer from my hand and pouring it into the kitchen sink. He was funny and made me feel at ease.

"Do you need help? I can wash the potatoes or do anything else that you prefer," I asked Matt.

"I prefer you go help Ann set the table and get out of my kitchen. No offense, but it's just too small and drives me crazy when I have to cook while trying to get around people in my way."

"No offense taken. Let's go set the table?" I asked Ann, feeling joyful.

The dinner was wonderful. Her friends were amazing and very welcoming. They made me feel so comfortable that I thought about repaying the kindness by inviting them to spend a few days in Marathon with me. It would be a wonderful opportunity for Ann and me to get to know each other better as well.

"Hey, guys, thank you very much for the wonderful time. In return, I wanted to invite you all to my place in Marathon for a couple of days."

"Marathon? Do you have a house in Marathon?" Ann asked skeptically. "I guess Marathon is getting popular now. I need to check it out."

"Yeah. It's not really mine. I rented it for the entire year. I have this friend in Chicago who told me how wonderful the Florida Keys were, so I had to check it out. Of course, I fell in love with the place and couldn't resist getting a little house for the weekends."

"For the weekends," Matt enforced.

"Well, the plan is to live there. I really don't have to go to the office every day; I can easily work from home and only go to the office for meetings and court days. Of course, I cannot do it now since I'm new in the office, but I'm sure I will convince the bosses. Don't you think, Ann?"

"I know nothing!" she said, smirking. "I would love to go with you…guys?" She looked at her friends.

"How many days are we talking about?" David asked.

"As many days you guys want to stay, I have an important meeting on Friday afternoon, but you can stay. I will go back afterward…"

"Yeah, of course, we want to go. What do you need from us? Should we go buy some groceries?" Matt added.

"We're going to the grocery shop now," Ann said.

"Now?" David asked. "Ok, let's go then."

The four of us went shopping for groceries. Matt and David were fun, and Ann was adorable as always. When coming back from the supermarket, Ann was worried about work. After all, it was only Tuesday.

"You can always call in sick," I suggested. "How many sick days have you taken so far?"

"None, I'm never sick."

"Ok, I won't tell anyone," I said, shaking my head.

"I guess I could call in sick. The office is kind of quiet now. There is not much to do, and Jane always takes time off, leaving me alone…"

"Great, I'll come over around 9:00 AM so everyone can be ready on time?" I said, parking the car in front of their houses.

Matt and David started to carry their groceries inside, arguing about what to take. They made me chuckle.

"They are awesome," Ann said, laughing at them as well and grabbing a few grocery bags.

"Yeah, I loved them. It must be nice to have neighbors like them."

"I can't tell you how many times they have helped me. I love them as brothers," she said, giving me a few bags and walking inside her house. I followed. She started putting the groceries away, giving me some to help her as we were already best friends, she made me feel relaxed.

"I had such a great time today! It feels like I have known you guys forever, really. I felt welcome and relaxed. Thank you!" I embraced her to look in her eyes. "Let's have a new start in Marathon. I really hope we can put that game stuff behind us…"

"Joe, you need to stop bringing that shit up, really. It turns me off every time I remember it. You know, I really liked you since the first day I saw you." *Did she just confess to having a crush on me?* "We can be good friends for sure…" She tried to amend it. So cute.

"But I want you," I murmured, and I kissed her, eager to start dating her.

"I guess I want you, too, but I'm not sure if we should get involved."

"Let's have a good time together, and then we'll see, ok?"

"Ok, see you tomorrow at nine!" she said, and I kissed her goodbye.

CHAPTER 68

I arrived on time. They were ready, waiting for me in front of their houses with (lots of) bags, sunglasses, beach hats, and dogs. Ann and Max came with me, and Matt and David followed with their dog, Luna. The trip was cool. Ann is very intelligent and easy to like; we could talk for hours about anything.

The house had only two bedrooms; I took Matt and David to the guest room and put Ann's things in the main bedroom. She looked at me without knowing what to say.

"I'll sleep in the living room," I told her, and she smiled, happy with my call. We spent the rest of the day talking, drinking, and putting our stuff away. It was already 3:00 AM when they went to bed. I stayed there, alone on the living room couch, but I was feeling good.

As anticipated, I couldn't sleep at all on the uncomfortable couch, so I got up and started making breakfast around 7:00 AM. Ann came down, probably after hearing noises in the kitchen and knowing that I was up.

"Morning…" she said, rubbing her eyes.

"Morning! Are you hungry? I'm making breakfast," I said energetically, ready to start the day.

"Starving," she said. "Can I have coffee? I can't function before having my coffee."

"Here, you can help me when you're done." I handed her a mug of freshly brewed coffee.

"What you want me to do?"

"You can set the table. Everything you need is in the upper cabinet above the counter, the first one to your right."

"K."

"Morning!" Matt and David came down saying.

After breakfast, we went to the beach for a walk with the dogs running around. When we came back, Matt cooked lunch, which was to die for, and after a lot of talking, laughter, and drinking, they went to take a kip. Ann went outside and sat by the firepit; I followed her.

"I shouldn't have eaten that much. I feel like a pig, a fat, lazy pig," I said, sitting close to her and tapping my swollen stomach.

"Me, too. I'm so full, but don't worry; the second round should start around five o'clock."

"Bloody hell! You got to be kidding me. I already ate for the whole month!" I said, making her laugh at me.

"Can we light up the firepit? It's kind of chilly," she asked.

"Sure." I lit the firepit and went inside to get her a blanket. I dragged a chair closer to hers and got under the blanket as well, embracing her in my arms. "So, did you like the house?"

"Yes, it's really nice."

"Would you live here—with me?" I looked at her, waiting for her reaction.

"I'll give it a thought. The house is nice, and you're adorable."

Satisfied, I smiled and kissed her. We stayed there talking, laughing, and making out until around five when Matt and David came down looking for what to do next.

"Firepit! Let's make s'mores! I'm sure I saw marshmallows

somewhere." Matt went to the kitchen to grab the ingredients.

"Didn't I tell you?" Ann said with a smirk on her face.

After dinner, we went for another walk under the stars. Matt and David cleaned up the kitchen and went to bed early. The dogs came along with us.

We strolled under the moonlight by the water; the ocean was flat and warm as the weather. The dogs were having fun running up and down, playing without a worry. I was feeling relaxed and happy to be there.

"I'm having a great time!" I said, smiling at her and grabbing her hand.

"Me, too. This place is really paradisaic." She also seemed happy and started swinging our intertwined arms playfully.

"Yeah, especially when you're in such good company." I winked at her, pleased with the moment. We walked for a little while and decided to come back to the house. It was getting late.

When we came back, Ann went upstairs, and I tried to make myself comfortable on the couch, which seemed impossible.

"Do you want a glass of water?" she asked me, coming down in her pjs.

"No thanks, I'm fine," I managed to say, tossing around on the uncomfortable couch and dropping my pillow on the floor. "Well, I'll buy a more comfortable couch tomorrow," I said, getting the pillow back and fluffing it in place to accommodate my head. She laughed at me.

"Why buy another couch? I thought you wanted me to move in with you. Do you want to sleep on your bed with me?" she said, looking down and then raising her sensual and bright brown eyes, looking straight into my soul, inviting me to join her.

I didn't wait for her to have a second thought and rushed up the stairs, taking her to the bedroom and laying her down on the bed. She was staring at me serenely but with desire. I kissed her affectionately, taking her pjs off, eager to have her. Her skin was soft against mine. Her small and hard breasts fit perfectly in my hand. I was crazy for her, longing to make love to her. We stared at each other with passion, saying nothing, letting our bodies speak for ourselves. We had such an incredible night. Ann is loving and mature, totally the opposite of Jane.

#

The next morning, on Friday, the weather had changed. It was raining. Matt, David, and I were in the kitchen preparing breakfast and making plans for the rainy day when Ann came down.

"What's up? What are we going to do today?" she asked, getting her coffee lazily.

"Eat!" Matt said, smiling. "What else?"

"Drink?" David complimented. "What else?"

"We could play cards. Do you guys play poker?" I suggested.

"Yeah! Let's play poker for real money when you come back from your meeting!" David said.

"Sounds like a plan!" I said, kissing Ann.

She went outside with the dogs, and not even a minute later, she was screaming.

"Joe! Joe! I think I broke my arm!"

"Ann! Oh! Ann, let me see." I rushed outside to check on her.

"What happened?" Matt and David said at the same time, rushing to check on her.

"Let's take her to a hospital!" David said.

I took her to the closest emergency room I saw. We were seen quickly, and thankfully, she had not broken her arm. It was just a hard sprain, but a cast was necessary, and painkillers were prescribed.

"Do you want to go home?" I asked when getting back two hours later.

"Yes, let's go. Right, Matt?" David said, looking at Matt, who nodded, confirming.

We changed, packed, and left. Matt and David took Max in their car since it would be difficult for Ann to handle him with the cast. We went straight to the office because I was already late for my meeting.

#

"What happened?" Jane asked when she saw Ann with a cast arm.

"Oh, nothing really. I fell over my arm. It's not really broken…"

I rushed into the conference room, where my client and Larry were already talking.

"I'm sorry for being late," I said apologetically, shaking the client's hand and introducing myself.

"Don't worry, we've just started," he politely said, smiling.

The meeting was fine and very productive. I'm glad I have a wonderful memory and remembered crucial details that impressed them all; they were satisfied with my approach to handling the case, and the meeting ended about a quarter past five. Ann was still in the reception waiting for me. "Sorry, I got out as soon as I could"

"No problem. Let's go," she said, grabbing her purse.

I drove her home since she needed to check on Max and leave her things. I was thinking about taking her to my place where I could pamper her all night long, but she had other plans.

"Sorry, Joe. I told Jane I was going out with her tonight"

"What?" I asked in disbelief.

"She asked what I was doing there in the office with you! I had to come up with an excuse. I said that I was bored and stopped by to see if she wanted to go to the movies or something."

"Oh, and then you got excited about going out with your little brat friend?"

"What? What are you talking about? Jane is not a brat; she's my friend. And she invited me to go out with her and her boyfriend."

"Her boyfriend?"

"Yes, why? I told her I wanted to go with them for the sake of our little secret."

"I don't want you to go. Stay with me?"

"Sorry, I have to go with her. We can talk tomorrow, ok?" she said.

But I was upset and didn't answer. I just looked at her, waiting for her to get out of the car. She knew I wasn't happy with her choice, but still went on with the plan to go out with Jane.

"Ok, you're mad at me. I'll call you tomorrow then," she said, getting out of the car.

Chapter 69

No need to even say that I was in a terrible mood for the entire weekend. Ann called several times, leaving voice and text messages; I didn't answer and was determined to break up with her as well. She's just like any other slut. I'm so tired of being betrayed and being everyone's second choice—and who was Jane's boyfriend? The bartender? I know he died. Is there another one already? *Fucking bitch!* Jane is a fucking trollop, I just wanted to fuck her again, and I have no regrets about saying this since everyone is apparently having their turn with her. *Whore!* And Ann, what the fuck was she thinking—*for the sake of our little secret?* I think she used that as an excuse to go have fun, as she always did. They're horny little bitches. I'm done.

The whole week, I was ignoring them, both of them. We were to have a professional relationship from now on. That was it. I could tell that they were somehow sad and upset with my attitude, but everyone behaved just as well as adults should. Or I thought they would…

Friday, at lunchtime, Jane came to my office.

"Hi!" she said, smiling and walking in without asking permission.

"Hi, Jane. Do you need anything?" I was feeling uneasy, not knowing what she was up to.

"Yeah, I miss you."

"Stop right there; we're in the office," I said, worried, and getting up to direct her out the door.

"I don't care. I need to see you after work."

"No, that will not happen. You must accept that our affair was a mistake," I whispered as I closed the door so no one could hear us.

"I can't."

"Listen, let's have lunch Sunday and talk as friends, but please don't make a scene here in the office. We both need our jobs."

"Ok, Sunday." And she left victorious.

I was dumbfounded by her courage and lack of respect for our workplace. *She's nuts!* When leaving for the day, I overheard them planning a night out in South Beach as they were ready for the next adventure in their lives with no regret for what they had done to me.

Feeling blue and in need of a drink, I stopped at the usual happy hour place on Las Olas and noticed that the dead bartender had already been replaced with a new one who was all smiling and flirting with the girls. How sad! I realized that everybody is replaceable and soon forgotten; life must go on. I had a few beers and decided to go after them. If Ann wants to move on with her life without me, fine, but she'll have to say that looking in my eyes. I was going to South Beach.

#

The place was crowded, and the music was loud. I saw Jane flirting with yet another guy who was not the alleged boyfriend. I could tell since they were not kissing or hugging, and she was charming the guy with shy smiles and cute faces. *I wanted to kill her; what a slut!* And Ann—all smiling with Justin. I felt like a freaking loser. I could care less about Jane, but I cared about Ann. I saw her getting up and going to the restroom, so I followed her.

"Are you having fun? I thought we had something special." I gripped her arm when coming out of the restroom.

"Joe! What are you doing here?"

"What do you think? I followed you. I needed to see with my own eyes that you are a little slut just like your bestie throwing herself at that guy over there," I said, pointing at Jane.

"What? You're drunk!"

"Can you tell?"

"Go home, Joe. I don't want to talk with you like this."

"Apparently, you don't care about how I feel. Wait, Jane is more important to you, right?"

"I called you. You never called me back or came over. So childish!" she said, pushing me off.

"Why did you have to go out with Jane last Friday? I wanted to stay with you and take care of you. You disgust me."

"Ok, Joe, you're not in the condition to have a conversation. Go home, and we can talk tomorrow. Justin and I have nothing; we're just friends for real." She pushed me away and left.

"Whore!" I yelled, but she was already far, getting back to the table.

At the same time, I saw Jane leaving the place alone. It was my chance. I followed her.

"Surprised?" I grabbed her by her arm, making her stop and look at me.

"What are you doing here?"

"What in the hell were YOU doing? I just can't understand you. Today, this very afternoon, you said you missed me, and now you are rubbing yourself all over that stranger? You're disgusting." I turned my back to leave her there.

"What? I was just dancing. There's nothing wrong with that, and I do miss you." She held my arm, making me stop.

"You know what? I know what you're up to. Let's get out of

here." I grabbed her arm again, pulling her through the crowded street, and asked where her car was parked. Once in the car, we drove away, if she wanted to fuck someone, that one would be me.

"Please, Joe, don't hurt me."

"Me, hurt you? Did I ever hurt you? I'm just giving you what you want."

I was so upset that I could not help speeding up a little. Suddenly, the guy with whom she was flirting with, passed us on a motorcycle. So, she was going to go somewhere with him, that is why she was leaving the place, to meet with him outside. *Fucking whore!*

"Do you want to hurt someone?" I said, passing the guy and cutting him off. The idiot fell. He wasn't even speeding and could not control the bike? He seemed pathetic.

"JOE, STOP! Are you insane? Stop the car right now." She was getting hysterical, taking her phone out to call 9-1-1.

"You aren't calling anybody. Accidents happen all the time." I took the phone from her hand.

"You're a monster. I want to go home."

I started to laugh at her comment. She called *me* a monster! "No, you don't want to go home. And at least you didn't kiss this one, but I could bet that you were ready to fuck him."

"What are you saying? Oh my God, oh my God, Fred! Please tell me you have nothing to do with Fred's death, please?"

"Fred, who? What the fuck are you talking about?"

"You killed him!"

"You're drunk. Shut up and be a good girl so we can play whore, would you?"

I took her to this rundown motel on Biscayne Blvd, which was exactly the kind of place she deserved. I parked, grabbed her purse and the car key, and said, looking at her, "I'm going to get a room for us. Don't try anything. If you try to escape, I'll hunt you down, and it won't be pleasant for you, do you understand?"

She nodded.

I went inside the motel's reception.

"Hi, I need a room for the night."

"How many people?"

"Two."

"Documents, please," the guy said without looking at me, checking the computer for an available room. He turned around and grabbed an old-fashioned key, which he handed to me. He took our driver's licenses from my hand and looked at my picture and my face. Then he leaned his head sideways to look at Jane in the car. He looked at the driver's licenses again and handed them back to me.

"Thank you," I said and left.

I opened the car door and grabbed Jane by the arm. She didn't fight me off. Once in the room, I looked at her, saying, "Let's start playing whore, shall we?" I pushed her on the bed and started taking her pants off.

She started slapping me all over, trying to get off the bed.

"Joe, wait. Let's talk."

"No talking, you little slut. Were you going to fuck that guy? Huh? Tell me, how many guys you fucked since we broke up?"

"I haven't been with anyone, Joe. Believe me."

"I don't believe you. And I know you have a boyfriend, and he isn't the guy on the bike."

"No, I don't have anyone! Who told you that?"

"It doesn't matter. What matters is that you're a scrubber." I flipped her over so I would not look at her angelic face.

"No, Joe. Please wait…"

She tried turning her face to look at me, but I held her down and fucked her from behind. It felt so good. When I was done, I got up and started dressing so I could get out of there. She sat up on the bed grabbing a pillow, holding it in her arms, tears running down her angry face.

"Joe, I don't know what you want from me. I have no one. You're the only one I want."

"Liar! I saw you many times flirting with other guys. You're a tramp and don't deserve compassion," I said, calling a taxi.

"I don't understand. You told me it was over, and then you get upset seeing me having fun, trying to move on with my life. You told me to do just that."

"See, you admit you were going to fuck the guy. You went outside to meet him and go somewhere where you could be his whore. Yes, move on with your life and leave me alone! Don't keep trying me, woman!"

"No! I went outside looking for Ann. She had disappeared, and I was worried about her. Juan Carlos is a nobody. He asked me to dance with him, that was all. Please believe me."

I looked at her with scorn and left.

Chapter 70

On Saturday morning, I was feeling wasted when Ann sent me a text.

Joe, I'm really worried about you and wanted to check if you got home safely last night. I shouldn't have let you drive intoxicated. Sorry. Please, please, call me. If you are still upset with me and don't want to talk, please just send me a text saying that you're well. Ann.

"We need to talk!" I called her back.

"Yes, I guess we need to!"

"Hi," I said when she opened the door for me.

"Hi!"

"I'm sorry about yesterday. I was drunk and upset."

"Upset about what?" She had a doubtful look on her face.

"About what? About you going out with Jane when all I wanted was to take care of you after we had such a wonderful time together. And you were hurt, remember? You shouldn't have gone out anyway. Then you go out on a date with that Justin guy? That's why!"

"I didn't want to tell Jane our secret, and she asked what I was doing in the office with you that Friday."

"Who said it's a secret? Did I ask you to keep it a secret?"

"No, but we don't want the whole office knowing just yet…right? Especially Jane."

"Why Jane? I don't get it. Did she say anything about me?"

"Like what?" She frowned.

"I don't know. I think she has a crush on me…" I wanted to know if Jane had said anything about us. I didn't trust her.

"Yeah, she does."

"You don't have to worry about her; she's not the type of girl for me. I want someone who I can trust and love. She's a slut!"

"She's not a slut! She's a little irresponsible and birdbrained, but she's my friend, and I love her very much."

"Ok, I take it back. I guess I'm jealous that you prefer her company over mine."

"You're wrong. I want to be with you, but I'm not sure about the office situation."

"What are you talking about? I know it can be a little weird, but we're adults, capable of keeping our professionalism at the office."

"I don't know. I have a bad feeling about the office, and I can't lose my job."

"Oh, you can't lose your job or your bestie, but it's ok to give up on me."

"I didn't say that! I need time to think…"

"You know what? I'm done. You can keep your job and your friend. And yes, I think she's a spoiled brat."

Matt and David showed up at the back door to check on us.

"What's up, guys? Is everything alright?" David asked.

"Yeah, I was leaving anyway," I said, turning around to leave.

"Wait! We haven't finished yet; I still have things to say to you." Ann grabbed my arm, making me stop.

"Guys, you need to calm down." David was worried about the situation.

"Yeah…why don't you come with me, Ann? Let's make coffee and give Joe a little time to chill. David will stay here with him."

"Yes! Good idea, Matt. Go with him, Ann. Joe and I will come over in a little while."

I came back and sat on the couch in silence, still annoyed but wanting to make peace with Ann. They left, and David looked at me, concerned about his friend's well-being.

"Hey, man, I'm not sure what happened between you two, but Ann is a wonderful being. She's lovely and has the kindest heart. Don't hurt her! If you're not sure of your feelings, let her go. I think she'll suffer a bit but will get over it eventually, but I want you to know that I won't let you hurt her further."

"I hear you. Thank you for being honest and a loyal friend to her. I don't want to hurt her. I really think she's the right woman for me. Even though I'm not sure about the office situation, I want to take our relationship to the next level. I'm serious about it."

"If you're sure about that, you definitely have to let her know. And, please, no more secrets."

"You're right; it's time for us to be together openly. I'll start sending resumes out and I'm sure I'll get another job before anyone can judge us."

"Well, I'm not sure about getting another job, but if you think it's better like this, then go for it! I'm sure you'll get another good job fast."

"Yeah, before the drama breaks out."

"What drama?"

"Never mind, I just think it'll be a little stressful when the truth comes out."

Ann walked in, and we locked eyes.

"Well, I guess Matt forgot to bring my coffee. I'll go. Bye." David left, leaving us there in silence.

"I'm sorry, Joe! I really am." She broke the silence.

"I'm sorry, too."

"I think I'm terrified of being hurt because someone hurt me really bad in the past. I'm scared of giving myself in and being betrayed again…"

"Shh, I understand. I have been hurt, too. Let's not talk about the past now." All I wanted was to make love to her. I kissed her affectionally, taking her to the bedroom.

"I'll never hurt you, Ann. I really want to be with you and take our relationship to the next level. I want you."

"No secrets?"

"No secrets," I promised, and we fell on the bed. I was eager to make peace with her.

Chapter 71

The next morning, I felt better and lazy after having a wonderful night with Ann. She was already up preparing breakfast; I could smell the freshly brewed coffee coming from the kitchen. She walked into the bedroom to check on me. I smiled at her, content.

"C'mon, time to get up, Mr. Garrison," she said, pulling the blanket off the bed and exposing my naked body. *"Ouh là là!"* she said, biting her lips, being adorable and sexy.

"Come here, you," I said, pulling her in the bed with me. Instead of kissing her as she expected, I asked, "Did you make coffee for us?"

"Whaaat?" she giggled, slapping me on the chest, trying to get up. I held her, getting myself on top of her, chuckling. She was smiling and waiting for my next move. I made her think I was going to kiss her again but stopped an inch from her mouth and said, "I would like some scrambled eggs too…" I looked at her seriously. "Do you have bacon?"

"Get up!" she said, pushing me off, laughing. "You can make your own eggs!" And with this, she left the room happily.

"Umm, I smell eggs and bacon. All that for me?" I said, smiling and kissing her good morning, walking in the kitchen. "You shouldn't have. I don't want to be any trouble," I teased her.

"You better eat everything I made," she said, smiling, sitting at the table, and starting to eat.

"So, what do you want to do about the office situation? As I said,

I'm open to whatever you decide," I asked her, helping myself with a cup of coffee.

"Well, I think we should start dating openly, but as if nothing has happened between us yet. Jane is my best friend, and she'll feel betrayed because I didn't tell her that you and I were seeing each other."

"How do you know she has no secrets? I mean, everybody does. She may be hiding something from you, too…"

"No, you don't know Jane. She's scatterbrained, naïve, and impulsive, but she has a great heart and is a loyal friend. I love her very much."

"I hope she loves you as much." I was worried about what Jane would say to her. If she really loved Ann, she would be quiet and let her friend be happy with me. After all, we broke up; I'm not cheating.

"Of course, she does. So, we can start showing that we're dating. We can go have lunch together; you can bring me candies, jewelry…" she said with a smirk. I chuckled at her jewelry comment.

"As I know her well, she's going to ask if you and I are seeing each other. I'll tell her *yes*, that you have asked me out, and we're dating. It'll be good to go slowly to check Mr. Poch's and Mr. McKee's reactions as well. I mean, if they say to you that they think it's not appropriate for us to get involved, we'll know how they feel about office romance and then decide what to do next."

"We could run away! Just leave town and no one would ever hear from us again. We can go to England. My mum will love you," I suggested.

"I wish…"

"Ok, I guess we have a plan then!" I said, taking a bite of my eggs and giving a piece of bacon to Max.

"I wonder why he loves you that much," she said, twisting her lips.

#

The next morning at the office, Ann and I were in the lunchroom making coffee when Jane arrived. She came into the room all smiling and was surprised to see me there with Ann that early, making coffee and talking joyfully.

"You?" She could not disguise the tension of having seen me there with Ann.

"Good morning, Jane. How was your weekend?" I asked her casually, hoping she would be quiet until I had the chance to talk with her and explain that I was dating Ann.

"I'm not feeling well," she said, leaving the room. Ann followed her.

I was feeling tense all morning, not knowing what was going on with Jane and Ann. What were they talking about? At lunchtime, Ann and I left for lunch as planned.

What's wrong with Jane?" I casually asked Ann at the restaurant.

"I don't know. She's distressed about something but didn't want to talk about it," she said.

Phew! Jane hasn't opened her mouth, so I guess she loves Ann after all. I thought I needed to talk to Jane before it was too late. I had to let her know that I was serious about Ann, that we're dating for real. If she loves her friend, she'll do nothing to hurt her.

Also, Jane can't say anything about Ann and me being together anyway since I know she has a boyfriend and was fucking other guys while having a good time with me as well. *Fucking whore—beautiful, sexy, stupid whore, that's what she is.* She's probably distressed about yet another guy; she makes me ill to my stomach.

#

After work, I ran to the garage to reach her before she could leave.

I found her crying in her car. I got in the car in the passenger seat and looked at her, striking her hair and wiping her tears. God, why does she have to be so beautiful and look so innocent?

"Why are you crying, Jane?"

"You're an evil, awful jerk. I hate you!" She started slapping me all over.

"Wow! Calm down, Jane," I said, holding her arms, preventing her from hitting me.

"Why are you doing this to me? Why are you doing this to Ann?" She kept crying.

"What? What are you talking about? Ann is my friend. I invited her for lunch, that's all. Are you jealous? Please don't cry. We need to talk. You're a big girl and must understand that I'm free to go out with whomever I want. You and I were just playing a game, which is over, by the way."

"I don't know what to think. What about Juan Carlos? You made him fall. You were jealous because I was dancing with him." She started talking nonsense.

"What are you talking about? Who is Juan Carlos?"

"That guy on the motorcycle. On Friday night, you made him fall."

"It was an accident, Jane. I swear to God. He wasn't hurt. I saw him getting up through the rearview mirror, and he rode away, maybe with a bruise or so, but that's all. You're driving me crazy!"

"What about Fred? You killed Fred."

"Who? I think you are hallucinating, Jane. Let me take you somewhere so you can calm down. I can't let you drive like this," I said, getting out of the car and going around to the driver's seat. "Scoot over."

She moved to the passenger seat, and I drove us out of there. I parked the car by Birch State Park; there was no one around. She had stopped crying.

"Babe, I don't know what's going on in your head, but I guarantee that I have nothing to do with the things you're accusing me of. I never hurt you or any of your boyfriends. You need help…"

"I know you did. And why are you charming my best friend now? Why are you trying to hurt everyone who gets close to me? You don't have to do that. You don't have to hurt anyone just to punish me."

"No, you're wrong. I'm not trying to punish you."

"Yes, you are! You like it when I misbehave, so you have an excuse to fuck me with fury. That's what you like. If I'm a whore, you are a pimp."

She was upsetting me, and I was getting turned on, wanting to fuck her again. Maybe I did want to punish her for being such a slut. Maybe she did bring out the pimp in me…

"You're wrong, and it's over. Please don't say anything to Ann. I like her for real, and if you tell her about us, she'll be very sad…and I'll be very angry."

"You see, you want me to make you angry."

"Don't be ridiculous. I want you out of my life! We started so well. We could've been together by now, but you kept spoiling everything."

"We can still be together."

"No way, we'll end up killing each other. Please leave me alone!" I said, trying to leave, but she held me back and started to kiss and touch me all over.

"I know what you want — me." she said, lifting her skirt and mounting on top of me. She unzipped my pants and started caressing and kissing me. "I can give you what you want," she whispered, kissing my ear and neck, rubbing her body against mine.

She unbuttoned my shirt and kissed my chest, then she looked at me, taking her shirt off and putting my hands on her breasts. Already desperate to have her, I could not stop. She's hot and turns me on like no one else. I kissed her, taking her panties off.

She sat on me, moaning. "Do you like this? Huh?" the little devil said, looking into my eyes and moving up and down, making me groan with pleasure. I could not stop. When she was done, she looked at me and said, "You know we belong together, and I won't let you go."

"Go home, Jane, and leave me alone. It doesn't matter we fucked again. I still don't want you. It's over!" I pushed her off, pulled my pants up, and fixed my shirt. I could not believe we fucked on the street again!

"Don't leave me here like this, please. Let me stay with you tonight. I won't say anything to Ann, I promise," she begged.

"You need to promise me you'll leave us alone."

"I promise."

"I don't know what to do with you. You're driving me insane."

"Please, I want to stay with you for the last time."

"Ok, but you promise it'll be the last time."

"I promise."

We went to this small boutique hotel in Lauderdale-By-The-Sea. We went to our room and asked for room service since I was starving. She was content and smiling, feeling victorious. I didn't want to say anything else. I took a shower and went to sleep. She came in, spooning me in the bed and kissing my cheek good night.

The next morning, she was taking a shower when I woke up. I was already dressed and ready to leave when she came out of the bathroom.

"Do we have to go now?" she asked, disappointed.

"Yeah, we need to go work. I have a very busy day ahead of me."

She didn't argue. She got dressed, and we left. I drove us to the parking garage where my car was parked, got out of the car, and left her there. She looked at me, sighed, and drove away.

Chapter 72

When arriving at the office around 10:00 AM, Larry and John called me into the conference room. I was nervous, wondering what they could possibly want with me. I thought that Jane might have said something and that I was going to be fired.

"Joe, dear boy, we called you here because we're very concerned about Jane. She's been behaving oddly lately, and we don't know what's going on. We know you are friends with the girls and may know something about why she's so distressed," John said, concerned.

"Yes, I noticed that, too, but honestly, I don't know. Ann told me she was having issues with her boyfriend." I pretended I knew nothing about her distress even though I might have been the cause of it.

"Yes, we thought it would be something like that. She's very young, and that's normal, but she needs to get over whatever is making her distressed. She needs to learn how to be professional," Larry added.

"I'm sure she'll be fine soon. Please give her a chance. She's a nice girl."

"Yes, Joe, you're right. I'm going to talk with her. Thank you, that's all we wanted to know for now," Larry said, leaving the room. John followed him out.

I stayed there for a minute to breathe in relief. I kept myself busy all day. I had a very important meeting with a client in the afternoon, which took hours. When we finished, it was already 5:30 PM, and the girls were gone. I went home feeling anxious. Where were they? I was impatient, trying to figure out what Jane would do, that little devil. Suddenly, my phone rang. It was Ann.

"Hey, Joe, I'm at Jane's. She needs a friend, and she's going to sleep over at my house. You know, girls' night. I think she needs to talk."

"What? Why? Did she get fired today? I heard a conversation that she wasn't doing well." I needed to know how the conversation went.

"Yeah, Mr. McKee called her in his office, but apparently, he gave her another chance."

"Really? I think it would be good for her to take a vacation; you know? Think things over."

"Yes, that's actually a good idea. I'm going to suggest it to her. I think she's having issues with her boyfriend."

"Boyfriend?"

"Yes, Mike. He's her next-door neighbor. She's there now talking to him; he seemed to be very upset with her. Hopefully, they won't fight. Poor Jane. I need to go. She's back. Bye."

"Ok, talk to you later."

What now? The little brat had me in her hands, and I had no idea what she was up to. I thought about quitting my job and going back to Chicago. Then, I thought about Amy. Why did she leave me? She's the reason I am going through this nightmare. I couldn't sleep all night, tossing and turning, thinking about the three of them, Amy, Ann, and Jane. Jane, the little liar, swore she didn't have a boyfriend. So, the guy's name is Mike, and he's her neighbor. I wanted to kill her. I couldn't stay in bed any longer. I got up, went to the gym for a run, took a shower, and was in the office before eight.

#

"Hi, girls," I greeted them with a cup of coffee in my hand when they finally arrived.

"Did you make coffee?" Ann asked, smiling and going to the lunchroom.

"I tried." I smiled at Ann and then locked eyes with the little devil.

"Let me try it; I'll tell you. Do you want some, Jane?"

Ann went to grab a cup for herself. Jane and I stared at each other without saying a word. I could feel in my soul that she was feeling victorious.

"Good, very good, actually," Ann said, coming back with two mugs. One was for Jane.

"Not bad, huh? See you later," I said, going to my office.

"Sure." Ann seemed happy, so I guess the little monster had not opened her fucking mouth. *Good.*

At lunchtime, as I was leaving to grab something to eat, I saw that Ann was alone in the reception.

"Were you going to have lunch with Jane?" I was confused since she said they had plans for lunch.

"No, Jane said she had other plans and left. I'm free if you are."

"Yeah, I'm ready to kiss you," I said, stealing a kiss.

"Let's go then?"

We went to this famous restaurant on Las Olas. It was crowded, but we got a table. After ordering our food and drinks, we started to talk about Jane. I was eager to know what they talked about last night.

"So, how's Jane? Is she ok?" I asked, sounding casual.

"No, I think she's going through a hard time, but she didn't want to talk about her troubles last night."

"Did you say she was having problems with her boyfriend? The neighbor?"

"Yeah, apparently, they're fighting a lot, which is confusing because she never cared for him that much, so I'm not sure why she's so distressed."

"Maybe she's having money issues?"

"No, she's stressed because of someone. I'm not sure if this person is Mike. He was asking where she went the night before, and apparently, she lied, saying that she was with me."

"I hope she gets better and really doesn't disturb the office peace. Mr. McKee was talking about letting her go, and to be honest, she may be better off somewhere else."

"Don't say that. She's my friend and I love her. I know she can be a pain sometimes, but I don't want her to leave."

"Well, I won't let her interfere in our relationship. If she keeps having an attitude, I'll agree with Mr. McKee about letting her go."

"I'll talk with her. I'm sure she'll be fine soon."

"You're an incredible friend. I just don't have your patience, and I'm not sure she deserves that much loyalty from you. I don't know, but I feel she's not sincere with you, and I think she wouldn't do the same for you."

"You don't know her."

"Maybe you're right. Enough talking about Jane. I miss you and can't wait to have you in my arms Friday night," I said, kissing her.

"Me too," she said, smiling and wiping the lipstick she had left on my lips with her thumb.

We then went back to the office.

Chapter 73

The rest of the week was very busy. I had a very important case to defend in court. It was a controversial case, an inheritance dispute where the father had disinherited one of his kids before dying. The hearing was very emotional and intense. The judge wanted to hear thoroughly from all sides of the issue; it was exhausting.

Friday afternoon, we had a break at the court, so I called Ann to let her know that I was still trapped in the courthouse, but I was going to pick her up as we had planned.

"Hey, love, how are you? I miss you so much. Can't wait to see you tonight. I'll pick you up at nine."

"Nine o'clock is fine. See you then."

#

We had planned for Ann to come and sleep at my place for the first time. I wanted her to feel that I was serious about our relationship. It was time for me to let her take over my space and leave her mark there. Whatever she wanted to do, I would let her.

When arriving at her house at around 9:00 PM, I saw a hooker blocking my way through. I had no choice but to slow down and check what she wanted.

"Hey, baby. Do you want company tonight?" she said, leaning on the car window.

"Get off, bitch!" I said, not looking at her.

"C'mon, I bet you'll have a lot more fun with me than with Ann," she said and smiled, batting her eyelashes when I looked at her.

"Jane? Is that you?" I couldn't believe it. She was disguised, wearing a very trashy and vulgar outfit, and had a long bleach-blond wig. Her makeup was exaggerated with huge eyelashes, and she had red lipstick on.

"Here," she said and tossed a piece of paper with this bar address at me. "I'll wait for you until ten o'clock. If you don't show, I'll tell Ann who you really are." And she left.

"What the fuck! BITCH! WHORE! SLUT!" I yelled, hitting the steering wheel several times with rage. I could not hold myself down as I was so angry. The fucking brat knows how to get me. She's a little devil, and I was going to kill her. I took a deep breath to calm down, counted to ten, and knocked on Ann's door.

"Hey, gorgeous!" I embraced and kissed her, taking her inside and closing the door behind us with my foot.

"Hey. I'm ready to go," she said, showing me her huge bag. I had to laugh.

"How long are you planning to stay?" I asked, chuckling.

"Forever!"

"Forever is good," I said and kissed her again. "I've got some not-so-good news."

"What happened?"

"Larry, Mr. Poch, called me, and he wants me to join him at the country club for a reception. He wants me to meet this new client. I'm sorry, I'll have to go and can't take you with me."

"Oh, no."

"I'm sorry, babe. I can come over afterward."

"That's ok. We can do something tomorrow. I'll cook for you, and we can invite Matt and David, too. What do you think?"

"Sounds like a plan!" I kissed her goodbye, and off I went to meet the devil in person.

#

I got to the address on the paper Jane had tossed me a few minutes before. It was a decadent bar with very frightening people. I went in and sat at the bar and asked for a beer. Jane was talking with this weird, huge, tattooed guy. She was laughing and apparently charming the poor guy when she saw me. She felt uncomfortable; I could tell. I stared at her with fury. She was acting vulgar and looked disgusting in that hooker outfit. I imagined her fucking that guy, rejoicing with pleasure. *What was she trying to do?* I was going to murder her.

When she got up after a little while and went to the bathroom, I thought about following her, but the big guy was still waiting for her to come back, so I had to think of another way to get to her. I left the bar and waited for her outside. I knew that if she had come that far with this ridiculous plan to provoke me, she would not leave before getting what she wanted. As I predicted, five minutes later, she came around the corner into the alley, looking for me.

"What the fuck are you trying to do? Do you want to get killed?" I said, grabbing her and trapping her against the wall. "I'm really tempted to do so right now," I said angrily and squeezing her throat, making her gasp for air.

"Please, Joe…" she tried to talk.

"What's that on your face? Look at you. You finally took on your real whore persona, huh?" I wiped her mouth, smearing her lipstick all over her face with my thumb, still holding her against the wall by her neck. My other hand got into her panties; she was wet. "You're a horny little bitch, and I know exactly what you want."

I fingered her until she started moaning. "Oh, Joe," she said and managed to unbutton and unzip my pants, grabbing my dick.

"That's what you want, eh?" I said, enraged.

"Yes…please, Joe…I love you," she said, groaning.

"No, you don't love me. You love my dick, you freak nymphomaniac." And then I gave her what she was so desperate to have. I fucked her very hard with no remorse.

"Ah…Joe…" She looked into my eyes, panting. "I'm the right woman for you, can't you see it? Let's get out of here, just you and me. I'll be your whore if you want me to," she said, kissing me all over. "You just have to leave Ann alone," she murmured. "I'll do anything for you, just don't leave me."

"No!" I got away from her, leaving her asking for more.

"Come back," she said, holding me.

"No! I don't want you! Can you understand that? Leave me and Ann alone. I'm warning you!" I shouted and walked away to my car, kicking the garbage bags in my way.

"I will not leave you alone! Do you hear me? I'm not going to let you go. You're mine, and you know it! JOE!" She stayed there crying and yelling. She is crazy!

What the fuck does she want from me? I couldn't think straight as I sat in my car. *What should I do next? How am I going to get rid of Jane?* Oh my God, I needed some time to think. I was already far beyond my limit and scared, not knowing what to do. *Fuck you, Jane!*

Chapter 74

I arrived at Ann's house around 11:30 AM with the mission of telling her that Jane was a psychopath and in desperate need of help. I would not let the little brat ruin my life. She needs to be locked in a mental institution.

"What happened? Is anything wrong?" Ann asked when she saw my preoccupied face.

"Yeah. I don't know how to tell you this, but I feel I need to. It's about Jane."

"What happened to her?"

"Well, yesterday, when I left the reception, I went to this club. Look, I know it can seem odd, but me and the guys usually go there for fun. We don't go there to pick up hookers. We just go for a good time. It's kind of cool; the people are great, and the girls are beautiful, but no lap dance for me, believe me."

"I'm not getting…"

"As I was saying, it's a strip club. Anyway, Jane was there, and she wasn't normal. She was wearing this very sexy, trashy outfit and a long bleach-blond wig…"

"No way!"

"Yes way. And there is more."

"What?"

"She was with this old, very scary, tattooed guy. I had to come closer to make sure that it was her, and it was. She panicked when she saw me. I tried to talk with her, but she left in a hurry."

"It can't be. I don't believe you."

"Believe me, I wouldn't tell you if I didn't think it wasn't serious. I told you I always thought that she was hiding something."

"Maybe that's the reason for her fights with Mike. He must have found out."

"It could be. I know she's your friend, but as I said, she doesn't hold you to the same standard."

"I need to digest this story. Thank you for letting me know anyway."

"Hey, guys! A little help here," David called us outside for help.

The barbeque was delicious. Matt was stressed out, trying to manage the grill and all, and even though he was clearly struggling to keep up with everything, he would let no one help him and mess with his cooking. He was funny; I liked him.

After we ate, drank, talked, and had a lot of fun together, it was time to clean up. Ann and I helped David and Matt, and when it was already getting dark outside, we went inside to relax.

"Do you want to go to my place as we had planned before?" I asked her.

"No, it's ok. I have Max to take care of, and I need to check on Jane tomorrow if you don't mind."

"Nope, I can go with you if you want."

"No, I'll talk with her alone. Actually, I want to talk with Mike first."

"Mike, who? The boyfriend?"

"Yes."

"Ok. *Muchacha, ven aquí con papi.*" I called her with my hands, trying to speak Spanish to impress her.

"Aww, you're so cute speaking Spanish. C'mon say more; you're turning me on…*papi.*" She sat on my lap, kissing me all over.

"*Guapa! Chica hermosa,*" I said, smiling and kissing her mouth. "*Te extraño.*" I was using all the Spanish words I knew to impress her.

"More…" she said, taking my t-shirt off and looking at me guilefully.

"That's all I know."

"Please keep going…don't stop."

"I promise I'll buy a Spanish dictionary tomorrow."

She laughed at me.

"*Te quero mucho,*" I said. "*Guapa, hermosa…*" I started to repeat the words I knew just to keep the mood going, laying her down on the couch and taking her t-shirt off.

"*Yo también te quiero,*" she said, unzipping my pants and starting to caress me.

"C'mon, *niña*… Let me show you, *papi.*" I took her pants off and kissed her all over. She was panting with pleasure.

"*Basta, ven aquí,*" she said, pulling me over her.

"What?"

"Shh, stop talking," she said, chuckling and getting me inside her.

"All right, say no more…" I kissed her tenderly, making love to her.

#

The next morning, I woke up and went for a run on the beach with Jamal. I missed my friend, and Ann was going to talk with Jane's boyfriend to try to understand what was wrong with Jane. I wasn't too worried about what Jane could and would say to Ann since she had kept her mouth shut until now. She clearly wanted me, and she knew that it would be the end of everything if she said anything.

"Hey, mate! Long time no see you!" I greeted Jamal at the Hollywood Beach boardwalk.

"Hey, Chicago! Where have you been? I miss you, man!"

"I've been busy, very busy."

"Work or girls?"

"Both!"

We started jogging.

"How's Jane?"

"Oh man, she's a nightmare!"

"No way! Tell me about it."

"No, I just want to forget about her. She's a little brat."

"It's getting interesting."

"No, man, it's getting out of hand. And I don't know how to get rid of her. What about you?"

"I'm well, met this girl, and we're getting along."

"Really? You're settling down with just one girl? I don't believe it."

"Yeah, man, she's incredible. Everything I always wanted…beautiful, sexy, independent, and bright."

"Good for you, Jamal, really. I'm happy you're happy."

It was a good run, and I was feeling relaxed. Back at Ann's place, I took a shower, and we went outside to meet David and Matt for another BBQ. We had a lot of leftovers from the day before.

#

In the afternoon, we sat outside, having beers, chips, and salsa.

Matt was quiet; he was still upset about yesterday's BBQ.

"I have never tried grilled watermelons before. It was delicious, really!" I tried to cheer Matt up.

"Thanks, Joe. I'm glad you liked it, but I'll never do that again; no more BBQs for me!"

We all laughed.

"What are you guys doing tonight?" David asked. "What about a movie night?"

"Thanks, David, but I have something to talk about with Joe," Ann said.

"What? I hope you guys are not fighting again," Matt said.

"No, it's about Jane."

"Oh, poor girl! You told me she is going through a hard time. Let us know if there is anything we can do to help her, ok?" David added.

"Sure, thanks."

Ann and I went inside and started putting the stuff away in the kitchen. I was dying to know what had happened with Jane and the boyfriend.

"What's up with Jane?" I tried to sound casual.

"I spoke with Mike this morning, the boyfriend."

"And?"

"And we had decided on an intervention session with her. We'll invite her over. Mike will be here, too. I'm not sure if tomorrow or when, so it's better that you don't come or sleepover for a couple of days. I'll let you know."

"Wait a minute—intervention like the TV show?"

"Yes, something like that!"

"I don't know."

"Well, Mike told me he saw her coming home Friday night, wearing the exact outfit you described, but worse—she was a mess. Her makeup smudged, and clothes torn..."

"Oh my God. I told you."

"I need to do something. She's my friend."

"I know! It's crazy." I felt that I had to tell her that Jane and I had had an affair, the whole story was getting out of control. "Ann, I need to tell you one thing before this intervention takes place."

"What?"

"Come sit down here on the couch with me."

"You're making me nervous. What is it?" She was getting apprehensive.

"Well, I didn't tell you before because I thought it wasn't important. In fact, if she didn't tell you, it's because she didn't want you to know."

"What?"

"I met Jane before starting to work in the office. We had a night out affair kind of thing. It was really nothing."

"How come you never told me?"

"I'm telling you now."

"How come she never told me, either?" She was confused, squinting her eyes and shaking her head.

"I don't know, but it's nothing you should care about. We know that her situation now is way more important than my affair with her. I just wanted to let you know before it comes up, and it seems like I was hiding something terrible from you."

"You hid a very important detail from me."

"You hid our relationship from her, too; that makes us equals."

"Equals how? I never lied to you."

"You hid our affair from Jane, your best friend."

"Because you wanted me to—you wanted to keep it a secret."

"I never asked you to keep our relationship a secret. You didn't want to tell her, not me."

"Maybe you're right. I was afraid that she could betray me like another best friend I had once…" She paused. "I need to think…"

"Ok, I'll see you tomorrow at the office."

I kissed her forehead and left.

Chapter 75

On Monday morning, I was apprehensive and nervous about the intervention thing. Jane is unpredictable, and I had no idea what she would do when under pressure. I thought I had to be there so she would feel intimidated. She must agree to go somewhere. I would happily pay for her to go on vacation somewhere and leave me alone.

When Ann arrived at the office, I was already there, waiting for some kind of news.

"Hi, babe. Are you still planning to go on with the intervention thing?" I asked, kissing her, trying to sound casual. But, at the same time, I was worried about Jane's situation.

"Yeah, definitely."

"Is there anything I can do? I mean, do you want me to be there, too?"

"No, you shouldn't be there. I'll call you afterward, ok?"

"Ok."

The day went well and smoothly. Jane seemed distressed and was unusually quiet. She was avoiding me, and we didn't make any eye contact all day long. I wanted to talk with her before their intervention meeting just to make sure she wasn't planning to say anything, but she was unapproachable. After work, I rushed to the garage, but her car wasn't there. I knew where she lived. I could go there, but the boyfriend is her neighbor. Well, I needed to relax and let it go. There was nothing I could do about it—only wait for the outcome. Around eight o'clock, Ann called me.

"Hey, Joe!"

"Hey, love."

"So, we're having the intervention thing tomorrow night, just to let you know."

"I think I should be there, too."

"No, you should not. I'll call you afterward, ok?"

"I'm not liking this shit."

"Everything is going to be fine. I love you."

"Love you, too. I'll wait for your call."

#

The night of the intervention, I was pacing back and forth in my living room, not knowing what to do. The fucking little brat had my life in her hands. Her beautiful and angelic face was a disguise. *She's evil!* I decided to go to South Beach and drink until passing out.

I walked on Ocean Drive. It was crowded as usual. People were having fun, not knowing my dilemma. Who knows what goes inside people's heads? I got a drink and sat on the wall dividing the Beach and Lummus Park. I stayed there, watching people passing by. Everyone seemed to be happy and having a good time. It was irritating.

I turned around to look at the ocean.

Suddenly, someone sat by my side and said with a heavy Russian accent, "Hey, you look so sad."

I looked at her and nodded. "No shit!" And I chuckled, looking away.

"My name is Tatiana. What's yours?"

"Joe."

"Hi, Joe. Why are you so pensive? Hard time? With money?"

"No."

"So, it must be a girl."

"Yeah, definitely." I chuckled and looked at her, nodding.

"I knew it! You must have many girls after you."

"Why is that?"

"Well, you're very handsome."

"Thanks, you're cute, too," I said, chuckling.

"Cute?"

"I meant beautiful," I corrected myself.

"Oh, much better!" she said, smiling and lighting a cigarette.

"You shouldn't smoke; beautiful girls don't smoke," I said, taking the cigarette from her hand.

"Russian girls do, but it's fine if you don't like it. Where are your friends?"

"Don't know. Where are yours?"

"Well, I'm on my break. I work over there." she said and pointed at this nightclub.

"Wow, what do you do there?"

"I'm a waitress."

"You don't look like a waitress. And you're definitely not dressed as a waitress."

"Yeah. We need to look sexy. Do you think I'm sexy?"

"No offense, but I don't want to start this conversation," I said, laughing, knowing what she wanted from me.

"Oh, I guess I'm just cute."

"No, you're beautiful. I'm the ugly one right now. Believe me, you don't want to get involved with me."

"I never said I wanted to get involved with you."

"So, what do you want, then?"

"To have a good time, to have someone to talk with, maybe have a drink after work."

"And?"

"I would sleep with you if you wanted."

I looked at her, mesmerized by her frankness. I laughed and kissed her.

"Why not? You got me, girl."

We went back to her nightclub. She was very busy serving tables. I sat by the bar counter and kept drinking, watching her. She was kind of beautiful in her own way. I think every girl has something beautiful about them. You just need to look for their special gift. Being beautiful outside doesn't mean the girl is also beautiful inside. Look at Jane. She's the most beautiful creature I have ever seen, but she's evil, crazy, and a lunatic.

I was going over the facts in my head. I'm a lawyer, and I knew I would not go to jail for sleeping with two girls who worked with me and were best friends. There is no law against free will. They're both adults and had sex with me willingly. However, I would get fired for that. I would have to move again, maybe out of the country, since no one would hire me knowing that I got fired for misconduct. Jane could ruin my life if she wanted to. So, let us drink to Jane! The little bitch won!

"Hey, Joe. Let's go?"

"Are you done? Can you leave now?"

"Yep, let's go," she said, pulling me out of my seat.

"Wait, I have to finish my drink," I said, drinking whatever was left in my glass at once. "Where do you want to go? Let's have a drink," I said, putting my arm around her and walking out of the club.

"I think you had enough to drink for tonight. What about we go to sleep?"

"Yeah. Let's go sleep, baby," I said, smiling and kissing her.

She took me to her apartment, which wasn't far from Ocean Drive. I was so drunk that I collapsed on her bed and blacked out until the next morning.

"Oh my God, what time is it? I have to go work!"

"Relax, it's only six in the morning. You have plenty of time to get to work," Tatiana said, giving me a cup of strong, bitter coffee. "Drink it, it'll wake you up."

"Thank you."

"Here, go take a shower." She handed me a towel.

"Thanks! Are you an angel? Am I dead?"

"I'm not, and no, you're not," she said, laughing at my comment.

"Why are you being so nice to me? You don't even know who I am."

"Yeah, I don't know you, but I could tell you needed someone last night."

"Thanks."

"No problem, just go!"

"Do you want to come and take a shower with me?"

"No, the magic is gone. Maybe next time," she said, smiling.

After a cold shower, I got dressed, kissed her goodbye, and rushed to Fort Lauderdale.

I was feeling awful.

Chapter 76

I got to the office late since I had to stop at my place to change. Everyone was already in but Jane. I was afraid to ask what had happened in the intervention meeting but eager to know the outcome.

"Hey, love, how was the intervention thing last night? Why didn't you call me?" I asked Ann when I saw her in the office.

"It wasn't good. I'm sorry I didn't call you after she left. She felt trapped and stormed out of the house."

"Wow. Did she say anything?"

"She said that you're evil."

"I think she needs professional help." So, she did try to say something about me. The little slut!

"Yeah, we're coming to this conclusion, too. Mike is going to try to take her on a vacation to New York so she can at least calm down a bit."

"That's a wonderful idea. She needs to get out of here."

"I'm going to tell Mr. McKee that she called in sick, and I'm planning to go to her house after work."

"I can go with you." I needed to stop Jane from opening her mouth.

"No, Mike and I have her under control. She's jealous of us, and your presence will only stress her more."

"Ok, call me if you need anything," I said, sounding calm but still apprehensive.

I was safe, at least for now. After work, I waited patiently for Ann's call, but she was taking too long, so I went to her house and waited for her there. I saw her car parked in front of the house and figured she was inside. I knocked on the door, but she didn't open. I sat on the doorstep to call her when I saw her coming back from a walk with Max.

"Hey, love, I stopped by to check if you were home and saw your car. I knocked, and I was going to call you."

"Hey, babe, I'm fine. Mike just called me saying that she opened the door and agreed to go to New York with him. I'm relieved."

"Well, that's wonderful news. She really needs to get out of here. It's going to be good for her and, to be honest, good for us, too." I sighed with relief!

"Don't say that."

"I don't want to talk about Jane anymore. What if we order food delivery and have a nice, relaxing, loving night together—just you and me?" I said, embracing her from behind and walking with her inside the house. I was so happy with the outcome. It couldn't have been better. She was gone, the little brat was gone!

"I think it's a wonderful idea. I miss you." she said, turning around to face me.

"I miss you, too," I said, kissing her and taking her to the bedroom.

"Wait! Let's order the food?"

"Food, right," I said, getting my cell phone. "What are you in the mood for? Greek?"

She nodded, and I placed the order.

"Ok, it's done. Where were we?" I said, smiling and grabbing her again.

"We need to wait for the delivery guy," she said, trying to get out of my embrace.

"The guy said approximately one hour."

"One hour is not a lot of time, and sometimes they come faster…"

"Sometimes they come later. Anyway, I can do a lot of things to you in one hour," I said, pushing her onto the bed, holding her arms above her head, and trapping her legs between mine.

"You can do a lot of things *with* me," she said, smiling and trying to kiss me. I pulled my face away so she couldn't reach my mouth with her lips.

"No, I'll do things *to* you. You're going to be the passive receptor of my actions," I said, kissing her belly and nibbling at her belly button.

"Joe, stop. It tickles."

"Now, I'm going to unbutton your shirt. I'm using just one hand…see?" and I showed her my free hand while the other still held her hostage.

"No, Joe, wait. I want to take a shower. I need to brush my teeth."

"I like you dirty!" I whispered, looking into her eyes.

"Ah. Kiss me already!"

"No."

"Please, let me kiss you, let me touch you. You are torturing me."

"That's the intention," I said, kissing her naked breast and her neck and unzipping her pants with my free hand. "Do you like this?" I said, caressing her.

She was wet and warm; she was so ready for me.

"Do you want me to stop now?" I said, smiling, looking in her eyes an inch away from her face.

"No, don't stop." She murmured.

"On second thought, I think you're right. Let's wait for the delivery guy," I said, grinning, and let her go free. I sat up at the bed's edge.

"What? No fucking way! Come back here!" she said, grabbing me from behind and pulling me back to bed with her. She was on fire; I've never seen Ann like that. She took my shirt and pants off in a hurry to feel my skin on hers. Then she kissed all over my naked body. I had to hold myself back from grabbing her and taking control of the situation, but she was doing amazingly well, so I let her do as she pleased. She was panting with pleasure when she rode me, free of any shame. She was incredible. It was fantastic; I'll never forget this day for sure.

Chapter 77

The week passed by so fast. Everything was going well. Ann and I were doing wonderfully. The office was quiet, and to be honest, Jane wasn't even missed in the office. I could forget she existed and move on with my life. However, everything turned around the following Saturday.

"Morning, love!" I said, opening the bedroom curtain and handing Ann a freshly brewed coffee mug.

"Morning," she said, smiling and grabbing the coffee. "What do you want to do today?"

"I'm going for a run on the beach if you don't mind."

"Of course, I don't mind. I'll do some cleaning and laundry and chat with David and Matt a bit. I miss them, and I have to give some attention to my kid, Max, as well. So go and have fun."

"Ok, I'll grab lunch with Jamal. We can go out tonight if you want. Do you want to go dance?"

"Yeah, I guess we could do something different."

"Ok, bye," I said and kissed her before leaving.

#

The beach was wonderful, the ocean was calm, and the sun was not that hot yet. I went for a run feeling good and relaxed. After running, I stopped by my place to get some clean clothes and water my pet plants. They were not very happy; I could tell. I tried to give them love and talked with them. Some people say they are sensible to our feelings and thrive when they feel loved.

"Love you guys," I told them and decided to ask Ann if she would take them in…maybe David would. I knew he loved plants. Anyway, I got everything I needed and went to meet Jamal on Las Olas for lunch.

"Hey, Jamal, my friend. How's everything?"

"I am wonderful! What about you, man?"

"Everything is fine."

"Good to know. How's that chick—Jane? Still giving you a hard time?"

"No, she's gone. Thank God! She's a bad juju. I'm glad she's gone."

"Good to know."

"What about you? How's the wonderful woman who conquered your heart?"

"She's fine. I'm happy, man. I think she's the one."

"I'm happy for you, my friend."

"Apparently, we both found our soulmates."

"Not sure about soulmates, but I'll settle down with her. You?"

"Yeah, definitely."

"To the girls of our dreams!"

"Cheers!" And we drank to celebrate the new era coming for us. I was content and feeling good.

Then I went home to Ann.

#

"How was your day?" I asked her, going to the bathroom to take a shower.

"I did a lot. It was a busy day. Mike called; he said they're coming back today," she said, following me into the bathroom.

"Today?" I opened the shower box door to confirm the bad news she was giving me.

"Yes, they want to come over to talk, and they want you to be part of the conversation."

"No fucking way. I really thought the vacation would calm her down. We're not going to let her keep with this neurotic behavior."

"Yeah, I hear you. I'm upset, too."

"Let's go out and enjoy our Saturday night," I said, coming out of the shower and dropping my towel on the floor.

"I agree. Please don't leave the towel on the floor," she said, giving me the look.

"*¿Qué pasa, niña? Estás loca?*" I laughed, taking the towel from the floor and hanging it on the towel bar. I looked at her, saying, "I wasn't going to leave it on the floor."

"Better!" she said, going to the bedroom.

"*Hey, Chica, yo stoy hablando.* It's Spanish...don't you find it hot?" I smiled, showing her my naked body.

"It doesn't work when I'm mad. *Vete hombre,*" she said and, with her hand, gestured at me to go away.

"*Oí ¿Estás loca mujer?* Ok, I'm going, I'm going..." I started going back to the bathroom, laughing to myself, when her phone rang.

"It's Mike! I'll get it in the living room," she said, leaving the bedroom.

"Mike said they're coming over around eight o'clock and want to talk with us both," she told me as I entered the living room, combing my hair.

"No way, I'm out of here. Let's leave before they arrive." I was upset with the trap, and it was already 7:45 PM.

"I can't. Why don't you go for a drink? I'll let them talk, and we'll go out afterward."

"I'll give them one hour. If they're still here when I come back, I'll tell them to leave."

"Ok, one hour is more than enough."

#

It was already dark outside when I left the house. I was lost in my thoughts, thinking that the nightmare was going to start over. *I really am going to kill Jane if she doesn't stop with this nonsense. Wasn't a week with her boyfriend enough for her to forget about me?* I was so upset that I didn't recognize Jane waiting for me across the street.

"Joe," she called me.

"Jane? Bloody hell! What in the hell are you up to? Get in the fucking car. NOW!" I yelled at her, getting myself in the car as well. "What are you trying to do? What's this about? Have you lost your mind?"

"I just want to be with you, Joe," she said with an innocent face.

"It's over, Jane. Don't you get it? I'm not into you anymore. I'm tired of this game shit. Let's forget everything and pretend it never happened."

"I can't pretend it never happened. You've just turned my life upside down, and now you're trying to get my best friend's life also screwed. Sorry, but I can't let you."

"Jane," I said and looked at her, taking I-95 and heading south to Marathon. "You don't understand. If you don't let go, I'll have to make you."

"How? Are you going to kill me?"

"Don't try me, woman! And why are you wearing this trashy outfit again? Do you want to play whore?"

"I want you. I can be your whore if you like."

"I can't take this anymore. Jane, please leave me alone. For the last time, I'm asking you to LEAVE ME ALONE!"

"NO!"

I was getting very upset and grabbed her arm with force. I wanted to kill her.

"Don't hurt me, please," she said, pretending to be scared.

"Why do you keep saying that? I've never hurt you; it's all in your imagination. You keep pushing me over the borderline, testing my limits; you like to see me angry and out of control. We've had enough. I can't take it anymore. I really don't want to hurt you."

"You can't leave me. I don't know how to live without you. Where are you taking me?"

"Let's go to Marathon. You and I are going to talk and find a satisfactory solution that suits us both, ok?"

"You mean we're going to fuck," she said with a cynical smile on her face now.

"That, too! Isn't that what you want?"

"You can't play with people's minds. It's wrong. I'm a person, and I have feelings."

"You know what?" I was trying to keep my cool. "It was my mistake, really. I should've known that you were too weak for this type of thing. You're just a little spoiled brat; that's what you are."

"No, Joe. I'm the type of girl you like. I'm the right woman for you. You also can't live without me."

"NO, you're wrong; you disgust me. Look at you. You really like to be treated like a whore that you are. I'm just the one that fell for your angel's face and ended up bringing the slut out of you, didn't I?"

"Don't you understand? I'm doing what you wanted me to. You started treating me this way. I could've been just a girlfriend to you, just like Ann."

"Ann is not like you. She's a good girl."

"Why are you saying that? What do you know about her? She's a normal girl, just like me."

"No, she's nothing like you. She's genuine, and she has no hidden side like you do."

"WHAT? You really are a son of a bitch, a psycho, and an asshole. I can't believe you're saying that to me. I'm doing what you wanted me to do. I'm doing it for you. And you love it, you know that."

"For me? Give me a break, Jane; we were doing so well until you started playing dirty. I'm a guy; I can't control myself. You knew I was crazy for you, and you kept pushing my limits to see me furious. Say it…I want to hear you say that I made you hornier than you've ever been in your life, freaking bitch. You're playing with my mind; you're the psycho."

"I can't believe my ears. You're trying to make me feel guilty about everything that has happened to me since I met you."

"You're guilty, Jane; admit it. You can't have a normal relationship. It would make you bored. You like to incite and feel the adrenaline running in your veins, taking risks. You love to fuck in filthy alleys. You make me want to hurt you. And you like just that— to be abused by me. I couldn't see this side of you before it was too late." I was furious. "Is that your boyfriend following us?" I saw this car following us through the rearview mirror. "Is he not enough for you? Doesn't he fuck you like I do? Of course, he doesn't."

"You're insane! How could you think I wanted to be abused? I'm just playing your fucking game. You asked me to play with you. You said it was supposed to be sensual and thrilling, remember? You wanted to fulfill my fantasies, and I just wanted to fulfill yours. I had to provoke you because it was the only way to make you come to me; that's the way you liked it. And I didn't want our relationship to cool down. Mike is not my boyfriend. Please, I love you."

"Jane, I'm sorry, but I don't love you. I just wanted to have a good time; you're so beautiful and sexy, and it seemed to me you were up for enjoying some adventure…and I don't believe you. I bet you fucked the guy. And why is he following us?"

"They're following us so they can witness the jerk you are. Why did you go that far? Why did you try to hurt Juan Carlos and kill Fred if you were not jealous and desperately in love with me?"

"They who?" I tried to see who else was in the car, following us through the rearview mirror. "Are you insane?" The accusation astonished me.

"I never tried to hurt Juan Carlos and don't even know who Fred is. You need help." I pulled over to look into her eyes. "Jane, believe me; it's all in your head. I've done nothing to hurt anyone, not even you. I thought we were enjoying a good time together, but every time I tried to be nice to you, you turned the table to provoke me; that's what you wanted, not me."

"I did it for you, Joe. I would do anything for you, and I can't stand seeing you with Ann."

"So, then we have a problem. I really like her."

"NO! You'll not be with her, I promise," she said with conviction.

The boyfriend's car caught up and pulled over behind us.

Chapter 78

"Please, Joe. I need you. We can start over somewhere else," she begged, trying to kiss me.

"I wish we could, but no matter where we are, we can't change it, not anymore. It's too late for us. One of us has to go," I said, pushing her off me and holding her arms.

"NO! I won't let you go. You can't leave me. Please, please, don't say it's over. I'd rather die!" She suddenly changed her demeanor and was crying hysterically now that her boyfriend was nearby. The little brat was trying to make a scene, playing the victim.

"Jane! Listen to me; it is over. We must move on; there's no other way. And you're not going to die; you'll find someone else."

"NO!" she screamed, opened the car door and ran onto the highway. We were over a bridge on US1, just passing Key Largo. I ran after her, not noticing that Ann was behind me.

"Jane! Come back here." I caught her by the arm and held her tight. "Jane, please don't make a scene. I can't give you what you want," I said again, looking at her with rage.

"Why not? You said you loved me, too." She looked at me with her beautiful blue eyes, tearing up.

"It will not work. We can't see each other ever again. If you don't quit the office, I'll have to. I don't want to hurt you or anybody else." I was still holding her. "You need help, Jane; let me help you."

"Let her go!" The boyfriend yelled, approaching us with a

baseball bat in his hands. Ann was right behind him, dazed by the scene.

"What's going on? Jane, let's talk. We can clear all this misunderstanding, I'm sure," Ann said, approaching us slowly.

"Ann, Joe is a jerk. He hurt me and killed Fred, tried to kill Juan Carlos, and now he wants to hurt you! Believe me, he's a liar." Jane started lying to Ann and making me seem like a monster.

Ann stretched her hand to Jane. "Come here," she said, calling Jane to her.

I let her go, and she ran to Ann, who embraced her. Jane was crying hysterically.

The boyfriend was trying to keep me away from the girls. He was so pathetic, but I could see the confusion on his face. He wasn't sure of what was going on. However, it was obvious that he didn't know Jane that well. She probably fooled him into believing she was the victim and that I was a murderer.

"Well, what the fuck, man! What did you do this for? Why did you mistreat her like that? She's just a girl," the boyfriend said, still swinging the bat in his hands, trying to protect his girlfriend.

"I meant no harm." What else could I say?

"I guess it's too late, huh? Do you think you can just play a game of your choosing, set the rules, and end the game when you're tired? I don't think so, not with my girl. I love her and will not let this happen again. You're an asshole."

"I may be." I wasn't in the mood to argue with the guy and was afraid of what Jane was telling Ann. "Let's talk, all four of us, so we can clear up this freaking story, shall we?" I said aloud so everyone could hear me.

"Yeah," Ann said. "I want to clean this mess up." She looked at Jane, who nodded, agreeing.

"Ok, but you need to stay close to me," Jane said to Ann.

"I have a house in Marathon; it's about one hour from here; we can talk there. Follow me." I said, going to my car.

"Come with me, girls," the boyfriend said. "I don't trust the guy."

"No, I'll go with Joe. We need to talk," Ann said, coming in my direction.

#

Ann got in my car, looking overwhelmed. She didn't know what was going on, and I had no idea about what the boyfriend had told her on their way there. She didn't say a word, but she looked into my eyes with disbelief and disappointment.

"Listen, Ann, Jane is crazy. She's delusional, thinking I killed this Fred guy and tried to kill that other one, Juan Carlos, out of jealousy because she kissed one of them or both. I don't really know."

"Was it just a one-night-out affair, Joe?" Ann asked. She was serious and didn't look at me.

"It was more than that. She became obsessed with me and couldn't let go, especially when you and I started dating. I told her it was over, but she stalked me. She was everywhere—in the supermarket, in the garage, even in front of your house."

"Please tell me I'm sleeping and having a nightmare. This can't be true," she said with tears streaming down her face.

"She's mad, you saw her. I did nothing stricter because I was afraid that she could harm herself. I was really losing my patience with her when you and her boyfriend realized she was not acting normal and tried to get her the help she needed."

"Why did you lie to me?"

"I didn't lie."

"Why didn't you tell me?"

"Because I thought I could handle her and because she's your friend."

"I don't know what to think. What about the game? Don't keep lying to me…"

"I know, it was wrong. I shouldn't have proposed that freaking game to either of you, but it happened. Sorry…" I needed to convince her that the game stuff was a mistake and that I really fell for her. "Ann, please listen to me." I tried to make her look at me, lifting her face with my hand under her chin as tears ran down her face. "I do love you, don't forget that."

"I don't believe you; you're a liar. Jane is right; you're a jerk, and I can't trust you anymore. You had every chance to make it right, but you decided to keep your dirty little secret from me. Leave me alone, and don't touch me!" she said, pulling her face off my hand and looking out the window, sobbing.

"Please let me explain," I said, parking the car in front of the Marathon house. "Whatever happens, whatever they say, just remember that I love you." I tried to hold her back as she opened the car door to leave.

"Let me go. I have nothing to say to you." She got out of the car without looking back, rushing to Jane and Mike, who were arriving as well.

"Goddamnit!" I slammed the steering wheel and got out of the car.

Chapter 79

"I need to use the bathroom," Jane said.

"There's one on the second floor," Ann tried to tell her where the bathroom was.

"I know the house well," she said, climbing up the stairs.

Ann's face tweaked suspiciously when she heard that Jane knew where the bathroom was. Then she followed her upstairs, which made me nervous.

I was worried that Jane would tell Ann lies about me killing and hurting people. I couldn't trust her, so I followed them and knocked on the bathroom door. "Are you alright? Open the door. Jane? Ann?" And they opened the door.

"Jane, are you alright?" I asked, trying to look into her eyes, but she looked away from me.

"I'm ok," she said, looking at Ann.

"So, let's go down to the living room and talk. I ordered pizza for us," I said, going down the stairs. We all sat down and looked at each other. No one said anything until I broke the silence.

"I guess I owe you all an explanation and an apology. Believe me, I didn't mean for anyone to get hurt or heartbroken. It was a simple, naïve game that I play all the time. It's quite known, and people are playing it everywhere; it isn't a big deal." They were staring at me silently.

"Jane, I'm really sorry that I hurt you and broke your heart; it wasn't my intention. I thought we were having fun, but you twisted everything, making accusations that I hurt that guy and killed the other. You're delusional; it never happened. Yes, I saw Juan Carlos falling off his bike, but he was ok. I saw him getting up and riding away. I told you that, but you were hysterical. I don't know where you got this idea from, really. I really like you, but not the way you want, sorry. I know you'll find someone who loves you, too. Unfortunately, this person isn't me. I tried, we tried, but it didn't work out. I'm sorry."

Then I looked at Ann.

"Ann, I'm really sorry that initially, all I wanted was to have fun with you, too, but I really fell for you, and I wanted to know you better. I was being truthful when I brought you here to this house that weekend and told you I wanted to be with you. I do." I said, looking at Ann. Her eyes were tearing up.

"You're a jerk! Hellooo! I'm here, can't you see me? You know you broke my heart, and you're still trying to win Ann's heart?" Jane yelled, crying and playing the victim again.

The boyfriend, who was quiet until now, suddenly got up and came in my direction to punch me in the face. I dodged it.

"What the hell!" I said, getting up, ready to fight the son of a bitch. "Do you want to fight? Huh? Come on!"

"Stop it, stop it!" Ann and Jane screamed at us.

"Do you want to see what really hurts, you piece of shit? I'm going to hurt you really bad. This is for Jane, and this for Ann," the boyfriend said, pushing me hard. I lost my balance and fell on the chair.

"Mike, please stop!" Jane was trying to hold her boyfriend. Ann came to hold me down as I was about to get back on my feet to punch the idiot.

The doorbell rang. "Pizza!" Ann said, going to open the door. "How much?" she asked. She paid the guy and came back to the kitchen, grabbing plates and beer from the refrigerator.

"C'mon," Ann said, getting a couple of slices and a beer for herself. "Let's keep talking like grownups, shall we?" She sat down and started eating her pizza. We all did the same in silence.

"Sooo, Joe…" Ann started. "You wanted to play this game with both of us at the same time? How fun it was for you, right? One day with me, the other with her? Do we look like idiots to you?" She was looking at me with angry eyes. "I really liked you. I thought you were the love of my life. How could you?"

"Ann, forgive me. I didn't mean to hurt you. I met Jane first, and we started first. I didn't mean for it to go this far. I tried to talk with her and end everything, but she didn't let go. I'm sorry." I was almost begging her to believe me.

"Shut up, you son of a bitch!" The boyfriend started again. "Can't you see that Jane is hurting? Don't you have empathy for other people's feelings? I'm going to kill you! You hurt Jane. I love her, and you ruined it for us because you're a fucking selfish prick," he said, getting up to fight me again.

I was getting tired of him. He was disturbing my conversation with the girls; all he cared about was Jane. He was in love with her and felt deceived. I was a threat to him.

"Mike, stop, please!" Jane yelled at him, trying to get in between the guy and me.

Ann came to help her, and the guy pushed both girls out of the way to get back at me. I was furious and flew over to punch him. Jane and Ann started screaming for us to stop fighting.

The boyfriend yelled at me with anger. "Forgiveness? You want forgiveness? Yeah, maybe after I do some damage to your handsome face, you son of a bitch!" He tried to punch me in the face, but I dodged again and punched him. He lost his balance and almost fell.

Ann and Jane got in between the fight. Jane jumped on my back and started to slap and punch my head like crazy, and Ann was trying to push me out of the boyfriend's way. The boyfriend got up and came in my direction. I stepped back, pulling Jane out from behind my back, and she fell.

The boyfriend pushed me very hard, making me lose my balance. I fell, hitting my head on the fireplace mantel. I felt blood running down my face. I looked at them.

Ann and Jane rushed to me, screaming, "Joe! Joe!" I looked at Ann, feeling dizzy.

"Is he dead?" the boyfriend asked, sitting down on the sofa.

"No, he isn't, but he's hurt. I'll call an ambulance," Ann said, getting her cell phone.

"There is no need to call an ambulance. He's fine," the boyfriend said, looking at me. "Right, Joe?"

I got up, still feeling a little dizzy. Ann helped me. I sat down on the chair and saw a pool of blood on the floor by the fireplace. I touched my forehead and felt the blood still gushing down. I was furious.

"Let me see. Take your hand down. Let me clean the wound." Ann had gotten a wet towel to clean the blood and stop the bleeding.

"I'm sorry, Ann. I really am. Will you ever forgive me? Please, let's get out of here. They're crazy." I was trying to get Ann on my side.

She nodded.

"Ann, don't listen to him. He's evil. He's trying to hurt us both," the little freak started to talk again.

"Shut the fuck up, Jane!" I yelled at her.

"See, he's a monster." Jane started to cry, making the boyfriend angry again.

"Don't yell at her! I'll kill you for real," he said, getting up and coming in my direction again. Ann got in between us to prevent him from punching my face. He hit her instead, and she fell on the floor.

"Ann?" I was furious now. "You fucking asshole son of a bitch. You can keep the little devil; she's all yours. Just leave Ann and me alone! Get out of my house!" I had totally lost my patience now.

"Stop, Mike! You hurt Ann!" Jane was really concerned about Ann.

Ann got up crying and said, "Please, let's stop this nonsense. I want to go home, please."

"Ann, my love, I'm so sorry." I helped her up and put my arms around her. "Let's get out of here." We started to walk toward the door.

"No!" Jane screamed. "Ann, don't leave me."

"You're going nowhere until we have this clear. You don't get to choose one of them," the boyfriend started again.

"Hey, man, you have to go. I'm trying to get things cleared out with the girls, but you're getting in the way. Bye, go away!" I demanded, getting up to open the door for him.

"I'm not going anywhere." He came in my direction, getting the baseball bat he had brought inside with him.

I was still feeling dizzy as I tried to get out of his reach, but everything was spinning around. I held myself up in the fireplace mantel, when I remembered about the gun I had hidden there. I reached out behind the shaft dumper, and there it was.

"Stay back," I warned him.

"Joe!" the girls screamed.

"You're a coward. You aren't going to shoot me," the boyfriend said, still coming in my direction with the baseball bat ready to hit me. I pulled the trigger, and a shot sounded. I was just trying to scare him off, but he fell like a sack of potatoes.

EPILOGUE

JOE

I had to resign from my job and go through the justice system. However, everything was resolved, and I was free to go. I'm glad I was in my house, and Mike was threatening me with a baseball bat when I accidentally shot him, so it wasn't difficult to prove self-defense.

There's a stand-your-ground law in Florida that exempts people who kill someone trying to defend themselves inside their property from being prosecuted and convicted. The girls collaborated, giving testimony, but we haven't talked ever since I came back to England.

My father was devastated and worried that what had happened to me in America would affect his practice in England. My mum was glad that I was alive and back home. To her, my disillusion was a blessing. I had no option but to work in my father's office, which was exactly what I was trying to avoid by moving to America.

Jamal keeps me informed by telling me what goes on in the local news. Apparently, after six months, the tragedy was losing momentum, and no one was talking about the case anymore. According to him, the girls moved away, and no one heard from them again in Fort Lauderdale.

I really didn't want to know about Jane, but I couldn't forget Ann. I tried to call, text, and email her several times, but she was nonresponsive. Of course, she was still hurt about everything and couldn't forgive me.

If I could explain myself, I would tell her everything, including about Amy, who, by the way, was really concerned when she heard about the case. She called me from Syria to see if I was ok and invited me to stay with her in Damascus for a while until things calmed down. I thought it was nice of her and actually considered the offer until she told me she was married and pregnant. *Oh, Amy, you keep breaking my heart. All I wanted in my life was to be with you forever.*

It was a rainy Friday in London, and I was on my way to meet my old mates at the pub. I didn't want to go home to watch telly with my mum. Suddenly, my mobile rang. It was from an unknown number. I hesitated a bit but decided to take it.

"Hello!"

"Hi, Joe?"

"No way! How did you get my number, Jane? I really don't want to talk to you."

"Wait! Don't hang up. We need to talk. I'm in London and…"

"You what? You got to be kidding me."

"No, I'm not. And I know where you work. Can we just talk? Tomorrow?"

"Goddamnit, Jane!"

ANN

I had to make a huge effort to keep my sanity while the whole commotion was going on. We called 9-1-1 after Mike was shot, and it was like a scene from a movie when the police, ambulance, and reporters arrived.

The media is like vultures searching for tragedies that can make the news—the bloodier, the better. They care less about the people involved and don't hesitate to expose them to the whole world. The police tried to keep them away from us, but when leaving the hospital where we were taken, the reporters were everywhere, even in front of my house.

"Ms. Martinez, can you tell us why your boyfriend killed Mike Jones? Were you having an affair with Mike Jones?"

"Ms. Martinez, was your friend, Jane May, having an affair with your boyfriend, Joe Garrison?"

"LEAVE ME ALONE!" I rushed inside, crying, not knowing what to do or where to go. I wanted to disappear. I ran to my bed, wanting to stay there in the dark until the end of my days.

"Hey, Ann…" Matt came into my room, knowing I needed to be comforted. David came right after with a cup of chamomile tea for me. They sat on my bed. Matt reached for my hand and started to pat it, saying. "We're here to help you, Ann; we'll do anything to protect you from those evil scavengers."

"Yes, Ann. I think we need to take you out of here. You need to go far away from this nightmare. Being here is not going to make you feel any better," David said, handing me the tea.

"Thank you, guys. I don't know what to do. I have nowhere to go. What am I going to do?" I started sobbing again.

"We'll figure it out. It must be a place that you can go to without anyone knowing," David started to set up a plan.

"Yeah, maybe you can go to Missoula in Montana. I have a very nice cousin there. She lives on a farm, so no one will get close to you. What do you think?"

"Maybe. Are you guys coming with me? I can't go alone. And what about Max?"

"We'll all go!" David said. "I'll put our stuff in a storage, and we can sneak out during the night..."

"Wow, how exciting! I'm in!" Matt was happy with the plan. "I'll call my cousin to let her know."

"Wait. I'll have to wait until the process is over. The police said I couldn't go anywhere before being released by the court. They also said that I can't contact Jane or Joe during the process."

"Yeah, of course," David said. "We'll wait, but let's have everything settled for when you are released."

"Ok. I can't wait to get out of here and never see Joe's or Jane's face again."

JANE

"FUCK YOU! Leave me alone, you bastards!" I yelled, getting into my building and slamming my apartment door. There was nothing I could do to get those reporters off my back. They were everywhere. The only place safe was inside my apartment, which wouldn't be my home anymore if I didn't come up with the rent money within a week.

I tried to ask my mom, but she didn't want to talk or have anything to do with me. If our relationship was bad before, now it's even worse. She pretends she doesn't even know me. I have no one. Mike was the only person who really cared for me, and now he was gone.

The police told me I couldn't contact Ann or Joe until the court decided whether anyone was guilty of Mike's death. The wait for the justice system to finish the process took forever, and I waited to reach Ann and Joe back. I saw them briefly in court when giving my testimony, but I couldn't talk to them. I had to wait until it was over.

When the judge decided that Joe acted in self-defense and wasn't going to be prosecuted, I felt relieved. I tried to call Ann, but she didn't answer her phone. She wasn't home either when I went to check on her. The neighbor told me she had moved out but didn't know where to. The house was up for rent.

I tried Joe. I knew it would be a lot more difficult to get him to talk to me again, but I needed to try. He also didn't answer my calls, texts, or emails. I went to his building, and the receptionist told me he had moved out. They told me he had gone back to London.

I was desperate. I had no one to help me and was going to be evicted by the following week. I had to think of a way out. My only solution was to go back to the office and beg forgiveness from Mr. McKee.

"Thank you for seeing me, Mr. McKee. I really appreciate it."

"Ok, Jane, what can I do for you? I'm very disappointed about the whole story. However, I really blame Joe since he should have known better that what he did was inadmissible."

"I'm very sorry. I don't know what to do. No one wants to give me a chance, and I have nowhere to go," I started crying inconsolably.

"Don't cry, Jane. There must be someone somewhere that you can go and have a fresh start."

"I have no one."

"I can't take you back here. Where is Ann?"

"I don't know, she doesn't answer her phone. I don't think she wants to talk to me, and she moved out. No one knows where to."

"Family?"

"No… Actually, I have a cousin in England but have no money to go there," I lied to him, still sobbing. I would do anything to go after Joe in London.

"Well, that's something I can actually help you with. How much you think you need?" he said, sitting down and grabbing his checkbook.

"Oh, thank you, Mr. McKee. I'll never forget this. You saved my life!" I felt relieved and thankful. I took the check and went straight to the bank to cash it. I had to move fast since I wasn't planning to pay the late rent. So, within a week, I sold most of my stuff and took Ollie to be adopted. It broke my heart, but I had no other option. He'll be fine; he's a cat, and cats are jerks; all they want is a nice bed to sleep on and someone to feed them. I'll miss him, but he'll probably forget I exist as soon as I turn my back.

I got my ticket, and to London, I went. I loved the city and quickly learned to be extra careful when crossing the streets since the cars drive on the wrong way. I started looking for Joe right away and was very frustrated when I realized that Garrison is a somewhat common name in England. But how many could be lawyers? I knew his father was also a lawyer and had an office in London.

It took me a couple of days to make a list of possible offices. I called every single one asking, "May I talk with Mr. Joe Garrison, please?" just to hear someone saying, "Oh dear, I'm afraid you have the wrong number."

But, on Friday, I got lucky, and the person said, "He isn't in right now. May I take a message?"

"Oh! Thank you! Do you know what time he's coming back? I have an important envelope to give to him from the court in the United States."

"I'm sorry, I don't think he's coming back until Monday, but you can drop the envelope off here at the office."

"No, I can't. I need his signature. Do you have his address?"

"I can't give you his address, but I can give you his mobile number. He'll tell you where to meet him. Is that ok?"

"Sure, that will work!" She gave me his number.

I filled myself with courage, breathed deeply ten times, and called.

"Hello!" he answered.

"Hi, Joe?"

"No way! How did you get my number, Jane? I really don't want to talk with you…"

"Wait! Don't hang up. We need to talk. I'm in London and…"

"You what? You got to be kidding me."

"No, I'm not. And I know where you work. Can we just talk? Tomorrow?"

"Goddamnit, Jane!"

He hung up, but I was happy to have found him, and I knew it was just a matter of time for us to be together again.

The End

About the Author

M. S. Novaes lives in Miami Beach with her husband, 14-year-old son and her cat. She loves to walk on the beach, watch movies, and read good books.